Men have always feared the unknown, and have hated what they fear. Except for those of courage and high heart to whom the unknown is like flame to a moth. But there were few such left in Gwynedd. It was no longer safe to admit even to curiosity about the Deryni.

For the priests, seeing their young King Kelson place more and more trust in Duke Alaric Morgan, who blatantly boasted of his Deryni heritage, felt their own position threatened. And thus they plotted to destroy Morgan, encouraging reports of Deryni atrocity, compounding lies about the inexplicable powers of this race now called nonhuman, recklessly willing to risk even the King himself in their self-seeking drive to win control of Gwynedd.

Very few were unafraid of the Deryni. For the power was real—and it was no longer properly understood or controlled. It had killed wantonly. It could, and had, destroyed.

But for Duke Alaric Morgan, Deryni power was all that stood between the priests and his annihilation.

DERYNI CHECKMATE

Volume II in the Chronicles of the Deryni

Katherine Kurtz

A Del Rey Book

BALLANTINE BOOKS • NEW YORK

A Del Rey Book
Published by Ballantine Books

ISBN 0-345-30593-0

Mnaufactured in the United States of America

First Edition: May 1972
Ninth Printing: November 1981

Cover art by Darrell K. Sweet

For
JOHN G. NELSON

*who, like the Deryni,
strives to hold back the darkness—
of whatever kind.*

CONTENTS

DERYNI
CHECKMATE

CHAPTER ONE

Three things there are which defy prediction: a woman's whims, the touch of the Devil's finger, and the weather of Gwynedd in March.

—St. Veneric,
Triads

MARCH HAS long been a month of storms in the Eleven Kingdoms. It brings the snow sweeping down from the great northern sea to layer a last coat of winter on the silver mountains, to seethe and swirl around the high plateaus of the east until it finally funnels across the great Gwynedd plain and turns to rain.

March is a fickle month at best. It is the last stand of winter against the coming spring, but it is also harbinger of the greening, of the floods which yearly inundate the central lowlands. It has been known to be mild—though not recently. Still, it is spring—close enough for men to dare hope that winter *might* end early this year; it *has*, on occasion.

But those who know the ways of Gwynedd do not build their dreams on the chance of an early spring. For they have learned through hard experience that March is capricious, often cruel, and never, never to be trusted.

March in the first regnal of King Kelson of Gwynedd was to be no exception.

Nightfall had come early in Kelson's capital at Rhemuth. It often did in March, when the northern storms rolled in across the Purple March from the north and east.

This particular storm had struck at midday, pelting the brightly canopied stalls and shops of the market square with hail the size of a man's thumbnail and sending merchants and vendors scurrying for cover. Within an hour, all hope of salvaging the interrupted market day was gone. And so, amidst thunder and rain and the pungent lightning-smell which the wind carried, the merchants had reluctantly packed up their sodden wares, closed up their shops, and left.

By dusk, the only people to be found on the rain-swept streets were those whose business compelled them to be out on such a night—city watchmen on their rounds, soldiers and messengers on official errands, citizens scurrying through the wind and cold to the warm hearthsides of their homes.

Now, as darkness fell and the great cathedral bells in the north of the city rang Evensong, sleet and rain whined through the narrow, deserted streets of Rhemuth, slashing at the red-tiled roofs and cupolas and filling the cobble-lined gutters to overflowing. Behind rain-blurred windowpanes, the flames of countless evening candles shivered and danced whenever a gust of wind managed to force its way through cracks in wooden doors and shutters. And in houses and taverns, inns and roadhouses, inhabitants of the city huddled around their firesides to take their evening meals, sipped good ale and traded yarns while they waited for the storm to subside.

At the north of the city, the archbishop's palace was likewise under siege from the storm. In the shadow of palace walls, the massive nave of Saint George's Cathedral loomed dark against the blackening sky, stubby bell tower thrust brazenly heavenward, bronze doors sealed tightly against the onslaught.

Leather-cloaked household guards patroled the ramparts of the palace proper, collars and hoods muffled close against the cold and wet. Torches hissed and flared under sheltered eaves along the battlements as the storm raged and howled and chilled to the bone.

Inside, the Lord Archbishop of Rhemuth, the Most Reverend Patrick Corrigan, was snug and warm. Standing before a roaring fireplace, pudgy hands extended toward the flames, he rubbed his hands together briskly to further warm them, then pulled his fur-lined robe more closely around him and padded on slippered feet to a writing desk on the opposite side of the room. Another man, also in episcopal violet, was poring over an elaborate parchment manuscript, squinting in the light of two yellow candles on the desk before him. Half a dozen candle sconces placed around the rest of the room made a feeble attempt to further banish the gloom encroaching from the darkness outside. And a youngish-looking priest-secretary hovered attentively over the man's left shoulder with another light, ready to apply red sealing wax when he was told to do so.

Corrigan peered over the reader's right shoulder and watched as the man nodded, picked up a quill, and scrawled a bold signature at the foot of the document. The secretary dripped molten wax beside the name, and the man calmly imprinted the wax with his amethyst seal of office. He breathed on the stone and polished it against his velvet sleeve, then looked up at Corrigan and replaced the ring on his finger.

"That should take care of Morgan," he said.

Edmund Loris, Archbishop of Valoret and Primate of Gwynedd was an impressive-looking man. His body was lean and fit beneath the rich violet cassock he wore, and the fine silvery hair formed a wispy halo-effect around the magenta skull cap covering his clerical tonsure.

The bright blue eyes were hard and cold, however. And the gaunt hawk-face was anything but benificent at the moment. For Loris had just affixed his seal to a document which would shortly cause Interdict to fall upon a large portion of Royal Gwynedd. Interdict— which would cut off the rich Duchy of Corwyn to the east from all sacraments and solace of the Church in the Eleven Kingdoms.

It was a grave decision, and one to which both Loris and his colleague had given considerable thought in the past four months. For in all fairness, the people of Corwyn had done nothing to warrant so extreme a measure as Interdict. But nor, on the other hand, could the true cause of the measure be ignored or tolerated any longer. An abhorrent situation had existed and continued to exist within the archbishops' jurisdiction, and it must be stamped out.

And so the prelates salved their consciences with the rationalization that the threat of Interdict was not, after all, directed against the people of Corwyn, but against one man who was impossible to reach in any other way. It was Corwyn's master, the Deryni Duke Alaric Morgan, who was the object of sacerdotal vengeance tonight. Morgan, who had repeatedly dared to use his blasphemous and heretical Deryni powers to meddle in human affairs and corrupt the innocent, in defiance of Church and State. Morgan, who had initiated the boy-king Kelson into the forbidden practice of that ancient magic and loosed a duel of necromancy in the cathedral itself at Kelson's coronation last fall. Morgan, whose half-Deryni ancestry doomed him to eternal torment and damnation in the Hereafter unless he could be persuaded to recant, to give up his powers and renounce his evil heritage. Morgan, around whom the entire Deryni question now seemed to hinge.

Archbishop Corrigan frowned and picked up the parchment, his bushy grizzled brows knitting together in a single line as he scanned the text once more. He pursed his lips and scowled as he finished reading, but then he folded the document with a decisive crackle and held it flat on the desk while his secretary applied wax to the overlap. Corrigan sealed it with his ring, but his hand toyed uneasily with the jeweled pectoral cross on his chest as he eased himself into a chair beside Loris.

"Edmund, are you sure we—" He halted at Loris' sharp glance, then remembered that his secretary was still awaiting further instructions.

"That will be all for the moment, Father Hugh. Ask Monsignor Gorony to step in, please."

The priest bowed and left the room, and Corrigan leaned back in his chair with a sigh.

"You know that Morgan will never permit Tolliver to excommunicate him," Corrigan said wearily. "Do you really think the threat of Interdict will stop him?" Duke Alaric Morgan did not technically fall within the jurisdiction of either archbishop, but both were hopeful that the letter on the table would shortly circumvent that small technicality.

Loris made a steeple of his fingers and gazed across at Corrigan evenly. "Probably not," he admitted. "But his people may. Rumor has it that a band of rebels in northern Corwyn even now preaches the overthrow of their Deryni duke."

"Humph!" Corrigan snorted derisively, picking up a quill pen and dipping it into a crystal inkwell. "What good can a handful of rebels hope to do against Deryni magic? Besides, you know that Morgan's people love him."

"Yes, they do—now," Loris agreed. He watched as Corrigan began carefully inscribing a name on the outside of the letter they had written, watched with a hidden smile as the tip of his colleague's tongue followed each stroke of the rounded uncials. "But will they love him as well once the Interdict falls?"

Corrigan looked up sharply from his finished handiwork, then vigorously sanded the wet ink with pounce from a silver shaker and blew away the excess.

"And what of the rebel band then?" Loris continued insistently, eying his companion through narrowed lids. "They say that Warin, the rebel leader, believes himself to be a new messiah, divinely appointed to rid the land of the Deryni scourge. Can you not see how such zealousness could be made to work to our advantage?"

Corrigan pulled at his lower lip in concentration, then frowned. "Are we to permit self-appointed messiahs to go galavanting around the countryside without proper supervision, Edmund? This rebel movement smacks of heresy to me."

"I've given no official sanction yet," Loris said. "I've not even met this Warin fellow. But you must admit that such a movement could be highly effective, were it given proper guidance. Besides," Loris smiled, "perhaps this Warin *is* divinely inspired."

"I doubt it," Corrigan scowled. "How far do you propose to pursue the matter?"

Loris leaned back in his chair and folded his hands across his waist. "The rebel headquarters is reputed to be in the hills near Dhassa, where the Curia meets later this week. Gorony, whom we send to Corwyn's bishop, has been in touch with the rebels and will return to Dhassa when he finishes his current assignment. I hope to arrange a meeting with the rebel leader then."

"And until then, we do nothing?"

Loris nodded. "We do nothing. I do not want the king to know what we are planning, and—"

There was a discreet knock at the door, followed by the entrance of Corrigan's secretary and an older, nondescript-looking man in the travelling garb of a simple priest. Father Hugh lowered his eyes and bowed slightly as he announced the newcomer.

"Monsignor Gorony, Your Excellency."

Gorony strode to Corrigan's chair and dropped to one knee to kiss the archbishop's ring, then stood at Corrigan's signal to wait attentively

"Thank you, Father Hugh. I believe that will be all for tonight," Corrigan said, starting to wave dismissal.

Loris cleared his throat, and Corrigan glanced in his direction.

"The suspension we spoke of earlier, Patrick? We had agreed that the man must be disciplined, had we not?"

"Oh, yes, of course," Corrigan murmured. He rummaged briefly among the papers piled at one corner of the desk, then extracted one and pushed it across the desk to Hugh.

"This is the draft of a writ of summons I need as soon as possible, Father. When the official document is drawn up, would you return it for my signature?"

"Yes, Excellency."

As Hugh took the paper and headed for the door, Corrigan resumed his conversation with Gorony.

"Now, this is the letter you're to deliver to Bishop Tolliver. I've a barge waiting to take you to the free port of Concaradine, and from there you can take ship with one of the merchant fleets. You should be in Corwyn within three days."

Father Hugh de Berry frowned as he closed the door to the archbishop's study and began walking down the long, torch-lined corridor toward his chancery office. It was cold and damp, and the corridor was drafty. Hugh shivered and clasped his arms across his chest as he walked, debating what he should do.

Hugh was Patrick Corrigan's personal secretary. and as such was privy to information not normally accessible to one of his comparative youth. He was a bright man, if not brilliant. And he had always been honest, discreet, and totally loyal to the Church he served through the person of the archbishop.

Lately, though, his faith had been sorely shaken—at least his faith in the man he served. The letter he had copied for Corrigan this afternoon had helped to do that. And as he remembered, Hugh shivered again—this time, not from the cold.

Gwynedd was in danger. This had been apparent since King Brion fell at Candor Rhea last fall. It had been evident when Brion's heir, the boy Kelson, had been forced to battle the evil Charissa for his throne but a few weeks later. And it had been painfully obvious whenever Morgan, the boy's Deryni protector, had had to use his awesome powers to slow down the inevitable conflagration that all knew must follow on the heels of such events. And it would follow.

It was no secret, for example, that the Deryni tyrant Wencit of Torenth would plunge the kingdom into war by midsummer at latest. And the young king must certainly be aware of the unrest being generated in his kingdom by rising anti-Deryni sentiment. Kelson had begun to feel the brunt of that reaction ever since the disclosure of his own half-Deryni ancestry at the coronation last fall.

But now, with Interdict threatened for all of Corwyn—

Hugh pressed one hand against his chest where the original draft of Corrigan's letter now rested next to his skin. He knew that the archbishop would not approve of what he was about to do—in fact, would be furious if he found out—but the matter was too important for the king not to be made aware of it. Kelson must be warned.

If Interdict fell on Corwyn, Morgan's loyalties would be divided at a time when all his energies were needed at the king's side. It could fatally affect the king and also Morgan's plans for the war effort. And while Hugh, as a priest, could hardly condone Morgan's fearsome powers, they were nonetheless real and needed if Gwynedd was to survive the onslaught.

Hugh paused beneath the torch outside the chancery office door and began to scan the letter in his hand, hoping the copy could be entrusted to one of his subordinates. Skipping over the archbishop's standard salutation for such documents, he gasped as he read the name of the addressee, then forced himself to reread it—Monsignor Duncan Howard McLain.

Duncan! Hugh thought to himself. *My God, what's he done?* Duncan McLain was the young confessor to the king, and Hugh's own boyhood friend. They had grown up together, gone to school together. What could Duncan possibly have done to incur such action?

Knitting his brows together in consternation, Hugh read the letter, his apprehension increasing as he read.

> . . . *summarily suspended and ordered to present yourself before our ecclesiastical court . . . give answer as to why you should not be censured . . . your part in the scandals surrounding the king's coronation November last . . . questionable activities . . . consorting with heretics . . .*

My God, Hugh thought, unwilling to go on, *he's been tainted by Morgan too. I wonder if he knows about this.*

Lowering the paper, Hugh made his decision. Obviously, he must go to the king first. That had been his original intention, and the matter was of kingdom-wide importance.

But then he must find Duncan and warn him. If Duncan submitted himself to the archbishop's court under the present circumstances, there was no telling what might happen. He could even be excommunicated.

Hugh shuddered at that and crossed himself. For the threat of excommunication was, on a personal level, as terrible as Interdict was for a geographical area. Both cut off the transgressor from all sacraments of the Church and all contact with God-fearing men. It must not come to that for Duncan.

Composing himself, Hugh pushed open the chancery door and walked calmly to a desk where a monk was sharpening a quill pen.

"His Excellency needs this as soon as possible, Brother James," he said, casually placing the document on the desk. "Will you take care of it, please? I have a few errands to do."

"Certainly, Father," the monk replied.

CHAPTER TWO

I am the son of the wise, the son of ancient kings.

—*Isaiah 19:11*

"MORE VENISON, SIRE?"

The red-liveried squire kneeling beside Kelson held out a steaming platter of venison in gravy, but Kelson shook his head and pushed his silver trencher aside with a smile. His crimson tunic was open at the neck, his raven head bare of any royal ornament. And he had hours ago discarded his wet boots in favor of soft scarlet slippers. He sighed and stretched his legs closer to the fire, wiggling his feet contentedly as the squire removed the venison and began to clear the table.

The young king had dined informally tonight, with only Duncan McLain and his uncle, Prince Nigel, to share the table in the royal chambers. Now, across that table, Duncan drained the last dregs from his chased silver goblet and placed it gently on the table. Fire and taperlight winked from the polished metal, casting bright flecks on the table, on the violet-edged black of Duncan's cassock. The priest gazed across at his young liege lord and smiled, blue eyes calm, contented, serene; then he glanced behind to where Nigel was struggling to break the seal on a new bottle of wine.

"Do you need help, Nigel?"

11

"Not unless you can charm this cork with a prayer," Nigel grunted.

"Certainly. *Benedicte*," Duncan said, lifting his hand to make the sign that went with the blessing.

The seal chose that minute to crack, and the cork shot from the neck of the bottle in a rain of red wine. Nigel jumped back in time to avoid a royal dousing, and Kelson leaped from his chair before he too could be splashed, but Nigel's best efforts were not sufficient to spare the table or the wool carpeting beneath his booted feet.

"Holy St. Michael, you didn't have to take me so literally, Duncan!" the prince yelped, chuckling good-naturedly and holding the dripping bottle over the table while the squire mopped the floor. "As I've always said, you can't trust a priest."

"I was about to say the same for princes," Duncan observed, winking in Kelson's direction and watching the boy control a smile.

The squire Richard wiped Kelson's chair and the bottle, then wrung his cloth over the fire and returned to tackle the table. The flames hissed and flared green as the wine vaporized, and Kelson took his seat and helped pick up goblets and candlesticks so that Richard could wipe up. When the young man had finished, Nigel filled the three goblets and replaced the bottle in its warming rack close by the fire.

Nigel Cluim Gwydion Rhys Haldane was a handsome man. At thirty-four, he was a mature version of what his royal nephew would look like in twenty years, with the same wide smile, the grey Haldane eyes, the quick wit that marked every Haldane male. Like his dead brother Brion, Nigel was a Haldane to the core, his military prowess and learning known and admired throughout the Eleven Kingdoms. As he took his seat and picked up his goblet, his right hand moved in an unconscious gesture to brush back a strand of jet black hair, and Duncan felt a twinge of nostalgia at the familiar movement.

Only a few months ago, that gesture had been Brion's as well. Brion, whom Duncan had served in one capacity or another for most of his twenty-nine years. Brion, victim of the same battle of ideologies which even now threatened to rend the country and plunge the Eleven Kingdoms into war.

Now Brion was gone. And his fourteen-year-old son reigned uneasily with the power he had inherited from his illustrious sire. And the tension grew.

Duncan's gloomy thoughts were interrupted by the opening of the door from the outer corridor. As he looked up, a very young page in Kelson's crimson livery entered carrying a steaming silver bowl almost as big as he was. A snowy linen towel was draped over the lad's shoulder, and a faint scent of lemon reached Duncan's nostrils as the boy knelt beside Kelson and held out the bowl.

Kelson nodded grave thanks as he dipped his fingers in the warm water and dried his hands on the towel. The boy bowed his head shyly and moved to repeat the performance for Nigel, but he would not look up at the lean figure in royal blue. Nor, when he moved to Duncan's side, would he look at the priest.

Duncan controlled the urge to smile as he replaced the towel on the boy's shoulder. But when the boy had scurried from the chamber, he gazed across at Nigel with a mischievous grin.

"Is he one of your pupils, Nigel?" he asked, knowing that it was so. Nigel was in charge of the training of all the pages in the royal household, but Duncan knew that this one was special.

Nigel gave a proud nod. "Payne, my youngest," he replied. "He has much to learn, but so does every new page. This was his first time to serve officially."

Kelson smiled and picked up his goblet, idly twirling the stem between his long fingers so that the faceted sides caught the reflection of tunic and fire and tapestried walls.

"I remember when I was a page, Uncle. Not so very long ago, either. The first time you allowed me to serve my father, I was scared to death." He leaned his head against the tall chair-back and continued dreamily. "There was no reason to be afraid, of course. He was the same, and I was the same, and the mere fact that I wore court livery shouldn't have made any difference.

"And yet, it did. Because I was no longer a boy serving his father; I was a royal page serving the king. There's a big difference." He glanced across at Nigel. "Payne felt that tonight. Even though I've known him all his life, used to play with him and the other boys, he knew the difference. Tonight I was his king—not a familiar playmate. I wonder if it's always like that?"

The squire Richard, who had been turning down the State bed on the other side of the room, approached Kelson's chair and made a short bow.

"Will there be aught else, Sire? Anything I may bring ye?"

"I don't think so. Uncle? Father Duncan?"

The two shook their heads and Kelson nodded.

"That's all for tonight, then, Richard. Check with the household guard before you leave. There should be a coach standing by later on to take Father Duncan back to the basilica."

"You needn't bother," the priest protested. "I'll be fine on foot."

"And catch your death of cold? Certainly not. The night's not fit for man nor beast. Richard, there will be a coach ready for Father Duncan. Understood?"

"Aye, My Liege."

Nigel drained his goblet and gestured toward the door as it closed behind Richard. "That's a fine young man, Kelson," he said, reaching behind to retrieve the wine bottle and pour himself another cup. "He'll be ready for knighthood soon. One of the finest lads I've ever had the pleasure to train. Alaric concurs in that judgement, by the way. Anyone else?"

He proffered the wine bottle, but Kelson shook his head. Duncan inspected his goblet and found it half empty, held it out for more. As Nigel replaced the bottle, Duncan leaned back in his chair and thought out loud.

"Richard FitzWilliam. He's about seventeen now, isn't he, My Prince?"

"Almost eighteen," Kelson corrected. "He's the only son of Baron Fulk FitzWilliam, up in the Kheldish Riding. I'd planned to knight him and a dozen others before we begin the summer campaign in Eastmarch. His father will be pleased."

Nigel nodded. "He's one of the best. What news of Wencit of Torenth, by the way? Any further word from Cardosa?"

"Not for the past three months," Kelson replied. "The city has a strong garrison, as you know, but they'll be snowbound for a few more weeks at least. And once the high passes are clear, Wencit will be hammering at the gates again. We can't possibly get relief troops there until the spring flooding is done, and it will be too late by then."

"So we lose Cardosa," Nigel sighed, gazing into the depths of his cup.

"And the treaty dies, and war comes," Duncan added.

Nigel shrugged and began running the tip of his finger along the rim of his goblet. "Hasn't that been apparent from the start? Brion certainly knew there was that danger when he sent Alaric to Cardosa last summer. And when Brion died and we had to recall Alaric or lose you, Kelson—well, I still think it was a fair exchange: a city for a king. Besides, we haven't lost Cardosa yet."

"But we will, Uncle," Kelson murmured, lowering

his eyes. "And how many lives will be lost in the exchange?" He twined his fingers together and studied them for a moment before continuing. "I sometimes wonder how to weigh those lives against my own, Uncle. Sometimes I wonder if I'm worth it."

Duncan reached across to touch Kelson's arm reassuringly. "Kings will always wonder about such things, Kelson. The day you stop wondering, stop weighing the lives that hang in the balance—on that day, I shall mourn."

The young king looked up with a wry grin. "You always know what to say, don't you, Father? It may not save cities or lives, but at least it soothes the conscience of the king who must decide who survives." He lowered his eyes again. "I'm sorry. That sounded bitter, didn't it?"

Duncan's reply was cut short by a knock at the door, followed by the immediate entrance of young Richard FitzWilliam. Richard's handsome face was tense, almost nervous, and his dark eyes flashed as he made an apologetic bow.

"Beggin' your pardon, Sire, but there's a priest outside who insists he must see ye. I told him ye'd retired for the night, that he should come back tomorrow, but he's most persistent."

Before Kelson could reply, a dark-cloaked cleric pushed his way past Richard and darted across the room to fling himself on his knees at Kelson's feet. A stiletto had appeared unobtrusively in Kelson's hand as the man approached, and Nigel half-rose from his chair, also reaching for a weapon. But even as the man's knees hit the floor, Richard was straddling his back, one arm across the man's throat in a chokehold, the other with a dagger at the jugular vein, a knee in the small of the man's back.

The man grimaced under Richard's rough handling, but made no move to defend himself or to threaten Kelson. Instead, he closed his eyes tightly and extended his empty hands to either side, tried to ignore the pressure of Richard's arm across his windpipe.

"Please, Sire, I wish you no harm," he croaked, wincing slightly as Richard's cold blade touched the side of his neck. "I'm Father Hugh de Berry, Archbishop Corrigan's secretary."

"Hugh!" Duncan exclaimed, leaning forward anxiously as he recognized the man and signaling Richard to release him. "What the Devil? Why didn't you say so?"

Hugh had opened his eyes with a start at Duncan's voice, and now he stared pleadingly at his brother priest, his eyes betraying his fear but also his resolution. Richard released his stranglehold and stepped back a pace at Duncan's repeated gesture, but he did not relax his vigilant pose, nor did he sheath his dagger. Nigel warily took his seat again, but Kelson continued to finger the slim stiletto he had produced when the man approached.

"You know this man, Father?" Kelson asked.

"He is who he claims to be," Duncan replied cautiously, "though I cannot speak for his intent after such an entrance. An explanation, Hugh?"

Hugh swallowed with difficulty, then glanced at Kelson and bowed his head. "I beg forgiveness, Sire, but I had to see you. I have certain information I could trust to no one else, and—"

He hazarded another glance at Kelson, then began withdrawing a folded piece of parchment from inside his damp cassock. His heavy black cloak was dark across the shoulders where the rain had soaked through, and his thinning brown hair glistened with a mist of fine droplets in the dancing taperlight. His fingers trembled as he handed the parchment across to Kelson. He averted his eyes again as he folded his hands inside his sleeves to hide their shaking.

Kelson frowned and replaced his dagger in its hid-

den wrist sheath before unfolding the parchment. As
Nigel moved a candle closer, Duncan came around to
read over the boy's shoulder. The priest's face darkened as he scanned the lines, for the formula was
familiar, and what he had often feared. Restraining
his rising anger, he straightened and glanced at Richard, his blue eyes stormy, grim.

"Richard, would you please wait outside," he murmured, flicking his gaze to Hugh's bowed head. "I
will vouch for this man's conduct."

"Aye, Father."

As the door closed behind Richard, Duncan returned to his chair and sat wearily. He continued to
study Hugh across the goblet between his hands,
looked up as Kelson finished reading and laid the
parchment on the table.

"I thank you for this information, Father," Kelson
said, motioning Hugh to rise. "And I apologize for
your rough handling. I hope you will understand the
necessity under the circumstances."

"Of course, Sire," Hugh murmured self-
consciously. "You had no way of knowing what I
was. I thank God that Duncan was here to save me
from my own impetuosity."

Duncan nodded, his eyes hooded and dark, but it
was obvious he was not thinking about Hugh. His
hands were clasped tightly around the silver goblet on
the table before him, and the knuckles were white.
Kelson did not seem to notice as he glanced at the
parchment again.

"I assume this letter has gone out by now," he said,
catching Hugh's affirmative nod. "Father Duncan,
does this mean what I think it does?"

"*Satan doom them both to nine eternal torments!*"
Duncan whispered under his breath. He looked up
sharply, suddenly aware he had spoken aloud, then
shook his head and released the goblet. It was oval
now instead of round.

"Forgive me, My Prince," he murmured. "It means that Loris and Corrigan have finally decided to do something about Alaric. I've been expecting some kind of action for months now, but I never dreamed they'd dare to interdict all of Corwyn for the actions of one man."

"Well, apparently they have dared," Kelson said uneasily. "Can we stop them?"

Duncan took a deep breath and forced himself to control his anger. "Not directly. We have to remember that Loris and Corrigan see Alaric as the key to the whole Deryni question. He's the highest placed of any known Deryni in the kingdom, and he's never tried to hide what he is. He was never blatant in his use of his powers. But when Brion died, circumstances forced his hand and he had to use his powers or see you die."

"And to the archbishops," Nigel interjected, "magic is evil, and that is that. Also, don't forget how Alaric repeatedly made fools of them at the coronation last fall. I rather imagine that has as much to do with the present crisis as any high-sounding motives they may say are behind the move."

Kelson slouched in his chair and studied a ruby ring on his right forefinger. "So it's to be war against the Deryni, is it? Father Duncan, we can't afford a religious dispute on the eve of a major war. What can we do to stop them?"

Duncan shook his head. "I don't know. I'll have to discuss it with Alaric. Hugh, do you have any further background for us? Who's delivering the letter? And how?"

"Monsignor Gorony, from Loris's staff," Hugh replied promptly. His eyes were round with wonder at what he had just seen and heard. "He and an armed escort are taking a barge as far as the Free Port of Concaradine, and will sail with a merchant fleet from there."

"I know Gorony," Duncan nodded. "Was anything added to the final draft of the letter? Anything that isn't in here?" He tapped the parchment with a well-manicured forefinger.

"Nothing," Hugh replied. "I made the final copy from this one," he gestured toward the letter on the table, "and I watched both of them sign and seal it. I don't know what they told Gorony after I left. And of course I have no idea what they may have said to him in advance."

"I see." Duncan turned the information over in his mind and nodded. "Is there anything else we should know?"

Hugh looked at his feet and wrung his hands together. There was another message, of course. But he had not counted on Duncan's earlier angry reaction, and he was not sure just how he should phrase the second matter now. It would not be easy, no matter how he phrased it.

"There—is something else you should know, Duncan." He paused, unable to look up. "I had not thought to find you here, but—there is another matter which came under my pen tonight. It—concerns you personally."

"Me?" Duncan glanced at Kelson and Nigel. "Go on. You may speak freely here."

"It—isn't that." Hugh swallowed with difficulty. "Duncan, Corrigan is suspending you. He's calling you to answer before his ecclesiastical court for dereliction of duty, probably tomorrow morning."

"What?"

Duncan stood, hardly aware that he did, and his face was ashen against the black of his cassock. Hugh could not raise his eyes.

"I'm sorry, Duncan," he whispered. "Apparently the archbishop thinks you were responsible for some of what happened at His Majesty's coronation last fall— begging your pardon, Sire," he glanced at Kelson. "He gave me his draft of the writ not an hour ago, asking to have it as soon as possible. I gave it to one of my clerks to copy and came straight here, intending to find you after I'd told His Majesty about the other matters."

He dared to look at Duncan finally, and whispered, "Duncan, are you mixed up in magic?"

Duncan moved toward the fireplace as one in a trance, his blue eyes wide, all pupil. "Suspended," he murmured disbelievingly, ignoring Hugh's question. "And called before his court."

He looked at Kelson. "My Prince, I must not be here tomorrow when that writ is served. It's not that I'm afraid—you know that. But if Corrigan takes me into custody now . . ."

Kelson nodded gravely. "I understand. What do you want me to do?"

Duncan thought a moment, looked guardedly at Nigel, then at Kelson. "Send me to Alaric, Sire. He must be warned of the threat of Interdict anyway, and I'll be safe from Corrigan at his court. It may even be that I can sway Bishop Tolliver to delay implementation of the Interdict."

"I'll give you a dozen of my best men," Kelson agreed. "What else?"

Duncan shook his head, trying to formulate a plan of action. "Hugh, you say that Gorony took the sea route. That's a three-day journey by ship, possibly less in storm weather if they pile on all canvas. Nigel, how are the roads between here and Alaric's capital this time of year?"

"Terrible. But you should be able to make it ahead of Gorony if you change horses along the way. Also, the weather gets a little better as you go south."

Duncan ran a weary hand through his short brown hair and nodded. "All right, I'll have to try it. At least I'll be out of Corrigan's jurisdiction once I cross the Corwyn border. Bishop Tolliver has been a friend of sorts in the past. I doubt he'd arrest me on Gorony's word alone. Besides, Gorony hopefully won't know about Corrigan's summons, even if he does get there ahead of me."

"It's settled, then," Kelson said, standing and nodding in Hugh's direction. "Father, I thank you for your loyalty. It shall not go unrewarded. But will it be safe for you to return to the archbishop's palace after what you've told us? I can offer my protection, if you like. Or you could go with Father Duncan."

Hugh smiled. "My thanks for your concern, Sire, but I believe I can serve you best if I return to my duties. I'll not have been missed yet, and I may be able to tell you more at a later date."

"Very well," Kelson nodded. Good luck to you, Father."

"Thank you, Sire," Hugh bowed. "And Duncan," he paused to clasp Duncan's hand and search his eyes, "be careful, my friend. I don't know what you've done and I don't want to know, but my prayers will be with you."

Duncan touched his shoulder in reassurance and nodded, and then Hugh was gone. As soon as the door had closed behind him, Duncan picked up the parchment and began refolding it, the crisp rustle the only sound in the still room. Now that he had a plan, his initial anger and shock were well under control, but he watched Kelson as he slipped the letter into his violet cincture. The boy was standing beside his chair, staring unseeing at the door and apparently oblivious to the fact that there was anyone else in the room. Nigel still sat at the table across from Duncan, but he too had withdrawn into a private world.

Duncan picked up his goblet and drained it, noticing the bent rim and realizing that he must have done it. He replaced the goblet silently and looked toward Kelson.

"I plan to take Hugh's letter with me if you have no objections, My Prince. Alaric will want to see it."

"Yes, of course," Kelson replied, shaking himself out of his reverie. "Uncle, will you see about the escort? And tell Richard he's to go along. Father Duncan may have need of a good man."

"Certainly, Kelson."

Nigel rose catlike and moved toward the door, slapping Duncan's shoulder as he passed. Then the door was closed, and there were only the two of them. Kelson had moved to the fireplace as Nigel left, and now he stared intently into the flames, resting his forehead on folded forearms along the edge of the mantel.

Duncan clasped his hands behind him and studied the floor uncertainly. There were things that only he and Kelson and Alaric had ever talked about, and he sensed it was something of this nature that was troubling the boy now. He had thought at the time that Kelson had taken this evening's events far too calmly, but he didn't dare wait much longer to get on the road. Corrigan just might decide to serve that writ tonight. And the longer Duncan waited, the farther ahead Gorony would be with the fateful letter.

Duncan cleared his throat gently, saw Kelson's shoulders stiffen at the sound.

"Kelson," he said quietly, "I have to go now."

"I know."

"Is there—any message I should take for Alaric?"

"No." The boy's voice was husky, strained. "Just tell him—tell him—"

He turned toward Duncan, his face pale, desperate. Duncan moved to his side in alarm, took him by the shoulders and gazed deeply into the wide, frightened eyes. The boy stood stiff and straight, fists clenched tightly at his sides, not in defiance but in fear. And the grey eyes filling with unbidden tears were no longer the eyes of a brave young king who had vanquished evil to keep his throne, but those of a child forced too soon and too long to function as an adult in a complex world. Duncan sensed all of this in less than a heartbeat, and he stared down at the boy in compassion. For all the young king's maturity, he was still a boy of fourteen—and a frightened one at that.

"Kelson?"

"Please be careful, Father," the boy whispered, his voice trembling on the brink of tears.

On impulse, Duncan pulled the boy to him and held him close, felt the proud young shoulders shudder convulsively as he surrendered to the rare luxury of tears. As Duncan stroked the raven head, he felt the boy relax, heard the stifled sobbing diminish. He hugged the boy closer still in a short gesture of comfort, then began to speak softly.

"Shall we talk about it, Kelson? It isn't nearly as terrifying if you look it in the eye."

"Yes it is," Kelson sniffed, his voice muffled against Duncan's shoulder.

"Well, now, I don't like to contradict kings, but I'm afraid you're wrong this time, Kelson. Suppose we consider the worst that can possibly happen and work up from there."

"V-very well."

"All right, then. What's on your mind?"

Kelson pulled away slightly and looked up at Duncan, then wiped his eyes and turned toward the fireplace, still in the protective circle of Duncan's left arm.

"What—" he whispered tremulously, "what will happen if you and Alaric are taken, Father?"

"Hmm, that depends on when and by whom," Duncan answered lightly, trying to reassure the boy.

"Suppose Loris captures you?"

Duncan considered the question. "Well, first I'd have to answer before the ecclesiastical court. If they could prove anything, which is open to debate, they could degrade me from the priesthood, strip away my orders. I might even be excommunicated."

"What if they found out you were half-Deryni?" the boy persisted. "Would they try to kill you?"

Duncan raised a thoughtful eyebrow. "They wouldn't like it at all if they were to discover that," he agreed, skirting the issue. "I should imagine I'd be excommunicated for sure if that were to happen. However, that's one very good reason I don't plan to let myself be taken. It would be awkward to say the least."

Kelson smiled in spite of himself. "Awkward. Yes, I suppose it would. Could you kill them if you had to?"

"I'd rather not," Duncan replied. "Another reason for not allowing them to catch me in the first place."

"What about Alaric?"

"Alaric?" Duncan shrugged. "It's difficult to say, Kelson. So far, Loris seems willing to settle for repentance. If Alaric renounces his powers and vows never to use them again, Loris will call off the Interdict."

"Alaric will never recant," Kelson said fiercely.

"Oh, I'm certain he won't," Duncan agreed. "In that case, the Interdict falls on Corwyn and we will begin to get political as well as religious repercussions."

Kelson looked up startled. "Why political? What will happen?"

"Well, since Alaric is the stated cause of the Interdict, the men of Corwyn will probably refuse to rally under his banner for the summer campaign, thus costing you approximately twenty percent of your fighting force. Alaric will be excommunicated, along with me, I'm sure. And that brings you further into the picture."

"Me? How?"

"Simple. Once Alaric and I are anathema, we carry excommunication with us like a plague. Anyone who associates with us is included in the decree. So that leaves you with two choices. You can obey the dictates of the archbishops and banish me and Alaric, thereby losing your best general on the eve of war. Or you can say the Devil with the archbishops and receive Alaric—and end up with all of Gwynedd under Interdict."

"They wouldn't dare!"

"Ah, but they would. Up until now your rank has protected you, Kelson. But I fear that even that will end shortly. Your mother has seen to that."

Kelson hung his head, remembering the scene a week before—how, unwittingly perhaps, his mother had set the stage for all that was now happening.

"But I don't understand why you have to go so far," Kelson was arguing. "Why St. Giles? You know that's only a few hours' ride from the Eastmarch border. There's going to be heavy fighting there in a few months."

Jehana calmly continued her packing, choosing garments from her wardrobe and handing them to a lady-in-waiting who was putting them in a leather-bound trunk. She was still in mourning for her dead husband, for it had been only four months since Brion's death. But her shining head was uncovered, the long auburn hair cascading smoothly down her back in a streak of red-gold, held only by a simple gold clasp at the nape of the neck. She turned to glance at Kelson, and Nigel frowning behind him, then returned to her work, her outward manner calm and dispassionate.

"Why St. Giles?" she answered. "I suppose because I stayed there for a few months many years ago, Kelson—before you were born. It's—something I have to do if I'm to be able to live with myself."

"There are a dozen places that would be safer if you feel you absolutely have to go," Nigel replied, pleating and unpleating a fold of his dark blue cloak in a disturbed gesture. "We're going to have enough to worry about without wondering if some raiding party has come and carried you off—or worse."

Jehana smiled and shook her head gently, looking the royal duke in the eyes. "Dear Nigel, brother, how can I make you understand? I have to go. And I have to go to Shannis Meer. If I were to stay here, knowing what's coming, knowing that Kelson will use his powers when and where he must, I would be tempted to use my own to try to stop him.

"I know in my mind that I dare not—not if he's to survive. And yet my heart, my soul, everything I've ever been taught—all tell me he must *not* be permitted to use those powers under any circumstances, that they're corrupt, evil." She turned to Kelson. "If I stayed, Kelson, I might destroy you."

"Could you really, Mother?" Kelson whispered. "Could you, a full Deryni despite your efforts to renounce that fact, truly destroy your own son because he is forced by circumstances to use the powers you gave him?"

Jehana reacted as though she had been struck, turned her back to Kelson and leaned heavily against a chair, head bowed as she strove to control her trembling. "Kelson," she began, her voice small, childlike, "don't you see? I may be Deryni, but I don't *feel* Deryni. I feel human. I think human. And as a human, I've been taught all my life that to be Deryni is to be evil, wrong." She turned to Kelson, her eyes wide and frightened.

"And if the people I love most are Deryni, use Deryni powers—Kelson, don't you see how it's tearing me apart? Kelson, I desperately fear that it's going to be human against Deryni again, as it was two hundred years ago. I don't think I can bear to be in the middle of it."

"You're already in the middle of it," Nigel snapped, "whether you like it or not. And if it *does* come to human against Deryni, you don't even have a side!"

"I know," Jehana whispered.

"Then why St. Giles?" Nigel continued angrily. "That's Archbishop Loris' bailiwick. Do you think he can help you resolve your conflict—an archbishop who's known for his anti-Deryni persecutions in the north? He's going to act soon, Jehana. He can't ignore what happened at the coronation much longer. And when he does make his move, I doubt that even Kelson's position will protect him for long."

"You can't change my mind," Jehana said steadily. "I'm leaving for Shannis Meer today. I intend to go to the sisters of St. Giles to fast and pray for guidance. But it has to be that way, Nigel. Right now, I am nothing. I can't be human and I can't be Deryni. And until I can discover which I am, I'm of no use to anyone."

"You're of use to me, Mother," Kelson said quietly, gazing across at her with hurt grey eyes. "Please stay."

"I cannot," Jehana whispered, choking back a sob.

"If—if I commanded you as king," Kelson quavered, the cords in his neck rippling as he fought back the tears, "would you stay then?"

Jehana stiffened for an instant, her eyes clouding with pain, then turned away, her shoulders shaking. "Don't make me answer that, Kelson," she managed to whisper. "Please don't ask me."

Kelson started to move toward her, to try to entreat her further, but Nigel put his finger to his lips and shook his head. Motioning Kelson to follow, he moved to the door and opened it quietly, waited as Kelson reluctantly joined him.

But the steps of both had been slow and heavy as they left the room. And the quiet sobbing closed behind the door still lingered in Kelson's mind.

Kelson swallowed hard and studied the flames in the fireplace before him. "Do you think the archbishops will attack me, then?"

"Perhaps not for a while," Duncan said. "So far, they've chosen to ignore the fact that you're Deryni too. But they won't ignore it if you defy an interdict."

"*I could destroy them!*" Kelson murmured, fists clenching and eyes narrowing as he considered his powers.

"But you won't," Duncan stated emphatically. "Because if you use your powers against the archbishops—whether or not they deserve it—that will be final proof to the rest of the Eleven Kingdoms that the Deryni do, indeed, intend to destroy Church and State and set up a new Deryni dictatorship. You must give the lie to that charge by avoiding a confrontation at all costs."

"Then, is it stalemate, Father? Me against the Church?"

"Not the Church, My Prince."

"Very well, then. The men who control the Church. It's the same thing, isn't it?"

"Not at all." Duncan shook his head. "It's not the Church we fight, though it may seem that way at first glance. It's an idea, Kelson. The idea that different is evil. That because some men are born with extraordinary powers and talents, those men are evil, no matter to what purpose they put those powers.

"We're fighting the idiotic notion that a man is responsible for the accident of his birth. That because a few men made grave errors in the name of a race over three hundred years ago, the whole race is damned and must forever suffer the consequences, generation after generation.

"That's what we're fighting, Kelson. Corrigan, Loris, even Wencit of Torenth—they're merely pawns in the larger struggle to prove that a man is worth something for himself alone, for what he does with his life, whether for good or for evil, with the talents he was born with, whatever he may be. Does any of that make sense?"

Kelson smiled self-consciously and lowered his eyes. "You sounded like Alaric just then. Or my father. He used to talk to me that way."

"He'd be very proud of you, Kelson. He was very fortunate to have a son like you. If I had a son . . ." He looked down at Kelson and a glance passed between them. Then Duncan squeezed the boy's shoulder reassuringly and stepped back to the table.

"I'm going then, My Prince. Alaric and I will make every effort to keep you informed of our progress or lack thereof. Meanwhile, trust Nigel. Rely on him. And whatever you do, don't intimidate the archbishops until Alaric and I have time to circumvent them."

"Don't worry, Father," Kelson smiled. "I won't do anything hasty. I'm not afraid any more."

"Just as long as that Haldane temper doesn't get out of hand," Duncan admonished with a grin. "I'll see you in Culdi in a week or so. The Lord keep you safe, My Prince."

"And you, Father," Kelson whispered as the priest disappeared through the door.

CHAPTER THREE

I am a man: I hold that nothing human is alien to me.

Terence

" 'AND OF the total, a two-fold increase over the last year's harvest, owing to good weather. Thus endeth the account of William, Reeve of the Ducal Estates at Donneral, rendered in March, the fifteenth year of the Duke's Grace, Lord Alaric of Corwyn.' "

Lord Robert of Tendal looked up from the document he had been reading and frowned as he glanced across at his employer. The duke was gazing out the solarium window to the barren garden below, his thoughts miles away. His booted feet were propped casually on a green leather footstool, and his blond head rested lightly against the high back of the carved wooden chair. It was obvious from the younger man's expression that he had not been listening.

Lord Robert cleared his throat tentatively, but there was no response. He pursed his lips and regarded his duke wistfully for another moment, then picked up the account roll from which he'd been reading and let it fall from a height of about two feet. Its impact echoed in the confines of the narrow chamber, rustling the documents and account rolls assembled on the table and breaking the duke's reverie. Lord Alaric Anthony Morgan looked up with a start and tried in

vain to cover a sheepish grin as he realized he'd been
caught daydreaming.

"Your Grace, you haven't heard a word I've said,"
Robert muttered reprovingly.

Morgan shook his head and smiled, rubbed a lazy
hand across his face. "I'm sorry, Robert. I was thinking of something else."

"Obviously."

As Robert reshuffled the documents he'd disturbed
in his outburst, Morgan stood and stretched. He ran
an absent hand through his close-cropped blond hair
as he glanced around the sparsely furnished solarium,
then sat down again.

"Very well," he sighed, leaning forward to probe at
the parchment halfheartedly with a ringed forefinger.
"We were doing the Donneral accounts, weren't we?
Do they seem to be in order?"

Robert pushed his chair back a few inches and
flung down his pen. "Of course they're in order, Alaric. But you know we have to go through this formali-
ty. These accounts represent a sizeable portion of your
land holdings—holdings which you will shortly be
losing as part of the Lady Bronwyn's dowry. And
even if you and Lord Kevin are inclined to take each
other's words in such matters, Kevin's father the duke
is *not!*"

"Kevin's father the duke is not marrying my sister!" Morgan retorted. He glanced sidelong at Robert
for a long moment, then let his wide mouth relax in a
smile. "Come, Robbie, be a good fellow and let me go
for the rest of the day. You and I both know those
accounts are correct. If you won't let me out of reviewing them altogether, let's at least postpone until
tomorrow."

Robert tried to look very stern and disapproving,
then gave in and threw up his hands. "Very well,
Your Grace," he said, gathering up his account rolls
and tallies. "But as your chancellor I am constrained

to point out that the wedding is less than two weeks away. And you have court tomorrow, and the Hort of Orsal's ambassador arrives tomorrow, and Lord Henry de Vere wants to know what you intend to do about Warin de Grey, and—"

"Yes, Robert; tomorrow, Robert," Morgan said, assuming his most innocent expression and only barely controlling a grin of triumph. "And now may I be excused, Robert?"

Robert rolled his eyes heavenward in a silent appeal for patience, then waved dismissal with a gesture of defeat. Morgan jumped up and bowed with a certain ironic flourish, then turned on his heel and strode out of the solarium to the great hall beyond. Robert watched him go, remembering the slender, tow-headed boy who had become this man—Duke of Corwyn, Lord General of the King's Armies, King's Champion—and a half-Deryni sorcerer.

Robert crossed himself furtively at that last thought, for Morgan's Deryni heritage was one thing he preferred not to remember about the Corwyn family he had served all his life. Not that the Corwyns had not been good to him, he rationalized. His own family, the lords of Tendal, had held the hereditary chancellorship of Corwyn for two hundred years now, since before the Restoration. And through all those years, the dukes of Corwyn had been fair and honest rulers, even if they were Deryni. Being strictly objective, Robert found he had no complaints.

Of course, he had to put up with Morgan's capricious whims occasionally, like today. But that was all a part of the game they played. The duke probably had good reason for insisting on adjournment this afternoon.

Still, it would have been nice to win occasionally. . . .

Robert gathered up his documents and stored them neatly in a cabinet near the window. Actually, it was just as well the duke had curtailed the accounting for the afternoon. For though Morgan had probably conveniently forgotten about it, there was to be a state dinner in the great hall tonight. And if he, Robert, did not coordinate it, the affair was sure to be a resounding failure. Morgan was notorious for eschewing formal functions unless they were absolutely necessary. And the fact that a number of eligible ladies would be present who keenly desired to become the next Duchess of Corwyn was not going to improve the duke's disposition.

Whistling lightly under his breath, Robert dusted his hands together and headed toward the great hall the way Morgan had gone. After this afternoon's session, it would be a distinct pleasure to watch Morgan squirm under the scrutiny of those ladies tonight. Robert could hardly wait.

Morgan scanned the courtyard automatically as he left the great hall. Far across the yard by the stables, he saw a stable boy running beside a huge chestnut destrier, one of the R'Kassan stallions the Hortic traders had brought in last week. The great horse was barely trotting, one of his long strides making three or four of the boy's. And to the left by the forge, Morgan's young military aide, Sean Lord Derry, was talking earnestly with James the blacksmith, apparently trying to agree on how the animal should be shod.

Derry saw Morgan and lifted a hand in greeting, but he did not cease his wrangling with the smithy. Horses were a very important subject with young Derry. He considered himself an expert; and, in fact, he was. Consequently, he was not to be bullied by a mere blacksmith.

Morgan was glad that Derry didn't join him. Astute as the young marcher lord might be, he did not always understand the moods of his commander. And while Morgan enjoyed Derry's company, he didn't feel like talking just now. That was why he'd fled

Lord Robert's account briefing, why he'd bolted outside at the first opportunity. There would be enough of pressure and responsibility later tonight.

He reached a side gate to the left of the great hall and let himself through. The gardens were still dead from the long winter, but that would probably mean he could be alone for a while. He saw a man cleaning the falcon mews far to the left, close by the stable area, but he knew he wouldn't be disturbed from there. Miles the falconer was a mute—though his eyes and ears were doubly sharp, as seeming compensation for the handicap—and the old man preferred the clicks and whistles of his falcons, which he could imitate, to the speech of men. He would not bother with a lonely duke who sought the solitude of the deserted gardens.

Morgan began to walk slowly down a path away from the mews, his hands clasped behind him. He knew why he was restless today. Part of it was the political situation, only delayed, not solved, by Kelson's defeat of the Shadowed One last fall. Charissa was dead, and her traitor accomplice Ian, too, but an even more formidable adversary now prepared to take her place—Wencit of Torenth, whose scouting parties were already reported along the mountains to the northeast.

And Cardosa—that was another problem. As soon as Wencit could get through the snow, which would be soon, he would be hammering at the gates of the mountain city once again. The approach through the high passes east of Cardosa was not difficult after the first week of spring flooding. But on the west, the direction from which relief must come, the Cardosa Pass would be a raging cataract from March to May. There could be no aid for Cardosa until the thaws were nearly over—two months hence. And that would be too late.

He paused by one of the reflecting pools in the

dead garden and gazed absently into the depths. The gardeners had cleared away the winter's debris and restocked the pond, and now long-tailed goldfish and tiny polliwogs swam in the currentless water, drifting across his field of vision as though suspended in time and space.

He smiled as he realized he could call them if he wished—and they would come. But the thought did not amuse him today. After a moment, he let his eyes focus on the surface of the water, let himself study the reflection of the tall blond man who started back at him.

Wide grey eyes in an oval face, pale from the winter dimness; hair glistening gold in the wan spring sunlight, cropped to only a few inches for ease of care in the battlefield; full, wide mouth above the squared-off chin; long sideburns accentuating the lean cheekbones.

He tugged at the bottom of the short green doublet with annoyance, glared at the reflection of the golden gryphon blazoned aesthetically but incorrectly across his chest.

He didn't like the outfit. The Corwyn gryphon should be green, proper on black, not gold on green. And the little jeweled basilard stuck in his belt was a travesty of weaponry—an elegant but useless accoutrement his wardrober, Lord Rathold, had insisted was essential to his ducal image.

Morgan scowled darkly at the pompous image in the water. When he had a choice—which he had to admit was most of the time—he preferred dark velvets covering mail, the supple sleekness of riding leathers, not the bright satins and jeweled toadstickers people seemed to think appropriate at a ducal court.

Still, he supposed he must make a few dress concessions. The people of Corwyn did not have their duke in residence for much of the year, what with service at the court in Rhemuth and such. When they did, they had a right to expect that he would dress befitting his rank.

They need never know that his compliance was not complete. For while they would not be surprised to find that the jeweled plaything at his waist was not his only weapon—there was a stiletto in a worn leather scabbard on his left forearm, as well as other aids—still, they would doubtless be chagrined were they to learn that he would wear light mail under his finery at dinner tonight. Quite chagrined. For to humans that betokened a mistrust of one's guests—a terrible breach of etiquette.

At least this would be one of the last state dinners for a while, Morgan thought, as he began walking again. With the spring thaws coming, it would soon be time to head back to Rhemuth and the king's service for another season. Of course, this year it would be a different king, with Brion dead. But his latest dispatch from Kelson indicated—

His train of thought was interrupted by the sound of footsteps in the gravel far to his right, and he turned to see Lord Hillary, the commander of the castle garrison, approaching at a brisk walk, his blue-green cloak whipping behind him in the breeze. His round face was puzzled.

"What's wrong, Hillary?" Morgan asked as the man drew near and sketched a hasty salute.

"I'm not sure, Your Grace. The harbor lookout reports that the Caralighter fleet has rounded the point and will be docking by nightfall, as soon as the tide shifts. Your flagship, *Rhafallia*, is in the lead, and she's flying royal dispatch signals. I think it could be the mobilization order, m'lord."

"I doubt it," Morgan shook his head. "Kelson wouldn't entrust that important a message to ship transport. He'd send a courier." He frowned. "I thought the fleet went only as far as Concaradine this trip."

"Those were their orders, m'lord. And they're back a day early at that."

"Strange," Morgan murmured, almost forgetting Hillary was there. "Still—send an escort to meet *Rhafallia* when she docks and bring back the dispatches. And let me know as soon as they've arrived."

"Aye, m'lord."

As the man moved off, Morgan ran a puzzled hand through his hair and began walking again. That Kelson should send dispatches by ship was strange indeed. He almost never did that. Especially with the uncertainty of the weather farther north this time of year. The whole thing had an ominous ring to it, like—like the dream!

He suddenly remembered what he'd dreamed last night. In fact, now that he considered it, that was another part of what had been bothering him all day.

He'd slept badly, which was unusual since he could generally turn sleep off and on at will. But last night he'd been plagued by nightmares—vivid, frightening scenes which had made him wake in a cold sweat.

He'd seen Kelson, listening tensely to someone whose back was all that he could see—and Duncan, his usually serene face drawn, troubled, angry, very unlike his priestly cousin. And then the ghostly, cowled visage he'd come to associate with legend last fall—Camber of Culdi, the renegade patron saint of Deryni magic.

Morgan looked up to find himself standing before the Grotto of the Hours, that dim, cavernous recess which had been the private retreat and meditation place of the Corwyn dukes for more than three hundred years. The gardeners had been at work here, too, burning leaves they had swept away from the doorway itself. But there was still debris just inside the entrance, and on impulse Morgan swung back the creaking iron gate and stepped inside. Taking a lighted torch from the wall bracket by the gate, he raked away the winter's debris with his boot and made his way into the cool interior.

The Grotto of the Hours was not large inside. Outside, its bulk reared a scant twenty feet above the level of the garden, the outer outline disguised as a rocky outcropping of stone in the midst of the garden paths. In spring and summer, small trees and bushes flourished green on the outside of the mass, with flowers of every hue. Water trickled down one side in a perpetual waterfall.

But inside, the structure had been fashioned to look like a natural cave, the walls irregular, rough, damp. As Morgan stepped into the inner chamber, he felt the closeness of the low ceiling arched above him. A swath of weak sunlight streamed through a high barred and grilled window on the opposite side of the chamber, falling on the stark black marble sarcophagus which dominated that side of the room—the tomb of Dominic, Corwyn's first duke. A carved stone chair faced the tomb in the center of the chamber. There was a candlestick with a stump of candle on the sarcophagus, but the metal was dulled by a winter's disuse, the candle stump mouse-nibbled and burned down.

But Morgan had not entered the grotto to pay homage to his ancient ancestor today. It was the rest of the chamber he was interested in—the side walls of the cavern, smoothed and plastered, then inlaid with mosaic portraits of those whose special favor was thought to be on the House of Corwyn.

Scanning briefly, Morgan saw representations of the Trinity, the Archangel Michael slaying the Dragon of Darkness, Saint Raphael the Healer, Saint George with his dragon. There were others, but Morgan was interested in only one. Turning to the left, he took three practiced steps which carried him to the opposite side of the chamber, then held his torch aloft before the portrait of—Camber of Culdi, the Deryni Lord of Culdi, *Defensor Hominum.*

Morgan had never quite resolved his strange fascination for the being of the portrait. In fact, he had only really become aware of Camber's importance last fall, when he and Duncan were struggling to keep Kelson on the throne.

He'd had "visions" then. At first there had been only the fleeting impression of that other's presence, the eerie feeling that other hands and powers were assisting his own. But then he had seen the face—or he *thought* he had seen the face. And it had always appeared in connection with something concerned with the legendary Deryni saint.

Saint Camber. Camber of Culdi. A name to resound in the annals of Deryni history. Camber, who had discovered, during the dark days of the Interregnum, that the awesome Deryni powers could sometimes be bestowed on humans; Camber, who had turned the tide for the Restoration and brought the human rulers of old back to power.

He had been canonized for it. A grateful people could not find high enough praise for the man who had brought the hated Deryni dictatorship to an end. But human memory was short. And in time the sons of man forgot that salvation as well as suffering had come from the hands of the Deryni. The brutal reaction which swept through the Eleven Kingdoms then had been a thing most humans wished to forget. Thousands of innocent Deryni perished by the sword or in other, more perverse ways, in supposed retribution for what their fathers had done. When it was over, only a handful survived—most of them in hiding, a few under the tenuous protection of a minute number of powerful human lords who remembered how it had really been. Needless to say, Camber's sainthood had been one of the first casualties.

Camber of Culdi, *Defensor Hominum.* Camber of

Culdi, Patron of Deryni Magic. Camber of Culdi, at whose portrait a descendant of that same race of sorcerers now gazed with impatient curiosity, trying to fathom the strange bond he seemed to have acquired with the long-dead Deryni Lord.

Morgan held his torch closer to the mosaic and studied the face, trying to force finer detail to emerge from the rough texture of the inlay. The eyes stared back at him—light eyes above a firm, resolute chin. The rest was obscured by the monkish cowl draped around the head, but Morgan had the distinct impression that the man would have been blond, had the hood been permitted to fall back. He couldn't say why. Perhaps it was a carryover from the visions he'd encountered.

Idly, he wondered whether the visions would ever resume, felt a shiver of apprehension ripple down his spine as the thought crossed his mind. It couldn't be Saint Camber really. Or could it?

Lowering the torch, Morgan stepped back a pace, still looking at the mosaic portrait. While not irreligious by any means, he found that the idea of divine or semidivine intervention on his behalf bothered him. He didn't like the idea of Heaven being that watchful of him.

Still, if not Saint Camber, then who? Another Deryni? No human could do the things the being had done. And if Deryni, why didn't he say so? Surely he must realize what Morgan would be thinking about such manifestations. And he seemed to be helping; but why the secrecy? Maybe it was Saint Camber.

He shuddered and crossed himself self-consciously at the thought, then shook himself back to sanity. Such thinking was getting him nowhere. He must pull his thoughts together.

Abruptly, he heard a commotion ensuing in the courtyard on the other side of the garden, and then running footsteps coming through the garden in his direction.

"Morgan! Morgan?"

It was Derry's voice.

Slipping back through the access way, Morgan jammed his torch into the wall bracket and stepped out into the sunlight. As he did, Derry spotted him and changed course, running across the grey garden toward the duke.

"M'lord!" Derry yelled, his face alight with excitement. "Come out to the courtyard. See who's here!"

"*Rhafallia*'s not in port already, is she?" Morgan called as he headed toward the young man.

"No, sir," Derry laughed, shaking his head. "You'll have to see for yourself. Come on!"

Mystified, Morgan started back across the garden, raising an inquiring eyebrow as he reached Derry and fell into step beside him. Derry was beaming from ear to ear—a reaction which could indicate the presence of a good horse, a beautiful woman, or—

"Duncan!" Morgan finished aloud as he stepped through the gate and saw his cousin across the courtyard.

There was Duncan swinging down from a huge, mud-splattered grey destrier, his black cloak damp and wind-whipped, the edge of his riding cassock torn and muddied. Ten or twelve guards in Kelson's royal crimson livery dismounted around him, and Morgan recognized Kelson's own squire, young Richard FitzWilliam, holding the grey's bridle as Duncan dismounted.

"Duncan! You old reprobate!" Morgan exclaimed, striding across the damp cobblestones of the courtyard. "What the Devil are you doing in Coroth?"

"Visiting you," Duncan replied, blue eyes twinkling with pleasure as he and Morgan came together in a quick embrace. "Things weren't exciting enough in Rhemuth, so I thought I'd come pester my favorite cousin. Frankly, my archbishop was overjoyed to be rid of me."

"Well, it's good he can't see you now," Morgan said, grinning widely as Duncan pulled a pair of saddlebags from the grey's back and slung them casually over his arm. "Just look at you—covered with mud and smelling like horses. Come on and let's get you cleaned up. Derry, see that Duncan's escort is taken care of, will you? And then see if you can get my squires to draw him a bath."

"Right away, m'lord," Derry said, smiling and bowing slightly as he backed a few steps in the direction of the riders. "And welcome back to Coroth, Father Duncan."

"Thank you, Derry."

As Derry moved among the guards and began issuing orders, Morgan and Duncan bounded up the steps and into the great hall. The hall was a flurry of activity in preparation for the coming banquet, and scores of servants and workmen were setting up heavy trestle tables and benches, rehanging the costly tapestries which had been removed and cleaned for the occasion. Kitchen varlets swarmed through the hall, sweeping hearths and readying spits for the roasting of meats. And a group of pages was industriously polishing the ornate wooden chairs at the high table.

Lord Robert stood by to oversee the entire operation. As the workmen finished setting up each table, Robert directed kitchen wenches in the wiping down with oil to bring out the rich patina of age and supervised the placing of the great pewter candelabras and service from the ducal treasury. To his right, Lord Hamilton, the balding seneschal of Castle Coroth, had been arranging the placement of musicians for the evening's entertainment. At the moment, he was engaged in a heated argument with Morgan's chief talent for the evening, the much acclaimed and celebrated troubadour Gwydion.

As Morgan and Duncan approached, the little performer was almost dancing in his anger, resplendent as a peacock in his full-sleeved orange doublet and hose. His black eyes snapped in outrage as he stamped his foot and half-turned away from Hamilton in disgust. Morgan caught his eye and crooked his finger for Gwydion to approach, and the troubadour threw Hamilton one final haughty look of contempt before gliding to Morgan's side to bow curtly.

"Your Grace, I cannot work with that man any longer! He is arrogant, boorish, and has no artistic rapport whatsoever!"

Morgan tried to conceal a smile. "Duncan, I have the somewhat dubious honor to present Master Gwydion ap Plenneth, the latest and most illustrious addition to my court. I might also add that he sings the finest ballads in the Eleven Kingdoms—when he's not quarreling with my staff, that is. Gwydion, my paternal cousin, Monsignor Duncan McLain."

"Welcome to Coroth, Monsignor," Gwydion murmured formally, ignoring Morgan's implied reprimand. "His Grace has spoken of you often and well. I trust your stay will be a pleasant one."

"I thank you," Duncan replied, returning the bow. "Back in Rhemuth, you're reputed to be the finest troubadour since the Lord Llewelyn. I trust you will see fit to prove that reputation before I must leave."

"Gwydion shall play tonight if he is permitted to arrange the musicians as he wishes, Monsignor," the troubadour bowed. He glanced at Morgan. "But if Lord Hamilton persists in his malicious persecution, I fear I shall develop a splitting headache. That, of course, would make it quite impossible for me to perform."

He drew himself up haughtily and folded his arms across his chest in a theatrical gesture of finality, then contemplated the ceiling with studied nonchalance. It was all Morgan could do to keep from laughing.

"Very well," the duke said, clearing his throat to cover his smile. "Tell Hamilton I said you can arrange things any way you like. I want no more quarreling, though. Do you understand?"

"Of course, Your Grace."

With a curt nod, he turned on his heel and strode back across the hall to where he had been working, arms still folded across his chest. As he approached, Lord Hamilton saw him and glanced at Morgan as though asking for support, but Morgan merely shook his head and gestured toward Gwydion with his chin. With a sigh that was almost audible even across the room, Hamilton nodded acquiescence and disappeared through another door. Gwydion took over where Hamilton had left off, directing the complete rearrangement of the musicians' area and strutting like a bantam rooster.

"Is he always that temperamental?" Duncan asked, somewhat taken aback, as he and Morgan continued on through the hall and up a flight of narrow stairs.

"Not at all. He's usually worse."

They came to the top of the staircase and Morgan opened a heavy door. A few feet beyond that was another door, heavy walnut inlaid with an enameled Corwyn gryphon. Morgan touched the eye of the beast with his signet, and the door opened silently. Inside was Morgan's private study, his chamber of magic, his *sanctum sanctorum*.

It was a round room perhaps thirty feet in diameter, perched atop the highest tower in the ducal castle. The walls were of heavy stone, pierced only by seven narrow green glass windows which extended from eye level to ceiling. At night, when the candles burned late in the round tower room, the tower could be seen for miles around, its seven green windows glowing like beacons in the night sky.

There was a wide fireplace in the wall ninety degrees to the right of the doorway, with a raised hearth which extended six to eight feet to either side. Above the mantel hung a silk banner of the same Gryphon design which graced the door, and various other objects rested along the top of the mantel. A tapestry map of the Eleven Kingdoms covered the wall directly opposite the door, with a wide, heavily laden bookcase beneath it. There was an immense desk with a carved wooden chair to the left of the bookcase, and a wide couch covered with a black fur throw to the left of that. Immediately to the left of the door was the tiny portable altar Duncan had known he would find, with a plain, dark wood prie-dieu before it.

All these things took but an instant to assess, however. For Duncan's attention was drawn almost immediately to the center of the room, which was bathed in a misty emerald glow from a high, round skylight. Beneath the skylight was a small table perhaps an arm's length across, flanked by two comfortable-looking chairs with green leather cushions. In the center of that table, a small, translucent amber sphere about four inches in diameter rested in the upraised claws of a golden Corwyn gryphon.

Duncan whistled lightly under his breath and crossed to the table, never taking his eyes from the amber sphere. He started to reach out to touch it, then changed his mind and merely stood there admiring. Morgan smiled as he joined his cousin and leaned against the back of one chair.

"How do you like it?" he asked. The question was strictly rhetorical, for Duncan was obviously enthralled with the thing.

"It's magnificent," Duncan whispered, with the awe in his voice of any artisan looking at a particularly fine tool of his trade. "Where did you ever find such an enormous—it *is* a *shiral* crystal, isn't it?"

Morgan nodded. "The very same. The Hort of Orsal found it for me a few months ago—at an outrageous price, I might add. Go ahead. Touch it if you like."

As Duncan slipped into the nearer of the two chairs, the forgotten saddlebags slung across his arm bumped against the table. He looked down with a start, as though just remembering he had them, and his handsome face went tense, guarded. He lifted the bags to the table and started to speak, but Morgan shook his head.

"Go on with the crystal," he urged, seeing Duncan's discomfiture. "I don't know what you've got in there that you think is so important, but whatever it is it can wait."

Duncan bit his lip and looked across at Morgan for a long moment, then nodded acquiescence and eased the bags to the floor. He took a deep breath and pressed his palms together for an instant, then exhaled and reached out to surround the crystal with his two hands. As he relaxed, the crystal began to glow.

"Beautiful," Duncan breathed, the tension draining away as he moved his hands lower on the crystal to better expose it. "With a crystal this size, I ought to be able to form images without half trying."

Concentrating anew, he gazed deeply into the crystal and watched the glow intensify. The sphere lost its opacity and became a transparent amber, clouded briefly as though breathed upon from within. Then a shape began to form in the mist, which gradually solidified and took on human aspects. It was a tall man with silvery hair, wearing an archbishop's robes and miter and wielding a heavy jeweled crozier. He was very angry.

Loris! Morgan thought to himself as he leaned forward to inspect the image. *What the Devil is he up to now? He certainly has Duncan riled, whatever it is. . . .*

Duncan snatched away his hands as though the crystal had suddenly become hot to the touch, and a look of disgust contorted his features for an instant. As his hands left the sphere, the form vanished and the sphere again became translucent. Duncan rubbed his hands against his cassock as though wiping away something distasteful, then forced himself to relax, folded his hands neatly on the table. He looked at his hands as he spoke.

"I suppose it's fairly obvious that this isn't just a social call," he murmured bitterly. "I couldn't even hide it from the *shiral* crystal."

Morgan nodded understandingly. "I realized that when you got off your horse." He studied the gryphon signet on his right forefinger and rubbed it absently. "Do you want to tell me what has happened?"

Duncan shrugged and sighed. "There isn't any easy way to say it, Alaric. I—I've been suspended."

"Suspended?" Morgan's jaw dropped in amazement. "What for?"

Duncan forced a wry smile. "Can't you guess? Apparently Archbishop Loris convinced Corrigan that my part in the coronation battle was more than just that of Kelson's confessor. Which, unfortunately, is true. They may even suspect that I'm half-Deryni. They were going to call me before an ecclesiastical court, only a friend found out and warned me in time. It's what we always feared might happen."

Morgan exhaled and lowered his eyes. "I'm sorry, Duncan. I know how much the priesthood means to you. I—I don't know what to say."

Duncan smiled weakly. "It's worse than you suspect, my friend. Frankly, if it were only the suspension, I don't think I'd be so worried. I find that the more I function as a Deryni, the less important my vows seem to become." He reached to the saddlebags beside his chair and withdrew a folded piece of parchment which he placed on the table between them.

"This is a copy of a letter now enroute to your bishop, Ralf Tolliver. A friend of mine who's a clerk in Corrigan's chancery risked a lot to get it for me. The point of the letter is that Loris and Corrigan want Tolliver to excommunicate you unless you recant your powers and 'take up a life of repentance.' Those are Archbishop Corrigan's words, I believe."

"Me, recant?" Morgan snorted, an incredulous half grin on his face. "They must be jesting." He started to slide the letter across the table and pick it up, but Duncan held his wrist.

"I still haven't finished, Alaric," he said quietly, holding Morgan's gaze with his own. "Unless you do recant and comply with their orders, they'll not only excommunicate you—they'll put all of Corwyn under Interdict."

"Interdict!"

Duncan nodded and released Morgan's wrist. "Which means that the Church will effectively cease to function in Corwyn. There will be no Mass, no marriages, baptisms, burials, no last rites for the dying—nothing. I'm not sure how your people will react."

Morgan set his jaw firmly and picked up the letter. He unfolded it and began reading, and as he read his grey eyes went cold and steely: " '*To His Most Reverend Excellency Ralf Tolliver, Bishop of Coroth ... Reverend Brother, it has come to our attention ... Duke Alaric Morgan ... heinous crimes of magic and sorcery contrary to the laws of God . . . if said duke does not recant his Deryni powers . . . excommunicate . . . Corwyn under Interdict . . . hope that you will do this . . . sign of good faith . . . *' Damn!"

Swearing explosively, Morgan half-crumpled the parchment in anger and threw it down on the table.

"May nameless maledictions pursue them to the depths of Hell-slime! May lyfangs devour the last of their line, and thirteen devils forever haunt their sleep! Damn them, Duncan! What are they trying to do to me?"

He sat back in his chair and exhaled explosively, and Duncan grinned.

"Do you feel better?"

"No. You realize, of course, that Loris and Corrigan have me exactly where they want me. They know that my influence in Corwyn is based not on pro-Deryni feeling, but on my people being pro-Morgan. If the Curia of Gwynedd declares me anathema because I'm Deryni, they know full well that my people will go along rather than see Corwyn put under Interdict. I can't ask my people to give up their faith for me, Duncan."

Duncan slumped back in his chair and gazed expectantly across at his cousin. "So, what are we going to do about it?"

Morgan smoothed the crumpled letter and looked at it again, then pushed it back across the table as though he had seen enough of it.

"Has Tolliver seen the original of this letter yet?"

"I don't see how. Monsignor Gorony sailed aboard the *Rhafallia* two days ago. If my calculations are correct, he should be arriving sometime tomorrow."

"More likely about three hours from now, when the tide shifts," Morgan retorted. "Gorony must have bribed my captains to pile on more sail. I hope they made him pay!"

"Is there any chance of intercepting the letter?"

Morgan grimaced and shook his head. "I don't dare, Duncan. If I do, I'm violating the immunity of the very Church I'm trying to protect in Corwyn. I have to let Gorony get through to Tolliver."

"Suppose I get there first, then. If I were to show Tolliver our copy of the letter and explain your concern for the situation, he might agree to delay for as much as several weeks before he takes action. Besides, I don't think he's going to like being dictated to by Loris and Corrigan. It's no secret that they consider him a backwater priest, country simpleton of sorts. We could play on his resentment—whatever it takes to keep the Interdict from falling. What do you think?"

Morgan nodded. "It might work. Go make yourself

presentable and tell Derry to saddle a fresh horse for you. While you're doing that, I'll write a second letter to Tolliver asking for his support. It's not going to be easy." He rose and crossed to his desk, already drawing out parchment and ink.

"Somehow I must strike just the proper balance between ducal authority, penitent son of the Church, and long-time friend—all without making the Deryni issue so strong he feels he can't in conscience go along."

A quarter of an hour later, Morgan scrawled his signature at the bottom of the crucial letter and added his paraph, the highly personal flourish at the end of the stroke to guard against forgery. Then he applied sealing wax in a bright green blob below his name, pressed his gryphon seal into the hot wax.

He could have done without the wax. With a little help, the Deryni signet was easily capable of imprinting without benefit of wax. But he didn't think it would be much to the bishop's liking. The Most Reverend Ralf Tolliver had nothing against the Deryni personally, but there were bounds beyond which even Morgan dared not go. A flagrant, or even minor, act of magic at this stage could entirely undo whatever good the letter, so painstakingly drafted, might accomplish. Morgan was folding the letter to seal it again when Duncan returned, a heavy wool riding cloak flung over one arm. Derry was with him.

"Finished?" Duncan asked, crossing to the desk and peering over Morgan's shoulder

"Almost."

He dripped sealing wax on the overlap to seal the letter closed and quickly stamped it with his seal. He looked up as he blew on the hot wax to cool it, then handed it to Duncan.

"Do you have the other letter?"

"Umm." Duncan snapped his fingers. "Derry, bring me that, would you?"

He pointed to the letter on the central table and Derry brought it, watching as the priest tucked it into the cincture of his clean cassock.

"Do you want an escort, Father?" Derry asked.

"Not unless Alaric does. Personally, I think that the fewer people who know about this, the better off we are. Alaric, do you agree?"

Morgan nodded. "Good luck, Cousin."

Duncan gave a quick grin, a nod, then was out the door and on his way. Derry stared after him for a moment, then turned back to Morgan. The duke had not moved from where he sat, but he seemed to be in a world of his own. It was with some hesitancy that Derry ventured to interrupt that world.

"M'lord?"

"Hmm?" Morgan looked up startled, almost as though he had forgotten the young man was there— though Derry was sure he hadn't.

"May I ask a question, sir?"

Morgan shook his head and grinned sheepishly. "Of course. You probably have no idea of what's going on right now."

Derry smiled. "It's not quite that bad, m'lord. Is there anything I can do to help?"

Morgan studied the young lord, his chin resting on one hand, then nodded tentatively. "Perhaps there is," he said, sitting forward in his chair. "Derry, you've been with me for a long time now. Would you be willing to become involved in magic for me?"

Derry broke into a broad grin. "You know I would, sir!"

"Very well, then. Come over to the map with me."

Morgan moved to the tapestried map covering the near wall, then ran his fingers along a broad finger of blue until he found what he was looking for. Derry watched and listened attentively as the duke began to speak.

"Now, here's Coroth. Here's the estuary arising from the two rivers. Up the Western River which forms our northeastern border with Torenth is Fathane, the Torenthi trading town. It's also a staging area for all of Wencit's raiding expeditions along this segment of the border.

"What I want you to do is to ride upriver toward Fathane, on the Torenthi side, then loop west along our northern border and back here. Your mission is to gather information, and there are three areas I'd like you to concentrate on: Wencit of Torenth's plans for the war in this area; anything you can find out about this Warin rascal in the north; and any leak of the threatened Interdict. Duncan told you about that, didn't he?"

"Yes, sir."

"Very well. You can choose your own disguise, but I think a fur trader or trapper would be good· cover. I'd rather you weren't recognized as a fighting man."

"I understand, sir."

"Good. Now, here's where the magic comes in."

He reached along the side of his neck until he found a slender silvery chain, which he then proceeded to pull outside his emerald tunic. As the last of the chain emerged and Morgan slipped it off over his head, Derry could see that there was a silver medallion of some sort attached to the chain. He bent his head slightly so Morgan could loop the long chain over his head, then looked down curiously at the medallion which now dangled at mid-chest level. It seemed to be a holy medal of some kind, though Derry couldn't identify either the figure depicted or the legend inscribed around the edge. Morgan turned the medallion to face forward, then leaned back against the bookcase beneath the tapestry map.

"All right, now I'm going to ask you to help me

establish a special kind of Deryni rapport. It's akin to Mind-Seeing, which you've seen me do a number of times, but not nearly as tiring because you remain in control. Just relax and try to let your mind go blank. It's not unpleasant, I assure you," he added, seeing Derry's momentary discomfiture.

Derry nodded and swallowed.

"Good. Now watch my finger and relax."

As Morgan held up his right index finger, he began moving it slowly toward Derry's face. The young man's eyes tracked the finger almost until it touched the bridge of his nose, then fluttered shut. He exhaled softly and relaxed as Morgan's hand rested on his forehead.

Morgan held that position for perhaps half a minute, nothing outwardly happening, then reached out and enclosed the medal in his other hand, closed his eyes. After another minute he released the medallion and looked up, dropped his hand from Derry's forehead. Derry's eyes popped open with a start.

"You—talked to me!" he whispered incredulously, his voice tinged with awe. "You—" He looked down at the medallion in amazement. "I can really use this to communicate with you all the way from Fathane?"

"Or farther, if necessary," Morgan agreed. "Just remember that it's a difficult operation. Being Deryni, I *could* call you any time it became necessary—though it would take a great deal of energy. But you have to confine your calls to the times we agree upon. If I'm not trying to reach you, you haven't the strength to summon me yourself. That's why it's important that you keep track of the time. I'll expect your first contact about three hours after dark tomorrow night. You should be in Fathane by then."

"Aye, m'lord. And all I have to do is use the spell you taught me, and that will put me into rapport?" His blue eyes were wide, but trusting.

"Correct."

Derry nodded and started to tuck the talisman into his tunic, then stopped and pulled it out to look at it again. "What kind of medal is this anyway, M'Lord? I don't recognize the inscription or the figure "

"I was afraid you'd ask," Morgan grinned. "It's a very old Saint Camber medallion dating from just after the Restoration. It was left to me in my mother's will."

"A Camber medal!" Derry breathed. "What if someone recognizes it?"

"If you keep your clothes on, no one will even see the medal, much less recognize it, my irreverent friend!" Morgan retorted, slapping Derry's shoulder and chuckling. "No wenching for you on this trip, I'm afraid. This is strictly business."

"You always have to take the fun out of everything, don't you?" Derry muttered, tucking the medallion inside his tunic with a grin as he turned to leave.

Darkness was approaching as Duncan guided his tired mount back toward the city of Coroth, and the night chill of the mountain country was already beginning to settle in the glens.

The meeting with Tolliver had been at least partially successful. The bishop had agreed to delay his answer to the couriers from Rhemuth until he could evaluate the situation, and had promised to keep Morgan advised of any further action regarding his eventual decision. But the Deryni aspect of the case had bothered Tolliver, as Duncan had known it would. And the bishop had warned Duncan to dabble no more in magic if he valued his priesthood and, indeed, his immortal soul.

Duncan pulled his cloak around himself more closely and urged his horse to a faster pace, remembering that Alaric would be impatient for word of the outcome. Also, he mused, there would be a state dinner awaiting him. And unlike his ducal cousin, Duncan loved ceremony. If he hurried, he should be able to make it in time for the main course. It was not yet dark.

As he rounded the next bend, not really thinking about anything in particular, he was suddenly aware of a tall dark form standing in the road not ten yards ahead of him. It was difficult to make out any details in the failing light, but as Duncan drew rein to avoid riding the man down, he noted that the pedestrian was clad in the garb of a monk, a peaked cowl pulled over his head and a staff in his hand.

Something was not as it should have been, however. Almost unconsciously the warrior in Duncan guided his right hand to the hilt of the sword strapped beneath his left knee. The figure turned his head toward Duncan—he could not have been more than ten feet away—and Duncan jerked his mount to a halt, his heart in his throat.

For the face which gazed serenely up at him from beneath the grey cowl was one he had come to know quite well in the last months, though never in the flesh. He and Alaric had studied it a hundred times as they searched the musty volumes for information on an ancient Deryni saint. It was the face of Camber of Culdi.

Before Duncan could speak, or even react beyond a mindless shock, the man nodded courteously and extended an empty right hand in a token of peace.

"Hail, Duncan of Corwyn," the stranger murmured.

CHAPTER FOUR

And the Angel that spoke in me, said to me . . . .

Zechariah 1:9

DUNCAN'S THROAT went dry and he had difficulty swallowing. For the man had called him by a name he had thought known to only three living men: himself, Alaric, and the young King Kelson. There was no way that this person could know that Duncan was half Deryni, that his mother and Alaric's had been twin sisters, of the high Deryni born. It was a secret Duncan had guarded zealously all his life.

And yet the man before him had called him by his secret name. *How could he know?*

"What do you mean?" he managed to whisper, his voice a quarter octave higher than normal. He cleared his throat. "I'm a McLain, of the lords of Kierney and Cassan."

"And you are also a Corwyn, of your sainted mother's right," the stranger contradicted gently. "There is no shame to being half Deryni, Duncan."

Duncan shut his mouth and managed to regain most of his composure, then wet his lips nervously. "Who are you?" he asked, holding his ground, but unconsciously letting his hand drop from the sword hilt he had clutched until now. "What do you want?"

The man chuckled amiably and shook his head. "No, of course you don't understand, do you?" he

57

murmured almost to himself, still smiling easily. "You needn't be afraid. Your secret is sealed within me. But, come. Dismount and walk with me awhile. There is something I would have you know."

Duncan hesitated for an instant, a trifle uncomfortable under the man's serene gaze, then complied. The man nodded gravely.

"You may consider this a warning, Duncan—not a threat from me, for it is not that, but for your own good. In the weeks to come, your powers will be sorely tested. More and more you will be called upon to use your magic in the open, to either accept your birthright and take up the fight as is your duty, or else to forever renounce it. Do I make myself clear?"

"You do not," Duncan whispered, his eyes narrowing. "To begin with, I am a priest. I am forbidden to practice the occult arts."

"Are you?" the man asked quietly.

"Of course I'm forbidden to practice magic."

"No. I mean, are you a priest?"

Duncan felt his cheeks begin to burn, and he had to avert his eyes. "According to the rite by which I was ordained, I am a priest forever, 'unto—'"

"'Unto the order of Melchizedek,'" the man quoted. "I know what the scripture says. But are you *really* a priest? What happened two days ago?"

Duncan looked up defiantly. "I'm merely suspended. I've not been degraded from the priesthood, nor excommunicated."

"And yet, you yourself said that the suspension didn't really worry you, that the more you use your powers, the less important your vows become."

Duncan gasped, instinctively drawing closer to the man, and his horse tossed its head in alarm.

"How do you know that?"

The man smiled gently and reached his hand to the horse's bridle to keep it from stepping on his sandaled feet. "I know many things."

"We were alone," Duncan murmured, almost to himself. "I would have staked my life on it. Who are you?"

"The power of the Deryni is by no means evil, my son," the man said in a conversational tone. He dropped his hand and began walking slowly down the road. Duncan shook his head in dismay and moved his horse along with him, straining to hear what he was saying.

". . . necessarily good, either. The good or evil is in the soul and mind of him who uses the powers. Only an evil mind can corrupt the power for evil." He turned to glance at Duncan as they walked—and continued.

"I have observed your use of the power so far, Duncan, and I find it most judicious. You need have no qualms as to whether your motivation is righteous. I understand the struggle you have undergone to be able to use it at all."

"But—"

"No more," the man said, holding up his hand for silence. "I must leave you now. I ask only that you continue to examine your motives in that other matter I mentioned. It may well be that you are called in other ways than you had thought. Think you on it; and the Light go with you."

With that, the man was gone; and Duncan stopped in confusion.

Gone!

Without a trace!

He looked down at the ground beside him where the man had been walking, but there were no footprints. Even with the lowering darkness, he could see his own tracks extending back the way he had come, the horse's hoofmarks firmly imprinted in the damp clay of the road.

But of the other's passage there was no trace.

Had he only imagined it?

No!

It had been too real, too chillingly threatening to have been in his mind alone. Now he knew what Alaric must have felt like when he'd had his visions. That sense of unreality, yet the certainty that he had been touched by someone or something. Why, this had been as real as—as that shining apparition that he and others of Deryni blood had seen at Kelson's coronation, supporting the crown of Gwynedd. Now that he thought about it, it could even have been the same being! And if so—

Duncan shuddered and pulled his cloak around himself again, then mounted and touched spurs to his beast. He wasn't going to find any more answers on this deserted road. And he had to tell Alaric what had happened. His cousin's visions had come at times of cusp, when grave crises were brewing. He hoped this wasn't a portent.

It was three miles back to the courtyard of Castle Coroth. It would seem like thirty.

At Castle Coroth, the night's festivities had begun with the setting of the sun. As darkness descended, richly clad lords and their resplendent ladies had begun to fill the ducal hall with color and sound as they awaited the arrival of their duke. Lord Robert, true to his word, had managed to transform the usually gloomy government chamber into an oasis of light and cheer, a welcome respite from the damp and darkness of the moonless evening.

Beaten bronze chandeliers suspended from the ceiling blazed with the light of a hundred tall candles. Light gleamed from the facets of fine crystal and silver goblets, reflected on the mellow wink of polished pewter and silver service on the dark tables. A dozen pages and squires in emerald green livery scurried around the long trencher tables putting out bread and decanters of mellow Fianna wine. And Lord Robert, stationed near the head of the table, kept a watchful eye out for his lord's appearance as he chatted with two beautiful ladies. Lute and recorder warbled as a festive undertone to the chatter of the guests.

As the guests mingled, Morgan's trusted surgeon, Master Randolph, circulated casually among the assembled nobility and gentry, nodding greeting and pausing occasionally to chat with those he knew. His task tonight, as it usually was on such occasions, was to feel out the mood of his master's subjects and to later report items of interest. As he made his way across the room, he picked up snatches of conversation.

"Well, I wouldn't give ye a copper fer a Bremagni mercenary," one portly lord was saying to another as his eyes followed a stately brunette across the room. "They can nae be trusted!"

"An' what about a Bremagni lady?" the other murmured, nudging his companion in the ribs and raising an eyebrow. "Do you think *they* can be trusted?"

"Ah—"

The two exchanged knowing nods and continued to inspect the lady in question, not noticing Master Randolph's slight smile as he moved on.

"And that's what the king just doesn't seem to understand," said a bright-faced young knight who looked barely old enough to have won his spurs. "It's all so very simple. Kelson knows how Wencit will move once the thaws begin. Why doesn't he just—"

Yes, why doesn't he? Randolph thought with a wry smile. *It's all so very simple. This young man has the answer to everything.*

"And not only that," a striking red-haired lady was saying to her companion, "it's rumored that he only stayed long enough to change, and then he was back on a horse and riding out for God knows where. I do hope he gets back in time for dinner. You've seen him, haven't you?"

"Ummm," the blond woman sighed approvingly. "I certainly have. What a pity he's a priest."

Master Randolph rolled his eyes in dismay as he continued past the women. Poor Father Duncan was always being sought after by the ladies of the court—almost as much as the duke himself. It was positively disgraceful. It would be different if the priest encouraged them. But he didn't. If the good father was lucky, he wouldn't get back before dinner was over.

Scanning the crowd casually, Randolph noticed three of Morgan's border lords in an earnest conversation over to his right. Morgan, he knew, would be vitally interested in what they had to say. But Randolph dared not go too close. The men knew him to be in Morgan's confidence and would surely change the subject if they thought they were being too candid for outside listeners. He edged as close as he dared and pretended to listen to two older men discussing falcons.

"Aye, ye dasn't hae th' jesses too tight, or ye'll—"

". . . and so this Warin fellow rides right into my granary yard and says, 'Do ye like paying taxes to His Grace?' Well, I tells him that sure, nobody likes taxes, but by God, the duke's tenants gets their money's worth of protection and good government!"

"Humph!" another growled. "Hurd de Blake was telling me just the other day how he'd had four acres of spring wheat burned out by the scoundrel. It's been a dry winter up north by de Blake's place, and the wheat burned like Hades. Warin ordered him to make a contribution to the cause, and de Blake told him to go to the Devil!"

". . . nah, I like th' smaller tyrrits mysel', so ye can get yer hands around th' jesses rightlike . . ."

The third man scratched at his beard and shrugged as Randolph strained to hear. "Still, this Warin fellow has a point. The duke is half Deryni, an' makes no secret o' the fact. Suppose he's plannin' to join with

Wencit in another Deryni coup, t'put Corwyn under another Interregnum. I dinnae want my manors blasted with heathen Deryni magic when I deny their heretical teachings."

"Ah, now, ye know our duke would never do a thing like that," the first lord objected. "Why only the other day . . ."

"My peregrine . . ."

Master Randolph nodded to himself and moved on at that, satisfied that the lords were no immediate threat; were, indeed, only talking about the things others were discussing tonight. Certainly, the people had every right to be curious about what their duke had planned, especially since he was getting ready to go off to war again, taking the flower of Corwyn's fighting men and leaving the others to more or less fend for themselves.

This continued mention of Warin and his band was disturbing, though. In the past month, Randolph had heard far more about the rebel leader and his band than he cared to remember. And apparently the problem was getting worse rather than better. Hurd de Blake's lands, for example, were more than thirty miles inside the border, much deeper than Randolph had ever heard Warin to penetrate before. The situation was becoming more than just a border problem. Morgan would have to be briefed before court in the morning.

Randolph glanced across the room to see slight movement behind the drapes from which Morgan would make his entrance—the duke's signal that he was about ready to come in. Randolph nodded and saw the curtain move again as he began to make his way slowly back in that direction.

Morgan let the heavy velvet drapes fall back into place and straightened, satisfied that Randolph had seen his signal and was on his way. Behind him,

Gwydion was bickering with Lord Hamilton again, in a low but penetrating tone. Morgan glanced around.

"You stepped on me!" the little troubadour was whispering furiously, pointing down at one elegantly pointed shoe which now bore a decided scuff mark on the side of the toe. His entire outfit was in shades of deep violet and rose, and the dust of Hamilton's misstep shone like a beacon on the rich suede of the left shoe. Gwydion's lute was slung across his back with a golden cord, and a sweeping hat with a white cockade was perched atop his thick black hair. The black eyes danced angrily in the swarthy face.

"Sorry," Hamilton murmured, starting to bend down and brush off the offending dust rather than argue in Morgan's presence.

"Don't touch me!" Gwydion yelped, dancing back a few steps and drawing his hands up against his chest in a show of horrified distaste. "You blundering fool, you'll only make it worse!"

He bent down to dust his own shoe, and the long tippets on his flowing violet sleeves dragged the floor so that he had to dust those too. Hamilton looked vindictive, and grinned malice as Gwydion discovered the new dust, then realized Morgan had seen the whole proceedings and cleared his throat apologetically.

"Sorry, m'lord," he muttered. "It really wasn't intentional."

Before Morgan could comment, the curtains parted briefly and Randolph slipped into the alcove.

"Nothing urgent to report, Your Grace," he said quietly. "There's a lot of talk about this Warin character, but nothing that can't wait until morning."

"Very well," Morgan nodded. "Gwydion, if you and Hamilton can stop fighting long enough, we'll go in now."

"My lord!" Gwydion gasped, drawing himself up

indignantly. "It was not I who started this silly quarrel. This oaf—"

"Your Grace, am I required to submit to this—," Hamilton began.

"All right, both of you! I don't want to hear any more!"

The lord chamberlain came to attention as the curtains moved beside him, and the room became hushed. Three slow raps of the long staff of office echoed hollowly through the quieting hall, and the chamberlain's voice rang out.

"His Grace, Lord Alaric Anthony Morgan: Duke of Corwyn, Master of Coroth, Lord General of the Royal Armies, and Champion of the King!"

As the musicians trilled a short fanfare, Morgan stepped through the parted curtains and paused in the doorway. A murmur of appreciation rippled through the assembled guests as all bowed respectfully. Then, as the musicians resumed their playing, Morgan acknowledged the tribute with a nod and began to move slowly toward his place at table, his entourage falling into place behind him.

Morgan was all in black tonight. Duncan's unsettling news from Rhemuth had brought with it a note of solemnity which had put him totally out of the frame of mind necessary for following the dictates of a temperamental master of wardrobes. So he had discarded the brilliant green of Lord Rathold's choice and worn black instead, and the Devil with what anyone thought.

Severely plain black silk tunic, sleek and close to body and wrists; over that, a sumptuous black velvet doublet trimmed in jet, high and close around his neck and with wide sleeves slashed to the elbow to show the silk of the tunic beneath; silk hosen disappearing into short black boots of softest leather.

And against this setting, the few articles of jewelry that Morgan permitted himself in such a mood: his gryphon signet on the right hand, emerald inlay of the beast glowing out against its onyx background; on his left, Kelson's Champion ring with the golden lion of Gwynedd etched on a field of black and gleaming gold. And on his head, the ducal coronet of Corwyn, hammered gold in seven delicate points, crowning the golden head of the Deryni Lord of Corwyn.

He appeared unarmed as he strolled toward his place at the head of the tables, for the ruler of Corwyn traditionally had no need to go armed among his dinner guests. But beneath Morgan's rich attire was the gleam of supple mail protecting vital organs, the slim stiletto in its worn wrist sheath. And the cloak of his Deryni power surrounding him like an invisible mantle wherever he went.

Now he must play the gracious host and settle down to the bore of a state dinner, while he inwardly seethed with impatience and wondered what had happened to Duncan.

It was well after dark when Duncan finally returned to Coroth. His horse had gone lame the last two miles, and he had been forced to go on foot the rest of the way, controlling the almost overpowering urge to force the animal to continue at a normal pace despite its pain. He had controlled that impulse. For whatever advantage the hour's difference in his return might make, it was doubtful that it would be worth ruining one of Alaric's best saddle horses. Besides, it was not in Duncan's soul to purposely torture any living thing.

And so, when he and the animal finally limped into the courtyard, he leading, the tired horse following slowly, it was to enter an almost deserted area. The gate guards had passed him without question, since they had been warned to expect his return, but there was no one in the courtyard to take his horse. At the invitation of the duke, the squires and pages who would normally have been manning the stable had slipped inside to the back of the hall to hear Gwydion sing. Duncan finally found someone to take the animal, then made his way across the courtyard to the entrance to the great hall.

Dinner was over, he soon learned, and as he passed among the servants crowded in the doorway he could see that the entertainment was already in progress. Gwydion was performing, seated on the second step of the raised dais at the far end of the hall, his lute cradled easily in his arms. As he sang, Duncan paused to listen. The troubadour apparently deserved his reputation he held throughout the Eleven Kingdoms.

It was a slow, measured melody, born of the highlands of Carthmoor to the west—the land of Gwydion's youth. And it was filled with the rhythms, the modulations to minor keys, that seemed to characterize the music of the mountain folk.

Gwydion's clear tenor floated through the still hall, weaving the bittersweet tale of Mathurin and Derverguille, the lovers of legend who had died in Interregnum times at the hands of the cruel Lord Gerent. Not a soul stirred as the troubadour spun his song.

> *So how shall I sing to the sparkling morn?*
> *How to the children yet unborn?*
> *Can I survive with heart forlorn?*
> *My Lord Mathurin is dead.*

As Duncan scanned the hall, he saw Morgan sitting at his place to the left of the dais where Gwydion sang. To Morgan's left, Lord Robert was flanked by two beautiful women who gazed fondly at Morgan as the troubadour sang. But the seat to Morgan's right, closest to Duncan, was vacant. He thought he might be able to make his way there without creating too much disturbance if he were careful.

Before he could do more than move in that direction, however, Morgan saw him and shook his head, then rose quietly and made his way to the side of the hall.

"What happened?" he whispered, pulling Duncan behind one of the pillars and looking around to be certain they were not being overheard.

"The part with Bishop Tolliver went well enough," Duncan murmured, "He wasn't enthusiastic about the idea, but he agreed to delay his answer to Loris and Corrigan until he can evaluate the situation. He will let us know when he makes a decision."

"Well, I suppose it's better than nothing. What was his general reaction? Do you think he's on our side?"

Duncan shrugged. "You know Tolliver. He's squeamish about the whole Deryni aspect of things, but then, everyone is. For now, he seems to be with us. There's something else, though."

"Oh?"

"I—ah—think we'd better not talk about it here," Duncan said, glancing around meaningfully. "I had a visitor on the way back."

"A v—," Morgan's eyes went wide. "You mean, like mine?"

Duncan nodded soberly. "Can I meet you in the tower room?"

"As soon as I can get away," Morgan agreed.

As Duncan moved on toward the door, Morgan took a deep breath to compose himself, then crossed quietly back to his seat. He wondered how long it would be before he could extricate himself gracefully.

In the tower room, Duncan paced back and forth before the fireplace, clasping and unclasping his hands and trying to calm his jangled nerves.

He was much more upset than he had realized, he knew now. In fact, when he had first entered the room a short while earlier, he had had a violent fit of shaking as he thought about his visitation on the road, almost as though an icy wind had blown across his neck.

The attack had passed, and after throwing off his damp riding cloak he had collapsed at the prie-dieu before the tiny altar and tried to pray. But for once, it hadn't worked. He couldn't force himself to concentrate on the words he was trying to form, and he had had to give it up as a lost cause for the moment.

The pacing was not helping either, he realized. As he stopped before the fireplace and held out one hand, he realized that he was still shaking in a delayed reaction to what had happened earlier.

Why?

Taking hold of himself sternly, he crossed to Alaric's desk and unstoppered a crystal decanter there, poured himself a small glass of the strong red wine Alaric kept for just such emergencies. He drained that glass and poured another, then took it over beside the fur-draped couch against the left-hand wall. Unbuttoning his cassock halfway to the waist, he loosened his collar and stretched his neck backwards to get the kinks out, then lay back on the couch, the glass of wine in his hand. As he lay there, sipping the wine and forcing himself to review the situation, he began to relax. By the time the gryphon door opened and Alaric entered, he was feeling much better—almost unwilling to get up or talk at all.

"Are you all right?" Morgan said, crossing to the couch and sitting down beside his cousin.

"Now I think I may survive," Duncan replied dreamily. "A little while ago, I wouldn't have been so sure. This thing really disturbed me."

Morgan nodded. "I know the feeling. Do you want to talk about it?"

Duncan sighed heavily. "He was there. I was riding along, I rounded a bend in the road about three or four miles from here, and there he was, standing in the middle of the road. He was wearing a grey monk's habit, holding a staff in his hand, and—well, his face was almost identical to those portraits we've found in the old breviaries and history books."

"Did he speak to you?"

"Oh, yes," Duncan agreed heartily. "Just as clearly as you and I are talking right now. And not only that, he knows what I am. He called me by my mother's name—Duncan of Corwyn. When I objected and said I was a McLain, he told me that I was also a Corwyn—'of my sainted mother's right,' I believe he put it."

"Go on," Morgan said, getting up to pour himself a glass of the red wine.

"Ah ... next he said that the time was approaching when I would be sorely tested, and would be forced to either accept my powers and begin to use them out in the open, or else forget them. When I objected and told him that as a priest I was forbidden to use those powers, he asked if I were really a priest. He knew about the suspension, and he—knew what we'd discussed earlier this afternoon. Remember, when I said that the suspension didn't really matter that much, that the more I used my Deryni powers, the less important my vows seemed to be? Alaric, I've never told that to anyone else, and I know you didn't. How could he have known that?"

"He knew what we talked about this afternoon?" Morgan said, sitting down again in amazement.

"Almost verbatim. And he didn't Truth-Read me, either. Alaric, what am I going to do?"

"I don't know," Morgan said slowly. "I'm not sure what to think. He's never been that talkative with me." He rubbed his eyes and thought a minute. "Tell me, do you think he was human? I mean, do you think he was really there? Or just an apparition, a visual phenomenon?"

"He was there in the flesh," Duncan stated promptly. "He put his hand on the bridle to keep from getting stepped on." He frowned. "And yet, there were no footprints where he walked. After he'd disappeared, there was still enough light to see my tracks going back the way I'd come. But none of his."

Duncan raised up on one elbow. "Now I really don't know, Alaric. Maybe he *wasn't* there at all. Maybe I imagined all of it."

Morgan shook his head and stood abruptly. "No, you saw something. I wouldn't even presume to guess what at this point, but I think something was there." He stared at his feet for a moment, then looked up. "Why don't we sleep on it, eh? You can stay here, if you like. You look as though you're very comfortable."

"I couldn't move if I wanted to," Duncan grinned. "See you in the morning."

He watched until Morgan had disappeared through the gryphon door, then reached to the floor beside the couch and discarded his glass.

He *had* seen someone on the road to Castle Culdi. He wondered again who it could have been.

And why?

CHAPTER FIVE

*Who is she that looketh forth in the morning, fair
as the moon, clear as the sun, and terrible as an
army with banners?*

Song of Solomon 6:10

As THE cathedral bells tolled Sext in Coroth, Morgan
suppressed a yawn and shifted slightly in his chair,
trying not to look as bored as he felt. He was reviewing court rolls from cases he had judged the day
before, and Lord Robert was working industriously
on an account roll across the table from him.

Lord Robert always worked industriously, Morgan
thought to himself. Which was probably a good thing,
since somebody had to do the blasted things. It didn't
seem to bother Robert at all to sit poring over obscure
records for hours at a time when things were crumbling around their ears. Of course, that was his
job. . . .

Morgan sighed and tried to force himself to return
to his job. As Duke of Corwyn, one of his primary
official duties when he was in residence was to hear
local court presentments once a week and to render
decisions. He usually enjoyed it, for it enabled him to
keep in touch with what was going on in his duchy, to
keep abreast of what was troubling his subjects.

But he had been restless for the past few weeks.
The long inactivity forced by almost two months of

nothing but attention to administrative detail had left him restive, eager for action. And even daily workouts with sword and lance, occasional forages into the countryside on hunting expeditions, had not been able to entirely take the edge off his discomfiture.

He would be glad when he could leave for Culdi next week. The honest fatigue of the four-day ride would be welcome change after the glittering but sterile life he had led for the past two months. And it would be especially good to see old friends again. The young king, for one, would be a particularly welcome sight. Even now, Morgan longed to be at his side, protecting and reassuring him in the face of the new crises which were developing daily. Kelson was almost like a son to him. He had a fair idea what sorts of worries must be going through the boy's mind right now.

Reluctantly, Morgan returned his attention to the correspondence in front of him and scrawled his signature at the bottom of the first sheet. Part of his problem this morning was that the cases he was reviewing seemed so trivial compared to what Morgan knew were the real issues. The writ he had just signed, for example, set a small fine on one Harold Martham for allowing some of his beasts to graze on another man's lands. As he recalled, the man had actually been upset over the judgement, even though there was no contesting that he had been in the wrong.

That's all right, friend Harold, Morgan thought to himself. *If you think you've got troubles now, just wait until Loris and Corrigan lower the Interdict. You don't know what trouble is.*

It was beginning to look as though there would, indeed, be an Interdict. Yesterday morning, after getting all the guests away, he had sent Duncan to see Bishop Tolliver again, to find out what the messengers had said when they delivered the archbishops' letter the night before. Duncan had returned hours later with a long face and a troubled mind, for the bishop had been almost secretive this time, in contrast to his previous amiable reception. Apparently the messengers had scared Tolliver. At any rate, Duncan had been able to discover nothing.

As Morgan moved his writ to the completed pile, there was a quick, sharp knock at the door, followed by the entry of Gwydion, lute slung over his back. The little troubadour was dressed in the simple brown homespun of the common folk, his swarthy face streaked with dust and perspiration, and he looked very serious as he strode across the polished floor to bow curtly by Morgan's chair.

"Your Grace, may I have a word with you?" He glanced at Robert. "Alone?"

Morgan leaned back and put his pen down, then gave Gwydion a long searching look. The foppish poppinjay that was the public Gwydion had been replaced by a thin-lipped, determined little man. And there was something in his manner, in his black eyes, that made Morgan realize Gwydion was deadly serious for a change. He glanced at Robert and motioned him to leave, but the chancellor frowned and did not move.

"My lord, I must protest. Whatever it is, I'm certain it can wait. We have only a few more rolls to go, and after that—"

"Sorry, Robert." Morgan replied, looking back at Gwydion. "I have to be the judge of whether it can wait or not. You can come back as soon as we're finished."

Robert said nothing, but he scowled vexedly as he stacked his papers and pushed back his chair. Gwydion watched until he had disappeared through the door and the door had closed, then strolled toward the window and eased himself down on the padded window seat.

"I thank you, Your Grace. There are many lords

who would not have taken the time to indulge the whims of a mere spinner of tales."

"I sense you have more than tales to spin, Gwydion," Morgan said quietly. "What is it you wanted to tell me?"

Gwydion unslung his lute and began tuning it, gazing out the window dreamily as he spoke.

"I was out in the city this morning, my lord," he said, strumming his instrument and toying with the pegs. "I've been collecting songs that I thought might please Your Grace's ears. I fear, now that I've found them, though, that they won't please you at all. Would you like to hear one?"

He turned and looked Morgan full in the eyes, his own gaze glittering with anticipation, and Morgan nodded slowly.

"Very well. This song is one I thought you'd be especially interested in, my lord, since it's about Deryni. I can't vouch for the tune or the lyrics, since they're not my arrangement, but the thought is there."

He strummed a few introductory bars, then launched into a spirited and lively melody reminiscent of a child's play tune.

"*Hey, hey, riddle me, do:*
Why are Deryni becoming so few?
Hey, hey, riddle me right:
Why should the gryphon be wary tonight?
Deryni are fewer since many are dead,
So, gryphon, beware, or you'll lose yer green head!
Hey, hey, ye've riddled me well.
Riddle again and see what I'll tell."

As Gwydion finished the verse, Morgan sat back in his chair and steepled his fingers, his eyes hooded, dark. He sat quietly for a moment, his grey eyes studying the singer, then spoke in a low tone.

"Is there more of this?"

The troubadour shrugged. "There are other verses, Lord, other versions. But the poetry is inferior, and I fear they all display more or less the same vitriolic humor. Perhaps you would be interested in 'The Ballad of Duke Cirala.'"

"Duke Cirala?"

"Yes, m'lord. Apparently he's a villain in every sense of the word—evil, blasphemous, heretical, a liar who deludes his subjects. Fortunately, the song does offer some hope for the poor oppressed people. I might also mention that the name Cirala is quite familiar if one only spells it backward: C—I—R—A—L—A—A—L—A—R—I—C. At any rate, the poetry is a little better than the other one."

Again he strummed an introductory chord, this time setting the mood for a slow, sedate, almost hymnlike piece.

"*Offenses hath Cirala made before the Lord Most High.*
The servants of the Lord must smite his gryphon from the
sky.
Facades of gold and radiance deceive the eyes of men,
But Duke Cirala's heresies are known by Lord Warin.

O men of Corwyn, lend your aid to mend Cirala's ways.
Cirala's heresy must stop, or all of Corwyn pays.
If naive men, in innocence, condone the Devil's deeds.
They still are doomed. 'Tis on false faith that evil often
feeds.

And so the day of judgement comes. Cirala's time is near.
The servants of the Lord must rise, and put aside their fear.
God's Chosen is the noble Warin, powerful and wise.
Rise, men beneath the gryphon's claws, and still Cirala's
lies!"

"Humph!" Morgan snorted when the troubadour had finished. "Where the Devil did you ever dredge that one up, Gwydion?"

"In a tavern, Lord," the troubadour replied with a dour grin. "And the first was taught me by a ragged street singer near Saint Matthew's Gate. Is my lord pleased with what I have brought him?"

"Not pleased with the content, but I am pleased that you told me. How much of this is about, do you think?"

Gwydion gently placed his lute on the cushioned seat beside him and leaned back against the side of the window, hands clasped behind his head. "It is difficult to say, Lord. I was out for only a few hours, but there are several versions of both songs, and probably others totally different that I did not hear. If my lord will heed some advice from a spinner of tales, you should combat this with other songs. Shall I attempt to compose something worthy?"

"I'm not certain that would be wise just now," Morgan said. "What do you—"

There was a discreet knock at the door, and Morgan looked up in annoyance. "Come."

Robert opened the door and stepped through, disapproval written all across his face. "Lord Rather de Corbie is here to see you, Your Grace."

"Ah, send him in."

Robert stepped aside, and a contingent of men in the sea green livery of the Hort of Orsal marched in in a double row. Behind them walked the redoubtable Rather de Corbie, Ambassador Extraordinaire of the Hort of Orsal. Morgan stood at his place and smiled as the double file split and lined up in front of him and Rather stopped and bowed.

"Duke Alaric," the man boomed, in a voice that simply did not match his five-foot stature. "I bring felicitations and greetings from His Hortic Majesty. He trusts you are well."

"Indeed, I am, Rather," Morgan said, shaking the man's hand enthusiastically. "And how is the old sea lion?"

Rather rumbled in laughter. "The Orsal's family has just been blessed with yet another heir, and the Orsal himself hopes that you will soon be able to come to see him." He glanced at Gwydion and Robert and then continued. "There are certain matters of navigation rights and defense he wishes to discuss, and he hopes that you will bring your military advisors with you. Spring is upon us, you know."

Morgan nodded knowingly. Between the two of them, he and the Hort of Orsal controlled water passage from the Twin Rivers to the sea, a route of extreme tactical advantage should Wencit of Torenth decide to invade along the coast. And since Morgan would be away with the army in a few weeks, arrangements must be made with the Orsal to protect Corwyn's sea approaches in his absence.

"When does he want me to come, Rather?" Morgan asked, knowing that the Orsal's request was fairly urgent, yet aware that he could not go until tomorrow at the earliest because of the impending contact with Derry tonight.

"Today, with me?" Rather asked cagily, watching Morgan for reaction.

Morgan shook his head. "How about in the morning?" he asked. He motioned Robert and Gwydion to leave them. "_Rhafallia_ is in port. I can sail with the tide and be there by Terce. That would give us the rest of the morning and all afternoon until I have to return. What do you say?"

Rather shrugged. "It's fine with me, Alaric. You know that. I only carry messages back and forth. Whether the Orsal will agree or not is something only the Orsal knows."

"Good, then," Morgan said, slapping Rather on the shoulder in a comradely gesture. "How about something to eat before you and your men leave? My cousin Duncan is visiting, and I'd like you to meet him."

Rather made a short bow. "I accept with pleasure. And you must promise to tell me what news you hear from the young king. The Orsal is still chagrined that he had to miss Kelson's coronation duel, you know."

Later that afternoon when amenities with Rather de Corbie had been concluded and the feisty old warrior was on his way home, Morgan found himself once again the reluctant captive of Lord Robert. Robert had decreed that today must see the completion of Bronwyn's dowry arrangements, and so he and Morgan had cloistered themselves in the solarium with the documents in question. Duncan had wandered out to the armorer's pavilion an hour earlier to inquire about the progress of a new sword he was having made, and Gwydion was out combing the city for more songs of unrest.

As Robert's voice droned on and on, Morgan tried to force himself to pay attention. He reminded himself for at least the fifteenth time this week that this was a necessary if tedious part of governing; and the realization did about as much good as the previous fourteen reminders had. He would rather have been doing just about anything at the moment.

" 'Rendering of the account of Corwode manor,'" Robert read. " 'They say that Corwode was wont to be in the hands of the king. And the Lord King Brion, father of the king who now is, gave the aforesaid manor to Lord Kenneth Morgan and his heirs. And it is held of the king by service of three men at arms in time of war.'"

Just as Robert drew breath to begin the next paragraph, the solarium door opened and Duncan padded in breathing heavily. Bare-legged and clad only in a damp linen exercise tunic and soft boots, the priest had evidently been trying the balance of his new blade with the armorer. He flung a rough grey towel around his shoulders and wiped his face with a corner of it as he strode across the room, his left hand clutching a folded and sealed piece of parchment.

"This just came in by courier," he said, grinning and tossing the parchment to the table. "I think it's from Bronwyn."

He perched on the table edge and nodded greeting to Robert, but the chancellor laid his pen aside with a sigh and sat back with a very vexed expression. Morgan chose to ignore the reaction, and broke the seal in a shower of red wax shards. His eyes lit with pleasure as he scanned the first few lines, and he leaned back in his chair and smiled.

"Your illustrious brother definitely has a way with women, Duncan," the duke said. "Listen to this. It's so typical of Bronwyn."

" 'My dearest brother Alaric, I scarce can believe it is happening at last, but in just a few short days I shall be the Lady Bronwyn McLain, Countess of Kierney, future Duchess of Cassan, and most important of all, wife to my beloved Kevin. It hardly seems possible, but the love we have always shared seems now to grow even stronger with each passing hour.' "

He looked up at Duncan and raised an indulgent eyebrow, and Duncan shook his head and grinned.

" 'This will probably be the last letter before I see you in Culdi, but Duke Jared is urging me to be brief. He and Lady Margaret have been showering us with gifts, and he says that today's is especially impressive. Kevin sends his love and wonders whether you were able to arrange for the troubadour Gwydion to perform at our wedding feast. Kevin was so impressed when he heard him sing at Valoret last winter, and I too am very eager to hear him.

" 'Give my love to Duncan and Derry and Lord Robert, and tell them that I look forward to seeing them at the wedding. And hurry to share the happiest day of your loving sister, Bronwyn.' "

Duncan wiped his sweating face again and smiled, then took the letter and scanned it again.

"You know, I never really believed I'd see Kevin so domesticated. At thirty-three and still unmarried, I was beginning to think *he* should have been the priest instead of me."

"Well, it certainly wasn't Bronwyn's fault," Morgan laughed. "I think she decided when she was about ten that Kevin was to be the only man in her life. Only a provision of our mother's will has kept them apart this long. The McLains may be hard-headed, but they can't compare to the stubbornness of a half Deryni wench who's determined to get what she wants."

Duncan snorted and headed for the door. "I think I'll go and badger the armorer some more. Anything is easier than trying to argue with a man who thinks his sister is perfect!"

With a chuckle, Morgan leaned back in his chair and put his booted feet up on the leather stool, his spirits restored.

"Robert," he said, smiling out the window at nothing in particular, "remind me to tell Gwydion he's leaving for Culdi in the morning, will you?"

"Yes, m'lord."

"And let's get back to those accounts, shall we? Really, Robert, you're getting insufferably lax these days."

"I, Your Grace?" Robert murmured, looking up from the note he had made.

"Yes, yes, let's get on with it. If we work hard, I think we can finish these blasted things by nightfall and I can ship them out with Gwydion in the morning. I can't remember when I've been more bored."

Lady Bronwyn de Morgan, however, was far from bored. At that moment, she and her future mother-in-law, the Duchess Margaret, were selecting the gowns that Bronwyn would take to Culdi in the morning for the wedding festivities. The ornate dress that she would wear for the ceremony itself was carefully laid out on the bed ready to be packed, its flowing skirt and sleeves aglisten with tiny silver paillettes and rose-flashing balasses.

Several other bright garments were also laid out neatly on the bed. And on the floor were two leather-bound trunks, one of which was nearly packed and ready to be closed. Two serving maids were busy adding the last touches to that chest before starting on the second, but Bronwyn kept finding last minute items to add that forced the maids to redo half the packing.

It was an unusually sunny day for March. Though it had rained hard during the night, the morning had dawned in a burst of lemon-streaked glory. Now, at mid-afternoon, the ground was almost dry. Pale sun-light streamed into the chamber through open balcony doors. And near those doors, three ladies-in-waiting stitched industriously on Bronwyn's trousseau, their nimble fingers moving quickly over the fine linens and silks. Two of them worked on the fine gauze veil their mistress would wear for her marriage, applying delicate lace to the edges with steady hands. The third embroidered Bronwyn's new McLain crest in gold on a pair of supple leather gloves.

Behind the ladies, next to the fire, two young girls curled up on velvet cushions, the older of the two strumming and playing a crewth. As she caressed the strings and hummed an accompaniment, her younger companion kept time with a timbrel and sang the lower, contrapuntal portion of the song. A fat orange cat dozed peacefully at their feet, only a slightly twitching tail betraying the fact that he was alive.

Now, brides are traditionally beautiful, especially daughters of nobility. And Bronwyn de Morgan was certainly no exception. But of all the ladies in the room that afternoon, even the bride to be, it would have been difficult to find a lady of gentler breeding or character than Lady Margaret McLain.

Lady Margaret was Duke Jared's third duchess—lady of that twice-bereft lord who had thought that he could never love again after the death of his second wife Vera, the mother of Duncan. He had hardly known his first bride; the Duchess Elaine had lived but a day after the birth of Jared's first son, Kevin. But his marriage to the Lady Vera three years later had been a long and happy one—twenty-six years of joy in an age when marriages of state were rarely more than affectionate matches of convenience, and almost never touched by romantic love.

The marriage had brought more children: first Duncan, then a daughter who had died in infancy, and then young Alaric and Bronwyn Morgan, when their wardship descended to Jared on the death of his cousin Kenneth, the children's father.

Then, four years ago, all that had ended. Lady Vera had contracted a strange wasting disease which drained her of vitality and left her helpless. Not even her Deryni powers (for she was full Deryni, the sister of Morgan's mother, though no one knew) could keep life from gradually ebbing away.

And then there was the Lady Margaret—a woman of no great physical beauty, a childless widow of forty who would never bear Jared another heir, but a quiet lady of gentle soul who could offer the one thing Jared sought above all else—Lady Margaret McLain, who had taught Jared how to love again.

So now that same lady fussed over Bronwyn's wedding arrangements as though Bronwyn were her own daughter, watching over the serving maids and supervising activities with a mother's sharp eye. Since Duncan had chosen not to wed, only Kevin and his wife would carry on the McLain line now. There would be no more McLain daughters born or married into the family until Bronwyn bore heirs. So the preparations for this marriage would have to last a long time.

Margaret glanced aside at Bronwyn and smiled, then slipped over to a carved wooden cabinet and unlocked it with a key from the jeweled chatelaine at her waist. As she began searching its shelves, Bronwyn took up a jeweled kirtle of rose watered-silk and held it in front of herself, walking thoughtfully to a large mirror standing in the corner of the room.

Bronwyn de Morgan was a beautiful woman. Tall and slim, with rich golden hair flowing sleekly down her back, she was the embodiment of all the best qualities of her Deryni mother, the Lady Alyce. The wide eyes in the oval face were a pale blue, bordering on grey when her moods changed. The rose gown she held in front of her accentuated the pale, flawless complexion, the bloom of roses in cheek and lip.

She studied her reflection carefully for a moment, weighing the effect the garment could be expected to produce, then nodded approvingly and laid it on the bed beside her wedding gown.

"I like this one for the ball the night we arrive in Culdi, don't you, Lady Margaret?" she asked, smoothing the folds of the dress and looking across to see what Margaret was doing. "Kevin has seen it before, but that doesn't matter."

Margaret took a gold velvet-covered box from a shelf in the cabinet and brought it over to Bronwyn. It was about ten inches square and a hand-width deep, and she handed it to Bronwyn with a gentle smile.

"Here is something else Kevin has seen before, my dear," she said gently, watching for Bronwyn's reaction as the girl began to open it. "It's been in the McLain family for many years. I like to think it brings luck to the women who wear it."

Bronwyn lifted the lid and gasped in wonder. A high tiara heavy with diamonds glittered brilliantly against a bed of black velvet, throwing a shower of flashing fire on Bronwyn's simple blue gown.

"It's magnificent!" Bronwyn breathed, carefully setting the box on the bed and lifting out the tiara. "This is the McLain nuptial crown, isn't it?"

Margaret nodded. "Why don't you try it on? I want to see how it will look with your veil. Martha, bring the veil, will you, please?"

As Lady Martha and her companion brought the veil, Bronwyn moved to the mirror again and stared at the reflection of the tiara in her hands. Margaret and Martha draped the unfinished veil over Bronwyn's golden hair and fussed with it until it hung to suit them, and then Margaret took the tiara and placed it gently atop the veil.

Lady Martha handed her a smaller mirror so she could see the back, and as Bronwyn turned to look she was startled to see two men standing in the doorway of the room. One was her future father-in-law, Duke Jared. The other was only vaguely familiar.

"You look absolutely enchanting, my dear," Jared said, crossing toward her with a smile. "If I were Kevin, I'd have carried you off years ago, and damn your mother's will."

Bronwyn lowered her eyes selfconsciously, then ran to Jared and flung her arms around him in an enthusiastic hug.

"Lord Jared, you are the most wonderful man in the whole world! Next to Kevin, of course."

"Oh, of course," Jared replied, kissing her forehead and then holding her carefully away from him to avoid crushing the veil. "I must say, my dear, you make a lovely McLain. This tiara only graces the heads of the Eleven Kingdoms' comeliest ladies, you know." He joined Margaret and kissed her hand affectionately, and Margaret blushed.

Jared had been holding court for most of the day. Like most land magnates of his stature, much of his time was not his own and must be spent attending to the official duties of his overlordship. He had come directly from a session of the ducal court this afternoon, and he still wore his ducal coronet and a brown velvet robe with McLain tartan sweeping from the shoulder. An enameled silver brooch with the McLain lion *dormant* secured the plaid on the left, and a heavy silver chain of office with links the size of a man's hand was draped around his broad shoulders. His blue eyes were mild and relaxed in the lined face and he brushed aside a stray lock of greying hair as he gestured toward the other man who had remained standing in the doorway.

"Rimmell, come in here. I want you to meet my future daughter-in-law."

Rimmell bowed and crossed toward his master.

The most extraordinary single feature about Rimmell at first glance was his snow-white hair. Rimmel was not an old man—he was but twenty-eight—nor was he an albino. He had, in fact, had perfectly ordinary brown hair until the age of ten. Then, one warm summer night, it had suddenly and inexplicably turned white while he slept.

His mother had always blamed it on the "Deryni witch" who was permitted to live on the outskirts of the village. And the village priest had vowed the boy was possessed, and had tried to exorcise the evil spirits. But whatever the reason, and despite all they did to try to change it, Rimmell's hair had remained white. And it was only this, coupled with eyes of a startlingly brilliant blue, which rescued him from the anonymity of very ordinary features and a slightly stooped posture.

He wore a grey tunic and high boots, a grey velvet cap with Jared's sleeping lion badge sewn to the front, and carried a scuffed grey leather equipment pouch slung across his chest on a long leather strap. Several long rolls of parchment were tucked under his arm, and he clutched them nervously as he reached Jared's side and bowed again.

"Your Grace," he murmured, removing his cap and keeping his eyes lowered. "My ladies."

Jared glanced conspiratorily at his wife and smiled. "Bronwyn, this is my architect, Rimmell. He's drawn up a few sketches I'd like your opinion on." He gestured toward a table near the fire. "Rimmell, let's spread them out over there."

As Rimmell crossed to the table and began unrolling his parchments, Bronwyn took off tiara and veil and handed them to a serving maid, then walked curiously to the table. Jared and Rimmell were opening out a number of parchment documents which appeared to be plans of some sort, and Bronwyn's brow wrinkled in puzzlement as she leaned closer to inspect them.

"Well, what do you think?"

"What are they?"

Jared grinned and straightened, folded his arms across his chest in anticipation. "They're plans for your new winter palace in Kierney, my dear. Construction has already begun. You and Kevin should be able to hold Christmas Court there next year!"

"A winter palace?" Bronwyn gasped. "For us? Oh, Lord Jared, thank you!"

"Consider it the only proper wedding present we could think of for the future duke and duchess of Cassan," Jared replied. He put an affectionate arm around his wife and smiled down at her. "Margaret and I wanted you to have somewhere for the grandchildren to play, something to remember us by when we're gone."

"You!" Bronwyn teased, hugging them both. "As if we needed an old palace to remember you by! Come. Show me the plans. I want to know about every last cubbyhole and stairway."

Jared chuckled and, bent down beside her, began pointing out the features of the structure. And as he proceeded to regale his audience with tales of the palace's splendor, Rimmell withdrew a few paces and tried to study Bronwyn unobtrusively.

He did not approve of the coming marriage of his master's heir with this Deryni woman. He had never approved, from the first time he set eyes on her seven months ago. In those seven months he had never spoken to Bronwyn. Indeed, he had only seen her a handful of times. But those were enough.

They were enough to make him realize the gap between them—she a lord's daughter and heiress of many lands; he a commoner, an architect, of no family at all. And they were enough for him to realize that he was falling hopelessly, helplessly in love with this exquisite Deryni woman.

He told himself that he disapproved of the coming match for other, more aesthetic reasons than the true ones. He told himself he disapproved because Bronwyn was half-Deryni, and therefore had no business marrying the young Earl Kevin, that she was not good enough for one so high. But whatever his objections, they always came back to the one inescapable, irreconcilable fact: he was in love with Bronwyn, Deryni or no. And he must have her or die.

He had no quarrel with Kevin. Kevin was his future master, and Rimmell owed him the same allegiance as he did his father. But neither could he allow the earl to marry Bronwyn. Why, even the thought was beginning to make him hate the sound of the young lord's voice.

His pondering was interrupted by a voice outside the balcony window—the voice of the hated earl himself.

"Bron?" the voice called. "Bronwyn, come here. I want to show you something.

At his call, Bronwyn hurried through the balcony doors and peered over the edge of the railing. From his spot near the table, Rimmell could just see the tips of pennants on lances above the balcony, and the shadowy shapes of riders on horseback through the narrow slits in the balcony railing. Lord Kevin had returned with his men.

"Oh!" Bronwyn called out, her face bright with excitement. "Jared, Margaret, come and see what he's got! Oh, Kevin, she's the most beautiful palfrey I've ever seen!"

"Come down and try her," Kevin shouted. "I bought her for you."

"For me?" Bronwyn squealed, clapping her hands like an excited child. She glanced back at Jared and Margaret, then turned back to blow Kevin a kiss.

"We're coming, Kevin," she called gathering her skirts around her as she flew across the room to join the McLains. "Don't go away!"

As the three hurried from the room, Rimmell stared after Bronwyn hungrily for a moment, then moved slowly across to the balcony. There in the courtyard below, Kevin, in full skirmish attire, was seated on a great roan destrier with McLain tartan on the saddle. A page had taken his lance and helmet, and he had pushed back his camail so that his brown hair was rumpled and tousled. In his right hand he held the lead rein of a cream-colored palfrey, caparisoned with green velvet hangings and a white leather side-saddle. As Bronwyn appeared at the head of the stairs, he tossed the lead to another page and moved his destrier to the steps, then reached up and lifted Bronwyn to the saddle in front of him.

"There, wench! What do you think of that?" he laughed, crushing her against his mailed chest and kissing her heartily. "Is that or is that not a horse fit for a queen?"

Bronwyn giggled and snuggled closer in the protective circle of his arm, and Kevin guided his mount back toward the palfrey. As Bronwyn reached out to touch her new prize, Rimmell turned away in disgust and stalked back to the table.

He didn't know how he was going to do it, but he must stop this wedding from taking place. Bronwyn was his. She must be his. If only he could find the right moment, he was sure he could convince her of that, could make her love him. It did not occur to him that he had just stepped across the border from fantasy into madness.

He rolled up his plans and scanned the room carefully, noting that all the ladies-in-waiting and servants had moved to the balcony to watch the spectacle in the courtyard below. Unless he was gravely mistaken, some of the women watched with more than a little jealousy. Could he, perhaps, play on that jealousy in some way? Perhaps one of the ladies could tell of a way to win a woman's love. At any rate, it bore closer watching. Since he truly meant to stop the marriage and take Bronwyn for himself, he must not miss a single possibility. Bronwyn must be his!

CHAPTER SIX

They also that seek after my life lay snares for me.

Psalms 38:12

"ANOTHER ROUND!" Derry said thickly, slapping a silver coin down on the bar and gesturing magnanimously around him. "Drinks for all o' these fine gentlemen! When ol' John Ban'r gets drunk, all his friends get drunk too!"

There was a roar of approval as a half-dozen rough-looking men in hunters' and sailors' garb lurched back to the bar around Derry, and the taverner snatched up a huge oak pitcher and began refilling the brown earthen mugs with fragrant ale.

"Thash a good boy, Johnny-lad!" one called, spitting amiably toward Derry's feet as he held out his mug.

"Fill 'er up!" another hollered.

It was early yet. Darkness had just fallen. But already the Jack Dog Tavern in Fathane was almost filled to capacity, its patrons as loud and boisterous a mob as any in the Eleven Kingdoms. Over against one wall, a sailor in the worn jerkin of a top rigger was leading an old sea chanty to the accompaniment of a reed pipe, an out-of-tune lute, and two heavy trestle tables which had become the percussion section. Around the group, which was growing larger and noisier by the minute, more serious drinkers were having to raise their voices more and more to compete with the singing. But they knew better than to express displeasure at the noise and risk a brawl with the crusty sailors.

Fathane, just at the mouth of the river isthmus, was predominantly a sailing town Ships from Torenth and Corwyn across the river traded there regularly, and it was also a point of departure for hunters and trappers going farther up river to the great Veldur forests. The combination of interests made Fathane a very lively town.

Derry took a long pull from his fresh mug and turned unsteadily toward the man on his right, apparently listening to his story.

"An' so this man says, 'Wa'd'ye mean, Lord Varney's wine shipment? Thash mine, an' I paid fer it,' an' the Devil take Lord Varney!' "

There was a roar of laughter at that, for the storyteller was evidently one of the most respected spinners of yarns in the village. But Derry had to fight hard to restrain a yawn.

He had gained a great deal of information in the past three hours of drinking and storytelling, not the least of which was the fact that Torenthi royalist troops were gathering somewhere north of here near a place called Medras. The man who'd told him of it hadn't known just what their purpose was—he was not the brightest of informants, and he'd been half-drunk by the time Derry got to him—but he had said there were as many as five thousand men being mustered there. And evidently the information was supposed to be secret, for the man had suddenly clammed up when a Torenthi soldier poked his head in the door while making his rounds.

Derry had pretended not to be interested, and had quickly changed the subject. But he had carefully filed the information away with the rest of the things he'd learned that afternoon. The mission thus far had been a highly fruitful one. A decided pattern was beginning to form.

He looked into the depths of his ale mug, affecting that morose brooding attitude so often exhibited by men who are very drunk, and considered his next move.

It was almost totally dark now, and he'd been drinking all afternoon. He wasn't drunk—it took more than ale to do that—but in spite of a capacity for spirits which Morgan assured him bordered on the prodigious, he was beginning to feel the effects. It was time he got back to the room he'd taken at the Crooked Dragon. He didn't want to miss his rendezvous with Morgan.

"An' so I says to the lass, 'Darlin', what's yer price?', an' she says, 'More 'n you've got, sailor. You couldn't even keep me in petticoats!'"

Derry took one last swig of the cold ale, then pushed himself back from the bar and straightened his leather jerkin with an exaggerated motion. As he placed another small coin on the bar, a man on his left lurched and nearly poured his ale down Derry's boot, but Derry managed to sidestep and steady the man without looking too sober.

"Careful, mate," Derry slurred, helping the man back to the bar and guiding his mug to the surface. "Here, you finish mine. I gotta get shome shleep." He poured the remnants of his drink into the man's mug, purposely slopping half of it over the side, then patted the man reassuringly on the shoulder.

"Now, you drink up, m'friend," he said, pushing himself away from the bar again. "An' I wish you a pleashant—g'night!"

"Aw, yer not leavin' yet, are ye, ol' buddy? Ish early."

"Come on, Johnny-lad. One more fer th' road?"

"No," Derry shook his head, drawing himself to

exaggerated attention. "I am too drunk. I ha' had enough, an' thash that."

He attempted a precise pivot, stumbled against another man behind him, then managed to weave his way to the door without major mishap. He kept an eye out as he staggered through the door, hoping he wasn't going to be followed. But no one except his former drinking partners even seemed to notice he was gone, and they were fast forgetting he'd ever been there.

As the noise of the raucous Jack Dog Tavern faded into the distance, Derry's hearing gradually began to return to normal. He tried not to collide with too many pedestrians as he lurched along the street—at least none bigger than himself—but when he reached a darkened alley he ducked into the shadows and peered back the way he had come. He had just about decided it was safe to drop his drunk routine when he heard a footstep in the alley behind him.

"Who'shat?" he grunted, dropping into character again as he turned, and hoping it wasn't necessary. "Who'sh there?"

"Hey, fella, are you all right?" said the man approaching him, his voice sounding strangely smooth and cultured in the filthy alley.

Damn! thought Derry as he recognized the man. He'd seen the fellow in the tavern earlier this afternoon, drinking rather quietly with another man in the corner. Why had the man followed him? And where was his drinking partner?

"I rememer you," Derry said, slurring his words and pointing at the man rather shakily as he tried to decide how he was going to handle this. "You were inna tavern, weren't ya? Whash matter? Can't pay yer bar bill?"

"My friend noticed you were awfully shaky when you left," the man replied, stopping about four feet from Derry and studying him carefully. "We just wanted to make sure you were all right."

"Yer frien'?" Derry questioned, trying to look around without seeming too coherent. "Whysh yer frien' so worried 'bout me?" he asked, craning his neck suspiciously as he saw the other man approaching from the street side. "Wha' ish thish anyway?"

"Don't be alarmed, my friend," the first man said, moving closer to Derry and taking his arm. "We're not going to hurt you."

"Now, lishen," Derry began, protesting more loudly as the man started to lead him further into the dark alley. "If it's money ya want, fergit it. I spent my lash copper back a' th' tavern."

"We don't want your money," said the second man, grabbing Derry's other arm and helping his companion half carry Derry along the alley.

Mumbling and whining under his breath, Derry continued to play his drunk role to the hilt, stumbling and falling with every other step to slow them down while he tried to form a plan. The men were obviously up to no good. But whether they suspected him for what he really was or merely wanted to roll him for his money was immaterial right now. What was important was that they believed him to be drunk. He could tell by the way they held his arms that they didn't think him any serious threat. Maybe there was still a way to salvage the operation after all.

"This is about far enough," said the first man, when they had dragged him, stumbling and staggering, some thirty or forty feet into the alley. "Lyle?"

The second one nodded, taking something small and shiny from his tunic. "This won't take a minute, my friend."

It was too small to be a weapon. As Derry watched the man fiddling with it, he realized it was a vial of some murky orangish liquid. He peered curiously as the man tried to worry the stopper out with his fingers, again revising his estimation of the situation.

They were going to drug him—whether to kill or to interrogate, he didn't know, but he didn't particularly care to find out. The first man was holding both his arms, but his grip was only firm enough to support him. Apparently they still believed him to be just a drunk. That would be their fatal mistake.

"What ish that?" Derry murmured amiably as the man pulled out the stopper. "Ish a pretty pink."

"Yes, my friend," said the man, bringing the vial toward Derry's face. "This will just help to clear your head. Drink it down, now."

It was the moment for action.

In a sudden movement, Derry wrenched his arm away from the man behind him and dashed the liquid over his shoulder into the man's face. At the same time he dropped slightly and kicked the second man in the groin, then rolled with the force of the kick and came up on his feet, sword half-drawn.

Before he could clear the scabbard, the first man was already leaping for his arm, wrenching the blade out of his grasp. And as he fought for control of the weapon, the second man launched himself into the fray and landed on his partner's back, thinking it was Derry in the dim light. The first man went limp and the sword fell from his hands; the second jumped back cursing, then lunged at Derry again.

Now the odds were more to Derry's liking, though it still would not be easy. While Derry knew he was most decidedly not drunk, neither was he entirely sober. His reflexes were slowed down, and the man before him was obviously an expert with a dagger. Derry whipped his own dagger from his boot top and sparred with the man briefly, each feinting several times. Then they closed.

After a frenzied scuffle, Derry finally managed to disarm the man and get him into a chokehold. But even as he eased the unconscious form to the ground he realized that he would have to kill the man. He didn't dare leave him in the alley this way, nor could he allow him to talk. The man would have to die.

Crossing quickly to the first man, he felt for a pulse; but the body was already growing cold, a gaping wound in its side. That, at least, saved one killing. But the other ...

He dragged the second man over beside the first and turned him face up, then went through his pockets quickly. He found another vial like the one they'd tried to drug him with, some papers he didn't have time to read just now, and some gold coins. Morgan would be interested in the vial, and possibly the papers, so he pocketed those. But the coins he replaced. He wasn't a thief. And whoever found the bodies in the alley later on would hopefully think the men had killed each other over the money. At least, they would not be looking for a robber. A search of the other man's clothing turned up a similar set of papers and more money, but again Derry kept only the papers.

The unconscious man moaned, starting to come to, and Derry was forced to silence him again. He found himself feeling rather squeamish as he picked up the other man's knife, for he had never killed a man in cold blood before. But his own life was in danger if he did not; there was nothing else to be done. He must look upon it as an execution.

Taking a deep breath, Derry pulled the man's head back and placed the blade against the throat, then drew it across in one quick gesture. Then he dropped the knife by the other man's hand, picked up his sword, and fled down the alley. He had seen and heard men die before, and by his own hand. But then it had been in battle, in open warfare. He had never thought he would become a killer in the dark.

He staggered out the other end of the alley and into the street, forced himself to resume his previous role of a drunk. He got about another block before he had to stop and retch over a gutter. Passers-by glanced at him in disgust or sympathy as they walked by, thinking he was just another drunk.

But Derry knew better. And by the time he reached his room at the Crooked Dragon, he was a very sober young man.

Morgan leaned back against the tall headrest of the carved chair and closed his eyes. He was in his tower room, and he was alone. He could hear and feel the fire roaring in the fireplace to his right, and if he opened his eyes, he knew he would see the high vaulted ceiling, the seven bars of green glass set in the high walls which gave the place its name—the Green Tower. In front of him was the *shiral* crystal, shining coldly on its gryphon stand in the center of the table. His hands rested lightly on the chair arms as he relaxed and cleared his mind. There was a knock at the door, but he did not move or open his eyes.

"Yes?"

"It's Duncan. May I come in?"

Morgan sighed and looked at the ceiling, then sat forward so he could turn to glance at the door.

"The door is open."

He saw the latch turn, and then the door opened and Duncan slipped through.

"Lock it," Morgan said, turning and leaning back in his chair once again.

Duncan crossed to the small round table and sat in the chair opposite Morgan. His cousin's face was calm, serene, and Duncan realized he must already have been casting about for Derry's signal.

"May I help, Alaric?" he asked quietly. "It's still a bit early, you know."

"I know," Morgan sighed. "I don't want him to try early and get discouraged, though. This is all rather new to him."

Duncan smiled. "And it isn't exactly routine to us, either, is it?" he said, leaning his elbows on the table and lacing his fingers together. "Are you sure you won't let me link with you and augment your power? It will save energy and another telling. And Derry will have to know about me sooner or later anyway."

Morgan grinned half-heartedly. "You win. How much longer?"

"Whenever you're ready," Duncan replied. "Go ahead. I'll follow one step behind you."

Morgan took a deep breath and exhaled slowly, then sat forward and cupped his hands around the *shiral* crystal. Another deep breath keyed the first response in the Thuryn trance, and he closed his eyes. There was a moment of silence, and then the *shiral* crystal began to glow faintly. At that, Duncan reached across and grasped Morgan's wrists firmly, his own arms resting easily on the table to either side of the crystal. He exhaled—and joined Morgan in trance.

The *shiral* crystal glowed brightly, then took on an indeterminate smoky amber hue. Neither man was aware of that fact.

He's getting ready, came Morgan's clear thought. *He's thinking about forming the link.*

I feel it, Duncan responded. *Where is he? Do you know?*

"I can't tell. A long way away.

In a tiny room at the back of a rather dowdy village inn, Derry sat down gingerly on the edge of the bed and doused one of the two candles in the room. He had read the papers he took from his two would-be assailants, and what he had learned had removed some of the taint of having killed in cold blood. For the men had been agents of Torenth, sent on special commission to ferret out information concerning Morgan's troop activities—precisely what Derry was doing, but on the other side. They had only been on their way through Fathane, but that was enough. And they would have killed Derry, had their positions been reversed.

So now they were dead and he was alive instead. It would take a while for the local authorities to identify them without papers. But once it was discovered that they were royalist agents, the hue and cry would be raised in tiny Fathane, and all strangers would be suspect. Derry didn't see how he could be linked with the deaths, but he must be on his guard. Stranger things had been known to happen, and he was totally alone in Fathane.

No, not totally alone, he reminded himself, as he laid back on the bed and pulled the medallion Morgan had given him out of his shirt. At least he would be able to tell Morgan what had happened, give him the information he had gathered thus far.

He cupped the medallion in his hands and studied it for a moment, then closed his eyes and murmured the words of the spell Morgan had taught him. He felt a fleeting sense of dizziness as he slipped into that strange and almost frightening sleep. And then he was aware of a familiar presence surrounding him, backed by another known almost as well. The spell had worked!

Congratulations, Derry. You're an apt pupil. Did you have any trouble reaching us?

Morgan?

That's right. And Duncan too.

Father Duncan?!

Are you surprised?

Surprised is hardly the word.

We'll explain later. What have you learned?

A great deal, Derry replied, smiling widely even though he knew his commander could not see the expression. *One, Torenthi royalist troops are gathering somewhere north of here—about five thousand strong, if rumor is correct.*

Where is "here"? Morgan interrupted.

Sorry. I'm in Fathane—an inn called the Crooked Dragon, for some reason I haven't been able to fathom yet.

I know the place. Go on.

Anyway, they're gathering near a place called Medras, about a half-day's ride north and inland from here. I thought I'd ride up that way in the morning. Good hunting has been reported in that direction, too.

Which is also a good cover for you, Morgan agreed. *How about our situation here in Corwyn?*

Ah ... a little rumbling about Warin de Grey, but not much. Since the Torenthi have a Deryni ruler, they can hardly be expected to be enthusiastic about an anti-Deryni religious fanatic. He's apparently made a few raids across the border here, but didn't have much success. I'll keep my ears open as I head back west.

Do that, Morgan replied. *Anything else? You've done a fine job, but I don't want to tax your strength any more than necessary.*

Yes! came Derry's emphatic reply. *I had to kill a man in cold blood tonight, m'lord. He and his partner were Torenthi agents, and they were trying to drug me with something.*

Do you know what it was?

No, but I have it here. I was going to bring it back for you.

Get it, Morgan ordered. *You can open your eyes without breaking rapport. Describe it to me.*

Derry opened his eyes cautiously, then reached across and picked up the vial. He looked at it carefully, then closed his eyes once more.

It's a small, cloudy crystal vial with a brownish stopper. The fluid inside seems to be orangish and kind of thickish-looking.

All right. Open it carefully and smell it. Don't spill any of it on you.

Right.

Derry sat up and opened the vial, then took a cautious sniff.

Again, Morgan commanded.

Derry obeyed.

Do you recognize it, Duncan?

I'm not sure. It could be bélas. The R'Kassans use the drug as a truth potion. But it will only work on humans, and then only when they're very drunk.

Derry, were you drunk? Morgan asked.

They thought I was, Derry replied with a smile. *Would it have hurt me?*

That depends on whether you're telling the truth about being sober. How do you know the men were Torenthi agents, by the way?

I took their papers. Garish de Brey and Edmund Lyle, late of His Majesty's court at Beldour. They were on their way to spy on you.

How inhospitable of them, Morgan retorted. *Anything else before we break rapport?*

No, sir.

All right. First of all, I want you to destroy those papers and the bélas. Either could be your death warrant if you're caught. I must go to the Hort of Orsal tomorrow, but I'll listen for your call tomorrow night at this time in case you need to get in touch with me. Don't try unless your information is vital, though, because we can't afford the energy drain on a regular basis. And see what you can find out about the Interdict. Other than that, just be careful and get back in the next two days. Have you got all that?

Yes, sir. Contact tomorrow night if it's important, and return in two days.

Good luck, then.

Thank you, sir.

Derry shuddered slightly as the contact was broken, then opened his eyes and looked around the room. He felt tired, drained of energy, but it was a good tired; and the experience had been much better than he'd expected. He'd apparently been apprehensive over nothing. One of these days he would learn to believe what Morgan told him about magic the first time.

He looked wistfully at the open vial in his hand, then emptied it into the chamberpot under his bed. Then he ground the vial to powder under his heel and put flame to the papers. Ashes followed the drug into the chamberpot, and then he urinated over the entire mess for good measure.

There. He defied even a Deryni to make sense of that mess—if anyone even thought to look.

That settled, he unlaced his leather jerkin and pulled off his boots. Pulling back the shabby blanket on the bed, he flopped down on the mattress and covered himself, moving his dagger under his pillow where he could reach it in a hurry. Then, as an afterthought, he tucked Morgan's medallion back inside his shirt.

Wouldn't want anyone to walk in and see that, he thought to himself as he dropped off to sleep.

CHAPTER SEVEN

Let destruction come upon him unawares . . .

Psalms 35:8

IT WAS JUST past sunup when Morgan, Duncan, and the ducal entourage arrived at the quay to board *Rhafallia*. The air was chill, damp, heavy with the bitter salt tang of the sea.

Since the visit to the Hort of Orsal was to be an official one, Morgan was decked out in quasi-formal attire—knee-length black leather surcoat with the Corwyn gryphon blazoned on the chest in green suede, this over light mail encasing his body from neck to knee. Hard leather boots took up where the mail left off, the heels adorned with silver ceremonial spurs—though Morgan would not be going near a horse. A rich green woolen cloak of a nubby texture hung from his broad shoulders, secured right of center with a carved silver clasp. And since this was a state visit and not a military maneuver, the ducal coronet of Corwyn crowned his golden head. His broadsword swung at his side in a well-worn leather scabbard.

Duncan, too, had made dress concessions for his visit to the Hort of Orsal, finally discarding all pretense of clerical garb in favor of a high-collared black doublet and cloak over mail. He had debated whether he should don the plaid of his McLain ancestors—he knew that Alaric kept one on hand for just such

104

events—but he had decided that such a move might be premature. Few people knew of his suspension as yet. And until they did learn of it, there was no need to advertise the fact. As long as he wore black, he would arouse no attention. People would see what they expected to see.

But meanwhile, he realized wryly, he would have little difficulty fitting into society as a layman again. Lord Duncan Howard McLain was first and foremost a nobleman's son, well-schooled in the fighting traditions of the aristocracy. And though the new blade hanging at his waist might be virgin just now, there was little doubt in Duncan's mind that it would serve him well the first time the need arose.

The dense coastal fog was lifting as Morgan and Duncan approached the *Rhafallia*, and they could see her tall mast looming suddenly in the greyness. The brilliantly decorated and stitched mainsail was furled loosely along the single wide yardarm, and Morgan's black-green-black maritime banner hung limply from a short standard at the bow. As they watched, a sailor ran up Kelson's colors on the mast, a flash of crimson and gold against the grey morning sky.

Rhafallia was not Morgan's largest ship, though at a mere fifty tons she was one of the fastest. Double-ended and clinker-built like most ships that plied the Southern Sea in trade, she carried a crew of thirty men and four officers, with room for perhaps half that many men-at-arms or passengers, in addition to cargo. When the wind blew and blew from the right direction, she could make four to six knots with little difficulty; and recent rigging innovations copied from the Bremagni merchant fleets to the south now made it possible to tack as close as forty degrees to the wind with a new forward sail called a jib.

If the wind failed, or did not blow from the proper direction, there were always the oars. And even without sail, the narrow and high-riding *Rhafallia* could easily make the crossing to the Hort of Orsal's island port and back in less than a day.

Morgan glanced up at the mast again as he and Duncan approached the gangplank and noticed that sailors were already swarming the rigging in preparation for departure. A lookout was supervising from a vantage point in the fighting castle at the top of the mast, and Morgan could just see the bright knit caps of the deck crew scurrying in the slightly lower level of the rowing gallery. He hoped that they would not have to rely too heavily on oars this morning, though. He wanted to be back on land well before noon.

As he considered the dismal possibility of a protracted crossing, a tall man in well-worn brown leather breeches and jerkin came striding up, his neck and shoulders muffled by a rough wool cloak of faded crimson. He wore the peaked leather cap of a ship's master, with the green cockade of Morgan's sea service jutting gaily from the brim. He grinned broadly as he saw Morgan, and a bushy rust-colored mustache and beard bristled when he talked.

"Good morning, m'lord!" he boomed, rubbing his hands together briskly and glancing around as though he were thoroughly enjoying the cold, the fog, and the early hour. "Isn't it a beautiful morning?"

Morgan raised a droll eyebrow. "It is if you like to sail blind, Henry. Will the wind pick up by the time the tide shifts, or are we going to have to row?"

"Oh, there'll be wind," the captain assured him. "It's going to be a beautiful day for sailing. Only one tack out of the harbor. How many are you bringing aboard, by the way?"

"There'll be nine in all," Morgan replied, glancing around distractedly. "Ah, this is my cousin, Monsignor Duncan McLain. Duncan, Captain Henry Kirby, Master of the *Rhafallia*."

Kirby touched the brim of his hat. "Pleased to meet

you, Monsignor." He turned back to Morgan. "Are you ready to come aboard then, m'lord?"

"Might as well. How long before the tide?"

"Oh, a quarter hour or so. We can start casting off and getting sail set as soon as you're aboard."

"Very well." Morgan turned and gestured to the knot of men standing farther back on the quay, then followed Duncan and Kirby aboard. Behind him, Lord Hamilton and his troupe came trudging down the quay seven strong.

Hamilton looked much more confident now that he was back in fighting harness. He was a warrior, not a courtier. And his close association with Gwydion and other more cultured personages for the past few days had been nerve-wracking, to say the least. Certainly none had been happier than he to see the fiery little troubadour packed off for Culdi this morning. It had started Hamilton's day most propitiously, and he was now in his element, presiding with singular aplomb as he herded his contingent aboard the ship.

Master Randolph was the first of the ducal party to go aboard, his handsome face alight with pleasure at the thought of the adventure he hoped awaited. As a physician, he was seldom included in court intrigue beyond that of the sort he had handled at the state banquet. And the fact that Morgan had invited him along on this trip was a constant source of wonder and delight.

At his side was young Richard FitzWilliam, the royal squire Duncan had brought with him from Rhemuth. Richard was enthralled with the prospect of seeing the Hort of Orsal's legendary court in person. Further, he idolized Morgan, had trained under his supervision at the court at Rhemuth. Fiercely loyal to the duke, he had risked harsh words and physical danger more than once to warn his mentor of impending danger.

In addition, there were four of Morgan's staff

officers from the castle garrison, serving the dual purpose of honor guard and military advisors for the strategy sessions which were the object of the visit. It would be the job of these men, under the leadership of Lord Hamilton who brought up the rear, to command the local defenses while Morgan was away leading the royal armies in the north. As such, they were a vital link in the defense of Corwyn.

When the last man was aboard, two crewmen in faded blue breeches and linen shirts drew in the gangplank and secured the rail on the side. Even now, a breeze was rising, the mist beginning to clear away in thin strips. Kirby began shouting orders, and lines were cast off, sails unfurled. As *Rhafallia* drifted away from the dock, a dozen rowers broke out their oars and began guiding her toward a patch of wind perhaps fifty yards from the quay. She cleared the last ships anchored in the vicinity of the quay and entered the wind, and her sails began to fill.

The breeze stiffened as *Rhafallia* cleared the harbor mouth, and she began to pick up speed. After a few hundred yards, she came about smartly and set a course for the Orsal's island capital. If the wind held, she would arrive at the other side in less than four hours, with a steady cross wind all the way.

As soon as the mechanics of getting under way were finished, Captain Kirby joined Morgan, Duncan, and Randolph on the afterdeck. Though *Rhafallia* was technically a merchant ship, she carried raised fighting platforms fore and aft. The helmsman steered the ship from the rear of the aft platform with a broad starboard steering oar, but the rest of the platform was ordinarily captain's country, used as a lounge and observation deck.

Sailors had brought folding camp stools of finely tooled Forcinn leather up the access ladder, and the four made themselves comfortable. The sun was shining strongly now, and as they looked back toward

Coroth, they could see the fog still shrouding the high cliffs of the coast, yet already beginning to melt away in the spring sunlight. Hamilton, the four lieutenants, and young Richard were lounging on the main deck about amidships, and those crewmen not engaged in the actual sailing of the ship were relaxing in the narrow, indented rowing galleries which ran the length of the ship on either side. A lookout stood watch on the forward fighting platform, and another in the castle atop the mast. The huge expanse of mainsail and wide jib obscured a large portion of the sky, the painted gryphon on the main fiercely surveying the entire scene.

Kirby sighed and leaned back against the railing on the aft platform as he inspected his ship.

"Ah, 'tis a beautiful day, just as I told you, m'lord. You really have to get out on the sea and taste the salt air to appreciate life. Can I interest you in a bit of wine to take the chill off your bones, perhaps?"

"Only if you have Fianna wine," Morgan replied, knowing that the vintage he requested was the most expensive, and also knowing that Kirby drank nothing else.

Kirby gave a wry grin and gestured expansively. "For you, m'lord, nothing but the best." He glanced over his right shoulder and into the starboard rowing gallery where a boy of seven or eight was whittling. "Dickon, come here a minute, lad."

The boy looked up attentively at the sound of his name, then put away his knife and scampered to the foot of the ladder. The ship rolled slightly in the brisk wind, but the boy held onto the ladder steadily. There was a look of pure hero worship in his eyes as he looked up at Kirby.

"Sir?"

"Bring up some cups and a new flask of that Fianna wine, will you, son? One of the hands can help you lift it down."

"My squire can give him a hand," Morgan said, moving to the rail beside the captain. "Richard, would you help this lad, please? Captain Kirby has graciously consented to treat us from his private stock of Fianna wine."

Richard looked up inquiringly from his post with the castle lieutenants and Lord Hamilton, then grinned and bowed acknowledgement. As Dickon turned on his heel and clambered down another ladder and into the hold, Richard glanced after him rather incredulously. He seemed somewhat taken aback at the boy's agility, for Richard himself did not profess to be a sailor, but he followed obediently, if a bit more gingerly.

Kirby watched the two disappear below decks and smiled. "My son," he stated proudly.

There was nothing Morgan could add to that.

Toward the bow, one of the crew had watched the preceding exchange with interest. His name was Andrew, auxiliary helmsman aboard the *Rhafallia*. And now he turned back to glower over the rail, squinting intently into the mist far ahead which shrouded the Hortic coast.

He would never reach those foam-drenched shores, he knew. Nor would he ever see his native Fianna again—that same Fianna whence came the wine which had just been the topic of discussion on the afterdeck. But he was resigned to that. It was small enough price to pay for the deed he was about to do. He had been ready for a long time.

He stood without moving for several minutes, then reached casually into his bleached homespun shirt and removed a small, crumpled scrap of cloth. Glancing around to be sure he was not being observed, he unfolded the cloth and cupped it in his hand, mouthing the syllables as he reread the words for the fifth or sixth time.

" 'The Gryphon sails with the tide in the morning.

He must not reach his destination. Death to all Deryni!' "

Below was an "R", and the sketchy emblem of a falcon.

Andrew glanced over his shoulder at the afterdeck, then turned back to face the sea. The message had arrived last night as the sun was sinking behind the misty mountains. As they had planned so long ago, the time at last had come when Morgan would sail again aboard his flagship *Rhafallia*—and meet his destiny. It would not be a pleasant death—not *that* for the Lord Alaric. But death it would be, and soon.

He pressed his right hand against his chest and felt the reassuring pressure of the vial on the cord around his neck. He would not shrink from his duty. Though his own death was certain, he had sworn the oath of the Sons of Heaven and he would keep it. Besides, Warin himself had promised that the end would not be painful. And Andrew would be richly rewarded in the Hereafter for killing the hated Deryni duke.

What matter if, in killing Morgan, he must take his own life? There could be no escape from the ship, even if he succeeded. And if he failed—well, he had heard what the Deryni could do to a man: how they could twist his mind, force him to open his soul to the powers of evil, even betray the Cause.

No, far better to drink the faithful poison and then strike down the Deryni. What price life if a man's soul be damned?

With a decisive gesture, Andrew crumpled the scrap of cloth in his hand and let it fall to the water below. He watched until it was lost from sight, then reached inside his shirt again and withdrew the tiny poison vial.

The elixir was very potent, Warin had told him. A few drops on the blade of his dagger, a small scratch on unprotected hands or face, and all the magic and mail in the world would not save the traitor Morgan.

He worried the stopper out of the vial, glancing around surreptitiously to be sure no one was watching, then let a few drops trickle down the blade stuck through his leather belt.

There. Let the Deryni defeat that, he thought to himself. *For, as I live and breathe, his blood will spill today. And with it spills his life!*

He recorked the vial and hid it in his hand, then turned and strolled casually toward the aft fighting platform to relieve at the helm. As he climbed the ladder and slipped past Morgan and the others to take the tiller, he tried to avoid looking at Morgan, as though a mere glance from the sorcerer might fathom his intent and foil the coming deed. His move was hardly noticed, for at that moment Richard and the cabin boy returned with worn wooden cups and a flask of wine. The flask, Andrew noted bitterly, still bore the Fianna seal of quality.

"That's a good lad," Kirby smiled, taking the flask and pouring all around after he broke the seal. "M'lord, you invariably have good taste in wine."

"I only follow your lead, Henry," Morgan smiled. He took a long draught. "After all, if I had no captains like you to import it, I'd never know such heaven on earth existed. An excellent year. But then, they all are." He sighed and stretched his legs in front of him, and the sun gleamed on his mail and his golden hair. He took the gold coronet from his head and laid it casually on the deck beside his stool.

Andrew took advantage of the activity to work the stopper out of the vial again with his thumb, then lifted it to his lips under the pretext of covering a yawn. The yawn quickly assumed the appearance of a cough as the liquid burned down his throat, and Andrew was hard pressed to cover his extreme discomfort. Kirby looked at him strangely, then returned his attention to his conversation. Andrew swallowed again with difficulty, but managed at last to regain his composure.

Hell's demons! Andrew thought as he wiped his streaming eyes, Warin hadn't warned him it would taste like that! He had almost given the whole plan away. He would have to act quickly now.

Straightening, he studied the configuration of men on the platform. Morgan was sitting on a stool about eight feet away, his back toward the helm. Kirby stood to his left and a few feet farther away, facing slightly sideways. The priest, Master Randolph, and the squire Richard were grouped to Morgan's right, also seated, and all were much more interested in the slowly emerging land to the east than in the movements of the ship's helmsman.

Andrew's lip curled in a sardonic smile as his hand crept to the hilt of his long dagger, and he carefully chose his target—the unprotected back of Morgan's head. Then, abandoning the tiller, he drew his knife and leaped toward his intended victim.

The outcome was not as anyone had planned. As Andrew leaped, young Richard FitzWilliam turned and caught the movement. In that fatal instant before Andrew could reach his target, Richard simultaneously shouted and launched himself between the two, throwing Morgan from his seat and sending leather stools flying. The ship lurched as it came around into the wind, throwing Andrew off balance and preventing him from stopping in time.

Even as Duncan and Kirby were leaping to disarm and subdue him, Andrew crashed into Richard and Morgan, his momentum carrying all three to the deck in a heap. Morgan ended up on the bottom of that heap, with Richard in his arms and a terrified Andrew on top of that.

He had failed!

Duncan and Kirby grabbed Andrew by the arms and wrenched him away as Hamilton and the four lieutenants swarmed up the access ladder to aid in the capture. Once Kirby saw that the man was in custody, he scrambled to the tiller and steered the ship back on course, shouting urgently for another seaman to come and take the helm. Randolph, who had pulled the boy Dickon to safety at the outset of the attack, watched half in a daze as Morgan struggled to a sitting position, fighting for wind and incredulously shifting Richard in his lap.

"Richard?" Morgan gasped, shaking the young man's shoulder urgently. The youth was a dead weight in Morgan's arms, and the duke's eyes went wide as he saw the dagger protruding from deep in Richard's side.

"Randolph, come here! He's hurt!"

Randolph was instantly at his side, kneeling to inspect the wound, and Richard moaned and opened his eyes with great effort. His face had an ashen, cyanic tinge to it, and he grimaced with pain as the physician touched the dagger. Duncan made certain his prisoner was secure, then hurriedly joined Randolph at the wounded man's side.

"I—I stopped him, m'lord," Richard gasped weakly, looking up at Morgan with trusting eyes. "He was going to kill ye.

"You did well," Morgan murmured, smoothing the youth's dark hair off his forehead and reading the agony etched there. "How is he, Ran?"

Randolph shook his head bitterly. "I think he's poisoned, m'lord. Even if the wound were not so critical, I—" He bowed his head in defeat. "I'm sorry, m'lord."

"Your Grace," Richard whispered, "may I ask a boon?"

"Whatever is in my power, Richard," Morgan said gently.

"Would—would ye tell my father I fell in your service, as your liege man? He—" Richard had to cough, and the movement sent another wave of pain wracking through his body. "He hoped I would be a knight some day," he finished weakly.

Morgan nodded, biting his lip and trying to keep his vision from bluring.

"Let me say the words, then, m'lord," Richard whispered, taking Morgan's hand and gripping it fiercely. "I, Richard FitzWilliam, do become your liege man of life and limb and of earthly worship." His eyes opened wider and his voice steadied as he continued. "And faith and truth I will bear unto you, to live and die, against all manner of folk," he grimaced in pain, his eyes squeezing shut, "so help me, God. . . ."

His voice trailed off with the end of the oath and his grip relaxed. The last breath died slowly. With a convulsive shudder Morgan held the dead youth to his chest for a moment, his eyes closed in sorrow. Beside him, he could hear Duncan murmuring the words of absolution.

He looked up at Kirby's drawn face, at his lieutenants holding the prisoner, at the prisoner himself, and his eyes went steely grey. Not taking his eyes from the man who stood there glaring down so defiantly, he gently lowered Richard to the deck and got to his feet. There was an overturned stool between him and the prisoner, and he forced himself to right it and set it carefully in place before moving closer to the man. His hands clenched and unclenched several times as he stood looking at the man, and he had to restrain the urge to smash the sneering face with his fist.

"Why?" he said in a low voice, not trusting himself to say any more at this point.

"Because you're Deryni, and all Deryni must die!" the man spat, his eyes flashing with a fanatic fire. "The Devil take you, you'll not escape next time! And there *will be a next time*, I guarantee it!"

Morgan stared at the man for a long moment, not

saying a word, and the man at last swallowed and dropped his gaze.

"Is that all you have to say?" Morgan said quietly, his eyes dark and dangerous.

The man looked up at him again, and a strange expression came across his face.

"You can't hurt me, Morgan," he said in a steady voice. "I tried to kill you and I'm glad. I'd do it again if I had the chance."

"What chance did Richard have?" Morgan said icily, watching as the man's eyes flicked nervously to the body lying behind him.

"He consorted with a Deryni," the man snapped. "He deserved what he got."

"The Devil take you, he deserved no such thing!" Morgan cursed, grabbing the front of the man's shirt and jerking his head to within inches of his own. "Who sent you to do this?"

The man grimaced with pain and shook his head, then smiled weakly. "It's no good, Morgan. I'm not telling you anything. I know I'm a dead man."

"You're not dead yet!" Morgan murmured through clenched teeth, giving the man's collar a slight twist. "Now who sent you? Who's behind this?"

As Morgan turned his Deryni gaze on the man, intending to Truth-Read, Andrew's blue eyes widened and a look of stark terror replaced the belligerence.

"Not my soul, you Deryni bastard!" the man croaked, wrenching his gaze from Morgan's and closing his eyes tightly. "Leave me alone!"

A shudder wracked through his body as he fought Morgan's power and he moaned in agony as he struggled to escape. Then he relaxed and slumped in the arms of his captors, head lolling loosely. Morgan made one last effort to probe his mind as he slipped away, but it was no use. The man was dead. Releasing the shirt, Morgan motioned for Randolph.

"Well," Morgan said, turning away in disgust, "did I kill him, or did he scare himself to death, or what?"

Randolph inspected the body the lieutenants lowered to the deck, then pried open the man's left hand. He took the vial and sniffed it, then stood up and held it out to Morgan.

"Poison, m'lord. Probably the same that was on the knife. He must have realized there was no hope of escape even if he'd succeeded in killing you."

Morgan glanced down at one of the lieutenants who was searching the body. "Anything?"

"Sorry, m'lord. Nothing."

Morgan looked down at the body for a moment, then prodded it with his toe. "Get rid of that," he said finally. "And take care of Richard. He'll be buried in Coroth with full honors, as my liege man."

"Yes, m'lord," A lieutenant said, taking off his green cloak and spreading it over the fallen squire.

Morgan turned away and walked to the rail, as far as possible from the two bodies, frowned as a splash told him there were no longer two. Duncan joined him and leaned against the rail to his left. He watched his cousin for a long moment before breaking the silence.

"'All Deryni must die!'" Duncan quoted softly. "Shades of the Inquisition. Does it remind you of anything else?"

Morgan nodded. "The songs they've been singing in the streets. Ran's reports from the banquet about the border raids. It adds up to one thing: this Warin affair is getting out of hand."

"That was a dedicated man standing there just now," Duncan observed. "This Warin fellow must have a great deal of charisma. I wonder what he told that sailor to make him take his own life for the cause?"

Morgan snorted. "It's not hard to imagine. 'By killing the Deryni monster, you aid all of humankind. There will be rewards for you in the Hereafter. Only through death can you escape the wrath of the Deryni, prevent him from defiling your immortal soul!' "

"Powerful persuasion for the common man, where superstition already runs rampant," Duncan commented. "And I'm afraid we're going to see a lot more of it, if and when the Interdict falls. It will bring all of this out in the open. This is only a taste."

"Well, I can't say I like the flavor," Morgan said. "We'll not stay long at the Orsal's court today, Duncan. I may not be able to do any more at home than I can there, but I at least want to be present when things start falling apart."

"Then you're finally convinced the Interdict *is* a serious threat."

"I never thought any different," Morgan agreed.

The sun had sunk into the sea and *Rhafallia* was churning her way back toward the Corwyn coast before Morgan at last had time to relax and ponder the day's events.

It had not been a good day. Aside from the obvious horror of attempted assassination and the death of Richard, even the meeting with the Hort of Orsal had been less than satisfying. His Hortic Majesty had been in a terrible disposition, for he had just received word that five of his prized R'Kassan stallions had been stolen from a breeding farm in his northern provinces. Torenthi border raiders had been responsible for the theft, and when Morgan and Duncan arrived the Orsal had been much more interested in recovering the animals and wreaking vengeance than in discussing mutual defense in a war that was still three months hence.

So the meeting had not been fruitful in that respect. Morgan visited with his old friend and his family and was coerced into allowing the Orsal's second heir, the eleven-year-old Rogan, to return with him to the ducal court for knightly training. But the defense plans so vital in the coming months were never settled to Morgan's satisfaction. When the duke boarded *Rhafallia* to go home, two of his castle lieutenants had stayed behind to wrangle with the Orsal's advisors and sea captains and work out final details of the protective alliance. Morgan did not like delegating such crucial responsibilities to others, but there was no real choice in this particular case. He could not personally afford to spend at the Orsal's court the days necessary to come to a final agreement.

The weather, too, had deteriorated during the day. When Morgan sailed at sunset, it was in name only. The air was so still that the ship could not even leave the quay without the aid of oars. The crew, with the good-natured resignation that was characteristic of the men on Morgan's ships, unshipped their oars and settled down to row. And as stars began to appear in the east, the crew's rough voices sang and hummed sea chanties as old as man's first ventures on the sea.

The ship was dark except for green steering lanterns fore and aft. On the afterdeck, Captain Kirby stood watchful guard beside the helmsman. Beneath him, under the shelter of the afterdeck, Master Randolph and the others of Morgan's party reclined on hard pallets and tried to sleep. The duke and Duncan were bedded down on the forward platform, sheltered against a light drizzle by a canvas canopy Kirby had rigged before they set sail.

But Morgan could not sleep. Gathering his cloak around him more closely, he leaned out from under the canopy to scan the stars. The Hunter had risen from the sea in the east, and his bright belt winked frostily in the chill March air. Morgan studied the other constellations distractedly, not thinking about what he was doing, before settling back on his pallet to sigh, hands clasped behind his head.

"Duncan?"

"Hmmm."

"Are you asleep?"

"No." Duncan sat up and rubbed a knuckled hand across his eyes. "What's the matter?"

"Nothing."

Morgan sighed again and clasped his knees against his chest, chin resting on folded arms. "Tell me, Duncan. Did we accomplish anything today besides the loss of a good man?"

Duncan grimaced, tight-lipped in the darkness, then tried to force a light tone. "Well, we saw the Orsal's latest offspring—number seven, I make it. And a 'lusty bairn,' as we say in Kierney."

"Hurrah for the lusty bairn," Morgan smiled half-heartedly. "We also saw little Orsals one through six, number three of which is now part of my entourage. Why didn't you stop me, Duncan?"

"I?" Duncan chuckled. "I thought you were desperately eager for a new Hortic squire at Castle Coroth, my Lord General. Just think—you can take the Orsal's son into battle with you."

Morgan snorted. "The Devil I can! If I take the second heir to the Hortic throne into battle and something happens to him, God forbid, I'll end up dying for my new squire, all right. But what could I say? I owed the Orsal a favor. And it would have been very difficult to bow out gracefully with the boy standing right there."

"You don't have to explain," Duncan replied. "If there's trouble, you can always put the lad on the first ship for home. I get the impression that young Rogan would like that anyway," he continued wistfully. "I don't think he's the warrior type."

"Yes, hardly the sort of son I'd pictured for the Hort of Orsal. He's second in line, and I have the feeling he's not even happy about being that close."

Duncan nodded. "A potential scholar or physician or monk if I ever saw one. It's a pity he'll never have the chance to pursue his true calling. Instead, he'll become some sort of minor functionary in his older brother's court when the time comes—never really happy, never knowing why. Or perhaps knowing why, yet unable to do anything about it. That's the saddest part of all, I think. I grieve for him, Alaric."

"So do I," Morgan agreed, knowing that Duncan, too, was feeling the futility of being trapped in a role he did not wish to play, forced by circumstances to veil his true potential and masquerade in a world he had not asked for or made.

With a sigh, Morgan leaned out of his pallet to study the stars once more, then edged closer to the bow where light was streaming from the forward steering lantern. Sitting back against the railing, he stripped off his right glove, smiled as the gryphon signet on his hand winked coldly in the green-tinged lantern light.

Duncan scooted across the deck on hands and knees to crouch beside his cousin.

"What are you doing?"

"It's time for Derry's report if he's going to make one," Morgan replied, polishing the ring against a corner of his cloak. "Do you want to listen with me? I'm only going to first level trance unless he calls."

"Go," Duncan said, sitting cross-legged beside Morgan and nodding his readiness. "I'm one step behind you."

As both men fixed their attention on the ring, Morgan inhaled deeply to trigger the earliest stage of the Deryni Mind-Touch, then exhaled slowly as he entered trance. His eyes closed; his breathing became slow and controlled. And then Duncan was reaching across to cover the gryphon seal with his cupped hand, to join in the rapport.

They cast around for perhaps fifteen minutes, at first touching only the consciousness of crew men and members of the ducal party aboard. As they extended their awareness, they caught the ghostly flickers of other minds, contacts so fleeting as to be almost undetectable, and certainly unreadable. But nowhere was there a sign of Derry. With a sigh, Morgan withdrew from the trance, Duncan following.

"Well, I suppose he's all right," Morgan said, shaking his head lightly to dispel the last vestiges of fogginess which such a search usually left behind. "Unless he's in serious trouble, I know he would have called if he'd had anything to report." He smiled. "I'm afraid our young friend Derry liked his first taste of magic far too much to pass up the opportunity for a repeat performance if there was the slightest excuse he could use. I think he's probably safe."

Duncan chuckled as he crawled back to his pallet. "It's a little surprising how easily he took to magic, don't you agree? He acted as though he'd been doing it all his life, hardly batted an eye when he found out I was Deryni too."

"Product of long indoctrination," Morgan smiled. "Derry has been my aide for nearly six years. And up until two nights ago, I never let him see me use my powers directly. He saw the fruits of those powers on occasion, though, if not the methods. So when the time finally came to get involved himself, there was no question in his mind as to whether being Deryni was a bad thing. He knew better. He shows remarkable potential, too."

"Could he be part Deryni?"

Morgan shook his head and lay down. "I'm afraid not. Which raises another interesting question. It makes one wonder what other humans could do, given the chance, if they weren't so damned convinced that magic is evil. Derry, for example, shows remarkable adaptability. There are a number of simple spells I could teach him right now if he were here, and he'd have no difficulty whatever in mastering them. And he doesn't even have ancestry through one of the original human families that carries the potential for receiving power—like Brion did, or like the Orsal's line."

"Well, I hope he's careful," Duncan murmured, rolling over and pulling his cloak over himself with a grunt. "A little knowledge can be dangerous, especially if it happens to be Deryni knowledge. And right now, the world can be a very dangerous place for Deryni sympathizers."

"Derry can take care of himself," Morgan said. "He thrives on danger. Besides, I'm sure he's safe."

But Derry was not safe.

CHAPTER EIGHT

*For there cometh a smoke out of the north, and there
is no straggler in his ranks.*

Isaiah 14:31

BUT DERRY was not safe.

That morning after leaving Fathane, he had decided to head north toward Medras to see what he could learn. He did not plan to go all the way to that city, for there was not sufficient time if he was to be back in Coroth by the following night as Morgan had ordered. But Medras was where Torenthi troops were reputed to be gathering. If he were prudent, he might be able to gain valuable information to relay back to Morgan.

Of course, he had reminded himself as he rode out the gates of Fathane, he would have to exercise a great deal more caution if he intended to do his work in another establishment like the Jack Dog Tavern of the night before. Last night's altercation in the alley had been far more brutal than he cared to repeat.

And that was yet another reason for quitting Fathane as soon as possible. He didn't want to be connected with those two bodies in the alley. He doubted that any of his drinking companions of the night before would even be able to remember him, much less connect him with the deaths. But witnesses had a bad habit of remembering things at the most inopportune times. And if, by some quirk of fate, those did—well, life would be neither easy nor long for one who had dared to kill two of Wencit's hand-picked spies.

So he had ridden north and inland toward the city of Medras, stopping occasionally at inns and wells to chat with the local folk and to peddle some of the furs in the pack behind his saddle. By noon he had reached the turn-off road to Medras, only minutes behind a large company of foot soldiers bound for that city. And he had very nearly been stopped and questioned by a pair of men from the rear guard of that troop.

If there had been any doubt in his mind before, that incipient threat convinced Derry that he had best, indeed, not go on to Medras. It was time to head west, back into Corwyn. Dusk found Derry crossing the rolling northern reaches of Morgan's territory, the fertile buffer region separating Corwyn from Eastmarch. The roads near the border were notoriously poor, and the one Derry had chosen was no exception, but he had made good time since crossing the Torenth-Corwyn border. Now, as darkness approached, however, Derry's horse stumbled and slowed on the rough footing. Derry sighed and forced himself to pay more attention to his riding.

It would soon be dark, but he had a definite destination in mind before he stopped for the night. For while this was Morgan country, it was also Warin country, if rumor was correct. There was a town ahead with a passable inn. Besides dinner, of which Derry was sorely in need, there might be valuable information to be gleaned.

Whistling a merry tune under his breath as he rode, Derry glanced at the horizon slightly to his left, then stared.

That was strange. Unless he was seriously mistaken, the sunset glow behind the next hill was not only in the wrong place (indeed he had seen the sun set thirty degrees farther to the right), but it was growing brighter instead of darker.

Fire?

Drawing rein to listen and sniff the wind, Derry frowned, then left the road and struck out across the open fields toward the hill. The bitter, acrid bite of smoke was strong in his nostrils now. And as he neared the crest of the hill, he could see the black clouds of smoke billowing into the still-pale sky ahead. Now, too, he was aware of shouts echoing on the chill night air.

Suspecting the worst, and hoping that he was wrong, Derry slipped from the saddle and covered the remaining few yards on foot. His face went grim as he dropped to his stomach to scan the scene below.

Fields were burning. Perhaps thirty or forty acres of winter wheat stubble were smoldering to the south, and actual flames were threatening a modest manor house just off the road Derry had left.

But it was not only fire which threatened the inhabitants of the manor house. There were armed horsemen plunging about in the manor courtyard, flailing about them with swords and lances, cutting down the green-liveried men on foot who tried futilely to ward off their blows.

All that was noble in Derry cried out in that instant. For one of the first precepts of knightly honor was to defend the helpless and the innocent. He wished desperately to go to the rescue.

Yet reason told him, rightly, that there was nothing one lone man could do against such odds except himself be cut down. And though he might very well have taken a number of marauders to the grave with him, it would be a useless death. Dying would not get word back to Morgan of what was happening here, or help the manor's occupants.

As Derry watched, sick at heart, his eye caught the

flicker of new fires starting to the north of the main one, and men on horseback with torches in their hands. As the new group rallied and waited at the road, Derry saw that the fighting was over in the courtyard, that all the liveried men were still. There was, he noted with satisfaction, another figure on the ground—one not in livery. But his comrades picked him up and put him across a horse, then waited until two other men with torches came running from the manor house to mount up and ride.

Smoke curled from the rear of the manor house— smoke from a place where there was no chimney— and Derry gritted his teeth and forced himself to wait as the last of the marauders galloped out of the courtyard and joined their companions, then disappeared over the hills to the west.

Cursing softly under his breath, Derry ran back to his horse, vaulted into the saddle, and began careening wildly down the hillside. The manor house was blazing strongly now, and there was no chance that it could be saved. But Derry had to be certain that there was no one left alive in that scene of carnage.

He was able to make his way to within fifty yards of the manor before flames from the burning wheat stubble forced him to return to the road. And then he had to blindfold his horse with his cloak before the animal would pass between the flames to either side of the manor gate. He steeled himself as he drew rein.

It had been the manor of a lord of modest means. The house was unpretentious, though well kept— what was left of it. And the lord's retainers had apparently made the best stand they could. There were half a dozen bodies in the yard, more on the porch: most of them old, all wearing blood-stained livery of the same green and silver as the coat of arms above the ruined gate.

Vert, three wheat sheaves proper on a chevron argent. Motto: *Non concedo*—'I do not concede.'

Surely these men did not concede, Derry thought as he picked his way across the courtyard and scanned the bodies. *I wonder of their lord, though. Where is he?*

He heard a moan from his left and saw a movement out of the corner of his eye. As he turned his horse to investigate, he saw a hand lift in supplication. He slipped from the saddle to kneel at the side of an old bearded man who also wore the green and silver livery.

"Who—who are you?" the old man gasped, clutching at Derry's cloak and pulling him closer to squint in the fire-lit darkness. "You're not one of them—"

Derry shook his head and eased the man's head against his knee. It was getting darker, and the man's face was scarcely more than a blur in the failing light, but it was enough for Derry to see that he was dying.

"My name is Sean Lord Derry, friend. I'm the duke's man. Who did this to you? Where is your lord?"

"Sean Lord Derry," the man repeated, his eyes closing against the pain. "I've heard of you. You—sit on the young king's Council, don't you?"

"Sometimes," Derry said, frowning in the darkness. "But right now it's more important that you tell me what has happened. Who's responsible for this?"

The old man lifted one hand and gestured vaguely toward the west. "They came out of the hills, my lord. A band of Warin de Grey's ruffians. My young master, the Sieur de Vali, is gone to Rhelledd to seek the duke's aid for all of the local landowners, but alas . . ."

His words trailed off and Derry thought he had lost him, but then the creaky old voice continued.

"Tell the duke we fought loyal to the end, my lord. Though we are but old men and boys, tell him we would not give in to the 'Holy One,' no matter what his minions threatened. We—"

He coughed, and dark blood trickled from a corner of his mouth. But then he seemed to gain strength from somewhere, and he raised his head a few inches, pulling himself up on Derry's cloak.

"Your dagger, my lord. May I see it?"

Derry frowned, wondering if the man meant to ask for the coup de grâce. It must have shown on his face, for the man smiled and shook his head as he relaxed against Derry's knee once more.

"I will not ask that of you, young lord," he whispered, his eyes searching Derry's. "I do not fear death. I but seek the solace of a cross to ease my passage into that other world."

Derry nodded, his face grave and solemn, and pulled his dagger from its boot-top sheath. Grasping it by the blade, hilt uppermost, he held it before the man's eyes, a faint shadow from the flame-light falling across the man's face. The man smiled and pulled the cross hilt down to touch it with his lips. And then the hand went slack, and Derry knew the man was dead.

Rest in peace, good and faithful servant, Derry thought, crossing himself with the hilt of the blade and replacing it in its sheath. *So Warin de Grey strikes again. Only this time, instead of threats and burning, there's murder, wholesale slaughter.*

Taking a last glance around the desolate courtyard, now illuminated only by the growing flames in the manor house, Derry stood and toyed with the ends of his reins in indecision, then remounted.

He should not really do what he was about to do. By all rights, he should go to a safe place and wait until it was time to contact Morgan. His commander would definitely not approve of the risk Derry was now considering.

But logic was not always the best answer, Derry

had found. Sometimes, in order to get things done, unorthodox methods must be used. Even at the risk of great personal danger.

Touching spurs to his mount, Derry clattered out of the courtyard and down the road the marauders had taken. If he was any judge of mobs, Warin's raiders would not go far tonight. It was late for travel on these roads, and there was no moon. Besides that, the riders had a dead or wounded man on their hands. If he was merely wounded, there was an excellent chance that they would stop before too long to tend his hurt.

In addition, there was the question of Warin himself. He had not been with the group at the manor. Derry had been fairly certain of that as he watched the carnage done. And the old man in the courtyard had not mentioned the presence of the dynamic rebel leader—only his men. Derry was certain Warin would have been recognized, had he been present.

Which meant that Warin was possibly somewhere in the vicinity, perhaps with another band. And that he might rendezvous with the rest of his men before the night was through. Derry must try to be there when that occurred.

The next hour was torture for Derry. As night descended, the sparsely populated countryside became darker and darker. And the quality of the roads had not improved on leaving the manor of the Sieur de Vali, either.

He apparently made much better time than he thought, however. For long before he expected, the dim, flickering lights of the village of Kingslake were winking cheerily in the darkness ahead. And as Derry guided his footsore mount along the main road through the village, he suddenly saw the bulk of the Royal Tabard Inn looming against the night sky. Here, if he was lucky, he could get a fresh horse before continuing his pursuit, perhaps even learn which direction the riders had taken—for the road forked beyond Kingslake.

The Royal Tabard Inn was two stories high, a sturdy wooden building nearly two hundred years old with accommodations for forty guests and a taproom renowned for miles around. It had been Derry's original destination before he came upon the burning manor, and now he wished he dared stop for a tankard of ale before continuing.

But as Derry approached the livery stable adjoining the inn, he noticed several dozen steaming horses tethered outside, a single man standing guard. The man was well armed, which was unusual since he wore only nondescript peasant garb. But there was a fierce, confident air about him, an aura of deadly purpose that made Derry look twice.

Was it possible that he was one of the raiders? That they had chosen the Royal Tabard as a resting place?

Scarcely daring to believe his unprecedented good fortune, Derry dismounted and led his mount into the livery stable. Arrangements for a fresh horse took only minutes, and then Derry was striding out of the stable toward the inn, his purpose a mug of ale, in case the guard should ask. He touched his cap and nodded amiably as he passed the man, and the man nodded pleasantly enough. But there was something strange about him, about the embroidered badges on his left shoulder and cap depicting a falcon. Derry was frowning as he entered the inn.

Inside, the scene was not at all what Derry had expected. He had thought, as he approached, that the inn was far too quiet for the number of horses tied outside. That many drinking men should have been more noisy. Even the mere patronage of local towns-folk should have provided at least a low hum of conversation on an ordinary night.

But it was not an ordinary night. The local citizens of the village and countryside were there; and they were drinking. Nor were they being molested by the men on the other side of the room—men who also wore the falcon badge—the same men Derry had watched at the de Vali manor.

But no one spoke. And the riders from the marauder band were hovering quietly around one of the long trestle tables which had been pulled to the left side of the room, watching over a still, blood-stained form which lay sprawled on that table.

As Derry made his way to a chair which seemed to be in neutral territory, he frowned. The man on the table—the same he had thought killed by de Vali's defenders—was apparently not dead yet; for a thin girl in peasant garb was bathing his head with towels wrung from a wooden basin at her side. He moaned as she worked, and her eyes darted nervously over the men who surrounded and watched her. But there, too, there was no word spoken.

Another girl brought a tray of earthen mugs filled with ale and distributed them to the riders, and some of them sat quietly and sipped at their drinks. But there was no conversation, no excessive movement. It was as though the men were waiting, listening. The townsfolk on the other side of the room sensed it too; and they waited.

Derry picked up the tankard of ale the proprietor brought and took a long pull, forced himself to gaze into the depths of the ale rather than stare at the raiders.

What was going on? he wondered. Were they waiting for Warin to come? And what did they hope to do for the man on the table, who was clearly near death?

There was the sound of horsemen drawing rein outside, perhaps as many as twenty, and shortly a second group of riders entered. These, too, wore the falcon badge on cloaks and hats. And their leader, after a whispered conference with one of the men attending the wounded man on the table, gestured for his own\ men to join their colleagues. Again, tankards were brought. And again, there was no further conversation. Apparently the new man was not Warin either.

Thus the situation remained for nearly half an hour, while Derry downed a second and third tankard of ale and tried to fathom what was happening. Then there was again the sound of hoofbeats on the road outside, this time only about a dozen. And as the horses stopped, amid snorts and jingling harness hardware, the room grew suddenly stiller yet. There was a taut, electric tension in the air. As Derry turned slowly toward the doorway, the door swung back to frame a figure who could only be Warin himself. Derry froze with everyone else in the room, not daring to breathe.

Warin was not a large man. In fact, were it not for his regal bearing, he might have been considered short. But this was totally overshadowed by the fact that the man had *presence*, which radiated outward from his person like a living entity.

The eyes were dark, almost black, with a wild, even reckless intensity which sent a shiver up Derry's spine as the man's glance touched him in scanning the room. (Derry had seen that look on Morgan's face once, and he shuddered anew as he remembered the consequences of the deeds which followed.) Warin's hair was brown and crinkled, a dusty dun color, closely cropped; and he wore a very short beard and mustache of the same dun hue.

Alone of all his men, Warin wore what could have been styled a uniform: a solid grey leather jerkin over tunic, hose, and high boots of the same shade—except that the falcon badge on his breast was large, covering most of his broad chest, and the cap badge on his close grey hat was silver rather than sewn. His grey leather riding cloak was full and long, almost brushing the floor. And he was totally unarmed as far as Derry could see.

There was a whisper of movement across the room, and Derry suddenly found himself able to breathe again. He hazarded a glance at Warin's men clustered around the table and saw that all had bowed their heads and brought closed right fists to their hearts on Warin's entrance. As Warin nodded acknowledgment, they looked expectantly at the man on the table and moved aside. Warin strode briskly into their midst, and the townspeople gathered courage and moved to the center of the room to see what the rebel leader would do. Derry cautiously made himself a part of that group.

"What has happened?" Warin asked. His voice was low, measured, crackling with authority.

"At the manor of the Sieur de Vali, Holy One," the spokesman of the first group said meekly. "De Vali had ridden to ask the duke's aid, and his men resisted. We had to put the manor to the torch."

Warin turned wide, dark eyes on the man. "That was unwise, Ros."

Ros fell on his knees, cowering, and buried his face in his hands. "Forgive me, Holy One," he whispered. "I have not your wisdom."

"See it does not happen again," Warin replied with a slight smile, touching the man's shoulder in a gesture of acceptance.

As the man scrambled to his feet, face transfigured with awe, Warin returned his attention to the wounded man and began stripping off his grey leather gloves.

"Where is the injury?"

"In his side, Lord," a man on the opposite side of the table murmured, drawing aside the man's rent tunic to show the wound. "I fear the lung may be pierced."

Warin leaned to inspect the wound, then moved to the man's head and lifted an eyelid. He nodded to himself, then straightened and tucked his gloves into his belt, glanced at the men who watched him so eagerly.

"With God's help we shall save this man," he said, spreading his arms to either side in a gesture of supplication. "Will you pray with me, brethren?"

To a man, Warin's followers dropped to their knees, their eyes riveted on their leader as he closed his eyes and began to pray.

"*In nomine Patris et Filii et Spiritus Sancti, Amen. Oremus.*"

As Warin intoned the Latin phrases, Derry watched wide-eyed and then forced himself to look even more closely. For unless he, too, was falling under the powerful charisma of the rebel leader, there was a faint glow beginning to surround Warin's head—a misty blue violet aura which resembled nothing so much as a halo!

Derry controlled a gasp, then bit his lip and tried to use the pain to break the illusion. There was no way this could be happening. Human beings did not have halos, and there were no more saints. But neither was his mind playing tricks on him. Morgan had taught him to see through illusion; but this was real, no matter how hard Derry tried to make it disappear.

". . . And therefore, O God, send thy healing spirit through these hands, that thy servant Martin may live to glorify Thee. Through Jesus Christ thy Son, our Lord, who liveth and reigneth with Thee in the unity of the Holy Spirit, God forever and ever, Amen."

As Warin finished speaking, he lowered his right hand to rest lightly on the wounded man's forehead, then let his left drop to cover the blood-frothed wound in the man's side. There was deathly silence for nearly a minute, and Derry's heart pounded as the light he was sure couldn't really be there seemed to extend itself down Warin's arms and into the still form beneath.

Then the man called Martin shuddered and exhaled

a long sigh, opened his eyes and blinked in amazement to find his leader standing over him.

Warin opened his eyes and smiled, then helped Martin to sit. There was a long murmur of awe as Martin stood down from the table and took the tankard someone offered. As he drained it, one of the townspeople gasped and pointed to the man's side. There was no sign of any wound except the bloody tear in his homespun tunic.

"Deo gratias," Warin murmured, crossing himself and lowering his eyes. The aura had all but disappeared now, and he glanced around curiously as he pulled his gloves from his belt and began to don them. There was blood on his left hand where he had touched Martin's wound, and one of his men noticed that fact and dropped to his knees beside Warin to wipe the hand with a corner of his cloak. Warin smiled and rested his hand on the man's head for just an instant, as though in blessing, then returned to his gloving without comment. The man got to his feet with a look of pure bliss on his face.

Warin's glance swept the room once more, and again Derry felt that chill sensation as the eyes touched his. Then Warin was moving toward the door. At his movement, his men drained their tankards and scrambled to their feet, gathering the belongings they had brought with them and crowding after him. One of Warin's lieutenants pulled gold coins from a pouch and paid the innkeeper. And as Warin reached the door one of the townsfolk suddenly threw himself to his knees and cried, "It's a miracle! The Lord has sent us a new messiah!"

Almost instantly, his words were taken up by half the people in the tavern, who fell to their knees and crossed themselves fervently. As Warin turned in the doorway, Derry knelt too—although he most certainly did not believe there had been any miracle involved.

The rebel leader scanned the room a final time, his

gaze calm, beneficent, then raised his right hand in benediction before disappearing into the darkness. As soon as the last Warin retainer had filed from the tavern, Derry jumped to his feet and ran to the window.

Now that Warin was out of the room and Derry could think clearly again, he realized what it was about the man which had been so disconcertingly familiar. It was that presence he had felt in men like Morgan, Duncan, Brion, the young King Kelson. That impression of raw power and command which almost always went with a talent not in the best of repute these days.

He peered through the misty glass of the tavern window and watched as Warin and his band disappeared down the road in a glow of torchlight. He would not follow them. With what he had learned, there was no need of that right now. Besides, he had to get this new information to Morgan as soon as possible.

It was quite late. He knew he had missed the appointed time for contact with his commander by well over an hour; but no matter, if he rode hard and met no further mishap, he could be back in Coroth shortly after noon tomorrow.

He could hardly wait to see Morgan's face when he told him he thought Warin might be a Deryni!

CHAPTER NINE

*And he will send them a savior, and a defender, and
he will deliver them.*

Isaiah 19:20

"WARIN IS what?" Morgan gasped. "Derry, you must
be joking!"

Morgan and Duncan were sitting under a tree in
the exercise yard adjoining the armory where they had
been sparring with broadswords when Derry had
thundered through the gates of Castle Coroth half an
hour before. Derry was tired and hungry as he
squatted on the grass beside his commander. But his
eyes glittered as he related all that had happened at
the Royal Tabard the night before.

Morgan wrapped his towel more closely around his
exercise tunic and mopped his face, for he was still
sweating from the workout Duncan had given him.
Derry did not challenge his outburst, and after a few
seconds the duke shook his head in disbelief.

"Well, this is certainly unexpected," he said, wiping
a hand across his forehead. "Derry, are you sure?"

"Of course I'm not sure," Derry replied, pulling his
hunt cap from his tousled brown hair and slapping
the dust from it in agitation. "But can humans do
what he did, m'lord?"

"No."

"Father Duncan, do you think Warin is a saint?"

"There have been stranger ones," Duncan replied enigmatically, thinking of his vision on the road.

Derry pursed his lips thoughtfully, then looked back at Morgan. "Well, he did heal that man, M'Lord. And from what you've told me, I had the impression that only Deryni could do that."

"I can do that," Morgan amended, scowling at the ground between his bare legs. "I don't know that other Deryni can. I'd never heard of it being done in recent times until I used it to save your life last year."

Derry bowed his head, remembering the attack on the guard detail he had commanded the night before Kelson's coronation. How they had been taken by surprise and overpowered in the darkness. The searing pain as a sword pierced his side and he fell, thinking never to rise again.

And then waking in his own quarters, his wound gone as though it had never existed. And a puzzled physician bending over him, unable to explain. And Morgan telling him, weeks later, how he had laid his hands on Derry's brow—and healed.

Derry looked up again, then nodded. "I'm sorry, m'lord. I meant no disrespect. But you are Deryni, and you can heal. And so can Warin."

"And so can Warin," Morgan repeated.

"Well, if he is Deryni, he certainly can't be aware of what he is," Duncan said, scratching his leg and cocking his head at his cousin. "Personally, I find it difficult to believe that the man of the rumors I've heard could be such a hypocrite—to persecute his own race."

"It's been done before."

"Oh, certainly it's been done before, and by experts. There are always some men who will sell out anything for the right price. But that's not the impression I get about Warin. He's sincere. He's convinced that his cause is just, that he has a divine calling. And what you've just told us, Derry, about healing the wounded man, his effect on his men—that simply confirms my impression."

"The trouble is," Morgan said, standing and retrieving his sword, "that Warin does the things saints and messiahs traditionally do. Unfortunately, those same deeds are not commonly attributed to Deryni, even though the legends of many Christian saints may have their origin in Deryni powers. Knowledge of this would certainly quell any thought of rebellion—but how do you impart this knowledge when Warin's people are as loyal and devoted as Derry says they are?"

Derry nodded his head. "That's right, m'lord. Already, his followers look on him as a Holy One, a saint. Those villagers in Kingslake are convinced they saw a miracle performed before their eyes, in the finest old biblical tradition. How do you fight something like that? How do you tell people their messiah is a fake? That he's the very thing he preaches against, only he doesn't know it? Especially if you want people to come out liking Deryni in the end?"

"You tell them very carefully, and by slow degrees," Morgan said softly. "And right now, you don't tell them at all. Because for now, unless we can do something about it, the people are flocking to his cause."

"And will flock even more when they find out what the archbishops have planned," Duncan added. "Derry, you didn't know this, but Archbishop Loris has summoned all the bishops of the realm to meet in conclave at Dhassa the day after tomorrow. Bishop Tolliver left this morning—he dared not refuse the summons. Nor will he dare to say no when Loris presents his decree of Interdict before the assembled Curia. I think you know what that means."

"Can they really lower an Interdict on Corwyn?" Derry asked. They began walking toward the main courtyard, Morgan and Duncan carrying their swords, Derry twirling his cap.

"They can, and they will unless something is done," Morgan replied. "Which is why Duncan and I are leaving for Dhassa tonight. Direct appeal to the Curia is probably hopeless; I doubt they would listen, no matter what I had to say. But Loris won't be expecting it. And I may at least be able to impress them enough to make them think about what they're doing. If the Interdict falls, with Warin as strong as he is now, I think the countryside will follow him in a holy war against Deryni. Even if I have to pretend to go along, submit myself to the Curia for penance, I can't allow that to happen."

"May I come with you, m'lord?" Derry asked, glancing up at Morgan hopefully as they walked along. "I could be a bit of help, I think."

"No, you've already been a great deal of help, Derry, and I have a more important task for you. After you've gotten a few hours sleep I want you to ride for Rhemuth. Kelson must be told what has happened, and Duncan and I can't do it if we're to reach the Curia before it's too late. If Kelson has already left for Culdi by the time you arrive, follow him there. It's vital that he be aware of all you've told us this afternoon."

"Aye, m'lord. Shall I try to contact you?"

Morgan shook his head. "If there's need, we'll contact you. Meanwhile, get some sleep. I want you on your way by dark."

"Right."

As Derry hurried away, Duncan shook his head and sighed.

"What's the matter?" Morgan asked. "Are you discouraged?"

"I'm certainly not encouraged."

"Cousin, you have read my mind again. Come. We'd better get cleaned up. Hamilton should have my officers ready for briefing in about an hour. I have a feeling it's going to be a very long afternoon."

Midway through that same afternoon Bronwyn walked leisurely along the terrace at Castle Culdi. The sun had shone brightly all day, drying out the damp of the past weeks' rain. The birds of the south had already begun to return from their winter sojourn, warbling their brave songs in the awakening garden.

Bronwyn paused at the balustrade and leaned over to look at a fishpond a few feet below, then resumed her stroll, luxuriating in the sweet, warm air and comfortable surroundings of the ancient palace. Twirling a strand of burnished hair between her fingers, she smiled to herself and let her thoughts ramble as she continued to walk.

The wedding party had arrived in the mountain city of Culdi the night before, after a pleasant, if damp, day's ride from Kevin's capital in Kierney. There had been a ball, and this morning had been spent in a hunt in honor of the bride and groom to be. She and Lady Margaret had passed the earlier part of the afternoon inspecting the budding gardens, with Bronwyn showing her future mother-in-law all the best-loved features of the familiar area.

There were fond memories in Culdi for Bronwyn, for she and Alaric, Kevin and Duncan, had spent many happy summers here in their childhood. The Lady Vera McLain, who had been a second mother to Bronwyn and her brother, had often brought the McLain and Morgan children to Castle Culdi in the summer.

Bronwyn remembered the romps through the flowering gardens, always in bloom at the time of the year they were there; the summer Alaric fell out of a tree and broke his arm; the stoic bravery with which the eight-year-old bore the pain. She remembered the many secret passages through the walls of the castle where she and the boys used to play hide and seek. And the quiet and serene chapel where their mother was buried—a place Bronwyn still liked to go to for meditation.

She had never known her mother. Lady Alyce de Corwyn de Morgan had died only a few weeks after the birth of her tiny daughter, victim of the milk fever which so often claimed the lives of young mothers. Alaric remembered her—or said he did. But Bronwyn's memories were only of the marvelous tales that Lady Vera spun about the lady who had borne them, and a hint of sadness that she had never been permitted to know this wonderful and shining lady.

Remembering the past, Bronwyn paused on the terrace, then headed resolutely back toward her chambers. It was still fairly early. If she did not dawdle, there would be ample time to visit the little chapel before she had to dress for dinner. But the chapel would be cool and damp this time of day. She would need her cloak.

She had almost reached the terrace doors to her chamber when she stumbled on a crack in the flagstone terracing, then recovered. As she leaned down to rub her foot in annoyance, she was not consciously listening for anything. But she suddenly became aware that there were voices—female voices—coming from her chamber.

"Well, I just don't understand why you defend her so," one was saying.

Bronwyn recognized the voice as that of Lady Agnes, one of her ladies-in-waiting, and she straightened and moved a little closer to the doorway as she realized they were talking about her.

"That's right," another said. "It isn't as though she's one of us."

That was Lady Martha.

"She's a woman like us," a third voice protested softly, her tone unmistakably that of Mary Elizabeth, Bronwyn's favorite. "And if she's in love with him and he with her, I see no shame in it for anyone."

"No shame?" Agnes gasped. "But she's—she's—"

"Agnes is right," Martha stated flatly. "The heir to the Duchy of Cassan ought to marry far higher than the daughter of a—"

"Than the daughter of a common Deryni!" Agnes chimed in.

"She never knew her mother," Mary Elizabeth interjected, "and her father was a lord. Besides, she's only half-Deryni."

"And that's half a Deryni too much to suit me!" Martha stated emphatically. "Not to mention that unspeakable brother of hers!"

"She can't help who her brother is," Mary Elizabeth interrupted, forceful but calm even in the midst of argument. "And other than being a bit more open with his powers than is, perhaps, wise, there's nothing wrong with Duke Alaric. He can't help being born Deryni any more than Lady Bronwyn can. And if it weren't for the duke, there's no telling who might be ruler of Gwynedd today."

"Mary Elizabeth, are you *defending* him?" Agnes gasped. "Why, that's close to blasphemy!"

"It *is* blasphemy!" Martha retorted. "Not only that, but it smacks of treason and—"

Bronwyn had heard enough. With a sick feeling in the pit of her stomach, she turned away from the chamber and moved quietly back along the terrace, finally going down the steps in the direction of the far garden.

Something like this always seemed to happen. She would go along for weeks, sometimes even months, without being reminded of that one dark spectre in her background.

And then, just when she began to feel she had perhaps lived down her Deryni heritage, that she had been accepted as herself, not some kind of scheming witch, an incident like this would occur. Someone would remember and use that remembrance to twist and turn the truth until it was something ugly, unclean. Why were humans so cruel?

Humans! she thought—then smiled bitterly as she hurried along the path. There she was, thinking in terms of *them* and *us* again. It happened every time she had an encounter like this.

But why did it have to start in the first place? There was nothing wrong with being Deryni, despite Church dictates to the contrary. As Mary Elizabeth had pointed out, one could not control the circumstances of one's own birth. Besides, she had never really used her powers.

Well, almost never.

She scowled as she walked along toward her mother's chapel, folding her arms across her chest against the sudden chill of the afternoon.

She had to admit that she had occasionally used her powers to heighten her senses of sight, hearing, smell, when the need arose. And she had formed a mind link with Kevin once, years ago when they were both young and the sport of doing something forbidden had outweighed their fear of punishment had they been caught.

Just as she sometimes called the birds to her hands in the gardens to feed them—though she made very certain that no one was watching when she did so.

But what could be wrong with that kind of magic anyway? How could they say it was wrong, evil? They were jealous—that was all!

As she considered this point, she became aware of a tall figure coming toward her on the path, his white hair and grey doublet identifying him unmistakably as the architect Rimmell. As she came abreast of him, the man withdrew to one side to let her pass, bowed low from the waist.

"My lady," he murmured as Bronwyn started to go by.

Bronwyn nodded pleasantly and continued walking.

"My lady, might I have a word with you?" Rimmell persisted, walking after her a few paces and stopping to bow again as Bronwyn turned to face him.

"Of course. Master Rimmell, isn't it?"

"Yes, m'lady," Rimmell replied nervously, nodding again. "I wondered how your ladyship liked the plans for the palace in Kierney. I did not have the opportunity to ask before, but I thought to get your ladyship's reaction while there is still time to make alterations in the plans."

Bronwyn smiled and nodded appreciatively. "Thank you, Rimmell. Actually, I was very pleased with the plans. Perhaps we could go over them some time tomorrow if you like. I can't think of anything I'd want changed, but I appreciate the offer."

"Your ladyship is most kind," Rimmel murmured, bowing again and trying to conceal his joy that Bronwyn was actually talking with him. "May—may I escort Your Ladyship anywhere? The afternoon grows chilly, and the mist comes early here in Culdi."

"No, thank you," Bronwyn replied, shaking her head and rubbing her arms as though in response to the suggestion of chill. "I was going to pay a visit to my mother's tomb. I'd rather go alone if you don't mind."

"Of course," Rimmell nodded understandingly. "Would Your Ladyship deign to accept my cloak, then? The chapel will be drafty this time of day, and Your Ladyship's dress, while perfectly suited to the warm sunshine, is hardly ample protection in the crypt."

"Why, thank you, Rimmell," Bronwyn said, smiling gratefully as Rimmell hung the grey cloak around her shoulders. "I'll have one of my servants return it later this evening."

"There's no hurry, my lady," Rimmell replied, backing off and bowing deferentially. "Good afternoon."

As Bronwyn continued on down the path, wrapped in Rimmell's cloak, he looked fondly after her for a moment, then turned back in the direction he had been going. As he was about to mount the steps to the terrace level, he saw Kevin come out of his quarters on the end and head down the steps.

Kevin was clean-shaven, his brown hair neatly combed, and he had exchanged his dusty hunt clothes of the morning and early afternoon for a short brown velvet doublet with the McLain tartan swinging jauntily from the left shoulder. As he clattered down the steps in a flash of freshly polished boots and spurs, scabbard and chains a-jingle, he saw Rimmell and hailed him, coming to a halt in the center of the stairway.

"Rimmell, I've finished with those plans you left me this morning. You can go into my quarters and get them if you want. You did a marvelous job, by the way."

"Thank you, m'lord."

Kevin started on, then paused. "Rimmell, have you, by any chance, seen my Lady Bronwyn? I can't seem to find her anywhere."

"I believe you'll find her at her mother's tomb, m'lord." Rimmell answered, "When I met her on the path a few minutes ago, she said she was on her way there. I gave her my cloak against the chill. I hope you don't mind."

"Not at all," Kevin said, slapping Rimmell on the shoulder in a casual gesture of friendship. "Thank you."

Raising a hand in farewell, Kevin bounded down the remaining steps and disappeared around a bend in the path, and Rimmell continued toward his master's quarters.

He had about decided the course of action he would have to take. Outright violence against this gracious young lord was out of the question. Besides, Rimmell was not a violent man. But he was in love.

That morning, Rimmell had spent several hours talking with some of the local townspeople about this dilemma, without, of course, naming the object of his heady passions. Being mountain people, and living here on the edge of the Connait and wild Meara, they sometimes had rather curious notions about how a man might woo his ladylove.

Rimmell hardly believed, for example, that hanging carilus flowers on Bronwyn's door and chanting the Ave seven times was likely to sway a Deryni girl in any way. Nor would putting a toad in Kevin's goblet help. The earl would simply fly into a rage that his servants had not been more careful.

But a number of folk had suggested that if Rimmell really wanted to win a lady's love, there was an old widow woman who lived in the hills—a holy shepherdess called Bethane—who had reputedly helped similarly distraught and lovesick young men. If Rimmell would take a sack of food and some gold up into the hills, perhaps Bethane could solve his problem.

So Rimmell had decided to try it. He had not paused to consider that he was indulging in a bit of superstitious practice he would never have considered had he not been smitten with love for the beautiful Bronwyn de Morgan. He was convinced that the widow Bethane would be his salvation, the way to win this fair creature he must either have or die. With a love potion or trinket from that esteemed and venerable holy woman, Rimmell could woo Bronwyn away from the Lord Kevin, make her love the builder instead of the baron.

He stepped into Kevin's quarters and glanced around, looking for his plans. There was little to distinguish the room from any other sleeping room in the castle, since all were merely temporary abodes for the current visitors. But there were a few things Rimmell could pick out as belonging to Kevin: the fold-

ing stool covered in McLain tartan, the tapestried rug
on the floor beside the bed, the comforters on the bed
itself—rich silk embroidered with the earl's crest—the
bed where Kevin would bring his beloved Bronwyn in
three days if Rimmell did not act soon.

He looked away from the bed, preferring not to
consider the possibility any further for the moment,
then saw his plans lying rolled up on a table near the
door. He had picked them up and was about to exit
the way he had come when his eye was drawn to
something glittering atop a small chest.

There were the usual jewels and badges of office
lying there—rings, brooches, chains. But one thing in
particular had caught his eye: a small oval locket on a
golden chain, too delicate and fragile to belong to a
man.

Without thinking about what he was doing, he
picked up the locket gingerly and opened it, glancing
out the door to be sure he was not being observed;
then he looked inside.

It was Bronwyn—the most beautiful likeness Rimmell had ever seen—her golden hair cascading down
her perfect shoulders, lips parted slightly as she gazed
fondly out of the portrait.

Not permitting himself to consider what he was
about to do, Rimmell stuffed the locket into his tunic
and bolted for the door, the rolled-up plans almost
crushed under his arm. He looked neither left nor
right as he fled down the stairs toward his own quarters. Observers, had they seen him, would have said
he went as a man possessed.

Bronwyn raised her head from the railing enclosing
her mother's tomb, then gazed dejectedly across at the
life-sized effigy.

She realized now that she was much more deeply
troubled by the overheard conversation than she had
allowed herself to believe at first. But she didn't know

quite what to do about it. She couldn't really confront the women and demand that they cease their gossiping. That would solve nothing.

She continued to study the effigy before her, finally seeing features now, and wondered what she would have done, marveled at the extraordinary woman who had been her mother.

Lady Alyce de Corwyn de Morgan had been an exceptionally beautiful woman in life, and her sarcophagus more than did her justice. Craftsmen from the Connait had carved the smooth alabaster with great skill, down to the most minute detail. It was so lifelike that even now, though Bronwyn was grown, she still had the feeling she'd had as a child; that the effigy lived; that only the right words need be spoken to make the statue breathe and the woman come alive.

The wide stained-glass window above the tomb was ablaze with light from the slowly sinking sun, bathing the small chapel with gold and orange and red, spreading a wash of color on the tomb, on Bronwyn's borrowed grey cloak, on the tiny ivory altar a few yards to her right.

Bronwyn heard the creak of the door opening behind her, and she turned slightly to see Kevin poke his head curiously through the doorway. His face brightened as he saw her, and he stepped inside and pulled the door shut. He bent his knee before the tiny altar before coming to kneel by her side at the tomb.

"I was wondering where you were," he said in a low voice, placing his right hand gently on hers. "Is anything wrong?"

"No—yes," Bronwyn shook her head, "I don't know." She looked down at her hands and swallowed with difficulty, and Kevin suddenly realized she was on the verge of tears.

"What's the matter?" he asked, putting his arm around her shoulders and pulling her toward him.

With a muffled sob, Bronwyn burst into tears and

buried her face against his chest. Kevin held her close and let her cry for a few minutes, stroking her soft hair with a soothing hand. Then he eased himself to a sitting position on the step and pulled her into his lap, to cradle her in his arms like a frightened child.

"There, now," he murmured in a low, calm voice. "It's all right. Let's talk about it?"

As her sobbing diminished, Kevin relaxed and leaned back against the railing, still stroking her hair as he watched their silhouettes blocking the jewel-light which spilled over their shoulders and onto the white marble floor.

"Remember when we were children and used to come here to play?" he asked. He glanced down at her and was relieved to see that she was drying her eyes. He pulled a handkerchief from his sleeve and gave it to her as he continued.

"I think we nearly drove my mother crazy that last summer before Alaric went to court. He and Duncan were eight, and I was eleven, and you were all of four or so, and very precocious. We were playing hide and seek in the garden, and Alaric and I hid in here, behind the altar cloth where it hangs down on the ends. And old Father Anselm came in and caught us, and threatened to tell Mother." He chuckled. "And I remember, he'd no sooner finished scolding us when you came wandering in with a handful of Mother's best roses, crying because the thorns had pricked your little fingers."

"I remember," Bronwyn said, smiling through her tears. "And a few summers later, when I was ten and you were a very grown-up seventeen, and we—" she lowered her eyes. "You persuaded me to form a mind-link with you."

"And I've never regretted it for an instant," Kevin smiled, kissing her forehead. "What's the matter, Bron? Is there anything I can do to help?"

"No, Bronwyn said, smiling wanly. "I was just feeling sorry for myself, I guess. I overheard some things I didn't want to hear earlier this afternoon, and it upset me more than I thought.

"What did you hear?" he asked, frowning and holding her away from him so he could see her face. "If anyone is bothering you, so help me, I'll—"

She shook her head resignedly. "There's nothing anyone can do, Kevin. I simply can't help being what I am. Some of the ladies were talking. That's all. They—don't approve of a Deryni marrying their future duke."

"That's unfortunate," Kevin said, holding her close again and kissing the top of her head. "I happen to love that Deryni very much, and I wouldn't have anyone else."

Bronwyn smiled appreciatively, then stood up and straightened her dress and wiped her eyes again. "You know just what to say, don't you?" she said, holding out her hand. "Come. I'm through feeling sorry for myself. We must hurry, or we'll be late for dinner."

"The Devil with dinner."

Kevin pushed himself to his feet and stretched, then put his arms around Bronwyn. "Do you know something?"

"What?" She put her arms around his waist and looked up at him fondly.

"I think I'm in love with you."

"That's strange."

"Why?"

"Because I think I'm in love with you, too," she smiled.

Kevin grinned, then leaned down and kissed her soundly.

"It's a good thing you said that, wench!" he said, as they headed for the door. "Because three days from now you're going to be my wife!"

And in a small room not far from there, Rimmell the architect, caught by the fascination of a beautiful and unattainable woman, lay stretched out on his bed and gazed at a small portrait in a locket. Tomorrow he would go to see the widow Bethane. He would show her the picture. He would tell the holy woman how he must have the love of this lady or die.

And then the shepherdess would work her miracle. And the woman would be Rimmell's.

CHAPTER TEN

Seek the aid of darker counsel . . .

IN THE DIM, predawn drizzle of a back street of Coroth, Duncan McLain gave the buckle on the girth a final tug and replaced the stirrup, then moved quietly back to his horse's head to wait. Another pair of reins looped over Duncan's left arm pulled gently as Alaric's riderless horse shook its head in the icy mist; and worn harness leather creaked beneath the oilskin saddle cover as the animal shuffled its feet. Beyond, a shaggy pack pony laden with bundles of untanned furs and skins lifted its head to snort inquisitively, then went back to sleep.

Duncan was getting tired of waiting. The rain which had begun at dusk had continued to fall throughout the night, most of which Duncan had spent catching fitful snatches of sleep in a tiny merchant's stall not far away.

But now a messenger had said that Alaric was on his way, that he would be there very soon. And so Duncan stood waiting in the rain, his rough leather cloak drawn up closely under his chin in the fashion of Dhassan hunters, the collar and hood muffled close against the icy wind and rain. The cape was already dark across the shoulders where the wet had soaked through. And Duncan could feel the chill of his mail hauberk even through the rough woolen singlet he

154

wore under it. He blew on gloved fingers and stamped his feet impatiently, grimacing at the feel of toes squishing in wet leather, and wondered what was taking Alaric so long.

As though on command, a door opened in the building to his right, and a tall, leather-clad figure was momentarily silhouetted in the path of light. Then Alaric was moving between the horses, clasping Duncan's shoulder reassuringly as he glanced up at the dismal grey sky.

"I'm sorry I took so long," he murmured, sweeping off the saddle protector and wiping the seat fairly dry. "Were there any problems?"

"Only damp feet and spirits," Duncan replied lightly, uncovering his own saddle and mounting up. "Nothing that getting out of here won't remedy. What kept you?"

Morgan gave a grunt as he checked the girth a final time. "The men had a lot of questions. If Warin should decide to move against me while we're gone, Hamilton will have his hands full. That's another reason I want to keep our departure a secret. As far as the people of Corwyn are concerned, their duke and his loyal cousin-confessor have gone into seclusion in the depths of the palace, so that said duke can examine his conscience and repent."

"You, repent?" Duncan snorted as his cousin swung into the saddle.

"Are you implying, dear cousin, that I lack the proper piety?" Morgan asked with a grin, collecting the pack pony's lead and moving his horse alongside Duncan's.

"Not I," Duncan shook his head. "Now, are we or are we not going to quit this dismal place?"

"We are," Morgan replied emphatically. "Come. I want us to be at old Saint Neot's by sundown, and that's a full day's ride in good weather.

"Wonderful," Duncan murmured under his breath,

as they moved out at a trot along the deserted streets of Coroth. "I've been looking forward to this all my life."

Later in the morning and many miles from there, Rimmell climbed a rocky hillside west of Culdi with more than a little trepidation. It was chill and windy in the high country today, with a nip of frost in the air even as the sun neared its zenith. But Rimmell was sweating in his sleek riding leathers in spite of the cold; and the canvas satchel slung over his shoulder seemed to grow heavier with every step. A horse whinnied in the hollow far below, forlorn at being left alone on the wind-swept valley floor, but Rimmell forced himself to continue climbing.

Rimmell's nerve was beginning to desert him. Reason, which had been his refuge through the long and sleepless night, told him he was foolish to be afraid, that he need not tremble before the woman called Bethane, that she was not like that other woman whose magic had touched him years before. But, still . . .

Rimmell shuddered as he remembered that night, at least twenty years ago now, when he and another boy had sneaked into old Dame Elfrida's yard to steal cabbages and apples. They had known, both of them, that Elfrida was rumored to be a witch-woman, that she despised strangers prowling about on her tiny plot of land—they had felt the swat of her broom often enough in the daytime. But they had been so certain they could outwit the old woman at night, so sure they would not be caught.

But then, there had been old Dame Elfrida, looming up in the darkness with an aura of violet light surrounding her like a halo, a blinding flash of light and heat from which Rimmell and his mate ran as fast as their legs could carry them.

They had escaped; and the old woman had not followed. But next morning when Rimmell awoke, his hair had been white; and no amount of washing or scrubbing or poulticing or dyeing could change it back to its original color. His mother had been terrified, had suspected that the old witch-woman had something to do with the affair. But Rimmell had always denied he was even out of the house that night, had always contended that he had simply gone to sleep and awakened that way—nothing more. And shortly, old Dame Elfrida had been run out of the village, never to return.

Rimmell shivered in the chill morning air, unable to shake the queasy feeling in his stomach that the memory always evoked. Bethane was a witch-woman of sorts—she had to be, to work the favors with which she was credited. Suppose she laughed at Rimmell's request? Or refused to help? Or demanded a price that Rimmell could not pay?

Or worse, suppose Bethane was evil? Suppose she tried to trick him? Gave him the wrong charm? Or decided, years from now, that payment had not been sufficient? Wreaked grievous harm on Rimmell, on Lord Kevin—even on Bronwyn herself?!

Rimmell shuddered and forced himself to abandon this line of thought. Such hysterics were irrational, with no basis in fact. Rimmell had thoroughly investigated Bethane's reputation the day before, talked with those who had used her services. There was no reason to believe she was anything but what people said she was—a harmless old shepherdess who had often succeeded in helping people in need. Besides, she was Rimmell's only hope for winning the woman he loved.

Shading his eyes against the sun, Rimmell paused to gaze up the trail. Beyond a scrubby stand of pines a few yards ahead, he could see a high, narrow opening in the barren rock, with a curtain of animal skins hanging just inside. A number of scrawny-looking sheep—mostly lambs and ewes—pulled at tufts of frost-burned grass among the rocky outcroppings to either side of the cave, and a shepherd's crook leaned against the rocks to the left. There was no sign of the owner of the crook.

Rimmell took a deep breath and steeled his courage, then scrambled the few remaining yards to the level space just before the cave entrance.

"Is anyone there?" he called, his voice quavering slightly in his uneasiness. "I—I seek Dame Bethane, the shepherdess. I mean her no harm."

There was a long silence in which Rimmell could hear only the faint spring-sounds of insects and birds, the sheep tugging at the tough grass all around him, his own harsh breathing. And then a voice rumbled, "Enter."

Rimmell started at the sound. Controlling his surprise, and swallowing hard, he stepped to the cave entrance and carefully pulled the curtain aside, noting that it looked—and smelled—like untanned goatskin. He glanced nervously around him a final time as the insane idea rippled through his mind that he might never see the sun again, then peered into the interior. It was pitch dark.

"Enter!" the voice commanded again as Rimmell hesitated.

Rimmell edged his way inside, still holding back the curtain to let light and air enter, and glanced around furtively for the source of the voice. It seemed to come from all around him, reverberating back and forth in the confines of the filthy cave; but of course he could see nothing in the darkness.

"Release the curtain and stand where you are."

The voice startled Rimmell even though he was expecting it, and he jumped and released the curtain in consternation. The voice had been in the darkness to his left that time—he was certain of it. But he dared not move a muscle in that direction for fear of disobeying the disembodied voice. He swallowed with difficulty, forced himself to stand straight and drop his hands to his sides. His knees were shaking and his palms felt damp, but he knew he dared not move.

"Who are you?" the voice demanded. This time the words seemed to come from behind him, a low and rasping tone, indeterminate of sex. Rimmell wet his lips nervously.

"My name is Rimmell. I am chief architect to His Grace the duke of Cassan."

"In whose name do you come, Rimmell the Architect? Your own or your duke's?"

"My—my own."

"And what is it you desire of Bethane?" the voice demanded. "Do not move until you are told to do so."

Rimmell had been about to turn, but now he froze again and tried to force himself to relax. Apparently the body connected to the voice could see in the dark. Rimmell certainly couldn't.

"Are you Dame Bethane?" he asked timidly.

"I am."

"I—" he swallowed. "I have brought you food, Dame Bethane," he said. "I—"

"Drop the food beside you."

Rimmell obeyed.

"Now, what is it you wish of Bethane?"

Rimmell swallowed again. He could feel sweat pouring from his brow and running into his eyes, but he dared not raise his hand to wipe it away. He blinked hard and forced himself to continue.

"There—there is a woman, Dame Bethane. She—I—"

"Go on."

Rimmell took a deep breath. "I desire this woman for my wife, Dame Bethane. But she—she is promised to another. She—will marry him unless you can help. You can help, can't you?"

He was aware of light growing behind him, and then he could see his own shadow dancing on the rock wall before him. The light was orange, fire-born, dispelling some of the gloom and fear of the narrow cavern.

"You may turn and approach."

With a scarce-breathed sigh of relief, Rimmell turned slowly toward the source of light. A lantern was resting on the stony floor perhaps a dozen paces away, an ancient crone in tattered rags sitting cross-legged behind it. Her face was seamed and weathered, surrounded by a mane of matted grey hair, once dark, and she was meticulously folding a dark cloth with which she had presumably muffled the lantern light. Rimmell wiped his sleeve across his eyes and crossed hesitantly toward the lantern, stood looking down apprehensively at the woman called Bethane.

"So, Master Rimmell," the woman said, her black eyes flashing and glowing in the flickering lantern-light. "Do you find my appearance offensive?"

Her teeth were yellowed and rotted, her breath foul; and Rimmell had to control the impulse to back away in disgust. Bethane chuckled—a reedy, wheezing sound—and gestured toward the floor with a sweep of a scrawny arm. Gold winked on her hand as she gestured, and Rimmell realized it must be a wedding ring. Yes, the townspeople had said she was a widow. He wondered who her husband had been.

Rimmell lowered himself gingerly to the rough stone floor of the cave and sat cross-legged in imitation of his hostess. When he had settled, Bethane gazed across at him for several moments without speaking, her eyes bright, compelling. Then she nodded.

"This woman—tell me about her. Is she beautiful?"

"She—," Rimmell croaked, his throat going dry. "This is her likeness," he said, withdrawing Bronwyn's locket and holding it out timidly.

Bethane extended a gnarled hand and took the locket,

opening it with a deft flick of one twisted and yellowed fingernail. One eyebrow rose almost imperceptibly as she saw the portrait, and she glanced back at Rimmell shrewdly.

"This is the woman?"

Rimmell nodded fearfully.

"And the locket is hers?"

"It was," Rimmell replied. "He who would wed her wore it last."

"And what of him who would wed her?" Bethane persisted. "Does he love her?"

Rimmell nodded.

"And she him?"

Rimmell nodded again.

"But, you love her too—so much that you would risk your life to have her."

Rimmell nodded a third time, his eyes wide.

Bethane smiled, a ragged parody of mirth. "I had such a man once, who risked his life to have me. Does that surprise you? No matter. He would approve, I think."

She closed the locket again with a click, held it by the chain in a gnarled left hand, reached behind and brought out a yellow gourd with a slender neck. Rimmell caught his breath and watched wide-eyed as Bethane removed the stopper with a flick of her thumb and moved the gourd toward him. The faint foreboding which had plagued him all morning again rippled across the surface of his mind, but he forced himself to disregard it.

"Hold out thy hands, Rimmell the architect, that the water may not spill to the thirsty rock and be forever lost."

Rimmell obeyed as Bethane poured water from the gourd into his cupped hands.

"Now," Bethane continued, setting the gourd aside, "watch as I trace the sacred signs above the water. Watch as the eddies of time and holy love breathe upon the waters and mark their passage. Watch as this which was hers now generates that which will be her downfall and make her that which is thine."

As she spun and swung the locket above Rimmell's cupped hands, tracing intricate patterns and symbols with its path above the water, she muttered an incantation that rose and fell, watched her subject's eyes as they trembled, heavy-lidded, and finally closed. Palming the locket, she dried away the water from Rimmell's hands with the dark cloth, that no moisture might escape while she worked and thus reveal the passage of time. Then she sighed and opened the locket again, searching her mind for the proper charm.

A love charm. And not just a love charm—a charm to transfer a woman's love from one man to another. Yes, she had worked a charm like that before—many times.

But that had been long ago, when Bethane was not so old, or toothless, or forgetful. She wasn't sure she could remember just how it went.

'Even havens rustle low?'

No, that was a charm for a good harvest. True, it might be applied to the lady at a later date, perhaps even to produce a son, if that was what Rimmell wanted. But it was not the charm that Bethane wanted now.

There was the call to Baazam—that was very powerful. But, no, she shook her head disapprovingly. That was a dark charm, a killing charm. Darrell had made her give up those things long ago. Besides, she would never wish that on the beautiful young woman of the locket. She herself might have looked much like that lady once. Darrell had told her she was beautiful, at any rate.

She squinted down at the portrait again as a ghost of remembrance flitted across her mind.

The woman in the locket—had she not seen her once before? It had been years ago, when her sight was better and she was not so old and crippled, but— yes! She remembered now.

There was a beautiful blond child, with three older boys who must have been her brothers or cousins. There had been a ride on mountain ponies, a leisurely meal on the green grass carpet which covered Bethane's hillside in the summer months. And the children were noble children, sons of the mighty duke of Cassan—that same duke whose servant now sat entranced on Bethane's floor!

Bronwyn! Now she remembered. The child's name had been Bronwyn. The Lady Bronwyn de Morgan, Duke Jared's niece, and half-Deryni. And she was the lady of the portrait!

Bethane cringed and looked around guiltily. A Deryni lady. And now she, Bethane, had promised to work a charm against her. Did she dare? Would her charm even work against a half-Deryni lady? Bethane would not want to hurt her. The child Bronwyn had smiled at her in the meadow many years ago, like the daughter Bethane had never had. She had petted the lambs and ewes and talked to Bethane, had not been afraid of the wizened old widow who watched her flocks on the hillside. No, Bethane could not forget that.

Bethane screwed up her face and wrung her hands. She had promised Rimmell, too. She did not like being put in a position like this. If she helped the architect, she might harm the girl; and she did not want to do that.

She glanced at Rimmell, and practicality crept back into her thoughts. The pouch at the builder's waist was heavy with gold, and the sack he had dropped on the floor by the entrance was filled with bread and cheese and other good things she had not tasted in months. Bethane could smell the fresh, savory aroma permeating the cavern while she debated with herself.

If she did not keep her promise, Rimmell would take the food, the gold, and go.

Very well. It would only be a little charm. Perhaps even a charm of indecision would do. Yes, that was the solution. A charm of indecision, so that the lovely Bronwyn would not be in such a hurry to marry her intended.

And who *was* her intended, Bethane wondered. A Deryni woman could not expect to marry high. Such was not the lot of that long-persecuted race in these troubled times. For that matter, so long as there was no high-born lord to risk offending, why couldn't Bethane work a more powerful charm, give Rimmell the results he desired?

With a decisive nod, Bethane climbed painfully to her feet and began rummaging through a battered trunk against the rear wall of the cave. There were dozens of items in the trunk that Bethane might use in her task, and she hunted agitatedly through an assortment of baubles, strangely-worked stones, feathers, powders, potions, and other tools of her trade.

She pulled out a small, polished bone and cocked her grey head at it thoughtfully, then shook her head and discarded it. The same process was repeated for a dried leaf, a small carved figure of a lamb, a handful of herbs bound with a twist of plaited grass, and a small earthen pot.

Finally she reached the bottom of the chest and found what she was looking for: a large leather sack filled with stones. She dragged the sack to the side of the chest, grunted as she hoisted it out and let it half-fall to the floor, then untied the thongs binding the bag and began sorting through the contents.

Charms for love and charms for hate. Charms for death and charms for life. Charms to make the crops grow tall. Charms to bring pestilence to an enemy's fields. Simple charms to guard the health. Complex charms to guard the soul. Charms for the rich.

Charms for the poor. Charms yet unborn, but waiting for the touch of the woman.

Humming a broken tune under her breath, Bethane selected a large blue stone embedded with blood-colored flecks, of a size to fit just comfortably in a man's hand. She rummaged in the chest until she found a small goatskin bag that would hold the stone, then replaced the large sack in the trunk and closed it. Then, taking stone and bag back to the lantern, she sat down in front of Rimmell once more and tucked stone and bag beneath the folds of her tattered robe.

Rimmell sat entranced in front of the guttering lantern, his cupped hands held empty before him, eyes closed and relaxed. Bethane took the yellow gourd, poured water into Rimmell's hands, and once again held the locket swinging above the water. As she resumed her chant, she reached gently to Rimmell's forehead and touched his brow. The architect nodded as though catching himself falling asleep, then began watching the locket once more, unaware that anything out of the ordinary had happened, that minutes had passed of which he had no knowledge.

Bethane finished the chant and palmed the locket, then reached beside her and produced the blood-flecked stone. She pressed the stone between her hands for a moment, her eyes hooded as she murmured something Rimmell could not catch. Then she placed the stone on the floor beneath Rimmell's hands, rested her taloned fingers on Rimmell's and looked him in the eyes.

"Open thy hands to let the water wash the stone," she said, her voice rasping in Rimmell's ears. "With that, the charm is accomplished and the stage is set."

Rimmell swallowed and blinked rapidly several times, then obeyed. The water washed over the stone and was absorbed by it, and Rimmell dried his hands against his thighs in amazement.

"Then, it is done?" he whispered incredulously. "My lady loves me?"

"Not yet, she does not," Bethane replied, scooping up the stone and placing it in the goatskin bag. "But she will." She dropped the bag into Rimmell's hands and sat back.

"Take you this pouch. Inside is that which you have seen, which you are not to remove until you may safely leave it where the lady is sure to come alone. Then you must open the pouch and remove what is inside without touching it. Once the crystal is exposed to light, from this moment on, you will have only seconds in which to remove yourself from its influence. Then the charm is primed, and wants only the lady's presence to be complete."

"And she will be mine?"

Bethane nodded. "The charm will bind her. Go now." She picked up the locket and dropped it into Rimmell's hand, and Rimmell tucked it and the pouch into his tunic.

"I thank you most humbly, Dame Bethane," he muttered, swallowing and fingering the pouch at his waist. "How—how may I repay you? I have brought food, as is the custom, but—"

"You have gold at your belt?"

"Aye," Rimmell whispered, fumbling with the pouch and withdrawing a small, heavy bag. "I have not much, but—" He put the bag down gingerly on the floor beside the lantern and looked at Bethane fearfully.

Bethane glanced at the bag, then returned her gaze to Rimmell.

"Empty the bag."

With a gulp that was audible in the still cavern, Rimmell opened the bag and spilled the contents on the floor before him. The coins rang with the chime of fine gold, but Bethane's gaze did not waver from the architect's face.

"Now, what think you the worth of my services, Master Rimmell?" she asked, watching his face for telltale signs of emotion.

Rimmell wet his lips, and his eyes flickered to the pile of gold, which was fairly substantial. Then, with an abrupt motion he swept the entire amount closer to Bethane. The woman smiled her haggled smile and nodded, then reached down and withdrew but six coins. The rest she pushed back to Rimmell. The architect was astonished.

"I—I don't understand," he quavered. "Will you not take more?"

"I have taken ample for my needs," Bethane croaked. "I but wished to test that you do, indeed, value my services. As for the rest, perhaps you will remember the widow Bethane in your prayers. In these twilight years, I fear I may need supplications to the Almighty far more than gold."

"I—I shall do that, Dame Bethane," Rimmell stammered, scooping up his gold and returning it to his pouch. "But, is there nothing else I may do for you?"

Bethane shook her head. "Bring your children to visit me, Architect Rimmell. Now leave me. You have what you asked, and so have I."

"Thank you, Dame Bethane," Rimmell murmured, scrambling to his feet and marveling at his luck. "And I shall pray for you," his voice floated back through the cave entrance as he slipped through the goatskin curtain.

As the architect disappeared into the outer world, Bethane sighed and slumped before the lantern.

"Well, my Darrell," she whispered, rubbing the gold band on her hand against her lips, "it is done. I have set the charm to give the young man his wish. You don't think I did wrong working against a Deryni, do you?"

She paused, as though listening for a reply, then nodded.

"I know, my darling. I have never used a charm against one of the occult race before. But it should work. I think I remembered all the proper words.

"It doesn't matter anyway—as long as we're together."

It was nearly dark when Morgan finally signaled for a stop. He and Duncan had been riding steadily since leaving Coroth early that morning, stopping at noon only long enough to water the horses and gulp down a few handfuls of travel rations.

Now they were approaching the crest of the Lendour mountain range, beyond which lay the fabled Gunury Pass. At the end of that pass lay the shrine of Saint Torin's, southern gateway to the free holy city of Dhassa. In the morning, when men and horses were rested, both men would pay their respects at Saint Torin's shrine—a necessary procedure before being permitted to cross the wide lake to Dhassa. And then they would enter the free city of Dhassa, where no crowned head dared go without approval of the city burghers, but where Morgan would enter anyway, in disguise. And they would confront the Gwynedd Curia.

Ruins were vaguely visible through the gloom of drizzle and lowering dusk, and Morgan reined his horse to a walk, shielded his eyes against the mist with a gloved hand. His grey eyes flicked from tower to steps to top of ruined wall, searching for signs of other occupancy; but there were no signs of recent habitation. They could safely stay the night.

Morgan slipped his feet from the stirrups and stretched his legs, sat back in the saddle and let his feet dangle as his mount picked its way across the rough terrain leading to the gateway. Behind him, Duncan steadied his own mount as the animal slipped on a patch of mud and recovered. The pack pony, following Duncan now, peered suspiciously at each new shadow-shape in the darkness ahead, shying and jerking at its lead with every sound or hint of movement on the wind-swept plateau. Men and beasts were travel-weary and chilled to the bone.

"Well, this is about as far as we go for tonight," Morgan said as they neared the ruined gate. The hollow squish-plop of the horses' feet in the mud changed to a simple splash as they reached the cobbled path entering the ancient courtyard. An eerie silence permeated the place despite the steady rain, and Duncan almost whispered in spite of himself as he moved his horse closer to Morgan's.

"What is this place, Alaric?"

Morgan guided his mount through a ruined doorway and ducked as he passed beneath a partially fallen beam.

"Saint Neot's. It was a flourishing monastery school before the Restoration, run by an all-Deryni brotherhood. The chapel was desecrated during the sacking, and several of the brothers were slain right on the altar steps. Local folk, such as there are, avoid it like the plague. Brion and I used to ride out here."

Morgan moved his mount into a dry, partially roofed corner and began pushing at random beams above his head, testing their stability, as he continued. "From what I've been able to learn, Saint Neot's ranked with the great university at Concaradine, or the Varnarite School at Grecotha when it was in its prime. Of course, being Deryni was respectable in those days."

He pushed at a final beam and grunted in satisfaction as it held. Then he sat back in the saddle and dusted his gloved hands together in a gesture of finality.

"Well, I guess this will do for a dry place to sleep. At least the roof won't collapse on us."

As he dismounted, he glanced around easily, obviously familiar with the ruin. In a few minutes he and

Duncan had unsaddled the horses and heaped their gear against a dry wall. And by the time Morgan returned from tethering the animals in a stabling area farther back in the ruins, Duncan had started the evening meal over a carefully tended fire in the corner. Morgan sniffed appreciatively as he stripped off his dripping cloak and gloves and rubbed his hands briskly over the fire.

"Hmmm, I was beginning to think I'd never be warm again. You've outdone yourself, Duncan."

Duncan gave the pot a stir, then began digging through one of the sets of saddlebags. "You don't know how close we came to not having a fire, my friend. Between the wet wood, and having to choose a place where no one could see the fire from outside— what was this room?"

"The refectory, I think." Morgan pulled several handfuls of branches out of dry crevasses and piled them near the fire. "Over to the right there were kitchens, stable facilities, and the brothers' sleeping quarters. It's in a worse state than I remembered. They must have had some hard winters up here since I was here last." He rubbed his hands together again and blew on them. "Any chance of building up the fire a little more?"

Duncan chuckled as he uncorked a wine flask. "Not unless you want everyone in Dhassa to know we're coming. I'm telling you, I had a Devil of a time finding a place for even a piddling fire like this one. Count your blessings."

Morgan laughed. "I appreciate your logic. I have no more wish to have my neck stretched or my throat slit than the next man." He watched as Duncan poured wine into two small copper cups, then dropped a small, glowing stone into each. The stones steamed and hissed as they hit the cold wine, and Morgan added, "As I recall, the Dhassans have some rather novel ways of dealing with spies, especially Deryni ones."

"Spare me the details!" Duncan retorted. He plucked the stones from the cups and handed one across to his cousin. "Here, drink up. This is the last of the Fianna wine."

Morgan flopped down beside the fire with a sigh and sipped the wine, hot and potent and warming all the way down.

"Too bad they don't drink this in Dhassa. There's nothing like Fianna wine when you're cold and tired. I gag to even contemplate the brew we'll be forced to imbibe for the next few days."

"You're assuming, of course, that we'll live that long," Duncan grinned. "And that the holy Dhassans won't recognize you before we can reach our esteemed archbishops." He leaned back against the wall to savor his drink. "Did you know that it's rumored Dhassans use *ale* in their sacrament, because the wine is so bad?"

"A poor joke, surely?"

"No, I have it on excellent authority. They use sacramental ale." He leaned forward to poke at the stew. "Are you ready to eat?"

A quarter hour later the two had found the driest spots for their bedrolls and were preparing to sleep. Duncan was trying to read his breviary by the dying firelight, and Morgan removed his sword and sat on his haunches staring out into the darkness. The wind whined through the ruins and mingled with the slackening sounds of rainfall. And close by in the darkness, Morgan could hear the scrape of iron-shod hooves against the cobbles in the stable area. From somewhere far in the distance, a night bird twittered once and then was silent. Morgan stared into the dying embers for a few more minutes, then stood abruptly and pulled his cloak around himself.

"I think I'll take a short walk," he murmured, fastening his cloak and moving away from the fire.

"Is anything wrong?"

Morgan glanced down awkwardly at his booted feet and shook his head. "Brion and I used to ride in these mountains years ago. That's all. I was suddenly reminded of that."

"I think I understand."

Pulling his hood close around his head, Morgan moved slowly out of the circle of firelight and into the damp darkness beyond. He thought vaguely about Brion, not yet willing to unleash the memories associated with this place, found himself at length standing beneath the open, burned-out ceiling of the old chapel. He glanced around almost surprised, for he had not intended to come here.

It had been a large chapel once. Though the right-hand wall and most of the chancel back had long since crumbled, either from the original fire or from the weight of years, and though the last shards of glass had fallen long ago from the high clerestories, there was still an odor of sanctity about this place. Even the sacrilegious murder of Deryni brothers in this very chamber had not entirely destroyed the pervading calm that Morgan always associated with consecrated ground.

He looked toward the ruined altar area, almost fancying he could discern darker stains on the steps before it, then shook his head at his own imagination. The Deryni monks who had died here were two hundred years dead, their blood long since washed away by the torrential rains which swept the mountains every spring and autumn. If the monks had ever haunted Saint Neot's, as the peasants' legends suggested, they had long ago found peace.

He turned and wandered through a doorway still standing at the rear of the ruined nave, then smiled as he saw that the stairway to the bell tower, though crumbling at the edges, was still passable. He eased his way up that stairway, staying close to the outer wall and picking his footing carefully, for it was dark and the treads were littered with debris. Then, when he reached the first landing, he inched along the outer wall to the window there, gathered his leather cloak more closely around him and sat down.

How long had it been since he'd last sat in this window, he wondered, as he looked around him in the darkness. Ten years? Twenty?

No, he reminded himself. It had been fourteen—and a few months.

He pulled his feet up and propped them against the opposite side of the window jamb, knees hugged against his chest—and remembered.

It was autumn—early November. Fall had come late that year, and he and Brion had ridden out of Coroth early that morning for one of their rare jaunts into the countryside before the bad weather set in. It was a clear, brisk day, just beginning to be tinged with the promise of winter to come, and Brion had been in his usual good humor. Thus, when he had suggested that Morgan show him through the old ruins, the young Deryni lord was quick to agree.

Morgan was no longer Brion's squire by then. He had proven himself at Brion's side the year before in the battle with the Marluk. Further, he was fifteen, a year past legal age by Gwynedd law, and Duke of Corwyn in his own right.

So now, riding at Brion's side on a spirited ebony warhorse, he wore the emerald gryphon of Corwyn on his black leather tabard instead of Brion's crimson livery. The horses blew and snorted contentedly as their riders drew rein at the entrance to the old chapel.

"Well, look at this," Brion exclaimed. He urged his white stallion into the doorway and shaded his eyes with a gloved hand to peer into the interior. "Alaric, the stairs to the bell tower seem to be sound. Let's have a look."

He backed his mount a few paces and jumped from the saddle, dropped the red leather reins so the animal could graze while they explored. Morgan dismounted and followed Brion into the ruined chapel.

"This must have been quite a place in its time," Brion said, climbing over a fallen beam and picking his way across the rubble. "How many were here, do you think?"

"In the whole monastery? About two or three hundred, I should think, Sire. That's counting brothers, servants, and students all together, of course. As I recall, there were well over a hundred in the Order."

Brion scrambled up the first few steps of the stairway, his boots sending shards of stone and mortar flying as he found each precarious foothold. His bright riding leathers were a splash of crimson against the weathered grey of the tower, and his scarlet hunt cap sported a snowy feather which bobbed jauntily over his shoulder as he climbed. He grunted as his boot slipped and he nearly lost his footing, then recovered and continued.

"Mind where you step, m'lord," Morgan called, watching Brion anxiously as he followed. "Remember that these steps are more than four hundred years old. If they collapse, Gwynedd will be minus a king."

"Hah, you worry too much, Alaric!" Brion exclaimed. He reached the first landing and crossed to the window. "Look out there. You can see halfway back to Coroth."

As Morgan reached his side, Brion cleared the windowsill of rubble and shattered glass with a sweep of his gloved hand, then sat easily, one booted foot propped against the opposite side.

"Look at that!" he said, gesturing toward the mountains to the north with his riding crop. "Another month and that will be covered with snow. And it will be just as beautiful then, in its snow-covered way, as it is right now with just the first burn of frost on the meadows."

Morgan smiled and leaned against the window jamb. "There would be good hunting up there about now, Sire. Are you sure you don't want to stay in Coroth a while longer?"

"Ah, you know I can't, Alaric," Brion replied with a resigned shrug. "Duty calls with a loud and persistent voice. If I'm not back in Rhemuth within a week, my council lords will go into a twitter like a pack of nervous women. I don't think they really believe that the Marluk is dead, that we're no longer at war. And then there's Jehana."

Yes, and then there's Jehana, Morgan thought morosely.

For an instant he allowed himself to visualize the young, auburn-haired queen—then dismissed the image from his mind. All hope of any civil relationship between himself and Jehana had ended the day she learned he was Deryni. She would never forgive him that, and it was the one thing he could not change, even had he wished to. It was pointless to belabor the issue. It would only remind Brion again of the disappointment over which he had no control, remind him that there could never be anything but loathing between his queen and his closest friend.

Morgan leaned out over Brion's outstretched foot to look over the windowsill.

"Look, Sire," he said, changing the subject. "Al-Derah's found some grass that didn't get burned by the frost."

Brion looked. Below, Morgan's black destrier was busily pulling at a patch of verdant grass some twenty feet from the base of the tower. Brion's stallion had strayed a few yards to the right and was contenting himself with nosing half-heartedly in a patch of brownish clover grass, one big hoof planted firmly on his red leather reins.

Brion snorted and leaned back in the window, folded his arms across his chest. "Humph. That Kedrach is so dumb, I sometimes wonder how he finds his own nose. You'd think the stupid beast would have enough sense to pick up his big feet and move. He thinks he's tied."

"I urged you not to buy horses from Llannedd, Sire," Morgan chuckled, "but you wouldn't listen. The Llanneddites breed for looks and speed, but they don't care much about brains. Now, the horses of R'Kassi—"

"Quiet!" Brion ordered, feigning indignation. "You're making me feel inferior. And a king must never feel inferior."

As Morgan tried to restrain a chuckle, he glanced out across the plain again. Half a dozen horsemen could be seen approaching now, and he touched Brion's elbow lightly as he came to full alertness.

"Brion?"

As the two watched, they were able to identify Brion's crimson lion banner in the hands of the lead rider. And beside him rode a stocky figure in brilliant orange which could only be Lord Ewan, the powerful duke of Claibourne. Ewan must have seen the flash of Brion's crimson leathers in the window at about the same time, for he abruptly stood in his stirrups and began a raucous highland war whoop as he and his band thundered toward the tower.

"What the Devil—?" Brion murmured, standing to peer down as Ewan and his companions drew rein in a cloud of dust.

"Sire!" Ewan yelled, his eyes sparkling with merriment and his red beard and hair blowing in the wind as he grabbed Brion's banner and brandished it aloft in triumph. "Sire, you have a son! An heir for the throne of Gwynedd!"

"A son!" Brion gasped, his jaw dropping in awe. "My God, it was supposed to be another month!" His eyes lit in elation. "A son! Alaric, do you hear?" he shouted, grabbing Morgan's arms and dancing him around in a half circle. "I'm a father! I have a son!"

Releasing Morgan, he looked jubilantly out of the window at his cheering escort and shouted again: "I have a son!" Then he scrambled back down the stairs, Morgan close at his heels, his voice echoing through the ruins in a paean of joy: "A son! A son! Alaric, do you hear? I have a son!"

Morgan sighed deeply and rubbed his hands across his face, refusing to let the sorrow overwhelm him, then leaned his head back against the window jamb once more. All that had been many years ago. The boy-man Alaric was now lord general of the Royal Armies, a powerful feudal magnate in his own right—if somewhat beset at the moment. Brion slept in the tomb of his ancestors beneath Rhemuth Cathedral, victim of a magical assassination which even Morgan had not been able to prevent.

And Brion's son—"*A son! A son! Alaric, do you hear? I have a son!*"—Brion's son was fourteen now, a man, and king of Gwynedd.

Morgan looked out across the plain the way he and Brion had done so many years before, fancying he could see the riders again, coming across the plain, then gazed up into the misty night sky. A gibbous moon was rising in the east, paling the few stars bright enough to penetrate the overcast. And Morgan gazed up at those stars for a long moment, savoring the serenity of the night, before turning his feet back to the floor to return to camp.

It grew late. Duncan would be worrying for his safety soon. And tomorrow, with its subterfuge and obdurate archbishops, would come all too early.

He picked his way back down the staircase, his

footing easier now that the moon was beginning to light the ruins, and headed back through the standing doorway to cut through the nave. He was perhaps halfway through that chamber when his eye caught a faint flicker of light in the far recesses of the nave— there, to the left of the ruined altar.

He froze and turned his head toward the light, frowned as it did not disappear.

CHAPTER ELEVEN

*I have raised up one from the north, and he is come
. . . and he shall come upon rulers as upon mortar,
and as the potter treadeth clay.*

Isaiah 41:25

MORGAN STOOD absolutely still for perhaps ten heartbeats, Deryni defenses raising automatically as he cast
about for danger. The moonlight was still very dim,
and the shadows were long, but there was definitely
something brilliant in the darkness to the left. He
considered calling out, for it could be Duncan. But,
no. His heightened senses would have identified
Duncan by now. If there was someone lurking in the
shadows, he was not known to Morgan.

Cautiously, and wishing he had thought to bring his
sword, Morgan eased his way left across the nave to
investigate, fingertips trailing the outer wall as he
glided down the clerestory aisle. The flicker had disappeared when he moved, and he could see now that
there was nothing extraordinary about that particular
corner of the ruins. But Morgan's curiosity had been
touched.

What could have shone that brightly after all these
years? Glass? A chance reflection of moonlight on
standing water? Or something more sinister?

There was a faint scuttling sound from the direction

of the ruined altar and Morgan whirled and froze,
stiletto flicking into his hand in readiness. That had
not been imagination, or moonlight on standing water.
There was something there!

Sight and hearing at full extension, Morgan waited,
half expecting the spectral form of some long-dead
monkish spirit to rise out of the ruined altar. He had
almost decided that his nerves were, indeed, playing
tricks on him when a large grey rat suddenly broke
from cover in the ruins and headed directly for him.

Morgan hissed in surprise and leaped out of the
animal's path, then exhaled with a sigh and chuckled
under his breath as the rat fled. He glanced back at
the ruined altar, chiding himself for his foolishness,
then began moving confidently down the aisle again.

The corner which had originally attracted Morgan's
attention was still partially roofed, but the floor was
rough and littered with rubble. A narrow altar-shelf
had been set in the back wall and remained, though
the edge was battered and cracked as from heavy
blows. Once there had been a marble figure in the
niche in the wall behind.

Only the feet of the statue remained now—those
and the cracked slab and the shards of glass and
stone—mute relics of that terrible day and night when
rebels had sacked the monastery two centuries before. Morgan smiled as his gaze passed over the feet,
wondering who the ill-fated saint had been whose
sandaled feet still trod the broken dreams of this
place. Then his eyes dropped to a sliver of silvered
glass still affixed to the base below the feet, and he
knew he had found his elusive light.

There were shards of silver and ruby on the littered
slab below, fragments of a shattered mosaic which had
once covered the pedestal directly above the altar. The
looters had smashed that, just as they had shattered
the statues, the stained glass in the high windows, the

marble and tile floorings, the precious altar furnishings.

Morgan started to reach his stiletto to pry out the elusive piece of glass, but then stopped and replaced his weapon in its wrist sheath, shaking his head. That one shard of silver, still clinging in its original place, had defied rebels, time, and the elements. Could the unknown saint in whose honor the glass had been placed make the same claim of his human adherents?

Morgan thought not. Even the saint's identity was lost by now. Or was it?

Pursing his lips thoughtfully, Morgan ran his fingers along the battered altar edge, then bent to inspect it more closely. As he had suspected, there were letters inscribed in the stone, their intricate whorls almost obliterated by the fury of the looters centuries past. The first two words were readable if one used a little imagination—JUBILANTE DEO— standard phraseology for such an altar. But the next word was badly damaged, and the next. He was able to trace out the letters S—CTV-, probably *sanctus*, saint. But the final word, the saint's name—He could make out a damaged C, an A, a shattered S on the end. CA——S. CAMBERUS? Saint Camber?

Morgan whistled lightly under his breath in surprise as he straightened. Saint Camber again, the Deryni patron of magic. No wonder the looters had done such a thorough job here. He was amazed they had left as much as there was.

He backed a few steps and glanced around distractedly, wishing he had the time to stay and explore further. If this had, indeed, been a corner of the church dedicated to Saint Camber, the odds were very good that there had been a Transfer Portal not far away. Of course, even if it still functioned—and that was doubtful after so many years of disuse—he had no place to go with it anyway. The only other Portals he knew of were back in Rhemuth, in Duncan's study

and in the cathedral sacristy, and he certainly didn't
want to go there. Dhassa was their destination.

It was probably a ridiculous notion anyway. A
Portal would have been destroyed long ago, even if
he could find it. Nor could he spare the time to look.

Stifling a yawn, Morgan took one final look
around, waved a casual salute to the feet of Saint Camber, then began crossing slowly back to camp. Tomorrow there would be answers to many problems, when
they confronted the Gwynedd Curia. But for now, it
had begun to rain again. Perhaps that would help him
to sleep.

But for Paul de Gendas there would be no sleep
tonight.

In the woods not many miles from where Morgan
and Duncan slept, Paul peered into the driving rain
and slowed his mount to a walk as he approached the
hidden mountain camp of Warin de Grey. His lath-
ered horse blew noisily, sending twin plumes of
steam into the cold night air. Paul, himself mud-
bespattered and soaked to the skin, swept off his
peaked hat and sat taller in the saddle as he came
adjacent to the first guard-outposts.

The move was worth the extra effort. For the sen-
tries with their hooded lanterns would no sooner ma-
terialize out of the darkness to challenge than they
would recognize the rider and melt back into the
shadows. Guttering torches ahead showed the dim
outlines of tents in the rain. And as Paul approached
the first tent at the perimeter of the camp, a young lad
wearing the same falcon badge Paul wore came running to take his horse, rubbing sleep from his eyes and
looking at the rider in puzzlement.

Paul nodded greeting as he slid shivering from his
horse, and he scanned the area of torchlight impatiently as he pulled his drenched and muddy cloak
around him.

"Is Warin still about?" Paul asked, slicking wet hair out of his face before replacing his hat.

An older man in high boots and hooded cloak had approached as Paul asked the question, and he nodded gravely to Paul and signaled the boy to be off with the weary horse.

"Warin is conferring, Paul. He asked not to be disturbed."

"Conferring?" Paul stripped off his soggy gloves and began moving along the muddy path toward the center of camp. "With whom? Whoever it is, I think Warin will want to hear what I've found out."

"Even at the risk of offending Archbishop Loris?" the older man asked, raising an eyebrow and smiling with satisfaction as Paul turned to gape. "I think the good archbishop is going to support our cause, Paul."

"Loris, here?"

Paul laughed unbelievingly, a grin splitting his rugged face from ear to ear, then pummeled his companion enthusiastically on the back.

"My friend, you have no idea of the uncanny good fortune of this night. Now I know Warin will welcome the news I bring!"

"You understand my position, then," Loris was saying. "Since Morgan has refused to step down and recant his heresies, I am forced to consider Interdict."

"The action you propose is perfectly clear," Warin said coldly. "You will cut off Corwyn from all solace of religion, doom untold souls to suffering and possible eternal damnation without benefit of sacraments." He glanced at his folded hands. "We are agreed that Morgan must be stopped, Archbishop, but I cannot condone your methods."

Warin was seated on a small portable camp stool, a fur-lined amber robe pulled loosely around him against the chill. In front of him, a well-tended fire blazed brightly in the center of the tent, the only portion of the floor not covered by tan ground cloths or rugs. Loris, his burgundy travel garb stained and damp from his ride, sat in a leather folding chair to Warin's right—the chair usually reserved for the rebel leader himself. Behind Loris stood Monsignor Gorony in stark black clerical attire, hands hidden in the folds of his sleeves. He had only just returned from his mission to Corwyn's bishop, and his face was inscrutable as he listened to the exchange.

Warin intertwined long fingers and rested his forearms lightly against his knees, then stared dourly at the rug beneath his slippered feet.

"Is there nothing I can say to dissuade you from this action, Your Excellency?"

Loris made a helpless gesture and shook his head solemnly. "I have tried everything I know, but his bishop, Tolliver, has not been cooperative. If he had excommunicated Morgan as I asked him to, the present situation might have been avoided. Now I must convene the Curia and—"

He broke off as the tent flap was pulled aside to admit a travel-stained man wearing the falcon badge on his muddy cloak. The man swept off his dripping hat and saluted with right fist to chest, then nodded apologetically in the direction of Loris and Gorony. Warin looked up distractedly and frowned as he recognized the newcomer, but he got up immediately and crossed to the entryway where the man was waiting.

"What is it, Paul?" Warin asked, running a hand through his already disheveled hair and guiding Paul closer to the tent flap. "I told Michael I didn't want to be disturbed while the archbishop was here."

"I don't think you'll mind this particular interruption when you hear the news, Lord," Paul said, controlling a smile and instinctively keeping his voice low so that Loris could not hear. "I saw Morgan on the road to Saint Torin's just before dark. He and one companion made camp in the ruins of old Saint Neot's monastery."

Warin grabbed Paul's shoulders and stared at him in amazement. "Are you certain, man?" He was obviously excited, and his eyes gleamed as he searched Paul's. "O my God, right into our hands!" he murmured almost to himself.

"It's my guess he's on his way to Dhassa, Lord," Paul grinned. "Perhaps a suitable reception could be arranged."

Warin's eyes glittered as he whirled to face Loris. "Did you hear that, Excellency? Morgan has been seen at Saint Neot's, on his way to Dhassa!"

"What!" Loris stood abruptly, his face livid with rage. "Morgan on his way to Dhassa? We must stop him!"

Warin did not seem to hear, had begun pacing the carpeting agitatedly, his black eyes gleaming in concentration.

"Do you hear me, Warin?" Loris repeated, staring at Warin strangely as the rebel leader paced the tent. "This is some Deryni trick he has devised to deceive us. He means to disrupt the Curia tomorrow. With his Deryni cunning, he may even be able to convince some of my bishops of his innocence. I know he does not mean to submit to my authority!"

Warin shook his head, a small smile playing on his lips, and continued to pace. "No, Excellency, I do not think he means to submit either. But neither is it my intention to allow him to disrupt your Curia. Perhaps it is time we met face to face, Morgan and I. Perhaps it is time to discover whose power is stronger—his accursed sorceries, or the might of the Lord. Paul," he turned back to the man in the entryway, "you are to hand pick a group of about fifteen men to ride to St. Torin's with me before dawn."

"Yes, Lord." Paul bowed.

"And once His Excellency leaves, I shall not wish

to be disturbed again unless it is absolutely vital. Is that understood?"

Paul bowed again and slipped out of the tent to do Warin's bidding, but Loris' expression was perplexed as Warin turned to face him again.

"I'm not certain I understand," Loris said, taking his seat and preparing to wait until he received some explanation. "Surely you don't intend to attack Morgan?"

"I have been awaiting such an opportunity to confront the Deryni for many months, Your Excellency," Warin said, staring down at Loris through hooded eyes. "At Saint Torin's, through which he must pass if he is to reach Dhassa, there is a way I might be able to surprise him, even take him captive. At worst, I think he will be dissuaded from interfering with your Curia. At best—well, perhaps you will not have to worry about this particular Deryni again."

Loris scowled darkly, then began pleating folds of his robe between nervous fingers. "You would kill Morgan without chance to repent his sins?"

"I doubt there is hope in the Hereafter for the likes of him, Excellency," Warin said sharply. "The Deryni were spawn of Satan from the Creation. I do not think salvation is within their grasp."

"Perhaps not," said Loris, standing to confront the rebel leader with his hard blue eyes. "But I do not think it is our place to make that decision. Morgan must be given at least a chance to repent. I would not deny that right to the Devil himself, despite the many reasons I have to hate Morgan. Eternity is a very long time to doom a man."

"Are you defending him, Archbishop?" Warin asked carefully. "If I do not destroy him while I have the chance, it may be too late. Does one give the Devil a second chance? Does one deliberately expose oneself to his power if one has the chance not to? 'Avoid the occasion of sin,' I believe someone once said."

For the first time since they had entered, Gorony cleared his throat and caught Loris' eye.

"May I speak, Excellency?"

"What is it, Gorony?"

"If Your Excellency will permit, there is a way that Morgan could be made helpless so that one could ascertain the worth of his soul. He could be kept from the use of his powers while it was decided how best to deal with him."

Warin frowned and stared at Gorony suspiciously. "How is this to be?"

Gorony glanced at Loris and then continued. "There is a drug, *merasha* the Deryni call it, which is effective only against those of their race. It muddles their thoughts and renders them incapable of using their dark powers until the drug has worn off. If some of this *merasha* could be procured, might it not be used to immobilize Morgan?"

"A Deryni drug?" Loris's brows furrowed in concentration and he frowned. "I like not the sound of it, Gorony."

"Nor I!" Warin spat vehemently. "I will have no traffic with Deryni trickery to trap Morgan. To do so would make me no better than he!"

"If your lordship will permit," Gorony said patiently, "we are dealing with an unorthodox enemy. Sometimes one must use unorthodox methods to defeat such a one. It would, after all, be in a good cause."

"This is true, Warin," the archbishop agreed cautiously. "And it would materially reduce the risk to you. Gorony, how do you propose to administer this drug? Morgan surely will not stand by while you drug his drink, or use some other subterfuge."

Gorony smiled, and his benign and nondescript face suddenly took on faintly diabolical overtones. "Leave that to me, Excellency. Warin has spoken of the shrine of Saint Torin as an ambush spot. I concur. With Your Excellency's permission, I shall ride imme-

diately to procure the *merasha*, and then on to rendezvous with Warin and his men at the shrine at dawn.
There is a certain brother there who will aid us in
setting the trap. You, Excellency, should return to
Dhassa with all haste, so that you may prepare for the
meeting of the Curia tomorrow. If, by chance, we
should not succeed, you would then be obliged to
continue with the Interdict proceedings."

Loris considered the proposal, weighing all the
ramifications, then glanced sidelong at the rebel
leader.

"Well, Warin?" he asked, raising an inquiring eyebrow. "How say you? Gorony stays to aid you in
Morgan's capture, stands by to hear his confession,
should he decide to recant; and then he is yours, to do
with as you see fit. If either of you succeeds, there
will be no need to lower the Interdict on Corwyn.
You would be able to claim the credit for averting
disaster in Corwyn, would in all probability be acclaimed as their new ruler. And I—I would be free of
the necessity for subjecting an entire duchy to the
censure of the Church because of the evil of one man.
The spiritual well-being of the people is, after all, my
chief concern."

Warin stared at the floor thoughtfully for a long
moment, then slowly nodded his affirmation.

"Very well, Your Excellency, If you say I shall
suffer no taint by using the Deryni drug to trap Morgan, I am obliged to accept your word. You are, after
all, Primate of Gwynedd, and I must accept your
authority in such matters if I am to remain a true son
of the Church."

Loris nodded approvingly and got to his feet. "You
are very wise, my son," he said, signalling Gorony to
withdraw. "I shall pray for your success."

He held out his hand with the amethyst signet, and
Warin, after a slight pause, dropped to one knee and
touched his lips to the stone. But the rebel's eyes were

stormy as he got to his feet again, and he kept his eyes averted as he escorted Loris to the portal.

"The Lord be with you, Warin," Loris murmured, raising his hand in benediction as he paused in the entry.

Then he was gone, and Warin stood silently in the doorway.

He turned and scanned the inside of the tent—rough tan walls, the wide camp bed covered with a grey fur throw, the folding camp chair and stool beside the fire, the hide-bound chest against the other wall, the stark wooden prie-dieu in the corner, its kneeler hard and well-worn in the dancing firelight.

Warin walked slowly to the prie-dieu and touched a heavy pectoral cross and chain draped across the arm rest, then let his hand tighten convulsively around the mass of silver.

Have I done right, Lord? he whispered, clutching cross and chain to his breast and closing his eyes tightly. *Am I truly justified in using Deryni aids to accomplish Your purpose? Or have I compromised Your honor in my eagerness to please You?*

He dropped to his knees on the hard wooden kneeler and buried his face in his hands, let the cold silver slip through his fingers.

Aid me, O Lord, I beseech You. Help me to know what I must do when I face Your enemy tomorrow.

CHAPTER TWELVE

When fear cometh as a storm . . .

Proverbs 1:27

It HAD been light for nearly three hours when Morgan and Duncan rode through the northern limits of Gunury Pass. The day was clear and bright, if a bit cold, and the horses picked up their feet smartly in the crisp morning air. They could smell water ahead, for Lake Jashan lay just beyond the trees surrounding the shrine of Saint Torin, but a half mile ahead. Their riders, rested after their long trip of the day before, surveyed the countryside idly as they rode, each immersed in his private speculations of what the day might bring.

The part of the marcher highlands where Dhassa nestled among the mountains was a forest area, covered with great trees and plentiful game, with teeming streams and lakes, but strangely enough with little native stone. To be sure, the highlands rested on a backbone of rock, and there were some areas where stone ruled and nothing would grow. But these were in the high peaklands of the mountain country, far above the timber line; and such places were not suitable for men.

Hence the people of Dhassa built their homes and towns of wood; for wood was plentiful and in great variety, and the dampness of the mountain air all but precluded the danger of fire. Even the shrine before which Morgan and his kinsman would shortly draw rein was build of wood—wood in all the myriad hues and textures the country could provide. It was altogether fitting and proper in this particular place; for Torin had been a forest saint.

Just how Torin had managed to earn his sainthood was a matter of conjecture. There were few facts available about Saint Torin of Dhassa, and many legends, some of dubious origin. He was known to have lived about fifty years before the Restoration, at the height of Deryni power in the Interregnum. It was believed that he was the scion of a poor but noble family of great hunters whose males had always been hereditary wardens of the vast forest regions to the north. But little else was known for certain.

He was said to have had dominion over the beasts of the forests he guarded, to have performed many miracles. It was also rumored that he had once saved the life of a legendary king of Gwynedd when that monarch was hunting in the royal forest preserves one stormy October morning—though no one could recall just how he had managed to do this.

Nonetheless, Saint Torin had been adopted as the patron of Dhassa soon after his death. And his veneration had become an integral part of the life of this mountain people. Women were exempt from service to this particular cult; they had their own Saint Ethelburga to intercede for them. But adult males of whatever country, desiring to enter the city of Dhassa from the south, must first make pilgrimage to the shrine of Saint Torin, there to receive the burnished pewter capbadge identifying them as one of the faithful. Only then, after paying their respects to Saint Torin, might they approach the ferrymen whose task it was to shuttle travelers across the vast Jashan Lake to Dhassa itself.

Not to make the pilgrimage was to court unwelcome attention, to say the least. For even if a boatman could be bribed to provide lake crossing—there was no other way to get around the lake—no innkeeper or tavern master was likely to serve anyone not wearing the prescribed pilgrim badge. And it was almost a certainty that attempts to carry on more serious business in the city would be met with similar resistance. Dhassans were very militant about their saint. And once it was learned that there were travelers in the city who did not exhibit the proper degree of piety, pressure could and would be brought quickly to bear. As a consequence, travelers rarely ignored the amenities at Saint Torin's shrine.

The waiting area to which Morgan and Duncan guided their horses was grassy and damp, a small, partially enclosed plot of ground just off the main road where travellers might rest themselves and their horses or prepare to pay their respects to Saint Torin. A rough, weathered wooden statue of the forest saint guarded the far side of the enclosure, its arms outstretched in benediction. And huge, dripping trees spread their gnarled branches over the heads of the pilgrims.

There were several other travelers in the enclosure, their cap devices indicating that they had already made the pilgrimage and were merely pausing here. Across the yard, a slight man in hunter's garb similar to Morgan and Duncan's doffed his cap and entered the outer door of the shrine.

Morgan and Duncan dismounted and secured their horses to an iron ring set in the low stone wall, then settled down to wait their turn. Morgan loosened the chin strap of the close leather cap he had pulled over his bright hair and bent his head to relieve the crick in his neck. He longed to remove the cap. But to do so would be to risk revealing his identity—a chance he could not afford to take if he hoped to reach the archbishops' Curia in time. Few men of Morgan's stature sported golden hair, and he dared not be recognized.

Duncan glanced at the travelers on the opposite side of the enclosure, then allowed his eyes to flick back to the shrine as he leaned slightly toward his cousin.

"Strange the way they use wood in these parts," he remarked in a low voice. "That chapel almost seems to grow from the ground itself, as though it weren't fashioned by human hands at all, but just grew up overnight like a mushroom."

Morgan chuckled, then glanced around to see if any of the other pilgrims had seen him. "Your imagination is running rampant this morning, Cousin," he chided mildly, hardly moving his lips as he continued looking around. "The Dhassans have been renowned for woodcraft for centuries."

"That may be," Duncan said. "Still, there's something eerie about this place. Don't you feel it?"

"Only the same aura of sanctity that surrounds any holy place," Morgan replied, glancing sidelong at his cousin. "In fact, there's perhaps less of that than usual. Are you sure you're not suffering pangs of priestly conscience?"

Duncan snorted softly under his breath. "You're impossible. Do you know that? Has anyone ever told you that?"

"Quite often, and with startling regularity," Morgan admitted with a smile. He glanced around the enclosure to see if they were attracting undue attention, then moved closer to Duncan, his face taking on a more serious expression.

"By the way," he murmured, his lips barely moving, "I neglected to tell you about the scare I had last night."

"Oh?"

"It seems the side altar at Saint Neot's was once sacred to Saint Camber. For a few moments there, I was afraid I was going to have another visitation."

Duncan controlled the impulse to turn and stare at his kinsman. "And did you?" he asked, keeping his voice low only with an effort

"I surprised a rat," Morgan quipped. "Other than that, I'm afraid it was just a case of nerves. So you see, you're not alone."

He glanced at a movement down the road which had caught his eye, nudged Duncan in the ribs.

Two horsemen had just rounded the bend—a fact which had probably first caught Morgan's attention because the men were walking their horses, not cantering. They wore identical livery of royal blue and white; and as Morgan and Duncan watched, the men were joined by a second pair, and then another and another.

They counted six pairs of outriders before the small coach rounded the curve—a coach paneled with blue between the dark sections of frame, and drawn by four matched roans, the horses blanketed and plumed in blue and white. The liveried men-at-arms alone would have attracted enough attention on the muddy Dhassa road this spring morning, but the presence of the lavish coach simply confirmed the first impression. Someone of importance was enroute to Dhassa. Considering the city's neutral status, it could be anyone.

As the coach and escort drew nearer, the pilgrim came out of the shrine and returned, the bright Torin badge winking softly from his peaked leather cap. Since Morgan had shown no sign of being ready to go next, Duncan unbuckled his sword and hung it over his saddle tree, then headed briskly toward the shrine. One did not bear steel into the shrine of Saint Torin.

The riders had drawn almost abreast of Morgan. As they moved past, he could see the gleam of satin tabards, hear the muffled clink of mail under those tabards, the jingle of bits and spurs and harness. The coach horses foundered in mud up to their knees as they drew even with the waiting enclosure. And then the coach was jerked to a jolting stop, a wheel bogged in the mud; and the horses could not pull it out.

The driver whipped at the horses and shouted (though he did not swear, which Morgan thought passing strange). A pair of riders took the bridles of the lead horses and attempted to urge them forward. But it was no use. The coach was stuck.

Morgan jumped down from his wall perch and peered attentively at the stalled cavalcade. He was about to be pressed into service, he knew. The satin-liveried riders would not want to muddy themselves getting the coach free—not when there were common folk to provide that service. And to all outward appearances, the duke of Corwyn was a commoner today. He must act no differently.

"You there," one of the riders called, moving his mount toward Morgan and the other travelers and gesturing with his riding crop. "Come and give a hand with her ladyship's carriage."

So it was a lady's carriage. No wonder the coachman had not sworn at his team.

With a deferential bow, Morgan hurried to the wheel and put his shoulder behind it, gave a mighty heave. The carriage did not budge. Another man braced himself against the wheel below Morgan and tensed for the next trial as several others joined on the other side.

"When I give the word," the lead rider called, moving to the front of the coach, "give the horses their heads and a little whip, and you men push. Ready, driver?"

The driver nodded and raised his whip, and Morgan took a deep breath.

"Now, go!"

The horses pulled, Morgan and his colleagues pushed with all their might, the wheel strained. And then the coach started climbing slowly out of the pothole. The driver let the coach roll forward a few feet, then pulled up. The lead rider backed his mount a few paces toward Morgan and the other pilgrims.

"Her ladyship's thanks to all of you," the man called, raising his crop in friendly salute.

Morgan and the other pilgrims bowed.

"And her ladyship wishes to add her personal thanks," said a light, musical voice from inside the coach.

Morgan looked up, startled, into a pair of the bluest eyes he had ever seen set in a pale, heart-shaped face of incomparable beauty. That face was surrounded by a smooth cloud of red-golden hair, swooped down on either side like twin wings of fire and then twisted into a coiled coronet around her head. The nose was delicate and slightly upturned, the mouth wide, generous, tinged with a blush of color which by rights should have belonged only to a rose.

Those unbelievably blue eyes locked on his for just an instant—long enough only to forever engrave her likeness on his mind. And then time resumed, and Morgan was recovered enough to stand back and make an awkward bow. He remembered only just in time that he was not supposed to be the suave and polished Lord Alaric Morgan, and modified what he had been about to say accordingly.

"It is the pleasure of Alain the hunter to serve you, my lady," he murmured, trying unsuccessfully not to let his eyes meet hers again.

The head rider cleared his throat and moved in, placing the tip of his riding crop lightly but firmly against Morgan's shoulder.

"That will be all, hunter," he said. His voice had taken on that edge associated with authority which fears it is about to be usurped. "Her ladyship is impatient to be off."

"Of course, good sir," Morgan murmured, backing off from the coach, but not quite taking his eyes from the lady as he did. "God speed you, my lady."

As the lady nodded and started to withdraw behind the curtains once more, a small, tousled red head poked up from below the window to stare wide-eyed at Morgan. The lady shook her head and whispered something in the child's ear, then smiled at Morgan as both disappeared from sight. And Morgan, too, grinned as the coach pulled out and continued down the road. Duncan came out of the shrine and buckled his sword around his waist, a Torin badge affixed to his hunter's cap. With a sigh, Morgan returned to the horses to remove his own blade. Then, with resolute step, he crossed the wide yard to enter the antechamber of the shrine.

The room was tiny and dim; and as Morgan stepped inside he surveyed the carved and pierced grillwork masking the walls on either side, noted the hollow echo of parquette flooring under his boots. There were heavily-carved double doors at the other end of the room, leading into the shrine itself. And there was a presence behind the grille on the right. Morgan glanced in that direction and nodded.

That would be the monk who was always stationed in the antechamber—both to hear the confessions of penitents who wished to unburden their souls, and to serve as guardian of the shrine, that only one unarmed pilgrim might enter at any one time.

"God's blessings on thee, Holy Brother," Morgan murmured, in what he hoped was his most pious tone.

"And upon thee and thine," the monk replied, his voice a harsh whisper.

Morgan made a short bow acknowledging the blessing, then moved toward the double doors. As he placed his hands on the door handles, he heard the monk shift position in his wooden cubbyhole, and the thought crossed his mind that perhaps he had rushed matters. He turned to glance in the man's direction, hoping he had not aroused the wrong kind of interest, and the monk cleared his throat.

"Didst wish to shrieve thyself, my son?" the voice grated hopefully.

Morgan started to shake his head and go through the doors, then paused to cock his head thoughtfully in the direction of the grille. Perhaps he had forgotten something. A small smile tugged at the corners of his mouth as he reached into his belt and withdrew a small gold coin.

"I thank thee, no, good brother," he said, controlling the urge to smile. "But here's for thy trouble anyway."

With a deliberately awkward and embarrassed movement, he reached across to the grille and placed the coin in a small slot. As he turned back to the doors, he heard the soft ring of the coin rolling down a groove, and then a not-too-carefully-masked sigh of relief.

"Go in peace, my son," he heard the monk murmur as he stepped through the doors. "Mayst thou find what thou seekest."

Morgan closed the doors behind him and allowed his eyes to adjust to the even dimmer light. Saint Torin's was not a terribly impressive shrine. Morgan had been in larger and more splendid ones, and ones built to far more august and holy personages than the obscure and strictly local forest saint. But there was a certain charm about the place which almost appealed to Morgan.

To begin with, the chapel was constructed entirely of wood. The walls and ceiling were wood; the altar was a huge slab cut from a giant oak. Even the floor was formed of thin strips of many different kinds and textures of wood, all inlaid in a striking chevron and cross-hatch pattern. The walls were rough-hewn, carved crudely with life-sized stations of the cross. And the high, vaulted ceiling was likewise beamed with rough cross-members.

It was the front of the chapel which impressed

Morgan the most, however. Whoever had done the
wall behind the altar had been a master craftsman,
had known every kind of wood his land had to offer
and how to best display and contrast each. Inlaid
strips ran inward from the sides and fountained behind the crucifix like a burst of wooden water frozen
timeless there, symbol of the eternal life awaiting. The
statue of Saint Torin, to the left, had been carved from
a single, gnarled branch of a great oak. And in contrast
was the crucifix before the altar—dark wood, pale figure; stiff, formal, the outstretched upper limbs in a
perfect T, the head upraised and gazing straight ahead.
King Regnant—not the suffering Man on the tree.

Morgan decided he didn't like this cold depiction of
his Lord. It sucked away the humanness, almost nul-
lified the air of life and warmth the living walls
provided. Even the glow of blue vigil and votive
lights, the golden wash of pilgrim candles, could
scarcely soften the cold, unyielding countenance of the
King of Heaven.

Morgan dipped his fingers distractedly into a font
of holy water to the right of the doors and crossed
himself as he started down the narrow aisle. His initial
impression of serenity had been shattered by his closer
scrutiny of the chapel, had been replaced by an air of
uneasiness. He missed his blade swinging at his side.
He would be glad to be away from this place.

Pausing at a small table in the center of the aisle,
he lit a yellow taper which he was required to carry to
the front of the chapel and leave by the altar. As the
wick flared, his mind flicked back for just an instant to
that same color of flame in sunlight that had been the
hair of the woman in the coach. Then his candle was
lit, and wax was dripping down his fingers, and it was
time to continue.

The gate in the altar rail was closed, and Morgan
dropped to one knee and nodded respect to the altar
as he reached for the latch behind the gate. The

candles of other pilgrims flickered on stands behind the altar rail, before the image of the saint, and Morgan stood as the latch gave with a sharp click. As he pulled away, the back of his hand scraped against something sharp, scratched on something that drew blood. Instinctively he put the wounded spot to his mouth, thinking as he stepped through the gate that this was a strange place for something that sharp.

He leaned down to take a closer look, still nursing his wounded hand. And the whole room began to spin. Before he could even straighten, he felt himself being drawn into a whirling maelstrom laced with all the colors of time.

Merasha! his mind shrieked.

It must have been on the gate latch—and then he had further carried it to his mouth! Worse, it was not just the mind-numbing effect of the Deryni-sensitive *merasha* he was fighting. Another presence was impinging upon his consciousness, a surging, powerful force which threatened to surround him, to drag him under into oblivion.

He fell to hands and knees and fought to escape it, fearing as he did that it was too late, that the attack had been too sudden, the drug too powerful.

And then there was a huge hand reaching down for him, a hand which filled the room, which blotted out the swimming, trembling light as it curled around him.

He tried to cry out to Duncan as pain engulfed his mind, tried in a final effort to shake the sinister force which was overpowering him. But it was no use. Though it seemed his screams could split the firmament, a detached part of him knew that they, too, were being absorbed by this *thing*.

He felt himself falling, and his scream was soundless, frozen as he slipped into the void.

And then there was darkness.

And oblivion.

CHAPTER THIRTEEN

Going down to the chambers of death . . .

Proverbs 7:27

THE SKY had darkened appreciably in the quarter hour since Morgan had entered the shrine of Saint Torin. The enclosure was empty except for Duncan and the three horses, and a damp, oppressive wind stirred Duncan's brown hair, blew long strands from the pack pony's tail across his face as he tugged at the animal's left hind foot. The pony finally lifted its foot, and the priest braced the hoof against his lap, using the crosspiece of his dagger as a hoof-pick to scrape away the last of the mud. Thunder rumbled low on the horizon, portending another storm, and Duncan glanced impatiently toward the shrine as he continued his work.

What was Alaric doing in there anyway? He should have been out long ago. Could something have gone wrong?

He eased the pony's hoof to the ground and stepped back, replacing his dagger in its boot sheath.

It wasn't like Alaric to be so long. His cousin wasn't irreligious by any means; but neither would he spend an inordinate amount of time in an obscure highland shrine when the entire Gwynedd Curia was preparing to convene against them.

Duncan frowned and leaned against the pony's pack, gazing across the animal's hindquarters to the chapel beyond. He removed his leather cap and toyed with the Torin badge pinned there, twirled the cap on his fingers. Maybe something was wrong. Maybe he should check.

With a resolute motion, Duncan jammed the cap back on his head and started to leave the enclosure. On second thought, he turned back to untie the horses—they might have to make a rapid departure— then crossed the yard toward the shrine. There was an astonished scurrying behind the right-hand grille as he entered the antechamber, and the creaky voice of the monk addressed him immediately.

"Thou mayst bring no weapons into this place. Thou knowest that. This is consecrated ground."

Duncan frowned. He had no desire to confound local custom, but neither did he intend to disarm under the circumstances. If Alaric was in trouble in there, Duncan might have to fight a way out for both of them. His left hand moved almost unconsciously to rest on the hilt of his sword.

"I'm looking for the man who followed me when I came here a little while ago. Have you seen him?"

Haughtily: "No one has entered the shrine since thou madest thy vigil. Now, willst thou leave with thine offensive steel, or shall I be forced to summon aid?"

Duncan stared keenly at the grille, sudden suspicion of the monk flaring. Then, carefully: "Are you trying to tell me that you did not see a man in hunting leathers and a brown cap come in here?"

"I have told thee, there is no one here. Now, go."

Duncan's mouth compressed into a thin, hard line.

"Then you won't mind if I take a look for myself," he stated coldly, crossing to the double doors and yanking them apart.

He heard an indignant yelp from behind as he stepped through and pulled the doors shut, but he ignored the monk's muffled protests. Bringing his Deryni sensitivity into play and casting about for danger as fully as he dared, Duncan ran quickly down the center aisle. As the monk had said, there was no one in the tiny chapel, at least not now. But with only one entrance and exit, where could Alaric have gone?

Approaching the altar rail, Duncan surveyed the area suspiciously, taking in every detail with his precise Deryni memory. No candles had been added to the rack by the altar, though there was a cracked and snuffed-out one lying close by the steps that he did not remember seeing before. But the gate—had that been closed when he came through?

Absolutely not.

Now, why would Alaric have closed that gate?

Correction: *Would* Alaric have closed that gate? If so, *why?*

He glanced back at the doors and saw them closing softly, caught a glimpse of a thin, tonsured figure in a brown monk's habit slipping back from sight.

So: the little monk was spying on him! And he would probably return with the reinforcements he had hinted in no time.

Duncan turned back toward the altar and leaned over the rail to release the catch on the gate. As he did, his eyes touched on something which had definitely not been there before, and he froze.

It was a worn, brown leather hunter's cap with a chin strap, lying crumpled and abandoned against the bottom of the railing at the other side.

Alaric's?

Chill suspicion nagging at a corner of his mind, Duncan started to reach for the cap, froze as his sleeve brushed the gate latch and caught. Bending down carefully to inspect the latch, he spied the tiny needlelike protuberance that had snagged him. He eased the sleeve free and moved his hand away, then bent to look more closely. Tentatively, he let his mind reach out to touch the latch.

Merasha!

His mind recoiled violently from the encounter, and he broke out in a cold sweat. Only with difficulty did he manage to control his shaking and avoid retreating as fast as he could go. He dropped to one knee and steadied himself against the railing, forcing himself to take deep, sobering breaths.

Merasha. Now he understood it all: the closed gate, the cap, the latch.

In his mind's eye he saw how it must have been: Alaric approaching the altar rail as Duncan had done, lighted candle in hand . . . reaching behind the gate for the hidden latch, alert to the greater dangers the place might hold, yet never dreaming that the simple latch held the greatest treachery of all . . . the barbed latch snagging bare flesh instead of sleeve, sending the mind-muddling drug coursing through the unsuspecting body.

And then, someone waiting in the stillness of ambush—waiting to attack the merasha-weakened defenses of the half-Deryni lord and spirit him away, to what fate he knew not.

Duncan swallowed hard and glanced behind him, suddenly aware how close he had come to sharing his kinsman's fate. He would have to hurry. The angry little monk would be back with reinforcements in no time. But he had to attempt contact with Alaric before he left this place. Because unless he could find some clue as to where his cousin had gone or been taken, he would not have the slightest idea where to look for him. How could he have gotten out of here?

Wiping his damp forehead against his shoulder, Duncan bent and pulled the leather cap through the spindles of the railing, cleared his mind and let his senses range forth. He felt the aura of pain, confusion, growing blackness that surrounded and clung to the cap clenched against his chest; caught a hint of the anguish which had driven his kinsman to pull the cap from his tormented head.

And then he was outside, briefly touching the anonymous flickers of thought that were the myriad travelers on the road beyond. He sensed soldiers of some kind approaching with purpose in their thoughts, though he could not read that purpose at such range; caught the sinister blackness of presence which could only be the little monk, his mind filled with fury at the interloper in his precious shrine.

And something else. The monk *had* seen Alaric! And he had *not* seen—nor did he expect to see—him leave!

Duncan broke his trance with a shudder, slumped dejectedly against the altar rail. He would have to get out of here. The monk, who was evidently a party to whatever had happened to Alaric, would be returning with the soldiers any minute. And if Duncan was to be any help to Alaric in the future, he dared not let himself be taken prisoner.

With a sigh, Duncan raised his head and scanned the chancel area a last time. He would have to leave, and now.

But where was Alaric?

He was lying on his stomach, his right cheek pressed against a cool, hard surface littered with something harsh and musty. And his first awareness as he regained consciousness was of pain—a throbbing ache which began at the tips of his toes and localized somewhere behind his eyes.

His eyes were closed, and he didn't seem to have the strength to force them open yet; but awareness was returning. And fiery needles surged through his head again with every pulse beat, making it almost impossible to concentrate.

He closed his eyes more tightly and tried to shut out the pain, trying to focus all his attention on moving some small part of his aching body. Fingers moved—he thought they were on his left—and he felt dirt and straw beneath his fingertips.

Was he out of doors?

As he asked himself that question, he realized that the pain had subsided somewhat in the region behind his eyeballs, so he decided to hazard opening his eyes. Much to his surprise the eyes obeyed him—though for a minute he thought that he was blind.

Then he saw his own left hand, only inches from his nose, resting on the—floor? Covered with straw? And he realized that he was not blind but merely in a darkened room, that a fold of his cloak had somehow fallen partway across his face, obstructing his view. Once his dulled senses adjusted to that fact, he was able to extend his gaze beyond the hand. He tried to focus, still without moving anything but his eyes—and found that he could now distinguish patterns of light and shadow, mostly the latter.

He was in what must have been an enormous chamber or hall, all of wood. His field of vision was very narrow without changing his position, but the portion he could see was a wall of high, deep arches, darkly illuminated by the guttering light of torches set in black iron brackets. In each archway, far in the recesses, he could barely distinguish a tall, motionless figure looming vaguely menacing in the shadows, each armed with a spear and holding an oval shield of some dark heraldic design. He blinked his eyes and looked again, trying to read the blazons—then realized that the figures were statues.

Where was he?

Rather too abruptly, as he immediately discovered, he tried to get up. He managed to get his elbows under him, and actually got his head a few inches off the floor. But then the waves of nausea returned and his brain began spinning worse than before. He cradled his head in his hands, trying to will the whirling to subside. And finally, through the fog, he was able

to recognize the symptom he was fighting—the dizzying aftereffects of merasha.

Memory returned in a rush. *Merasha*. It had been
on the gate in the shrine. He had stumbled into the
trap like a bumbling apprentice. And the flat after-
taste numbing his tongue told him he was still under
the influence of the mind-dulling drug, that whatever
his situation now, he would not be able to use his
powers to extricate himself.

Knowing the source of his discomfort, he found
that he could at least curb the physical symptoms to
some degree, control the numbness, stop some of the
spinning. He carefully raised his head a few more
inches to see a sweep of black wool robe a few feet to
his right, and then a motionless grey boot not six
inches from where his head had lain. His eyes darted
to either side—more boots, long cloaks trailing the
straw-littered floor, the tips of drawn broadswords—
and he knew that he was in danger, that he must get
to his feet.

Each move of a cramped limb was torture, but he
forced his body to obey; slowly raised himself first
to elbows, then to hands and knees. As he rose, concentrating on that boot before his face, he raised his
eyes also, knowing as he did that it was too much to
hope that the boot would be empty.

There was a leg protruding from the boot, and
another leg and boot beyond it, and a grey-clad body
attached to the legs. A falcon blazon on the chest
swam in Morgan's vision. And as he raised his gaze to
the piercing black eyes which glared down at him,
Morgan's spirits sank. Now he was surely doomed.

For the man in the falcon tunic could only be
Warin de Grey.

Duncan started to turn on his heel to leave the
chapel, then paused to scrutinize the chancel are?
again.

Something was still unanswered. Somewhere he had failed to evaluate all the information available—information which might still save Alaric's life. That candle he had seen when he first returned to the shrine. Where was it?

Leaning to peer over the altar rail once more, Duncan spied the candle lying near the altar steps to the left of the central carpeting. He started to reach for the gate latch, froze in mid motion as he remembered the danger there, then swung his leg over the rail and climbed in instead. Glancing nervously back at the double doors, he crouched down beside the candle and studied it in position, reached out to prod it with a cautious forefinger.

As he had suspected, the candle was still warm, the wax at the wick end still semisolid and malleable. He could feel just a whisper of Alaric's ordeal clinging to it yet, catch the faintest hint of pain and terror just before it was dropped.

Damn! All this pointed to something he had missed—he knew it. Alaric had to have been within the railing. The gate had been opened, and the candle lay too near the altar to have simply rolled there. But where could Alaric have gone from here?

Scrutinizing the floor around the candle, Duncan spied wax drippings on the bare wood, a fine trail of faintly yellow wax leading from the candle to a spot just left of the carpet approaching the altar. The wax was scarred and scuffed just beside the rug, as though someone had stepped on it before it had had time to congeal. And one of the droplets, a large one very near the edge of the carpeting, had a faint vertical line through it, almost as though—

Duncan's eyes widened with a sudden idea, and he bent to look more closely. Could it be that there was a crack in the wood floor there, a line not part of the floor's intricate design, but running along the edge of the rug toward the altar?

He scrambled across to the other side of the carpet on hands and knees, sending an apologetic glance at the altar for his unseemly behavior, then squinted at the floor on that side.

Yes! There was definitely a faint line running the entire length of the carpet from the chancel gate to the bottom step of the altar, more pronounced than the other joinings in the patterned flooring. And there appeared to be a seam in the carpet where it joined that portion covering the steps themselves.

A trap door beneath the carpet?

Crawling back to the left side, Duncan inspected the crack once more. Yes, the wax had been disturbed after it hardened, not before. It was lighter on one side of the line, as though one side of the crack had become lower, had dropped from under and then returned.

Hardly daring to believe it. might be possible, Duncan closed his eyes and extended his senses along the carpet, trying to fathom what lay beneath. He had the impression of space below, of a convoluted maze of slides and low corridors lined in polished wood through which a man, even an unconscious man, might slip for God knew how far. And the mechanism which controlled the opening of that space—that was a scarcely visible square in the patterned floor directly to the left of the carpeting, though he sensed that this was not the only center of control.

Scrambling to his feet, Duncan stared down at the carpeting, at the square. He could trip the device very easily. A hard stamp on the square would do that. But did the passage lead to Alaric? And if it did, was his cousin still alive? It was unrealistic to assume that the setters of the trap, whoever they were, would not have been waiting for Alaric when he reached the bottom, wherever that was. And if Alaric had gotten a strong dose of the merasha—and again, there was no reason to suppose to the contrary—then he would not be able to function normally for hours. On the other hand, if Duncan went down, armed and in full command of his faculties—which were not inconsiderable—Alaric might yet have a chance.

Duncan glanced once more around the chapel and made up his mind. He would have to be extremely careful. He really should drop into wherever he was going with drawn sword, ready to fight his way out. However, there was the question of the maze. He had no idea how far he would be going, how the maze would twist and turn before he got to the end. If he weren't careful, he could impale himself on his own weapon.

He fingered the hilt of his blade thoughtfully, then tipped the scabbard up under his left arm, hilt down. That position, sheathed and with the blade held in place by his sword hand, should suffice until he reached wherever he was going. And then a quick draw—

He heard sounds in the antechamber, and knew he must act at once if he hoped to avoid a confrontation with the treacherous little monk. Taking a tighter grip on his sword, he stamped on the square and crouched in the middle of the carpeting, felt the floor tipping out from under him. He caught a last glimpse of the heavy chapel doors crashing back on their hinges, of the little monk, who did not look nearly as little now, framed in the doorway with three mailed and armed foot soldiers.

And then he was sliding through the darkness, sword clutched to his side, faster and faster into what danger he knew not.

Powerful hands jerked Morgan roughly to his feet and immobilized him, pinning his arms behind him and throwing a choke hold around his neck. He struggled at first, as much testing the strength of his captors as trying to escape. But a few sharp jabs to kidneys and groin sent him quickly to his knees, doubled over with pain. A numbing pressure across his throat brought the darkness swimming dangerously near again as his wind was shut off.

Stifling a moan, Morgan closed his eyes and forced himself to relax in his captors' grip, willed the pain to recede as the men pulled him to his feet once more. It was clear he could not hope to win a physical contest against so many while in his present drugged condition. Nor, until the *merasha* wore off, could he rely on his powers. And as for normal thinking processes—ha! He couldn't even *think* straight at this point. It would be interesting to see if he could, indeed, salvage anything out of this fiasco.

He opened his eyes and forced himself to remain calm, to assess the current crisis as well as his befuddled senses would allow.

There were about ten armed men in the chamber: four holding him prisoner and the rest grouped in a semi-circle in front of him, swords drawn and ready. There was a strong light source behind him—probably a door to the outside—and it was reflected from the swords and helmets of the men before him. Two of the men also held torches aloft, the orange light spilling around them like fiery mantles. Between those two stood Warin and another man in clerical garb whom Morgan thought he recognized. Neither had spoken a word during the short scuffle, and Warin's face was impassive as he gazed across at his prisoner.

"So this is Morgan," he said evenly, with no emotion evident in voice or face. "The Deryni heretic brought to bay at last."

Folding his arms across the falcon blazon on his chest, Warin walked slowly around his prisoner and studied him from head to toe, his boots rustling the loose straw as he passed. Morgan, because of the choking arm across his throat, could not observe Warin in turn; nor would he have given the rebel leader that satisfaction had he had the chance. Besides, his attention had been diverted to the cleric ahead. Recognition of the man had brought with it a chilling suspicion.

The priest, if Morgan recalled correctly, was one Lawrence Gorony, a monsignor attached to Archbishop Loris' staff. And if that were, indeed, the case, then Morgan was in worse trouble than he had thought. For it could only mean that the archbishops had recognized Warin in some capacity, that they stood ready now to support the rebel leader's bid for power.

It betokened another, more immediate, danger, too. For the presence of Gorony at this ambush—not one of his high-ranking episcopal masters—perhaps indicated that the archbishops had washed their hands of Morgan, had written him off, that they were now prepared, after a token semblance of ministering to his soul, to give him over to Warin's authority.

Warin had never suggested anything but death for men of Morgan's race. Warin's mission, so he believed, was to destroy Deryni, however repentant they might be. And he was not likely to let Morgan, the arch-Deryni of all in his eyes, escape the fate he believed destined for all of his kind.

Morgan controlled a shudder (and mentally marveled that he was able to do it), then flicked his gaze back to Warin as the rebel leader returned to his original place. Warin's eyes were cold and stern and glistening jet as he addressed his captive.

"I shall not waste time, Deryni. Have you anything to say before I pronounce judgement on you?"

"Pronounce judge—" Morgan broke off in consternation, realizing he had spoken the words out loud, as well as in his mind, and trying with only partial success to mask the fear and indignation the words had invoked.

Khadasa! Had he gotten that strong a dose of *merasha*, that he could not even control his tongue? He must be wary, must try to stall for time until the drug began to wear off and he could think clearly.

And even as he thought it, he realized he was not thinking clearly at all, that he would be lucky at this rate to even last out the next few minutes without totally betraying himself. He wondered where Duncan was—his cousin would surely be looking for him by now—but of course, Morgan wasn't even sure when now was. He had no idea how long he'd been unconscious. Further, he might not even be at Saint Torin's any more. He dared not count on Duncan to rescue him. If only he could stall, could bluff until some measure of power returned.

"You were about to speak, Deryni?" Warin said, observing Morgan's face and beginning to realize that he did, indeed, have the upper hand.

Morgan forced a wry smile and tried to nod, but the arm across his throat was heavy and mailed, and he could feel the metal links bite into his neck as the guard tensed.

"You have me at a disadvantage, sir," he said shakily. "You know me, but I do not know you. Might one inquire—?"

"I am your judge, Deryni," Warin replied curtly, cutting Morgan off in mid-sentence and studying him with cold deliberation. "The Lord has appointed me to rid the land of your kind forever. Your death will be an important step in the accomplishment of that mission."

"Now I know you," Morgan said. His voice had steadied, but his knees quavered with the effort of concentration. He tried, successfully this time, to keep his tone light.

"You're that Warin fellow who's been raiding my northern manors and burning out crops. I understand you've been burning out a few people as well. Not in keeping with your benevolent image, I must say."

"Some deaths are necessary," Warin replied coolly, refusing to be rattled. "Of a certainty, yours is. I will grant you one thing, however. Against my better judgement, I promised that you should have the opportunity to repent your sins and seek absolution before you die. Personally, I feel that such is a waste of time for your kind; but Archbishop Loris disagrees. If you do wish to repent, Monsignor Gorony will hear your confession and attempt to salvage your soul."

Morgan shifted his gaze to Gorony and frowned, a further stalling technique coming to mind. "I fear you may have jumped to some hasty conclusions, my friend," he said thoughtfully. "If you had taken the trouble to ask before resorting to ambush, you would have found that I was on my way to Dhassa to submit myself to the archbishop's authority. I had already decided to renounce my powers and lead a life of penance," he lied.

Warin's black eyes narrowed shrewdly. "I find that highly unlikely. From all that I have heard, the great Morgan would never renounce his powers, much less do penance."

Morgan attempted to shrug, was heartened to find that the guards had relaxed their hold just a bit.

"I am in your power, Warin," he said, telling the truth now to give weight to the lie he had just told, and to the lies he intended to tell if necessary. "As whoever procured the Deryni drug will have told you, I am totally helpless under the influence of the *merasha*. Not only are my arcane powers suspended, but my physical coordination is hampered. Nor, I think, could I lie to you in this condition if I wanted to." That was a lie, for as Morgan had discovered when he told the first falsehood, he *could* lie under the influence of the *merasha*. Now, if Warin would only believe him.

Warin frowned and pushed at a clump of straw with his boot, then shook his head. "I don't understand what you hope to gain, Morgan. Nothing can save your life now. You shall burn at the stake in just a short while. Why do you compound your sins by perjuring yourself even as death approaches?"

The stake! Morgan thought, his face going ashen. *Am I to be burned as a heretic, without even a chance to defend myself?*

"I have told you I would submit to the archbishop's authority," Morgan said, incredulity edging his voice. "Will you not permit me to carry out that intention?"

"That possibility is no longer open to you," Warin said impassively. "You have had ample opportunity to amend your life and you have not taken it. Your life is therefore forfeit. If you wish to try to save your soul, which I assure you is the gravest of danger, I suggest you do it now, while my patience still holds. Monsignor Gorony will hear your confession if you wish it."

Morgan shifted his attention to Gorony. "Is it your intention to permit this, Monsignor? Will you stand by and be party to an execution without proper trial?"

"I have no orders other than to minister to your soul's needs, Morgan. That was the agreement. After that, you belong to Warin."

"I do not *belong* to any man, priest!" Morgan snapped, his grey eyes flashing in anger. "And I do not believe the archbishop can be aware of this gross miscarriage of justice!"

"Justice is not for your kind!" Gorony retorted. His face was dark and malevolent in the torchlight. "Now, will you or will you not make a confession?"

Morgan wet his lips and mentally kicked himself for losing his temper. Argument would do no good. He could see that now. Warin and the priest were blinded by their hatred of something they did not understand. There was nothing he could say or do which was likely to have any effect—except, perhaps, to hasten the execution if he wasn't careful. He *must* stall for time!

He lowered his eyes and made a visible effort to assume the proper contrite expression. Perhaps he could stretch the time. There must be hundreds of things he could confess over thirty years of life. And if he ran out, he was sure he could invent a few.

"I apologize," he said, bowing his head. "I have been rash, as so often in the past. Am I to be permitted private confession, or must I speak before all of you?"

Warin snorted disdainfully. "Surely you jest, sir. Gorony, are you prepared to hear this man's confession?"

Gorony pulled a narrow purple stole from the sleeve of his robe and touched it to his lips, draped it behind his neck.

"Do you wish to confess, my son?" he murmured formally, averting his eyes and taking a step toward Morgan.

Morgan swallowed and nodded, and his captors dropped to their knees, bearing him down with them. The arm across his throat was removed, and Morgan swallowed again with relief as he bowed his head. He tried to flex his left wrist experimentally as he settled on his knees—which was difficult because of the vise-grip on all his limbs—and amazingly there was the reassuring pressure of cold steel along his forearm: his trusty stiletto, which he did not think the men could detect through his mail hauberk. Apparently they had not bothered to search him—*Clumsy fools!* he thought triumphantly as he prepared to speak—which might also mean that he hadn't been unconscious for very long. Perhaps, if it came to that, he could at least take a few of these fanatics with him in death when the time came. For it appeared that there was, indeed, to be no escape.

"Bless me, Father, for I have sinned," he murmured, turning his attention back to Gorony standing before him. "These are my sins."

Before Morgan could even draw breath to begin his enumeration, there was a sudden rumbling in the beamed ceiling overhead. Heads jerked backward to gape incredulously as a lean figure in brown hunting leathers came hurtling through a narrow opening to land with a thump in the straw where Morgan had lain.

It was Duncan!

As the priest sprang to his feet, blade whipping from its scabbard, he slashed out at the unprotected knee of one of Morgan's guards. The man screamed and went down, clutching his leg in agony; and at the same time Morgan flung his full weight to the left, carrying two more of his captors to the floor with him. A fourth man, fumbling and caught off balance by the double offensive, tried to draw sword to protect his fallen comrade before Duncan could strike again. But his indecision cost him his life. Duncan cut him down before he could even get his weapon clear. And then the room erupted in confusion as Warin's men overcame their immobility and attacked.

Duncan fought with gusto, sword and dagger responding in his hands as though they were extensions of his own arms. Morgan, on the floor and still in the grip of two of his original captors, kicked viciously as one of the men attempted to rise. The man's anguished collapse threw the second man off guard long enough for Morgan to free his stiletto and dispatch him. And then Morgan was shouting and slashing wildly at another attacker who had come flying out of nowhere to land squarely on top of him with a dagger poised.

As he wrestled for possession of the weapon, he was dimly aware of Duncan almost straddling his feet and fighting ferociously with half a dozen swordsmen, and that they could not possibly hope to hold their own against such odds.

And then Gorony's harsh voice cut through the chaos shouting: "Kill them! The Devil take you, you must kill them both!"

CHAPTER FOURTEEN

What is the supreme wisdom of man?
Not to injure another when he has the power.

                                           St. Teilo

DUNCAN LUNGED and parried, feinted and recovered, as he strove to keep the attackers at bay. Blocking one assailant with the long dagger in his left hand, he lashed out with his foot to kick away another man's weapon.

But there was no time to press the advantage with four other swordsmen to take the place of one disarmed. A chance sword-thrust penetrated his guard on the right and would have finished him had it not been for the mail which deflected the blow. And before he could recover from that, another swung a flaming torch at his face.

He dodged and slipped on blood—luckily. For as he went down, a broadsword whistled past where his head had been—a blow which surely would have decapitated him had it connected. He rolled with the fall and came to his feet with a short upward thrust that nearly disemboweled one man, then cut down the wielder of the torch with a desperate slash that also wounded another. A fountain of blood from the man's half-severed neck showered Duncan and his attackers in a rain of crimson. And then a torch was falling from lifeless fingers to ignite the bloody straw.

The stench of burned blood was strong in Duncan's nostrils as he made an attempt to stamp out the flames, but it was impossible while he was under attack. As he retreated before fire and swords, he nearly tripped over Morgan and a struggling assailant. The two were grappling on the floor trying to choke one another, Warin's man on top. Morgan, in his drug-befuddled weakness, was getting the worst of it.

Duncan shoved an attacker onto the blade of one of his fellows and raised his sword to finish Morgan's opponent. As he did, his sword arm was grabbed from behind, and someone else flung an arm around his neck in an effort to pull him over backwards. Wrenching his right arm free, Duncan rammed it back in a short arc which caught Warin full in the stomach and sent him to the floor, sobbing for breath. He felt a dagger slide harmlessly off the mail covering his back, and then he was ducking to flip his second attacker over his head in a heap at his feet. It was Gorony.

Controlling a snarl of disgust, Duncan reached down and grabbed Gorony by the neck of his robe, stomped on the hand still holding the dagger until Gorony released it with an anguished cry. He jerked Gorony roughly to his feet to shield him from further attack, left arm across throat to force obedience. Warin's two remaining men fell back in confusion.

"Hold!" Duncan barked, raising his sword to Gorony's throat. "Come a step closer and I'll kill him!"

The men stopped, looked to Warin for guidance, but the rebel leader was still gasping for breath on the blood-drenched straw, in no condition to give orders. The man with the wounded leg had crawled to the side of a more seriously injured man and was trying to staunch his wounds. But there was no other movement in the chamber except for the growing flames behind them. Duncan, his reluctant captive in tow, edged his way back to Morgan, glanced down to see his cousin straddling a dead or unconscious assailant, exhaustedly beating the man's bloody head against the wooden floor.

Had he gone mad?

"Alaric!" he hissed, not daring to take his eyes from Warin's men for more than a few seconds. "Alaric, stop it! That's enough! Come, let's get out of here!"

Morgan froze and suddenly seemed to become aware of his surroundings again. He glanced at Duncan in surprise, then looked down at the battered form beneath him. Reason returned in a rush, and he wiped his hands against his legs in horror.

"Oh, my God," he murmured, staggering to his feet and steadying himself on Duncan's shoulder, shaking his head. "God, that wasn't necessary. What have I done?"

"No time for that now. I want to get out of here," Duncan said, eying the flames behind Warin's men and beginning to edge toward the doors with his human shield. "And these fine gentlemen aren't going to try to stop us, because killing a priest is very serious business. Almost as serious as killing two."

"You are no true priest!" Gorony rasped, clutching at Duncan's arm and trying to ease the pressure across his throat. "You are a traitor to Holy Church! When His Excellency hears of this—"

"Yes, I'm sure His Excellency will take appropriate action," Duncan said impatiently, watching Warin's men as he and Morgan reached the heavy barred doors. "Alaric, can you get this door open?"

The doors were heavy, ornate, grilled with iron at the top and barred with a stout oak beam across black iron clamps. Morgan struggled to lift the bar, grunting with the effort, then eased it free. But as he pushed against the door itself, then pushed harder, nothing happened. As Duncan glanced behind to see what was holding them up, Warin climbed shakily to his feet, assisted by his two surviving men-at-arms, and moved slowly toward them.

"It's no use," Warin said, his breathing still labored. "The door is locked."

"Then open it," Duncan said, "or he dies." His sword moved back to Gorony's throat and the priest whimpered.

Warin stopped about fifteen feet from Duncan and smiled as he spread his arms in a helpless gesture. "I can't open it. Brother Balmoric locked it from the outside, at my order. Gorony may have been your insurance, sir, but Balmoric is mine. I don't think you're going to escape after all."

He gestured behind him at the growing fire, and Duncan's heart sank. The flames were rising at an alarming rate, singeing the inlaid panels lining the chamber and licking at the ancient paint on the carved cornices and mouldings. Once the ceiling caught, which would be shortly, the flames would quickly eat their way up to the shrine itself. The place would be an inferno.

"Call Balmoric," Duncan said evenly, bringing his blade to rest lightly against Gorony's throat.

Warin shook his head and folded his arms across his chest.

"If we die, you die too."

Warin smiled. "It would be worth the price."

Duncan glanced at Morgan. "How are you feeling?"

"Oh, splendid," Morgan whispered, swallowing hard and gripping the bars of the door to keep from losing consciousness. "Duncan, do you remember what I did to another locked door once?"

"Don't be ridiculous. You're in no condition to—"

Duncan broke off and lowered his eyes, realizing what Morgan meant. Their only chance now was for Duncan to use his Deryni powers to master the lock. And to do so in Gorony's presence would be to reveal himself as Deryni forever. As the being in the vision on the road had warned, the time would come when Duncan must make a choice. That time was now.

He glanced across at Morgan and nodded slowly. "Can you handle our friend here?" He jutted his chin toward Gorony, and Morgan nodded.

"All right."

Transfering Gorony to Morgan's grasp, Duncan gave him the long dagger and resheathed his bloody sword. He raised an eyebrow at Morgan in inquiry as his cousin adjusted his grip, but Morgan seemed to have things under control. Duncan could guess what the effort must be costing Alaric in his weakened condition, but there was no other way. With a sigh of resignation, Duncan turned his attention to the door.

The wood was warm and sleek beneath his fingers, and looking through the upper grating he could see where the lock mechanism must be. Placing his hands lightly over the lock, he closed his eyes and allowed his awareness to surround the mechanism, began feeling out the inner workings. Sweat poured from his brow, and his hands grew moist as he worked. But then there was a click from deep inside the door, followed by another, and then another. With a glance behind at Warin and his men, who had remained spellbound all the while, Duncan gave the door a strong push—and it opened.

"Oh, my God, he's one of them!" Gorony murmured, his face going white as he squeezed his eyes shut. "A Deryni serpent in the very bosom of the Church!"

"Shut up, Gorony, or I may just stick you," Morgan said softly.

Gorony's eyes popped open and he gasped as Morgan's dagger pressed against his neck, but he did not say another word. Not so with Warin.

"Deryni? The Lord will smite thee for this, thou

spawn of Satan! His vengeance will seek thee out and—"

"Let's get out of here," Duncan muttered under his breath, taking Gorony and pushing his cousin through the door as Warin and his men pressed forward. "Get to the horses and ride. I'll catch up with you."

As Morgan began scrambling up a short slope toward the front of the shrine, Duncan dragged the protesting Gorony through the door and closed it behind him, giving the lock a mental nudge to set the pins again. Warin and his men immediately crowded to the door grating to peer out, Warin screaming maledictions as Duncan urged Gorony up the hill.

Almost at the top, Duncan found his kinsman collapsed, staring in horror at a tall stake set in the ground amid piles of kindling. Iron chains hung around the stake, ready to fetter an unwilling victim, and a torch smoked and guttered in the wind before Morgan's fascinated gaze.

"Alaric, let's go!"

"We must burn it, Duncan."

"Burn it? Are you mad? We haven't the time for— Alaric!"

At Duncan's protest, Morgan had begun to drag himself toward the torch, crawling painfully on hands and knees to reach the flame. With a grimace of indecision, Duncan glanced over his shoulder at the shrine, back at Alaric, then roughly jerked Gorony around to face him.

"I'm letting you go, Gorony. Not because you deserve to live, but because that man needs me more than I need vengeance for what you've done to him. Now, get out of here before I change my mind!"

With a shove, he sent Gorony sprawling down the incline, then scrambled the few remaining feet to Morgan's side. Morgan had reached the torch and was struggling to pull it from the ground, eyes glazed with the effort. With a cry Duncan wrenched the brand out of his cousin's grasp and flung it into the kindling around the stake, watched for just an instant as the wood caught and began to blaze. Then he set his shoulder under Morgan's arm and helped him to his feet, and the two began staggering the rest of the way up the slope.

Far to the right, the monk Balmoric and a handful of foot soldiers came running down the incline toward the barred door and Gorony. One made as though to break away and pursue the two escapees, but Balmoric gave a curt hand signal and snarled something Duncan could not catch. The man returned to the foot of the slope.

The shrine was burning. Through the confusion Duncan and Morgan finally made their way to the paddock area. As smoke billowed from the shrine, fed by the massive wooden foundations beneath the structure, Duncan boosted Morgan onto his horse and wrapped the reins around his hand, then vaulted into his own saddle. Guiding his horse only by the pressure of his knees, he led the way out of Saint Torin's yard, flying hooves throwing a shower of mud over travelers passing beneath the arms of the forest saint. Morgan galloped at his heels but a half-length behind, clinging to his horse's neck with a desperation born of the ordeal he had just undergone, eyes tightly closed. As Duncan glanced back, he could see Saint Torin's in flames, black smoke billowing up against the grey thunderheads; and the furious Warin and Gorony silhouetted against the blaze, shaking their fists at the retreating Deryni lords. There was no pursuit.

With a mirthless chuckle, Duncan leaned forward on his horse's neck to retrieve the dangling reins, then pulled up slightly so that Morgan's horse could draw even. His cousin was hardly in condition to even ride just now, much less to make critical decisions. But Duncan was sure he would agree that their best plan now lay in getting to Kelson as soon as possible. Once this morning's news reached the archbishops, Kelson would probably be the next target of ecclesiastical censure. And Duncan knew that Alaric would want to be at the boy's side when and if that happened.

Of course, any appeal to the Curia in Dhassa was out of the question after this morning's events. Both he and Alaric would probably be excommunicated and outlawed by nightfall. Nor could they return to Corwyn in safety. Once the Interdict fell—and there was little doubt now that it would—there was going to be civil war in Corwyn. And Alaric would be in no condition to cope with that for several days at least.

Duncan reached across and took Morgan's reins, touched spurs to his mount as thunder rumbled ominously. Alaric must rest before too long. Perhaps at Saint Neot's, where they had camped last night. In fact, if they were lucky, Duncan might even be able to locate a working Transfer Portal in the ruins. Alaric had mentioned an altar to Saint Camber. A Portal might not be far away. And it could save them more than a day's ride to Rhemuth and Kelson, if they could find it.

Large raindrops began to fall, and lightning flared across the darkening skies. Resigning himself to traveling in the rain, Duncan settled into his saddle to ride hard and keep a watchful eye on his cousin.

They would be riding into the storm in more ways than one now. In a very short while, Gorony would be telling the archbishops of Morgan's capture and escape, and how one Duncan Howard McLain had come to the rescue; and how that same Monsignor McLain, King's Confessor and one-time promising star of the lower ecclesiastical hierarchy, was a Deryni sorcerer.

He hated to even think of what Loris would say when he found out.

"I'll excommunicate him! I'll excommunicate the pair of them!" Loris was shouting. "Of all the false, deceitful, reprehensible—I'll strip him of his orders! I'll—"

Loris, Corrigan, several of their assistants and clerks, and a large number of the Gwynedd clergy had been informally assembled in the bishop of Dhassa's drawing room when the news came. Monsignor Gorony, his robes blood-stained and dripping with mud, had come staggering into the room at mid-afternoon and flung himself to the floor at Loris' feet. As the clergy listened with growing horror, Gorony had gasped out the story of the morning's ordeal: the thwarted capture, his personal peril, the perfidy of the two Deryni called Morgan and McLain.

Yes, he was sure Morgan's companion had been Duncan McLain. The suspended priest even knew he had been recognized, had known Gorony, called him by name, had actually threatened him with sacrilegious murder if he did not obey!

With that Loris had exploded, venting his spleen on Morgan, Duncan, the Deryni, and circumstances in general. Corrigan and the rest of the clergy had followed suit, indignation so heavy on the air that one could almost taste it. And now the dispute went on, in small, vehement groups. Though degrees might differ, there was little question that terrible things had happened at Saint Torin's, and that appropriate action must be taken.

Bishop Cardiel, in whose chambers the debate raged, cast a sidelong glance across the room at his colleague Arilan and then returned his attention to a side argument between the aging Carsten of Meara and Creoda of Carbury. Arilan nodded to himself and suppressed a small smile as he continued to study Loris and Corrigan in action.

Cardiel and Arilan, at forty-one and thirty-eight respectively, were Gwynedd's two youngest bishops.

Next after them came the fifty-year-old Tolliver of Coroth, Morgan's bishop, and then the rest of the clergy grouped predominantly in the late sixties.

But besides age, there was at least one other important difference between Cardiel and Arilan and most of the other bishops present. For the junior members of the Curia were finding Loris' unseemly outburst almost amusing. They were not amused by the threats Loris was making; both were secretly in sympathy with the Deryni general Morgan who had protected their young king so ably during the coronation crisis last fall. And Duncan McLain had, for a time, been a rather promising protegee of the fiery Bishop Arilan. Nor were they happy about this "Warin" whom Gorony had mentioned. Neither liked the idea of an anti-Deryni religious fanatic running around loose in the countryside, and they were somewhat annoyed that Loris had presumed to sanction Warin's movement, even if unofficially.

But on the other hand, it was amusing that the ineffable Morgan had once again managed to make Loris out an idiot. Cardiel, a relative outsider by dint of being Dhassa's traditionally neutral bishop, had only an academic interest in whether or not Loris was, indeed, a fool. But Arilan knew it was so, and relished this public proof of the fact. The young auxiliary bishop of Rhemuth had had to put up with what he considered fanatic foolishness far too many times to be impressed just because Loris was Primate of Gwynedd. Perhaps what Gwynedd needed was a new Primate.

Arilan had no delusions that he might be that new man. He would be the first to admit that he was far too young and inexperienced. But the scholarly Bradene of Grecotha, or Ifor of Marbury, or even de Lacey of Stavenham would be much superior to Edmund Loris as archbishop of Valoret. And as for Loris' colleague and Arilan's immediate superior, the

blustering Patrick Corrigan—well, perhaps the arch-
bishopric of Rhemuth could stand some new blood
too. And that was not necessarily out of Arilan's
reach.

Loris finally managed to curb his temper and stop
shouting. As he stood at his place and raised both
hands for silence, his clergy gradually ceased their
railing and took their seats. Younger priests and clerks
in the service of the bishops pressed closer to their
masters to hear what the Archbishop would say.
There was total silence except for the raspy breathing
of old Bishop Carsten.

Loris bowed his head and cleared his throat, then
looked up. His bearing was erect, composed, as he
swept his gaze around the room, for he was speaking
as Primate of Gwynedd now.

"My lords, we beg your indulgence for our recent
outburst. As you are doubtless aware, the Deryni
heresy has been a special interest of ours for many
years. Frankly, we are not surprised at Morgan's actions. Indeed, we could have predicted them. But to
discover that one of our own clergy, a nobleman's son
and member of the monsignori, at that, is a—," he
forced himself to say the word without embellishment,
"is a Deryni—" He paused to swallow his anger before continuing.

"Again we apologize for our excess of emotion, my
lords. Now, as reason returns, and we further contemplate what this discovery of deception in our midst
means to the Church in Gwynedd, we realize that there
is but one way to proceed from this point, at least
with the heretic priest McLain. And that is excommunication: excommunication, degradation from the
priesthood, and, if the Curia will allow it, execution as
the treacherous Deryni heretic that he is.

"We realize that the second and third sanctions
require time-consuming legislation by this august
body, and we are perfectly willing to accede to the

proper procedures." His sharp blue eyes scanned the room. "But it is within our jurisdiction as Primate of Gwynedd to declare that Duncan Howard McLain and his infamous cousin Alaric Anthony Morgan shall be declared anathema. Archbishop Corrigan, our brother of Rhemuth and McLain's immediate superior, supports us in this declaration. We hope that as many of you as see fit will join us for the rite of excommunication after Compline tonight."

There was a ripple of discussion around the room, but Loris cut it off with a sharp tone. "There surely can be no question of conscience in this matter, my lords. Morgan and McLain have this day most foully murdered good and loyal sons of the Church; have threatened the life of our servant Monsignor Gorony, an ordained priest; have used vile and forbidden magic in a consecrated place. Looking back, we must even surmise that McLain was probably responsible for much of what went on at the coronation of our beloved King Kelson last fall; for that, he and Morgan share double blame." His gaze swept the room once more. "Is there any dissension? If so, feel free to speak."

There was none.

"Very well, then," Loris nodded. "We shall expect all of you to assist in the excommunication rite this evening. Tomorrow we shall decide what further action, if any, is to be taken in this specific matter. In addition, we shall again discuss what is to be done with Morgan's Duchy of Corwyn. It may well be that we shall yet have to lower the Interdict we discussed today. Until this evening, my lords."

With a short bow, Loris took his leave of the clergy and glided out the door, followed by Corrigan, Corrigan's clerk Father Hugh de Berry, and a half-dozen other assistants and scribes. As soon as the door had closed behind them, the rest of the occupants broke into heated debate once more.

"Arilan?"

Bishop Arilan, following the discussion between Bishops Bradene and Tolliver, looked up at the sound of his name above the din and saw Cardiel signal from across the room. Taking his leave of the two senior bishops, he made his way through the throng of railing prelates and clerks surrounding his host bishop, and bowed formally.

"Did my lord Cardiel wish to see me?"

Cardiel returned the bow without batting an eye. "I had thought to retire to my private chapel to meditate on this grave crisis which has come upon us, my lord Arilan," he shouted in Arilan's ear, trying to make himself heard. "It occurred to me that you might care to join me. I expect the Curia chapel will be somewhat crowded by our elder brothers."

Arilan controlled a smile and inclined his head graciously as he waved dismissal to his attendants. "I should be most honored, my lord. And perhaps our joint prayers will be of some use in assuaging the anger of the Lord against our brother Duncan. To damn any priest of God, even a Deryni one, must needs be a serious matter. Do you agree?"

"We are in complete accord, my brother," Cardiel nodded as they slipped out through a private door. "I believe we might also meditate on the merits of this Warin person whom the good Monsignor Gorony mentioned in his somewhat hasty report. Don't you?"

Guarded nods were exchanged with a pair of monks passing in the corridor, and then they were entering the secluded and sound-proofed private chapel of the bishop of Dhassa. As the doors closed, Arilan finally allowed his smile to escape without restraint, leaned easily against the doors as Cardiel struck light to a candle beside him.

"Warin is not the real issue, you know," Arilan said, squinting as the candle fire flared. "But while we're discussing him, I'd suggest a careful study of this Interdict notion Loris seems determined to force upon us. I don't see how we can fail to support the excommunication and remain in good standing with the Curia. The facts are there, and Morgan and McLain are at least technically guilty as charged. But I totally reject the Interdict plan unless the people of Corwyn should refuse to honor the Curia's excommunication of their duke."

Cardiel snorted as he strode to the front of the chapel and touched his light to a pair of candles on the altar. "I'm not certain I could support the Interdict even then, Denis. Frankly, I'm not convinced that Morgan and McLain did anything but defend themselves. And even the inherent evil of Deryni magic is highly questionable, to my way of thinking."

"It's good you say that only to me," Arilan smiled, walking down the short aisle to join Cardiel. "Others among the Curia might not understand."

"But you do," Cardiel said confidently. He glanced at the red Presence lamp hanging from the ceiling and nodded toward it. "And He for whom that light burns understands. We three are enough for now."

Arilan smiled again and settled back in the front pew. "We are enough," he agreed. "So let us discuss how to make us more than three; what things might be done and said to change Loris' plans when the time is right."

CHAPTER FIFTEEN

The humans kill what they do not understand.

Unknown Deryni Monk

IT WAS STILL raining as Duncan and Morgan came down off the mountains. Lightning streaked in the west and paled the fading sunset, and thunder rumbled and echoed among the mountain peaks. The wind howled through the ruins of Saint Neot's, lashing rain against weathered grey stone and charred timbers as the two riders rode through the ruined courtyard.

Duncan squinted into the gloom and pulled his hood farther over his head. At his right, Morgan huddled in the saddle, gloved fingers locked on the high pommel and eyes closed as he nodded with the motion of his mount. He had slipped into semi-consciousness some hours ago, his stupor mercifully numbing him to the discomfort of the long ride, but Duncan knew his cousin could not last much longer without rest. Thank God they had finally reached shelter.

Duncan guided his mount into the protected corner where he and Morgan had spent the previous night, and reined in. Morgan swayed in the saddle, then jerked to awareness as the horses halted and Duncan jumped to the ground. His glazed eyes searched his surroundings uncomprehendingly.

"Where are we? Why have we stopped?"

Duncan ducked under his horse's neck and moved to Morgan's side. "It's all right. We're at Saint Neot's," he said, taking Morgan by the shoulders and helping him from the saddle. "I'm going to leave you here to rest while I look around. There should be a Transfer Portal somewhere about. That will get us as far as Rhemuth, if it's still working."

"I'll help you look," Morgan mumbled thickly, almost stumbling as Duncan led him to the driest corner of the old campsite. "It's probably by the Camber altar I told you about."

Duncan shook his head as he eased Morgan to the ground and knelt beside him. "If it's there, I'll find it," he said, pushing his kinsman back against the wall. "Meanwhile, you're going to get some proper sleep."

"Now wait a minute," Morgan protested, trying feebly to sit up. "You're not going to wander around out there by yourself while I sleep."

Duncan smiled indulgently, but his hand was firm as he pushed Morgan back against the wall and shook his head once again.

"I'm afraid that's exactly what I'm going to do, my friend. This time you haven't any say in the matter. Now don't fight me, or I'll have to force you to sleep."

"You would, too," Morgan muttered petulantly, slumping back against the wall with a sigh.

"I would indeed. Now relax."

As Morgan closed his eyes, Duncan stripped off his gloves and stuffed them into his tunic. Clasping his hands together for just an instant in preparation, he stared across at his cousin and collected his thoughts, his pale eyes going hooded. Then he reached across to place a hand on either side of Morgan's head, thumbs to temples.

"Sleep, Alaric," he whispered. "Sleep deep, sleep without dreams. Let slumber wash away fatigue and restore you."

He let himself slip into silent Deryni mind-contact as he continued.

Sleep deep, my brother. Sleep soundly, without fear. I shall not be far away.

Morgan's breathing became slow, regular; the handsome features relaxed. And then he slipped into a deep, dreamless sleep. Duncan dropped his hands and watched for a moment, satisfying himself that his cousin would not reawaken until he returned, then stood and pulled a blanket from his saddle to drape over the sleeping form.

Now for the Transfer Portal.

Duncan paused on the threshold of the ruined chapel and surveyed the place warily. Though night was falling, the rain had slackened so that he could see the half-fallen walls looming against the darkening sky. Over to the left, where portions of the roof still held, windows of the ruined clerestory stared down at him like empty eye sockets, their bright glass gone forever in the general destruction which had befallen the place. Lightning flashed, illuminating the once-proud chapel bright as day as Duncan made his way toward the main altar and chancel. Shallow puddles on the broken flooring flashed fragmented brightness whenever a new bolt of lightning seared its way across the heavens. Wind whined through the ruins, moaning protests of bygone ignominies and misadventures.

Duncan reached the bottom of the altar steps and paused, envisioning how it must have been in the days when the monastery had flourished, when the walls had soared above the heads of nearly a hundred Deryni monks, countless more teachers and noble students.

In those days, the processions would have approached the altar with reverence, voices raised in praise with the sweet, pungent smoke of incense and the glow of beeswax tapers. He could almost feel it.

Introibo ad altare Dei. . . . I will go up to the altar of God.

Lightning arced across the sky, illuminating the fallacy of Duncan's musings, and he smiled at himself. Mounting the altar steps, he moved to the ruined slab and gently placed his hands on it, wondering how many other hands, consecrated like his, had rested there before. In his mind's eye he saw the splendor of the place when the altar had been holy, bowed his head and genuflected in respect for that ancient time.

Then thunder crashed and he turned away from the altar, mindful once more of the problem at hand.

To locate a Deryni Transfer Portal—that was his task. To locate a place of magic in the ruins of a long-defunct Deryni monastery and hope that it would still function after two hundred years.

Where would one build a Transfer Portal if one were the architect of this chapel four hundred years ago? Would one follow tenets similar to those held by the builders of the Portals Duncan knew? How many Portals were there in the Eleven Kingdoms? Did anyone know?

Well, Duncan knew of two. There was one in his study, originally built so that the King's Confessor, traditionally Deryni in the old days, could have access to the cathedral at a moment's notice. And the second Portal was in the cathedral sacristy, a simple metal plate set in the floor beneath the carpeting of the vesting chapel. After all, one could never predict when it might become necessary to storm the gates of Heaven with prayers and supplications for the king— or so the old ones had believed.

So he was back to the original question: Where would such a Portal be, here at Saint Neot's?

Duncan scanned the nave to left and right, then on impulse turned to the right and picked his way across the broken flooring. Alaric had said that there was an old Camber altar at the left of the chancel—to the right, the way he was facing. Perhaps the answer lay there. Saint Camber was the patron of Deryni magic. What better location for a Transfer Portal made possible by that magic?

There was little left of the altar. It had only been a narrow shelf set in the wall to begin with, and heavy blows had battered and defaced the edge of the marble slab so that the lettering was almost illegible. But Duncan could trace out the *Jubilante Deo* at the beginning of the inscription; and imagination helped to fill in the name, *Sanctus Camberus*. The round-arched niche above the altar still held the broken-off feet of the Deryni saint.

Duncan's fingers caressed the worn slab as he turned to view the ruins from this vantage point, but after a moment he shook his head. He would not find a Transfer Portal here. Not out in the open. In spite of the general acceptance of magic before and during the Interregnum, when the monastery was built, the Deryni architects of Saint Neot's would never have placed a Transfer Portal out here, before the fascinated eyes of all comers. That was not the Deryni way.

No, it would be somewhere more secluded—nearby, perhaps, since the presence of Saint Camber would have been thought to offer some protection, but not out in plain view.

Then where?

Turning back to face the tiny altar, Duncan scanned the walls to either side, searching for an opening to the chambers and smaller chapels which should lie beyond. He found it—a crumbled doorway half-buried beneath fallen timbers and overturned stones—and without further ado, cleared a hole big enough to crawl through. He wriggled into the opening and found himself looking into a small lofty chamber which could only have been the sacristy.

Duncan squirmed the rest of the way through his passage and straightened cautiously, ducking to avoid

low beams which had fallen when the chapel burned.
The floor was littered with blocks of stone, rotting
wood, shattered glass. But over against the far wall
were the remains of an ivory vesting altar, fragments
of closets and chests and mouldering vestment presses
to either side. Duncan scanned the chamber with a
practiced eye, squinting as a particularly bright bolt of
lightning lit up the heavens.

Now, where would the ancients have located the
Portal in here? And with such large-scale destruction
as the ruins indicated, could anything have survived?

Kicking aside rubble and moving farther into the
chamber, Duncan closed his eyes and rubbed the back
of his hand across his forehead wearily, trying to open
his mind for impressions that might remain.

Beware, Deryni! Here lies danger!

Duncan's head whipped around in alarm and he
dropped to a crouch, sword half-drawn. Lightning
flashed again, sending eerie shadow-shapes chasing
across the walls, but there was no one in the chamber
besides Duncan. Straightening warily, he resheathed
his sword and continued to scan for danger.

Had he imagined the voice?

No.

Then, could the voice have been a mental one? One
left by the ancient Deryni masters of Saint Neot's?

Moving cautiously back to his original position beside the vesting altar, Duncan closed his eyes again
and willed himself to concentrate. This time the voice
was expected, if no less chilling. And it was definitely
in his mind.

*Beware, Deryni! Here lies danger! Of a full one
hundred brothers only I remain, to try, with my
failing strength, to destroy this Portal before it can be
desecrated. Kinsman, take heed. Protect yourself,
Deryni. The humans kill what they do not understand. Holy Saint Camber, defend us from fearful evil!*

Duncan eased his eyes open and glanced around, then tried again.

Beware, Deryni! Here lies danger! Of a full one hundred—

Duncan broke off the contact and sighed.

So. It was a message left by the last Deryni to hold this place. And he had tried to destroy the Portal as he lay dying. Had he succeeded?

Dropping to his haunches, Duncan studied the floor where he had been standing, then drew the dagger from his boot to sweep away the rubble. As he had suspected, there was the faint outline of a square inscribed in the floor, perhaps three feet by three feet. Like the Portal in the cathedral, it had probably been hidden beneath carpeting at one time, but of course that had all been destroyed long ago. As for the Portal itself . . .

Replacing his dagger, Duncan gently laid his hands on the square and extended his powers, hoping desperately that he would feel the faintly dizzying pressure which would tell him he was on the verge of transfer.

Nothing.

He tried again, and this time he caught a faint wave of blackness, of pain, the beginning of the message he had already heard.

And then nothing. The Portal was dead. The last Deryni had been successful.

With a sigh Duncan got to his feet and took a final look around, wiping his hands against his thighs. Now they would have to ride to Rhemuth after all. With the Portal destroyed they had no choice. And after that, they would probably have to continue on to Culdi; for Kelson would be journeying there for Bronwyn and Kevin's wedding.

Well, it couldn't be helped. He would go and wake Alaric and they would be on their way again. With any luck, they should reach Rhemuth by the following night, well ahead of any pursuers.

The bells were muffled and tolled leadenly as the bishops filed into Saint Andrew's Cathedral in Dhassa. The night was clear, crisp, tinged with new frost, with tiny ice crystals that swirled in the wind as the men gathered just inside the doors. Long tapers distributed by two young priests were lit from a guarded flame within the nave. The flames shivered in the draft which whistled through the half-open doors, danced weird patterns of candle-fire on the dark, frost-touched cloaks of the prelates.

The men glided down the clerestory aisles to take their places in the choir, two ragged lines of faceless men with fire in their hands. As the muffled bells ceased their tolling, a clerk counted heads unobtrusively, confirming the presence of all whose attendance was required. He disappeared up the darkened nave, and there was a hollow slam as the great doors closed. Three candles moved back down the clerestory aisle on the left as the clerk and two priests joined the others. There was a short pause, some coughing and shuffling of feet; and then a side door opened and Loris entered.

Loris was in full ecclesiastical regalia tonight. In a black and silver cope, with jewels encrusting the miter on his head, he held his silver crozier resolutely in his left hand as he strode through the transept and turned into the choir. Archbishop Corrigan and Bishop Tolliver flanked him to either side, with Bishop Cardiel bringing up the rear. A young crucifer carrying the archbishop's heavy silver cross led them all as they passed between the two lines of clergy.

Loris and his entourage reached the bottom steps of the sanctuary and stopped, bowed respect to the altar, turned to face the nave. As Cardiel moved to the right and took four candles from a waiting monk, he glanced aside at Arilan, his eyes grim. Then he returned to his place at Tolliver's side to give over the candles, passing the flame from his to Tolliver's and on to Loris and Corrigan. When Loris' taper was lit, Gwynedd's Primate stepped forward and drew himself to his full height. His blue eyes flashed cold fire as he swept the assembled clergy.

"This is the text of the instrument of excommunication," he said. "Hear and take heed.

"'Whereas Alaric Anthony Morgan, Duke of Corwyn, Master of Coroth, Lord General of the Royal Armies and Champion of the King, and Monsignor Duncan Howard McLain, a suspended priest of the Church, have willfully and repeatedly defied and scorned the dictates of Holy Church;

"'And whereas said Alaric and Duncan have this day slain innocent sons of the Church and threatened sacrilegious murder on the person of a consecrated priest of God, forcing him to witness vile and heretical acts of magic;

"'And whereas said Alaric and Duncan have caused desecration to the shrine of Saint Torin by their use of forbidden magic and caused its destruction, and have repeatedly used such forbidden magic in the past;

"'And whereas said Alaric and Duncan have shown no willingness to confess their sins and amend their ways;

"'Now therefore I, Edmund Loris, Archbishop of Valoret and Primate of Gwynedd, speaking for all the clergy of the Curia of Gwynedd, do anathematize the said Alaric Anthony Morgan and Duncan Howard McLain. We sever them from the bounds of the Holy Church of God. We expel them from the congregation of the Righteous.

"'May the wrath of the Heavenly Judge descend upon them. May they be shunned by the faithful.

May the Gates of Heaven close before them and any who would aid them.

" 'Let no God-fearing man receive them, or feed them, or give them shelter from the night, on pain of anathema. Let no priest minister to them when living, nor attend their funerals when dead. Cursed be they in the house, cursed in the fields; cursed be their food and drink and all that they possess.

" 'We declare them excommunicate, cast into the outer darkness with Lucifer and all his fallen angels. We count them among the thrice-damned, with no hope of salvation. And we confound them with eternal malediction and condemn them with perpetual anathema. So let their light be quenched in the midst of darkness.' So be it!"

"So be it!" the assembly chanted.

Taking his taper in front of him, Loris reversed it end-for-end and cast it to the floor, snuffing out the flame. And then, in unison, the assembled bishops and clergy followed suit.

There was a clatter of falling candles like hollow blocks, and then blackness as the lights died.

Except for one candle which burned still, guttering defiantly against the tiles.

And no one could say from whose hands the light had fallen.

CHAPTER SIXTEEN

For love is strong as death; jealousy is cruel as the
grave: the coals thereof are coals of fire, which hath
a most vehement flame.

Song of Solomon 8:6

"CATCH ME if you can!" Bronwyn taunted.

With a flirtatious wink, she raced off down the
garden path with her golden hair flying, blue skirts
whipping seductively around her long legs. As she
bolted, Kevin made an initial attempt to grab her
arm, missed, then bounded off after her with a de-
lighted laugh. His sword clanked against his boots,
threatening to trip him with every step, but he paid
little heed to that minor detail; merely steadied the
sword with a hand on the hilt as he chased her across
the grass.

The day was fresh, the sun gently warm, and
Bronwyn and Kevin had just returned from an early
ride in the greening hills outside Culdi. Cavorting in
the garden now like a pair of mischievous children,
they ran and dodged among the trees and statues of
the formal gardens for nearly a quarter of an hour,
Kevin the pursuer and Bronwyn the hunted. At length
Kevin managed to trap Bronwyn behind a small fountain, wagged a confident finger at her and chuckled as
they circled round and round.

It was Bronwyn who finally broke the impasse.

Sticking out her tongue in a defiant gesture, she began to dart for safety, only to slip on the grass and stumble to one knee as she cleared the fountain. Kevin, pressing his advantage, leaped to her side and threw his arms around her, carrying her to the ground with his weight as he bent to steal a kiss. As she relaxed in his arms and her lips parted under his, he almost lost himself in the heady ecstasy of the moment. Until he heard someone clearing his throat meaningfully behind him.

Kevin froze and opened his eyes, knowing he was caught, then ended the kiss. As he pulled away from Bronwyn, he saw her eyes widen slightly as she looked over his shoulder, and she suppressed a giggle. Then he was looking up at the face of his father. Duke Jared was smiling indulgently.

"I thought I might find you two here," his father said, noting Kevin's sheepish grin. "Stand up and greet your guests, Kevin."

As Kevin scrambled to his feet and gave Bronwyn a hand up, he saw that Jared was indeed not alone. Jared's seneschal, Lord Deveril, and the architect Rimmell were with him—Deveril restraining a smile, Rimmell deadly serious as usual—as were Kelson, Derry, and the red-bearded Duke Ewan, one of Kelson's council lords. Kelson, wind-blown but contented-looking in his scarlet riding leathers, smiled and nodded acknowledgement as Kevin and Bronwyn bowed, then stepped aside to disclose a seventh visitor— a small, wiry man with dark features and flamboyant rose and violet garb who could only be the great troubadour Gwydion. A round-bellied lute was slung over the musician's back by a golden cord, the fretted fingerboard worn satin-smooth by much use. And the troubadour's black eyes glittered attentively as he studied the young couple.

Kevin glanced at Kelson and returned his grin. "Welcome to Culdi, Sire," he said, brushing the grass from his clothes and including the others in his greeting. "You honor us with your presence."

"On the contrary, it is Gwydion who honors all of us, my Lord Kevin," Kelson smiled. "And if you would but introduce him to your lady, I believe he might be persuaded to give us an impromptu recital this afternoon."

As Gwydion bowed thanks to Kelson, Kevin grinned and took Bronwyn's hand.

"Bronwyn, I should like you to meet the incomparable Gwydion ap Plenneth, of whose prowess with lute and song you have already heard. Master Gwydion, the Lady Bronwyn de Morgan, my betrothed. It was she who, on your reputation alone, insisted I persuade Alaric to let you come."

"My Gracious Lady," Gwydion purred, doffing his vibrant rose cap with a flourish and bowing, his long sleeves brushing the grass. "For a glimpse of such rare beauty, I should have risked even the ire of your lord brother." He bent low to kiss her hand. "Forgive me if I stand speechless in your presence, wondrous Lady."

Bronwyn smiled delightedly and lowered her eyes, a faint blush of color staining her cheeks. "Methinks this minstrel has a courtly air about him, Kevin. Master Gwydion, would you indeed consent to play for us this afternoon? We have waited long to hear your tunes."

Gwydion beamed and made another sweeping bow. "I am yours to command, my lady." He gestured expansively. "And since this garden is so wondrous fair, and betimes a fit setting for the songs I would play, may we not avail ourselves of the bounteous nature of the Lord and tarry here awhile?"

"Your Majesty?" Bronwyn asked.

"He came to play for you, my lady," Kelson replied with a smile, folding his arms across his chest as he watched her delight. "If you wish it here in the garden, then here it shall be."

"Oh, yes!"

With a short bow Gwydion gestured to the grass beside the fountain and invited his audience to sit. As he unslung his instrument and sat on the edge of the fountain, Kevin removed his riding cloak and spread it on the ground. Bronwyn sank down on the plaid and curled her feet under her skirts contentedly while Derry and Deveril and Ewan made themselves comfortable. Kevin started to take his place beside Bronwyn, then saw Kelson trying to catch his eye and gave his place to his father. As Kevin and Kelson moved slowly away from the group, Gwydion strummed a chord and began delicately tuning his instrument. His audience listened with rapt attention as he told of the song he would sing.

Kelson glanced at the group assembled on the grass, then turned back to Kevin again as they walked. His face was serious, thoughtful, as he addressed the older man.

"Have you heard aught from your brother these past weeks, my lord?"

His manner seemed casual enough, but Kevin felt his body go tense, forced himself to control his apprehension. "You speak as though you have not either, Sire," he said evenly. "Has he not been with you?"

"Not for the past week and a half," Kelson said. "Ten days ago we received certain information that Duncan was to be suspended and called before the ecclesiastical court in Rhemuth. There was nothing we could do about the suspension, of course. That is a purely religious matter, one between Duncan and his superior. But all of us—Duncan, Nigel and I—were in agreement that he should not stand before the court."

Kelson stopped and studied the tips of his black leather boots before continuing.

"There was another matter which came to our attention at the same time—one of an even more serious nature than Duncan's suspension. Loris and Corrigan plan to place Corwyn under Interdict. This is their means to retaliate against Morgan and to end the Deryni controversy which has split these Eleven Kingdoms for the past two hundred years—or so the archbishops believe. Under the circumstances, Duncan felt that his place was with Alaric, both to deliver the news of the Interdict threat and to absent himself from the reach of Loris' ecclesiastical court. When Lord Derry left them four days ago both were well, but they were preparing to ride to Dhassa to make direct appeal to the Curia against the Interdict. I have had no word since then."

Kevin winced. "Suspension and Interdict? Has anything else gone wrong while I've been away from Court?"

Kelson gave a wry grin. "Since you ask, yes. There's a rebel force rising in the hills north of Corwyn, bent on starting a holy war against Deryni. They, of course, will be immensely aided if the Interdict falls. And Wencit of Torenth will be besieging Cardosa any day. Other than that, everything is wonderful. Your esteemed brother told me to remain calm, to bide my time, not to make any disturbances until he and Morgan can get back to advise me. He's right, of course. Despite my rank and power, I'm still too young in many ways and he knows it—I'm being very candid with you, Kevin. But it makes things very difficult, just to sit and wait."

Kevin nodded slowly, then looked casually back over his shoulder to where Gwydion was now singing. He could not distinguish the words, but the melody floated over the still spring air, pure and sweet. He shuffled his feet against the grass, arms folded across his chest, lowered his eyes.

"I assume the others don't know about all of this."

"Derry knows everything. And Gwydion suspects what he is not sure of. But the others—no. I'd appreciate it if you'd keep it that way. At this point their worrying can't alleviate the situation, and I would not wish to spoil your wedding celebration more than I already have."

Kevin smiled slightly. "Thank you for telling me, Sire. I'll say nothing to the others. And if there's anything I may do to help, you know my sword and my fortune are yours to command."

"I wouldn't have confided in you had I not known you were to be trusted," Kelson said. "Come. Let's go back and listen to Gwydion. This is supposed to be your celebration, after all."

"Ah, my lady," Gwydion was saying as they returned, "modesty is most becoming in a woman, but allow me to entreat you further. Lord Alaric has boasted so of your skill with the lute. Will you not send someone to bring your instrument?"

"Kevin?"

Before Kevin could respond, Rimmell roused himself from where he had been leaning against a nearby tree and bowed slightly.

"Permit me the honor, my lady," he said, trying not to let his eagerness show. "Lord Kevin has missed one song already. 'Twould not be fitting that he miss a second."

"My lady?" Gwydion questioned.

"Oh, very well," Bronwyn laughed. "Rimmell, Mary Elizabeth knows where I keep my lute. You may tell her I said to let you fetch it for me."

"Yes, m'lady."

Gwydion strummed another chord, modulated to a minor, and ran down a scale as Rimmell strode away. "'A faithful servant is a true and valued treasure,'" he quoted, caressing the strings and surveying his audience with a contented smile. "And now, while we wait, I would endeavor to sing another song—a love song this time, dedicated to the happy couple."

He rippled off a few introductory bars and began to sing.

Strains of Gwydion's new song echoed in Rimmell's hearing as he hurried across the palace courtyard. He had not wanted to leave Bronwyn there listening to love songs with Kevin; there were few enough times when he could be in her presence and watch her without being obvious. But he would never have a better chance than now to place the charm Bethane had given him. At this time of day Bronwyn's ladies would be finished in her rooms for the next few hours. And the next person to enter once he left was sure to be the lady herself.

As he bounded up the steps to the terrace level and Bronwyn's chambers, he pressed his hand against his chest and felt his heart pounding, felt the reassuring pressure of the pouch Bethane had given him the day before. In a few hours it would all be over and Bronwyn would be his. He could hardly believe it was really happening.

He hesitated and glanced around self-consciously before entering the chamber, for he had been told to look for Mary Elizabeth; but no one had seen him approach. Nor was there anyone in the room itself. He spied Bronwyn's lute hanging on a wooden peg beside the bed, but he ignored that for the present. First he must find a place to leave the crystal. Somewhere that Bronwyn would not notice until it was too late and the charm had worked its spell.

The dresser was the place, he decided, as he crossed to it and withdrew the pouch. Surely a woman would go to her dresser first when she entered a room, especially when she'd been riding most of the day. And there were other glittering things already on the dresser top. They would help to camouflage what he would leave.

Placing the pouch gently on the dresser, he started

to untie the leather thongs, paused as he remembered he would have only a few seconds in which to get himself out of range. He crossed to the peg and took down the lute, slung it over his shoulder, then returned to the dresser and loosed the thongs of the pouch, slid the cold blue-red crystal out on the surface.

Heart in throat, Rimmell snatched the leather bag and fled to the door, slowing to compose himself only as he reached the doorjamb. He hazarded a single look back at the dresser, but he could see no trace of blue amid all the other glitter there. Whistling a triumphant little marching tune, he walked casually back along the terrace walkway toward the garden, Bronwyn's lute slung over his shoulder. As he walked, he carefully withdrew the locket from his tunic, opened it and gazed fondly at the portrait inside, then closed it with a tiny click and replaced it in his tunic with a sigh. As he reentered the garden, he could hear Gwydion's song floating in the sunlight.

> "Good Lady, hear the fervent prayer
>   I offer thee this day.
> As I beseech, so let thy heart
>   be moved by what I say.
>
> Let not thy glance convey thy scorn.
> If thou denyst, I am forsworn.
> What man can live with heart forlorn,
>   Without thy gracious love?"

An hour later, Bronwyn paused in the doorway to her chamber to smile as Kevin pressed his lips to her palm.

"Half an hour?" she whispered.

"Half an hour," he agreed solemnly. "And if you're late," he broke into a grin, "I'll come and dress you myself!"

Bronwyn wrinkled her nose mischievously and

made a face. "Two more days, Kevin McLain," she taunted. "You'll survive until then."

"Will I?" he murmured, drawing her close and looking down at her with only partially feigned passion.

She giggled and hugged him briefly, then slipped out of his grasp and through the partially opened door.

"Half an hour," she admonished. "And see that you're not late, or I'll come and help you dress!"

"Do!" came Kevin's enthusiastic reply as she closed the door.

Bronwyn pirouetted gracefully and cradled her lute to her breast as she spun across the room, blissful in the sheer joy of being alive and loved. As she paused by her dresser, humming a few bars from Gwydion's last song, she bent to glance at herself in the mirror, smoothed a strand of dark golden hair off her forehead. Even as she tried to straighten, the treacherous spell began its work.

Bronwyn stumbled and clutched at the dresser edge for support, barely managing to keep her feet as she was engulfed a second time. In her desperate fight for consciousness, she let the lute slip from her numbed grasp and fall to the floor. The neck cracked in the fall, and one of the strings snapped with a taut ping.

The sound was sufficient to jar her Deryni senses into play, to set her analyzing the situation even as her outer mind spun. Eyes searching blankly, almost mindlessly, for a clue to the attack, she spotted the blue crystal pulsating amid the clutter of her dresser.

Magic! her mind shrieked. *O my God, who has done this thing?*

"Kevin! Kevin!" she managed to scream.

Kevin had not had time to go far. Hearing Bronwyn's terrified scream, he raced back down the corridor and flung himself at the door. It gave without resistance and he staggered into the room—halted in horror at what he saw.

Bronwyn had sunk to her knees beside the dresser,

fingers white-knuckled against the edge of the dark-stained top. The object of her terrified gaze was a strange blue crystal that glowed and pulsated among the jewels and trinkets on the dresser. And as Kevin watched, she reached slowly toward the thing to touch it, her lips moving in a silent repetition of Kevin's name.

Kevin acted. With a wordless cry, and without further thought than the need to get the crystal away from his beloved, Kevin shoved her aside and scooped the thing off the dresser with both hands, intending to fling it through the open terrace doors and out of range.

It was not to be. The spell had been ill-set to start, and never for the likes of a human lord like Kevin—indeed, the more deadly for that. As Kevin lifted the crystal he froze in mid-motion, a terrible expression of fear and pain washing across his features. In that same instant Bronwyn realized what he had done and tried to wrest the crystal from him, hoping that her Deryni blood would at least afford partial immunity where Kevin had none. But she, too, was transfixed as she touched him, the crystal beginning to pulsate wildly with their dual heartbeats.

Then both were engulfed in a flash of harsh white light which illuminated the entire room. It seared the carpets and the very air with its brilliance, cutting off the screams which reverberated through the palace as the white light faded.

And then there was silence. Until the guards, streaming into the room in response to the screams, halted aghast at the sight which awaited, drew back in confusion as Kelson arrived at a dead run and jerked to a halt in the doorway, Derry right behind him.

"Get back, all of you!" Kelson commanded, staring wide-eyed through the open door and motioning them to withdraw. "Hurry! There's magic afoot!"

As the guards obeyed, Kelson stepped cautiously

into the room and spread his arms to the sides, lips moving in a counterspell. As he finished the words, light flared faintly in the center of the room and died. Kelson bit his lip and closed his eyes briefly, controlling his growing apprehension, then forced himself to move slowly closer.

The couple lay sprawled near the open terrace doors, Kevin on his back, Bronwyn slumped face down across his chest, her golden hair spilling across his face in disarray. Kevin's arms outstretched to either side were black, the hands charred and burned with the terrible energy he had tried to quench. The McLain plaid fastened to his shoulder was singed at the edge where it lay partially across one slack hand. There was no sign of life.

Swallowing with difficulty, Kelson dropped to his knees beside the two and reached out to touch them, winced as his fingers brushed Kevin's arm, Bronwyn's silken hair. Then he sank back on his heels and bowed his head in sorrow, hands resting helplessly on his thighs. There was nothing he or anyone else could do for the two lovers now.

At Kelson's gesture of finality, Derry and the guards and Jared's Lord Deveril began to filter into the room, hushed and stunned in the wake of the unexpected tragedy. Lord Deveril's face went white as he saw the crumpled bodies; and then he was pushing his way back through the growing crowd to try to stop Duke Jared. He was too late.

"What's happened, Dev?" Jared whispered, craning his neck to see past his seneschal. "Has something happened to Bronwyn?"

"Don't, m'lord, please!"

"Let me through, Dev. I want to see what's—Oh my God, it's my son! Sweet Lord in Heaven, it's both of them!"

As the guards parted to admit Jared, Rimmell arrived and eased his way to the back of the crowd, gasped and clenched a fist to his open mouth as he saw what had happened. A violent fit of trembling overcame him as his fist tightened convulsively on the tiny filigree locket, and he was desperately afraid he was going to be sick.

O my God, what have I done? It wasn't supposed to end this way. Not like this. Dear God, it can't be true! They're dead! My Lady Bronwyn is dead!

As more guards and courtiers spilled into the chamber, Rimmell tried to shrink back against the wall and melt into the stonework, tried to force his eyes away from the awful sight, but could not. Then he crumpled to his knees and sobbed in bitter despair, not knowing or caring that the filigree locket cut his hands as he wrung them in anguish.

Lady Margaret arrived with Gwydion. She paled as she saw the bodies and looked as though she might faint. But then she was moving toward her husband, who stood numb and motionless beside them. She put her arms around him and clung wordlessly for a long moment, then led him gently to the terrace doors and turned him so he would not have to see the thing which tore at her heart. She talked to him then, softly, in words no one else could hear.

Gwydion picked up Bronwyn's discarded lute and looked at it wordlessly, its neck cracked and belly smashed from its fall. Moving slowly to Kelson's side, the little troubadour watched without comment as the young king unfastened his scarlet cloak and draped it over the two bodies, then absently plucked at one of the remaining strings. The note echoed discordantly in the stillness, and Kelson looked up with a start.

"I fear the music is shattered forever, sire," Gwydion murmured sadly, kneeling beside Kelson to lay the lute gently by Bronwyn's hand. "Nor can it ever be mended."

Kelson averted his gaze, knowing it was not the lute Gwydion spoke of. Gwydion allowed his slender fingers to caress the lute a final time, then folded his hands before him.

"May one ask how this came to pass, Sire?"

Kelson shrugged dully. "Someone set a *jerráman* crystal in the room, Gwydion. By itself that fact would not be terribly significant; *jerrámani* can be used for many things, some of them quite beneficial. You may have heard mention of them in some of the old ballads you sing."

His voice faltered as he went on. "But this one was not beneficial—at least it wasn't once a human like Kevin entered the picture. Alone, Bronwyn might have been able to overcome the spell, whatever its intent. She had the power, if her training was sufficient. But she must have called out or screamed, and no doubt Kevin heard and came to her aid. She could not save herself and him; and hence in the end she saved neither."

"Could she not have—"

Kelson cut off further discussion with a warning look and got to his feet, for Jared and Margaret had been joined on the terrace by the white-robed Father Anselm, Castle Culdi's aging chaplain. The young king bowed respectfully as Anselm approached with the bereaved parents, then stepped back to let them kneel beside the bodies. He crossed himself as Anselm began to pray, then began backing off slowly, signaling Gwydion to accompany him.

"Gwydion, Derry, let's clear away the unnecessary spectators, shall we? The family wishes some privacy just now."

As the men followed Kelson's orders, gently shepherding soldiers and weeping ladies-in-waiting from the room, Derry came at last to Rimmell. The architect knelt moaning softly in a corner, his white hair shaking as he wept, a fine golden chain spilling through his clasped fingers as he rocked slowly back and forth. As Derry touched his shoulder, Rimmell looked up with a start, his eyes red and streaming. Derry, ill-accustomed to dealing with hysterical men, noticed the golden chain and seized on it as an excuse to distract the man.

"Eh, what's this? Rimmell, what have you got there?"

As Derry caught his wrist, Rimmell tried to pull away, eyes wide as saucers as he staggered to his feet. His resistance only heightened Derry's interest, and the young Marcher lord renewed his efforts to pry open the hand.

"Come, now, Rimmell, I want to see what it is," Derry said, becoming a little irritated as Rimmell resisted all efforts to distract him. "Why, it's a locket. Where did you get—"

As he spoke, the locket slipped from Rimmell's grasp and fell to the floor, springing open even as Derry scooped it up. He started to return it to Rimmell, giving it only a cursory glance, then gasped as the portrait registered.

"*Khadasa,* it's my lady!"

At Derry's oath, Kelson frowned and turned, intending to reprimand Derry for his unseemly outburst. When he saw the stunned look on Derry's face, however, he crossed to the young lord and took the locket instead. Just as he realized who the portrait was intended to be, Lady Margaret saw the locket and dashed to his side, clutching his arm in horror.

"Where did you get that locket, Sire?"

"This?" Kelson looked confused. "Why, apparently Rimmell had it, my lady. Though how he came by it, I cannot imagine."

Margaret's hand quivered as she took the locket from Kelson, and she flinched as the metal touched her hands. She looked at the portrait inside for just an instant, then clutched it to her bosom with a moan.

"Where—," she swallowed with difficulty, "where did you get this, Rimmell?"

"My lady, I—"

"Bronwyn gave this locket to Kevin on their betrothal day. *Where did you get it?*"

With a wail of despair, Rimmell flung himself to his knees and clutched at her skirts in supplication, his white head shaking as he poured out his misery.

"Oh, my dearest lady, please believe that I never meant for this to happen!" he sobbed. "I loved her so much! I only wanted her to love me in return. Surely you can understand what it is to love!"

Margaret shrieked, drawing away in abhorrence as she realized the implication of Rimmell's words, and Derry and several guards grabbed the architect and forced him to release Margaret's skirts. Jared, who had watched the exchange uncomprehendingly, murmured his dead son's name once, but could not seem to make further sound or action.

"You!" Kelson gasped, hardly daring to believe what he had just heard. "You set the *jerráman*, Rimmell?"

"Oh, Sire, you must believe me!" Rimmell babbled, shaking his head pleadingly. "It was only to have been a love charm. Dame Bethane said—"

"Dame Bethane?" Kelson snapped, grabbing Rimmell's hair and yanking his head up to look him in the eyes. "This was Deryni magic, Rimmell. I know, because I had to neutralize what was left after it had done its deed. Now, who is this Dame Bethane you speak of? A Deryni?"

"I—I know not if she be Deryni, Sire," Rimmell stammered. He winced as his head was pulled back by the hair. "Dame Bethane lives in the hills north of the city, in—in a cave. The villagers say she is a holy woman, that she has often worked love charms and other favors in return for food and—and gold." He swallowed and blinked his eyes tightly. "I only wanted Bronwyn to love me, Sire. Besides, it was but simple magic Bethane used."

"Simple magic does not *kill!*" Kelson fairly spat the words as he released Rimmell's hair abruptly and wiped his hand against his thigh. "You, too, bear responsibility for those deaths, Rimmell. Just as surely as if you yourself had set the magic and watched them burn!"

"I'll kill him!" Jared screamed, flinging himself at a guard and snatching out the man's sword. "As God is my witness, he shall die for this wretched deed!"

As he darted toward Rimmell with lightning speed, glassy-eyed and with sword upraised, Margaret screamed "No!" and threw herself between them. Derry and a guard captain grabbed Jared's sword arm and forced it down as Margaret clung sobbing to his chest, but Jared continued to struggle and shout: "Take your hands off me, you fools! I shall kill him! Margaret, he has murdered my son! Don't interfere!"

"Jared, no! Hasn't there been enough killing? At least wait until you're not so distraught. Sire, don't let him do this thing, I beg of you!"

"Stop it, all of you!"

Kelson's words cut through the shouting like a sword, bringing instant silence save for the forlorn sobbing of Rimmell. All eyes turned to the young king as he let his stern glance roam the waiting faces, and there was much of his father in him as he turned to Derry.

"Release Jared."

"Sire?" Derry looked incredulous, and Lady Margaret stared at the king in horror.

"I asked you to release him, Derry," Kelson repeated evenly. "I believe the order was plain enough."

With a puzzled nod Derry relinquished his grip on Jared's arm and stepped back, held Margaret gently by the shoulders to keep her from interfering. Margaret watched horrified as Jared raised his sword again and moved toward Rimmell.

"Sire, I beseech you, do not let Jared kill him! He—"

"No, let him kill me, Sire!" Rimmell cried, shaking his head and closing his eyes in resignation. "I do not deserve mercy, wretched man that I am! I am unworthy to live. Kill me, Your Grace! I have destroyed the woman I love! Kill me horribly! I deserve to suffer!"

Jared froze, the glazed look leaving his eyes. He straightened up and lowered the sword in his hand, studied Rimmell's bowed head. He glanced at Kelson, at Margaret's taut, anxious face, then dropped the sword to the floor with a clatter and half-turned away in disgust.

"Lord Fergus?" he said, gazing calmly out the door to the garden beyond.

A heavy-set man wearing a baldric of minor command stepped from the throng and bowed. His expression was grim, determined, and he glanced down at the groveling Rimmell with a look of pure contempt.

"Your Grace?"

"This man is an admitted murderer. I want his head on Traitor's Gate within the hour. Do you understand?"

Fergus' eyes glittered triumphantly as he bowed. "Yes, Your Grace."

"Very well. I would see the evidence of your work before you leave the garden, Fergus."

Fergus nodded again. "I understand."

"Go then."

With a curt nod, Fergus signaled a pair of his men to take custody of the prisoner and began heading toward the terrace doors. As they walked Rimmell continued to whimper, "I deserve to die, I have killed her, I deserve to die." Fergus loosened his broadsword in its leather scabbard. Jared waited until they were gone, then staggered toward the two bodies, knelt to pull aside the scarlet cloak and touch Bronwyn's golden hair which still lay across Kevin's face. Margaret gazed after the departing soldiers and their prisoner disbelievingly, at her husband and Anselm kneeling beside the bodies, then moved to wring her hands before Kelson.

"Sire, you must not permit this! The man is guilty, of course. No one could deny that. But to slay him in cold blood—"

"It is Duke Jared's execution, my lady. Do not ask me to intervene."

"But you are king, Sire. You can—"

"I came not as king but as a wedding guest," Kelson interrupted, turning his grey glance on Margaret and fixing her with his stare. "I would not usurp Duke Jared's authority in his own house."

"But Sire—"

"I understand what motivates Jared, my lady," Kelson said firmly, looking at the kneeling duke. "He has lost a son. I have no sons yet, and like may never have one if the forces of darkness have their way. But I think I know how he feels. I have lost a father and many more. I think the anguish cannot be too different."

"But—"

There was a sickening thud from the terrace outside, the clang of steel striking stone flagstones, and Margaret's face went white. Footsteps approached the terrace doors with a measured tread, and then Lord Fergus was standing in the doorway with a heavy dripping burden held by a shock of red-stained white hair. It was Rimmell's head.

Jared looked up impassively as Fergus displayed the head aloft, only his hands clenching and unclenching in the folds of the crimson cloak to betray his emotion. Then his face blanched and he nodded dismissal. Fergus bowed and backed away from the doorway, leaving a trail of red that soaked into the stone paving as he disappeared around the corner. Only then did

Jared lower his eyes to the two beneath the cloak again.

" 'Vengeance is mine, saith the Lord,' " Father Anselm murmured, his voice slightly chiding as he gazed across at Jared.

"And I have avenged my children," Jared whispered. reaching out a trembling hand to touch Kevin's shoulder. "My son, my beloved daughter who was to be ... Now you shall sleep together forever, as was your wish. Yet, by my soul and by everything I hold precious. I never dreamed a tomb would be your bridal bed. I had thought to see you married two days hence."

His voice caught, and then he began to weep—dry, racking sobs which shook the proud old body in grief. With a muffled cry, Margaret ran to her husband and knelt beside him, wordlessly cradling his head against her breast and weeping with him. Kelson stared after them, reliving for a moment the anguish and despair that each one felt, then shook himself free and signaled Derry to come to his side.

"There is a mission to be undertaken which, by rights, should fall to me," Kelson murmured, "but I must not leave Lord Jared alone at this time. Will you undertake it for me, Derry?"

Derry nodded gravely. "You know I will, Sire. What would you have me do?"

"Go into the hills and search out this Dame Bethane. If she's Deryni, there may be danger. But I know that you are not afraid of magic. You're the only one here I would trust to go in my place."

Derry bowed. "I would be honored, Sire."

Kelson glanced around the room, then moved to the corner and signalled Derry to follow. The guards and ladies had all withdrawn, and only Gwydion and Lord Deveril and a few special servants still remained with the family. Father Anselm's prayers drifted in the stillness as Kelson looked Derry in the eyes.

"I would ask you this now as friend, not as king,"

Kelson said in a low voice. "I ask it as I believe Morgan would ask, giving full freedom to refuse if you so choose."

"Ask, then, Kelson," Derry replied softly, returning Kelson's gaze measure for measure.

Kelson nodded. "Will you allow me to place occult protection upon you before you seek Bethane? I hesitate to send you against her without some defense."

Derry lowered his eyes in thought, his right hand moving to his chest where Morgan's Camber medallion still hung. He considered Kelson's words for a long moment, then pulled the chain from beneath his tunic to cup the medallion in his hand.

"I am not totally uninitiated in the arts of magic, Sire. This medal was the instrument of Morgan's instruction. Saint Camber offers his protection even to humans, it seems."

Kelson glanced sharply at the medallion, then at Derry. "May I touch it? Perhaps my power can augment what you already have."

Derry nodded, and Kelson took the medallion in his hands. He stared at it in concentration for several seconds, then placed his right hand lightly on Derry's shoulder. His left hand still cupped the medal.

"Relax and close your eyes as Morgan taught you," Kelson instructed. "Open your thoughts to me."

As Derry obeyed, Kelson wet his lips and began to concentrate, a crimson aura forming around the medal as Kelson held it. Green flared with the crimson as Kelson's spell merged with that of Morgan. Then the light died and Kelson dropped his hands and sighed. The medallion gleamed silver against Derry's blue tunic.

"Well, that should be some help," Kelson half-smiled as he glanced at the medallion again. "Are you sure you don't have any Deryni blood, Derry?"

"None, Sire. I think that has Morgan puzzled too." He smiled, then lowered his eyes and sobered.

"And what about Morgan, Sire? Shouldn't he be told what has happened?"

Kelson shook his head. "What purpose would it serve? Would it bring him any faster? He's already on his way here, surely—riding once more to the scene of death, as he did for my father. At least let his ride be peaceful this time."

"Very well, Sire. And if I find this Bethane, and can capture her, shall I bring her back?"

"Yes. I want to know what her part was in all of this. But be careful. There was a mistake in her magic before, whether accidental or intentional. I would rather have you alive than she, if it comes to a choice."

"I can take care of myself," Derry smiled.

"So I've been told," Kelson replied, a half-hearted smile escaping his lips in spite of himself. "You'd best go now."

"At once, Sire."

And as Derry disappeared to do his king's bidding, Kelson turned once more to gaze at the scene of sorrow. Father Anselm still knelt with the family and household servants beside the bodies, and his voice whispered through the hushed room in the timeless words of the litany:

"*Kyrie eleison.*"

"*Christe eleison.*"

"*Kyrie eleison.*"

"*Pater noster, qui es in coelis . . .*"

Kelson dropped to one knee and let the familiar phrases wash over him as they had another time, when he knelt by the body of a man on the field of Candor Rhea. The man then had been his father Brion, also struck down unawares by magic. And the words now brought little more comfort than they had when he knelt on that windswept plain five months before.

"Eternal rest grant unto them, O Lord."

"And let perpetual light shine upon them. . . ."

Kelson suppressed a small sigh and rose, slipped out of the room to escape the murmur of death. He would hear the words again, two days hence; and they would be no more easy to accept then than they were now.

He wondered again if they would ever be easy to accept.

CHAPTER SEVENTEEN

*There must be also heresies among you, that they
which are approved may be manifest among you.*

I Corinthians 11:19

IT WAS edging on into the evening of that fatal
day—as Kelson mourned, and Morgan and Duncan
rode unwittingly toward the place of mourning—and
the Gwynedd Curia in Dhassa was still in session.

Loris had assembled his bishops in the great Curia
Hall at the center of the episcopal palace, not far from
where he and his colleagues had performed the rite of
excommunication the night before. But though the
session had begun shortly after dawn, with but a short
break for a noon meal and attention to personal
necessities, the discussion still dragged on, no closer to
resolution than it had been when they started.

The principal reason for this seeming deadlock was
in the person of two men: Ralf Tolliver and Wolfram
de Blanet, one of Gwynedd's twelve itinerant bishops
with no fixed see. Tolliver had begun the dissent with
the opening of the session—it was, after all, his diocese for which Interdict was threatened. But it was
Wolfram who had finally brought the matter out into
the open.

The gruff old prelate had arrived midway through
the morning session with seven of his colleagues in
tow, appalled to find that the Interdict question was

being seriously considered. He had made a noisy entrance—as ill-bred, itinerant bishops were wont to do, his enemies would have said—and had straightaway declared himself unalterably opposed to Loris' intended sanction against Corwyn. Corwyn's duke, as Arilan and Cardiel had agreed the day before, undoubtedly deserved censure of some kind for his actions at Saint Torin's, as did his Deryni cousin who had been masquerading in the guise of a priest for lo, these many years. But to punish the entire duchy for the sins of their master, especially when that master had been adequately dealt with already—why, that was nothing short of preposterous!

And so the debate had raged. Cardiel and Arilan, hoping to gain some insight into just how far the peppery old Wolfram would go, had held themselves aloof through much of the discussion, being careful to say nothing which might tip their hands before they were ready. But both realized that Wolfram could be just the catalyst they were seeking to make others bolt in their support—if the timing were right. It simply required a proper paving of the way.

Arilan folded his slender fingers on the table before him and scanned the assembly while old Bishop Carsten droned on and on about some obscure point of canon law touching the matter at hand.

Wolfram, of course, would support anyone who was against the Interdict. Which meant that he could be counted upon to follow Cardiel's lead when the time came. Of Wolfram's seven unattached colleagues, Siward and the dull-witted Gilbert would probably follow suit, with three more on Loris' side and the remaining pair undecided. Of the senior bishops, Bradene and Ifor would remain carefully neutral— you could tell just by the looks on their faces as they listened to the debates—but de Lacey and Creoda would follow Loris, as would the wheezing old Carsten. Corrigan, of course, was Loris' man from the start—which left only Tolliver among the senior bishops. Fortunately, there was no question where his loyalties lay.

That made eight for the Interdict; four neutral; and six against. Not very impressive odds, Arilan realized. For the four neutral men could not be counted upon to stay that way, and in any case would probably never break with the Curia if it actually came to that. Which meant, in effect, a count of twelve to six, unless someone had the courage to remain truly neutral. So if the six bolted, they would be cutting themselves off from the Church—self-imposed excommunication, in effect—possibly for good.

Arilan glanced across the table—it was large and horseshoe-shaped, with Loris seated between the arms of the horseshoe—and caught the gaze of Cardiel. Cardiel nodded almost imperceptibly, then returned his attention to Carsten's closing remarks. When the old bishop had taken his seat, Cardiel stood. It was time to make their move.

"My Lord Archbishop?"

Cardiel's voice, though low, cut through the whispered dissension Carsten's words had evoked, and heads turned toward the bend of the horseshoe table where he stood. He waited quietly, knuckles resting lightly on the table in front of him as the dissidents took their seats and gradually calmed down, then nodded toward Loris.

"May I speak, Your Excellency?"

"Very well."

Cardiel bowed slight in Loris' direction. "Thank you, my lord. I have been listening to this railing and dissension among Christian brothers for an entire day now, and as host bishop I wish to make a statement."

Loris frowned. "We have given you leave to speak, Bishop Cardiel." His voice held a hint of irritation— and suspicion.

Cardiel controlled a smile and allowed his gaze to sweep the assembly, noting the positions of his chief targets and touching the glances of Arilan and Tolliver as he passed. Corrigan's secretary, Father Hugh, looked up expectantly from his note-taking as Cardiel paused, lowered his head again as the bishop drew breath to speak.

"My Lord Bishops, brothers," he began coolly, "I speak to you this evening as brother, as friend, but also as host to this Curia. I have held my peace for the most part today, because the Bishop of Dhassa should, in most matters, remain carefully neutral, lest he sway those of lesser stature. But I believe that things have progressed to the point where I can no longer keep silent, when I must either speak or else betray the trust I assumed when I was consecrated bishop."

His eyes swept the assembly, and he could feel Loris's gaze boring into him. Hugh was scribbling furiously, his lank hair falling partially in his eyes as he wrote, but all other eyes were locked on Cardiel.

"Let me state it in my official capacity—and I hope that Father Hugh is inscribing all of this—that I, too, am opposed to the Interdict which our brother of Valoret has proposed to lay upon Corwyn."

"What!"

"Have you lost your mind, Cardiel?"

"He's gone mad!"

Cardiel waited patiently, watched as the protestors gradually took their seats, as Loris' fingers tightened on the arms of his chair, though the archbishop's expression did not change. Cardiel held up his hands for silence, got it, scanned his listeners again as he continued.

"This is not a decision which is lightly made, my brothers. I have thought and prayed about it for many days, since I first learned what it was that Loris proposed to bring before this Curia. And further discussion of the issue today has only strengthened my belief.

"The Interdict for Corwyn is wrong. The one the Interdict attempts to reach is already out of Corwyn by last reckoning. He met the brunt of your personal censure last night when you excommunicated him and his kinsman."

"You supported the excommunication, Cardiel," Corrigan interrupted. "As I recall, you sanctioned it by your presence in the procession with Archbishop Loris and myself. So did Tolliver, Morgan's own bishop."

"So I did," Cardiel replied evenly. "And as canon law is now written, Morgan and McLain were rightly proscribed. So they should remain unless they can bring evidence that they are not guilty of the charges in the edict, or can justify their actions to this assembly. The excommunication is not the issue."

"Then, what is the issue, Cardiel?" one of the itinerant bishops asked. "If you agree that Morgan and the priest are guilty as charged, then—"

"I made no such judgement as to their moral guilt or innocence, my lord. Indeed, they have done the things described in the proscription read out last night. But we're speaking of proscription for an entire duchy, proscription for many thousands of people who will be wantonly cut off from the sacraments of Holy Church for the actions of their duke. This is not just."

"It will bring the wicked to justice," Loris began.

"It is not just!" Cardiel repeated, striking the table with the flat of his hand for emphasis. "I will not condone it! Further, if you persist in advocating the lowering of this Interdict, I shall withdraw from this assembly!"

"Then do it!" Loris said, standing in his place, his face going red. "If you think you can intimidate me with threats to withdraw your support from this Curia, you are mistaken! Dhassa is not the only city in the Eleven Kingdoms. If the Curia does not meet here, it will simply meet somewhere else. Either that, or else Dhassa will shortly have a new bishop!"

"Perhaps it is Valoret which needs a new bishop!" Wolfram said, jumping to his feet and glaring at Loris. "And as for me, my lord, I have no diocese you can threaten to remove me from. While I live, I remain bishop. And not you nor any man can take away that which came to me through God! Cardiel, I follow you!"

"This is insane!" Loris spluttered. "Do you think the two of you can defy this Curia?"

"There are more than two of us, my lord," Arilan said, as he and Tolliver stood and moved to Cardiel's side.

Corrigan threw up his hands in dismay. "O Lord, deliver us from men with causes! Are we now to be schooled by our juniors?"

I am older than was Our Lord when he rebuked the scribes and the Pharisees," Arilan replied coolly.

"Siward? Gilbert? Do you stand with us? Or with Loris?"

The two glanced at one another, at Wolfram, then stood. "With you, My Lord," Siward said. "We like not this talk of Interdict."

"Do you like rebellion better?" Loris hissed. "You realize that if you do this, I could suspend you all, I could even excommunicate you—"

"For disobedience?" Arilan snorted. "I hardly think that makes us anathema, My Lord Archbishop. As for suspension—yes, that is within your prerogative. But our actions will not be affected by your words. And we shall continue to minister to the people who depend upon us."

"This is madness!" old Carsten whispered, searching them all with wide, rheumy eyes. "What can you hope to gain by it?"

"Say that we witness for our faith, my lord," Tolliver said, "and that we attempt to preserve the rights of the flocks the Lord entrusted to our care. We will not see an entire duchy put under Interdict for the deeds of one or two men."

"You will see it done here and now!" Loris raged. "Father Hugh, you have the instrument of Interdict ready for signature?"

Hugh's face drained white as he stared up at Loris—he had long since ceased taking notes—and then he pulled a parchment from the bottom of the pile and handed it across to Loris.

"Now," Loris said, taking Hugh's pen and signing his name with a flourish. "I hereby declare the Duchy of Corwyn, with all its cities and inhabitants, under Interdict, until such time as Duke Alaric Morgan and his Deryni kinsman, Lord Duncan McLain, are taken into the custody of this Curia for disposition. Who will sign with me?"

"I will," Corrigan said, pushing his way to Loris' side and taking the pen.

"And I," echoed de Lacey.

Cardiel watched in silence as Corrigan's signature rasped across the page. "Have you given thought to what the king will say when he learns of your actions, Loris?" he asked.

"The king is an impotent child!" Loris retorted. "He will not resist the entire Gwynedd clergy—not when his own condition is so highly suspect. He, too, will obey the Interdict."

"Will he?" said Arilan, leaning across the table in defiance. "He was not so impotent when he took control of the Regency Council last fall and freed Morgan, seated Lord Derry against your protests. Nor was he impotent when he defeated the sorceress Charissa to keep his throne. In fact, as I recall, you were the impotent one then, my lord!"

Loris reddened and glanced sharply at de Lacey,

who had halted, pen poised over the parchment, as Arilan spoke. "Sign, de Lacey," he whispered, returning his stare to Arilan. "We shall see how many support this young upstart and how many prefer to support the side of truth."

As de Lacey signed, eight of the other bishops made their way to Loris' chair to sit and add their signatures to the document, only Bradene remaining in his place when all had finished. Loris stared at Bradene and furrowed his brow, started to smile as Bradene rose slowly to his feet and made a slight bow.

"I rise, my lord Archbishop," he said quietly, "but not to sign your document."

Cardiel and Arilan exchanged glances in amazement. Was the great Grecotha scholar going to come to their side after all?

"Nor can I join these esteemed gentlemen to my right," Bradene continued. "For, while I do not support the Interdict for reasons of my own, neither can I bring myself to ally with men who would break with the Curia and destroy it—which is precisely what will happen if Bishop Cardiel and his colleagues carry out their threat to defy this assembly."

"Then, what do you propose to do, my lord?" Tolliver asked.

Bradene shrugged. "I must abstain. And since abstention in this case is useless to either side, I shall retire to my scholastic community in Grecotha to pray for you all."

"Bradene—" Loris began.

"No, Edmund, I shall not be swayed. Don't worry. I shall not be an embarrassment to you."

As the entire assembly watched in amazement, Bradene bowed farewell to both sides and glided out the door. As the door closed behind him, Loris turned to glare at Cardiel, his jaws working in fury as he began moving slowly into the horseshoe toward the six rebel bishops.

"I shall suspend the lot of you as soon as the papers can be drawn up, Cardiel. I shall not allow this assault on my authority to go unpunished."

"Draw up your papers, Loris," Cardiel challenged, leaning both hands on the table to return Loris' glare. "Without a majority of the Curia to sign, neither your suspensions nor your Interdict are worth any more than just that—paper!"

"Eleven bishops—" Loris began.

"Eleven of twenty-two does not constitute a majority," Arilan pointed out. "Of the eleven who have not signed, six are here to oppose you and will never sign, one has refused to play your game, and the other four are itinerant bishops with no fixed sees, out ministering to their flocks where they belong. It may take you weeks to find one of them, more weeks to convince one of them to sign."

"That does not concern me," Loris whispered. "Eleven or twelve, it makes little difference. This Curia will consider you outcast, and the people will seek out Morgan and deliver him to us to end this as soon as possible. And that, after all, is the object of this action in the first place."

"Are you sure it's not to stir up a new Deryni holy war, Archbishop?" Tolliver said. "Deny it if you can, but you and I both know that when Warin de Grey receives word that the Interdict has fallen—which I have little doubt he will, if you have anything to say about it—he will launch the blodiest anti-Deryni campaign this kingdom has seen in two hundred years. And he will have your sanction!"

"You're mad if you believe that!"

"Am I?" Tolliver retorted. "Was it not you who told us how you had met with this Warin and given him permission to dispose of Morgan if he could? Didn't you—"

"There's more to it than that! Warin is a—"

"Warin is a fanatic hater of Deryni, just as you

are," Arilan broke in. "Only the degree is different. He has become distressed, just as you have, that Corwyn has become a place of refuge for Deryni under Duke Alaric's rule; that many Deryni, some fleeing from your persecutions in Valoret, have found a haven in Corwyn where they can live quietly and unmolested. I don't think they'll stand by and let themselves be slaughtered as they were in the past, Loris."

"I am not a butcher!" Loris spat. "I do not prosecute without good cause. But Warin is right. The Deryni scourge must be erased from the earth. We will grant them their lives, but their evil powers they must forever consign to the outer darkness. They must renounce their powers, must render themselves incapable of ever using them again."

"Can the common man make that fine distinction between Deryni, Loris?" Cardiel asked vehemently. "Warin will tell him to kill, and he will kill. When that time comes, will he be able to sort out the Deryni apostates who have renounced their powers from those who refuse to give up their birthright?"

"It will not come to that," Loris protested. "Warin will obey my—"

"Get out!" Cardiel ordered. "Get out before I forget I am a priest and do something I may later regret! You sicken me, Loris!"

"You would dare—?"

"I said get out!"

Loris nodded slowly, his blue eyes blazing like coals in his snowy head. "Then it is war," he whispered. "And all who side with the enemy shall be counted as the enemy. There can be no other alternative."

"Loris, I'll have you thrown out if I have to. Tolliver, you, Wolfram, Siward, Gilbert, be certain they leave. Tell the guards I want them gone by midnight at the latest. And watch them."

"With pleasure!" Wolfram retorted.

Face white with rage, bearing stiff and restrained, Loris turned on his heel and stalked from the hall, followed by his bishops and clergy and Cardiel's four dissident bishops. When the doors had closed, only Cardiel, Arilan, and Hugh remained; and Hugh was huddled down in the chair where he had sat through the entire confrontation, his head bowed fearfully. Arilan was the first to notice his presence, and he motioned Cardiel to join him as he moved quickly to Hugh's end of the table.

"Staying to spy awhile, Father Hugh?" he asked quietly, taking Hugh's arm and raising him to his feet gently but firmly.

Hugh kept his gaze averted, twisted a fold of his robe as he studied his sandaled toes. "I am no spy, my lord," he said in a small voice. "I—I wish to join you."

Arilan glanced at his colleague, and Cardiel folded his arms cautiously across his chest. "What brings you to this change of heart, Father? You have been Archbishop Corrigan's secretary for some years."

"It's not a change of heart, Excellency—at least not a recent one. Last week, when I discovered that Loris and Corrigan meant to lower the Interdict, I warned His Majesty of the plan. I promised him I would stay to see what more I could learn. I could stay no more after today."

"I think I understand," Cardiel smiled. "Denis? Are you willing to trust him?"

Arilan grinned. "I'm willing."

"Good." Cardiel held out his hand. "Welcome to our group, Father Hugh. We aren't many, but as the psalmists tell us, our faith is strong. Perhaps you'll be able to give us some insight into what Loris and Corrigan are going to do next. Your help will be very valuable."

"However I may assist you, Excellency," Hugh

murmured, bobbing to kiss Cardiel's ring. "Thank you."

"Now, no ceremony," Cardiel smiled. "We have more important things to do. If you'll find my secretary, Father Evans, we can use both of you in about a quarter of an hour. We'll have some urgent correspondence to get out."

"Of course, Excellency," Hugh beamed, as he bowed and made his exit.

Cardiel sighed and sank down into a vacant chair, closed his eyes and rubbed his forehead wearily, then looked up at Arilan. The younger bishop had perched himself against the edge of the table, and grinned down at Cardiel with a look of grim resignation.

"Well, we've done it now, my friend. We've split the Church right down the middle on the eve of war."

Cardiel snorted and smiled wearily. "War with Wencit of Torenth and civil war. If you think that won't keep us busy. . . ."

Arilan shrugged. "It couldn't be avoided. I pity Kelson, though. Loris will be after him next. After all, he's half-Deryni the same as Morgan, with that extra power from his father thrown in to boot."

"Which simply means that Kelson will have to be living proof of how beneficent and pure a Deryni can be," Cardiel said. He sighed, laced his fingers behind his head and stared up at the ceiling. "What do you think about the Deryni, Denis? Do you think they're really evil, as Loris contends?"

Arilan gave a slight smile. "I think that there are some evil Deryni, just like anybody else. I don't believe that Kelson, or Morgan, or Duncan are evil, though, if that's what you mean."

"Hmmm. I just wondered. That's the first time I've ever gotten a straight answer out of you on the subject." He turned to twinkle at Arilan. "If I didn't know better, I'd sometimes swear that you were Deryni."

Arilan chuckled delightedly and clapped Cardiel on the shoulder. "You think of some of the strangest notions, Thomas. Come. We'd best get busy, or the real Deryni will be pounding on our door."

Cardiel shook his head and stood. "Heaven forbid."

CHAPTER EIGHTEEN

Stand now with thine enchantments, and with the multitudes of thy sorceries, wherein thou hast labored from thy youth.

Isaiah 47:12

DAWN OF the second day was but a few hours away when Morgan and Duncan came within sight of the walled city of Culdi. They had been riding steadily for nearly twenty hours, after only a brief stop in Rhemuth to confirm that Kelson had already gone on before them.

Nigel, managing Kelson's affairs in the capital in the absence of his young nephew, had been appalled at the tale Duncan told of the Dhassa debacle, had agreed that their only course of action now lay in getting to Kelson with the news as soon as possible. Once word of the episode at Saint Torin's reached Kelson, probably in the form of an official decree of excommunication from the Curia at Dhassa, the young king would be risking much to even receive the two fugitive Deryni. Meanwhile, Nigel would step up his mustering of troops for the coming campaign and prepare the army to move out. If the domestic crisis in the southeast continued to worsen, those troops might be needed to quell internal strife. Gwynedd might well be on the brink of civil war.

So Morgan and Duncan had ridden on toward

Culdi, little suspecting what that city held in store for them besides a worried young king. As they reined in before the main gates in the chill, early morning blackness, squinting against the torchlight on the rampart walls, a gate warder slid open a spy hole and inspected them suspiciously. After three days of riding, the two before the gates definitely did not look like types one would want to admit to a walled city in the predawn hours.

"Who seeks admittance to the city of Culdi before the rising of the sun? Identify yourselves or face the judgement of the city."

"Duke Alaric Morgan and Duncan McLain to see the king," Duncan said in a low voice. "Open quickly, please. We're in a hurry."

The gate warder held a hurried, whispered conference with someone Duncan could not see, then peered out again and nodded.

"Stand back please, m'lords. The captain is on his way."

Morgan and Duncan backed their horses a few paces and slouched in the saddles. Morgan glanced up at the ramparts and noticed a white-haired head on a pike above the gate. He frowned and touched Duncan's elbow, directing his attention toward the sight with a nod of his head, and Duncan looked up too.

"I thought that sort of execution was reserved for traitors," Morgan said, studying the head curiously. "That hasn't been up there for long, either. It can't have happened more than a few days ago."

Duncan knitted his brow and shrugged. "I don't recognize him. He looks fairly young, too, despite the white hair. I wonder what he did."

There was the creak of bars being raised behind the gates, a groan of steel hinges and clanking chains, and then a postern gate opened in the right half of the huge main doors, barely large enough to admit a man on horseback. Morgan glanced quizzically at Duncan, for as far as he remembered it was not the usual practice to admit visitors through the postern gate. On the other hand, he had never tried to enter the city before dawn, either. And there was no hint of danger behind the door. Morgan's powers had returned by now, and there was no treachery afoot that he could detect.

Duncan guided his horse through the gate and into the small courtyard beyond, and Morgan followed. Inside, two dark-cloaked city warders bearing torches were mounting up, holding their skittish horses in check before Morgan and Duncan. A guard captain wearing the insignia of Kelson's elite corps reached up to take hold of Morgan's bridle.

"Welcome to Culdi, Your Grace, Monsignor McLain," he said, bowing slightly but keeping his eyes averted as he moved to keep from being stepped on by Morgan's horse. "These men will escort you to the main keep."

The man released Morgan's horse and stepped back, signaling the warders to proceed, and Morgan frowned again. It was dark in the tiny courtyard, with only the meager torchlight to illuminate the area, but Morgan thought he had seen black crepe banding the man's arm above the elbow. It was very strange that one of Kelson's personal household should be in public mourning. He wondered who had died.

The mounted escort pulled out, holding their torches aloft, and Morgan and Duncan urged their tired horses after them. The streets of Culdi were empty at this hour of the morning, and the hoofbeats echoed on the cobbles and paving stones of the winding streets. They came at length to the main entrance to the keep, were readily admitted when the guards there saw their escort. But as Morgan and Duncan glanced up at where the royal suite was located, the rooms where the king always stayed when he visited Culdi, they were amazed to see lights burning at the windows there, with still more than an hour until dawn.

Now, that was truly strange. What could have aroused the young king at this hour? Morgan and Duncan both knew that the boy was an inveterate late sleeper, would not willingly have arisen at this hour unless something were urgently requiring his attention. What was going on?

The two drew rein and dismounted. A groom walking a sheeted and exhausted horse over to the left was muttering and shaking his head disgustedly every time he stopped to run his hands down the animal's legs, and the animal itself seemed on the verge of collapse.

A messenger must have arrived on that horse, Morgan concluded. A messenger with news for Kelson which could not wait. That was why the candles burned at Kelson's window.

As they hurried up the main steps, Morgan glanced at his cousin and realized he had reached the same conclusion. An ancient doorkeep whom both men recognized from their childhood admitted them and bowed, signaled two young pages to light their way to the upper floor. He was Jared's man, a faithful servant of the McLain family all his life, but he too would not meet their eyes or speak. And he, too, wore a black crepe armband.

Who has died? Morgan asked himself, a chill suspicion touching his heart. *Not the king, please God!*

Casting an anguished look at Duncan, Morgan bounded up the stairs three at a time, Duncan right at his heels. Both knew the way to their destination, for Castle Culdi was a familiar childhood haunt. But Morgan reached the door first and wrenched at the latch. The door flew open and crashed back against the wall.

Kelson sat at a writing desk near the windows in his nightclothes, haggard-looking and with raven hair disheveled. The desk was banked with candles, their light dancing over the table as the door flew open, and Kelson was writing absorbedly on a scrap of paper, studying a parchment document on the table before him. Behind him and to his left stood Derry in a hastily donned blue dressing gown, leaning over Kelson's shoulder to point out something on the parchment. A young squire was slumped exhaustedly on a hassock by the fireplace, one of Kelson's crimson cloaks thrown around his shoulders. He stared dully into the flames and sipped hot wine as two pages removed his boots and tried to offer him food.

Kelson looked up with a start as the door flew open, and his eyes widened as he saw Morgan and Duncan. All eyes had darted to the doorway as the two entered, and now as Kelson stood and put down his pen, Derry stepped back and watched quietly. Even in the candlelight, it was evident that something was grossly wrong.

Kelson signaled the pages and the squire to withdraw, not moving further until the door had closed behind them. Only then did he step from behind the table to lean dejectedly against the edge. No word had yet been spoken, and Morgan glanced first at Derry, then at Kelson.

"What's wrong, Kelson?"

Kelson studied the toes of his slippers, would not meet Morgan's eyes. "There's no easy way to tell you this, Alaric, Father Duncan. You'd better both sit down."

As Derry pulled chairs closer, Morgan and Duncan exchanged apprehensive glances and sat. Derry returned to his place beside Kelson's chair, his face unreadable, and Morgan returned his attention to Kelson as the boy sighed.

"First of all, there's this," the boy said, gesturing behind him to where the parchment lay on the table. "I don't know what you did at Saint Torin's—Father Hugh didn't give the details—but I think it will come as no surprise that both of you have been declared excommunicate."

Morgan and Duncan exchanged glances again and Duncan nodded.

"By Loris?"

"By the entire Gwynedd Curia."

Duncan sat back and sighed. "No, I can't say we're surprised. Gorony must have had some tales to tell. I suppose they mentioned that I had to reveal myself as Deryni?"

"It's all here," Kelson said, gesturing vaguely toward the parchment again.

Morgan frowned and sat forward in his chair, studying Kelson shrewdly. "There's something you haven't told us, Kelson. Something you found out before you got that message. What's wrong? Why is the staff in mourning? Whose head was that on the gate?"

"The man's name was Rimmell," Kelson said, not meeting Morgan's eyes. "You may remember him, Father Duncan."

"My father's architect," Duncan nodded. "But, what did he do? Beheading is usually reserved for traitors."

"He was in love with your sister, Alaric," Kelson whispered. "He found an old witch-woman in the hills to cast a love spell on her. Only the spell was badly done, and instead of making her love Rimmell, it— killed."

"Bronwyn?"

Kelson nodded miserably. "And Kevin. Both."

"O my God!" Duncan murmured, his voice choking off as he buried his face in his hands. Morgan, dazed, touched Duncan's shoulder in a mindless gesture intended to comfort and sank back in his chair.

"Bronwyn is dead? By magic?"

"A *jerráman* crystal," Kelson replied in a low voice. "Alone, she might have been able to overcome it. It was very poorly set. But it wasn't fashioned for a human's interference, and Kevin was there when it struck. That was two days ago. The funeral is to be today. I might have tried to get a message to you, but I knew you'd already be on your way. The least I could do was to spare you the same anguished kind of ride you had when my father died."

Morgan shook his head in disbelief. "It doesn't make sense. She should have been able to—who is this witch-woman Rimmell contacted? Deryni?"

Derry stepped forward and bowed his head sympathetically. "We don't know for certain, M'Lord. Gwydion and I spent the rest of that afternoon and all day yesterday searching the hills where Rimmell said to look. Nothing."

"It's partly my fault," Kelson added. "I should have questioned Rimmell more closely, Truth-Read him. As it was, all I could think was that—"

There was a knock at the door, and Kelson looked up.

"Who is it?"

"Jared, Sire."

Kelson glanced at Morgan and Duncan, then crossed to the door to admit Jared. Morgan rose and moved dazedly toward the window behind Kelson's desk, staring out through the streaked glass at the lightening eastern sky. Duncan was sitting slouched in his chair, hands clasped between his knees and staring at the floor. He looked up with a pained expression as he heard his father's voice, composed himself and stood to face the door as Jared entered.

Jared had aged years in the past few days. His usually immaculate hair was disheveled, streaked with more grey than Duncan remembered, and the heavy brown dressing gown with dark fur collar and cuffs only accentuated the new lines on his haggard face, added more years to a frame which now seemed almost unable to bear them.

He met Duncan's eyes briefly as he crossed the

room, then looked away to avoid breaking down in his son's presence. His hands wrung together uneasily in the long velvet sleeves.

"I—was with him when they brought word you had come, Duncan. I couldn't sleep."

"I know," Duncan whispered. "Nor could I in your position."

Kelson had wandered back to the table to stand beside Morgan now, and Jared glanced at him before turning to his son.

"May I ask a favor of you, Duncan?"

"Whatever I can do," Duncan replied.

"Would you preside at your brother's Requiem this morning?"

Duncan lowered his eyes, taken aback at the request. Apparently Jared had not been told of the suspension, much less the excommunication, or he would not have asked. A suspended priest was not supposed to exercise the powers of his sacred orders. And an excommunicated one—

He glanced at Kelson to confirm his suspicion about Jared, and Kelson deliberately turned the parchment face down and shook his head slightly.

So. Jared did not know. Apparently the only ones in Culdi who did know were in this room right now.

But Duncan knew. Of course, until the official notification of excommunication arrived from Dhassa, that could be construed to be mere rumor, and therefore not binding—though Duncan knew better. But the suspension—well, even that would not invalidate the sacraments Duncan would perform. Suspension did not take away a priest's sacerdotal authority— only his right to exercise it. And if he chose to defy suspension and perform his sacred functions anyway— well, that was between the priest and his God.

Duncan swallowed and glanced up at Jared, then put his arm around his father's shoulders reassuringly.

"Of course I'll do it, Father," he said quietly.

"Now, why don't we go back and see Kevin together this time?"

Jared nodded and blinked, trying to keep back the tears, and Duncan glanced at Morgan and Kelson. As Kelson nodded, Duncan inclined his head and moved on toward the door. Derry caught Kelson's eye and raised an eyebrow, inquiring whether he too should leave, and Kelson nodded yes. Derry followed Duncan and Jared and closed the door behind him softly, leaving Kelson and Morgan alone in the room.

Kelson watched Morgan from behind for a moment, then bent to blow out the candles on the desk. The sky was brightening steadily as dawn approached, and the light coming through the windows now was just sufficient to discern vague shadow-shapes, some features. Kelson leaned against the window casement to Morgan's right and gazed out over the city, hands in the pockets of his robe, not looking directly at Morgan. He could find no words to speak of Bronwyn.

"We have a few hours before you must make an appearance, Alaric. Why don't you rest?"

Morgan seemed not to have heard. "It's been like a very bad dream, my prince. The past three days have been unlike any I've ever endured, almost as bad as when your father died—perhaps worse in many ways. I keep thinking I'll wake up, that it can't possibly get any worse—but then it does."

Kelson lowered his head and started to speak, distressed to hear his mentor in such low spirits, but Morgan resumed almost as though Kelson were not there.

"Once the official notice of excommunication comes, you are bound not to receive us, Kelson, on pain of coming under excommunication yourself. Nor may you accept our aid in any way, for the same reason. And if Interdict falls in Corwyn, which it almost certainly will, I cannot even promise you the aid of my countrymen. Indeed, you may be faced with civil war. I—don't know what to tell you to do."

Kelson pushed himself away from the casement and touched Morgan's elbow, gesturing toward the state bed in the far corner. "Let's not worry about it for now. You're exhausted and you need rest. Why don't you lie down for a while, and I'll wake you when it's time. We can decide what to do later."

Morgan nodded and let himself be led to the bed, unbuckling his sword and letting it slip to the floor as he sank down on the edge. At last he spoke of Bronwyn.

"She was so young, Kelson," he murmured, letting Kelson unfasten the cloak at his throat and take it from his shoulders. "And Kevin—he wasn't even Deryni, yet he died too. All because of this senseless hatred, this differentness. . . ."

He lay down on the bed and closed his eyes briefly, gazed up exhaustedly at the brocaded canopy overhead. "The darkness closes in more every day, Kelson," he murmured, forcing himself to relax. "It comes from every side, all at once. And the only thing holding it back is me, and Duncan, and you. . . ."

As he drifted off to sleep, Kelson watched anxiously, easing himself to sit on the edge of the bed beside his friend when he was sure Morgan was asleep. He studied the general's face for a long time, clutching Morgan's mud-stained leather cloak against his chest, then reached out cautiously to place his hand on Morgan's forehead. Clearing his mind carefully, he closed his eyes and extended his senses over Morgan.

Fatigue . . . grief . . . pain . . . beginning with the first news when Duncan had appeared at Coroth . . . The peril of impending Interdict and Morgan's concern for his people . . . Derry's scouting expedition . . . The assassination attempt and the sorrow of young Richard FitzWilliam's death . . . Derry's report of Warin and the miracle of healing . . . Remembrances of Brion, of his father's pride the day Kelson was born ... The chilling search in the ruined chapel, disclosing nothing ...

Saint Torin's ... deception, treachery, whirling chaos and blackness, dimly remembered ... The terror of awakening totally powerless, in the grip of *merasha*, of knowing you are captive of one who has vowed to destroy you and all your kind ... Escape, long numb ride, mostly in a merciful haze of semi-consciousness while mind and powers return ... And then grief at the loss of a beloved sister, a much-loved cousin ... And sleep, merciful oblivion, at least for a few hours ... secure ... safe ...

With a shiver, Kelson withdrew mind and hand and opened his eyes. Morgan slept peacefully now, sprawled on his back in the center of the wide state bed, oblivious to all. Kelson stood and shook out the cloak he had been holding, spread it over the sleeping form, then snuffed out the candles beside the bed and returned to his desk.

The next hours would not be easy for anyone, least of all Morgan—and Duncan. But meanwhile the business of trying to preserve order in chaos must go on; and he must be strong now, while Morgan could not help him.

With a last glance at the sleeping Morgan, Kelson sat down at his desk and pulled the parchment document toward him, turned it face up, picked up pen and the scrap of paper he and Derry had been working on when Morgan came.

Nigel must be told now—the whole grim business. He must be told of Bronwyn and Kevin's deaths, of the excommunication, of the impending danger on two fronts once the Interdict fell. For Wencit of Torenth would not wait while Gwynedd ironed out its domestic problems. The Deryni warlord would take full advantage of the confusion in Gwynedd, the threat of holy war.

Kelson sighed and reread the letter. The news was grim, no matter how one tried to approach it. There was no way to tell it but to begin.

Duncan knelt alone in the small vesting chapel adjoining Saint Teilo's Church and stared into the flame of a Presence light beside the tiny altar. He was rested now. He had applied the Deryni methods of banishing fatigue about as often as he dared, and he felt as fit as could be expected. But though he was clean and shaven now, and had donned his priestly garb again, his heart was not in what he must do next. He no longer had the right to put on the black silk stole and chasuble, the sacred vestments he must wear to celebrate the Mass.

Celebrate, he thought ironically. There was more than one reason he was reluctant to put them on. For he knew in the back of his mind that this would likely be the last time, that he might never again be permitted to participate in the sacraments of the Church which had been his life for twenty-nine years.

He bowed his head and tried to pray, but the words would not come. Or rather, the words came, but they rolled through his mind as meaningless phrases, bringing no comfort. Who would ever have thought he would have to be the one to consign his own brother and Morgan's sister to the grave? Who would have thought it would come to this?

He heard the door open softly behind him and turned his head. Old Father Anselm was standing in the doorway in cassock and white lace surplice, his head bowed in apology at having disturbed Duncan. He glanced at the vestment rack beside Duncan, at the black silk chasuble hanging there, still undonned, then looked at Duncan.

"I don't wish to rush you, Monsignor, but it's nearly time. Is there anything I may do to help?"

Duncan shook his head and turned back to face the altar.

"Are they ready to begin?"

"The family is in place, the procession is forming. You have a few more minutes."

Duncan bowed his head and closed his eyes. "Thank you. I'll be there directly."

He heard the door close softly behind him and lifted his head. The figure above the altar was a beneficent, loving God, he was sure. He would understand what Duncan was about to do, why he must defy ecclesiastical authority just this once. Surely He would not judge Duncan too harshly.

With a sigh, Duncan rose and pulled the black stole from its peg, touched it to his lips and looped it over his head, secured the crossed ends under the silk cord binding his waist. Then he donned the chasuble, adjusting the folds to fall as they should. He paused and looked down at himself for a long moment, smoothed the silver-outlined cross blazoned heavy on the front of the black silk. Then he bowed toward the altar and moved to the door to join the procession.

Everything must be perfect this time, all as it should be: a perfect offering for what would, in all probability, be the last time.

Morgan sat numbly in the second pew behind the coffins, Kelson to his right, Jared and Margaret to his left, all in black. Behind were Derry, Gwydion, a host of Duke Jared's councilors and retainers, members of the ducal household; and behind them, as many of the people of Culdi as could squeeze into the tiny Church. Both Bronwyn and Kevin had been well loved in Culdi, and the people now mourned their deaths as did their families.

The morning was sunny but fog-shrouded outside, the air nipped with the last cold of the season. But inside, Saint Teilo's was dark, solemn, ghostly, with the dim flicker of funeral tapers instead of the nuptial candles which would have burned if things had happened differently.

Heavy funeral candlesticks were ranged to either side of the two coffins set in the center of the transept, and the coffins themselves were draped with black velvet palls. Painted shields of the two families rested on each sable-draped coffin. And Morgan forced himself to blazon each one in his mind, in grieving memory of those who lay within.

McLain: *Argent, three roses gules, 2, 1; in chief, azure, a lion dormant argent,* the whole surmounted by Kevin's mark of cadency—an argent label of three points.

Morgan: (Morgan's throat constricted, and he forced himself to go on.) *Sable, a gryphon segreant vert, within a double tressure flory counter-flory or*—this on a lozenge instead of a shield. For Bronwyn.

Morgan's vision blurred and he forced himself to look beyond the coffins to where candles blazed on the altar, winking and glowing from the polished silver and gold of the candlesticks and altar furnishings. But the altar cloths were black, the gilded figures shrouded in black. And as the choir began to intone the entrance chant, there was no way that Morgan could convince himself that this was anything but what it was: a funeral.

The celebrants began to process: cassocked and surpliced thurifer swinging pungent incense, crucifer with black-shrouded processional cross, altar boys bearing glowing silver candlesticks. Then the monks of Saint Teilo's, surplices over habits, with black stoles of mourning; and Duncan, who would celebrate the Mass, pale in his black and silver vestments.

As the procession reached the chancel, splitting to either side so the celebrant could approach the altar, Morgan watched dully, made automatic responses as his cousin began the liturgy.

Introibo ad altare Dei. I will go up to the altar of God.

Morgan sank to his knees and buried his face in his hands, unwilling to witness these last rites for those he loved. Only a few weeks ago Bronwyn had been alive, filled with joy over her coming marriage to Kevin. And now, to be struck down in the fullness of her youth by magic, by one of her own kind. . . .

Morgan didn't much like himself just now. He didn't like Deryni, he didn't like his powers, and he resented highly the fact that half the blood flowing in his veins came from the accursed race.

Why did it have to be this way? Why should Deryniness have to be hidden, forbidden so that one felt ashamed of one's powers, learned to hide them, perhaps for so long that generations later the skill to use those powers wisely was lost, but the power remained? Power which sometimes found its way to the hands of deranged, senile practitioners who would use the powers as something else, not even suspecting that the power came from an ancient and noble heritage, from men called Deryni.

And so a wizened and senile old Deryni woman who had not known, who had been forced, years ago perhaps, to sublimate her powers—or whose parents had—had tried to work simple magic for a lovesick young man—and had killed instead.

Nor was that the worst of it. Of all the problems facing them in the weeks and months to come, every single one could be traced in some way to the Deryni question. Deryniness was the issue which had put the Church at odds with magic for over three centuries, which now threatened to rend it further in all ill-timed holy war. Deryniness, and the violent hatreds it evoked in ordinary men, had led Warin de Grey to feel himself called to destroy Deryni, starting with Alaric Morgan. And that had brought them to the disastrous episode at Saint Torin's, culminating in his and Duncan's excommunications.

Deryniness had led to the crisis at Kelson's coronation last fall, when the sorceress Charissa had made her bid to "regain" the throne she believed her Deryni father should have occupied; had led Kelson to assume his father's Deryni-given powers to stop her; and made Jehana, fiercely loyal mother of the young king, stop at nothing to try to protect her son from the evil she believed inherent in the Deryni—though she herself was of the high Deryni born, and had not known.

And who could say that the impending war with Wencit of Torenth was not tied up in the Deryni question too? Was not Wencit a full Deryni lord, born to the total power of his ancient race in a land which accepted that magic? And was it not rumored that he was allying himself with other Deryni, that there might be truth to the fears of the common man that a rise of Deryni power in the east might lead once more to a Deryni dictatorship like the one three hundred years ago—to the detriment of the human population, it might be added?

All in all, whether one believed in the inherent evil of Deryniness or not, it was a difficult time to be Deryni, a difficult time to have to accept oneself as a member of the occult race. Right now, if Morgan had had the choice, he might very well have been tempted to cast out the Deryni part of himself and be just human, to deny his powers and renounce them forever, as Archbishop Loris had demanded.

Morgan raised his head and tried to pull himself together, forced himself to watch and listen as Duncan continued with the Mass.

He had been very selfish during the past few minutes, he realized. He was not the only Deryni suffering agonies of the soul right now. What of Duncan? What angel must he be wrestling, as he defied suspension and excommunication to appear in the guise and function of a priest?

Morgan was far too distraught to try to catch Duncan's thoughts as he presided at what might well be his last liturgical function. Besides, he would not have thought of intruding on Duncan's private grief. But there was no question in Morgan's mind, now that he considered it, that his cousin was enduring much as he went through the motions of the Mass. The Church had been Duncan's life until today. Now he was defying that Church, even though only Morgan, Kelson, and Derry knew he did so, to pay this last token of respect and love for a brother and almost sister who were dead. Duncan, too, would be finding it difficult to be Deryni.

"*Agnus Dei, qui tollis peccata mundi, miserere nobis,*" Duncan intoned. *Lamb of God, who takest away the sins of the world, have mercy on us.*

Morgan bowed his head and repeated the words under his breath with the congregation, though the words did not bring comfort. It would be long before he would be able to reconcile what had happened two days ago with the will of God; long before he would be able to be as certain again that there was good in the powers he had carried all his life. Right now, responsibility for what had happened to Bronwyn and Kevin weighed heavy on his soul.

"*Domini, non sum dignus . . .*"

Lord, I am not worthy that thou shouldst come under my roof. Speak but the word and my soul shall be healed.

The Mass dragged on and on, but Morgan was aware of little of it. Fatigue and despair and numb grief and a dozen lesser emotions washed over his mind instead, and it was with some surprise that he found himself standing outside the gate to the crypt below Saint Teilo's with the others; and knew that the gate had closed behind Bronwyn and Kevin for the last time.

He glanced around and realized that the gathering was dispersing, that the few members of the family and household who had been permitted at the interment were drifting away in little knots and talking among themselves. Kelson was still with Duke Jared and Lady Margaret, but Derry stood attentively at his elbow and nodded sympathetically as Morgan looked up.

"Don't you think you should get some rest, sir? It's been a long few days, and soon you won't have the opportunity."

Morgan closed his eyes and rubbed the back of a gloved hand across his forehead, as though to blot out the sorrow of the past few hours, then shook his head.

"Make some excuse for me, will you, Derry? I need a few minutes to myself."

"Of course, sir."

As Derry stared after him with concern, Morgan slipped away from the mourners and made his way into the palace gardens which adjoined the church. Wandering unseeing along the graveled paths, he came at last to his mother's chapel and let himself in through the heavy wooden door.

He had not been here for a long time—how long, he could not recall—but the chapel was a refuge, light and airy and shining; and someone had opened the stained glass panel above his mother's sepulcher so that the warm sunlight streamed in rich and golden, touching the alabaster effigy with warmth.

The sight conjured up happier memories, for this had always been Morgan's favorite time of day to visit his mother's tomb. He could remember coming here as a child with Bronwyn and his Aunt Vera to lay flowers at the feet of the effigy, and the heady, wondrous tales his aunt had told them of the Lady Alyce de Corwyn de Morgan. Then, as now, he had had the feeling that his mother had never really left them, that her presence

had lingered and watched over him and his sister as
they played in the chapel and in the gardens outside.

He remembered the quiet times—sitting alone in the
cool sanctuary of the chapel when the world outside
became too unbearable; or lying on his back in a pool
of color from the window above the sepulcher, listening
to the sounds of his breathing, to the wind in the trees
outside, to the stillness of his own soul. The memory
somehow brought a measure of comfort even now.
Abruptly he wondered if his mother knew that her only
daughter now lay in a stone tomb not far away.

The wide brass railing surrounding the sepulcher
shone in the sunlight, and Morgan let his hands linger
there for a long moment as he bowed his head in grief.
After a while, he slipped the hook of the chain which
formed the railing across one end of the enclosure and
stepped inside, let the chain slither leadenly to the
marble floor. As he ran a gentle finger along the carved
hand of his mother's effigy, he became aware of someone humming brokenly in the garden outside.

It was a familiar tune—one of Gwydion's most haunt-
ing melodies—but as he closed his eyes to listen, the
voice began to sing new words to the song—words he
had never heard before. The singing was Gwydion's, he
realized after a while, the troubadour's mellow voice
blending with the rich lute chords in a golden meld
of sheer beauty. But there was something wrong with
Gwydion's voice as he sang. And it took Morgan several
minutes to realize that the little troubadour was crying.

He could not catch all the words. The lilting song
was often lost in Gwydion's sobs. But the nimble fingers
filled in where the singer's voice failed, underscoring the
phrasing with a tender caring.

He sang of spring and he sang of war. He sang of a
golden maiden who had stolen his heart and was no
more; of a noble's son who had dared to love the maid
and had died. Sorrow must come, the poet sang. For
war was blind, striking down the innocent as well as

those who waged the war. And if dying must come, then man should take the time to mourn his losses. Only grief gave meaning to the deaths, made the need for final victory real.

Morgan's breath caught as he listened to Gwydion's song, and he bowed his head over his mother's tomb. The troubadour was right. It was a war they waged; and many more would die before battle was done. It was necessary if Light was to prevail, if the Darkness was to be overcome.

But those who fought must never forget why they held back the Darkness, or that the price of victory might often be measured in human tears. And that the tears, too, were necessary: to wash away the pain, the guilt, to free the heart and let the human part cry out.

He opened his eyes and stared up into the sunlight, then let the hollow emptiness wash over him, felt his throat constrict as he tasted bitter loss.

Bronwyn, Kevin, the beloved Brion, whom he had loved as father and brother, young Richard FitzWilliam —all were gone, all victims of this mad, senseless conflict which raged even now.

But now—now, when a lull in the storm gave brief respite from the fury of the wind—now a man might let himself mourn at last and lay the ghosts to rest.

The golden light swam before his eyes, and his vision blurred. And this time he did not try to hold back the tears which welled up. It was some minutes before he was aware that the singer was gone, that footsteps were approaching on the gravel path outside.

He heard them coming long before they reached the door, and knew it was he they sought. By the time the door was swung hesitantly open, he had had time to compose himself again, to don the face he must show to the outside world. He took a deep breath to steel himself and turned to see Kelson framed in the bright doorway, a muddy, red-tuniced courier standing at his elbow. Jared, Ewan, Derry, and a handful of other

military advisors had accompanied Kelson, but they
kept a respectful distance as their young monarch
stepped into the chapel. A much-folded square of
parchment with many pendant seals was in the royal
hand.

"The Curia at Dhassa has split over the Interdict
question, Morgan," the king said, his grey eyes searching Morgan's carefully. "Bishops Cardiel, Arilan, Tolliver, and three others have broken with Loris in
defiance of the Interdict decree, and are prepared to
meet us at Dhassa within a fortnight. Arilan believes
he can raise an army of fifty thousand by the end of the
month."

Morgan lowered his eyes and turned partially away,
twining his gloved fingers together uneasily. "That is
well, my prince."

"Yes, it is," Kelson said, frowning slightly at the brief
answer and taking a few steps toward his general. "Do
you think they would dare to go against Warin? And if
so, do you think that Jared and Ewan can hold Wencit
in the north if we must aid the rebel bishops?"

"I don't know, my prince," Morgan said in a low
voice. He raised his head to gaze distractedly out the
open window at the sky beyond. "I doubt Arilan would
go against Warin actively. To do so would, in effect,
acknowledge that the Church's stand on magic has been
mistaken for two hundred years, that Warin's crusade
against the Deryni is wrong. I'm not certain that any of
our bishops are willing to go that far—not even Arilan."

Kelson waited, hoping Morgan would add something more, but the young general seemed to have
finished.

"Well, what do you suggest?" Kelson asked impatiently. "Arilan's faction has expressed a willingness to
help us. Morgan, we need all the help we can get!"

Morgan lowered his eyes uncomfortably, reluctant
to remind Kelson of the reason for his hesitation. If the
young king continued to support Duncan and himself,

excommunication and Interdict would fall on all of
Gwynedd before the archbishops were finished. He
could not allow—

"Morgan, I'm waiting!"

"Forgive me, Sire, but you should not be asking me
these things. I should not even be here. I cannot allow
you to compromise your position by associating with
one who—"

"Stop that!" Kelson hissed, grabbing Morgan's forearm to stare at him angrily. "There's been no official
word of your excommunication from the Curia yet. And
until there is—and maybe not even then—I don't intend
to lose your services just because of some stupid archbishop's decree. Now, damn you, Morgan, you will do
as I say! I need you!"

Morgan blinked in astonishment at the boy's outburst, almost fancying for an instant that it was Brion
standing before him, king admonishing a blundering
page. He swallowed and lowered his eyes, realizing
how close he had come to dragging Kelson's safety
into his own self-pity; he realized too that Kelson
recognized the danger approaching—and was willing to
accept it. As he gazed into the stormy grey eyes, he saw
a familiar, determined look he had never seen there
before. And Morgan knew that he would never think of
Kelson as a boy again.

"You are your father's son, my prince," he whispered. "Forgive me for forgetting, even for an instant.
I—" He paused. "You do understand what this decision means, Kelson?"

Kelson nodded solemnly. "It means that I trust you
implicitly," he said softly, "though ten thousand archbishops speak against you. It means that we are
Deryni and must stand together, you and I, even as
you stood by my father. Will you stay, Alaric? Will
you ride the storm with me?"

Morgan smiled slowly, and then nodded. "Very
well, my prince. These are my recommendations. Use

Arilan's troops to protect the northeast border of Corwyn against Wencit's armies. There is a clear-cut danger there. They need not be compromised by being drawn further into the Deryni question.

"For Corwyn itself, use Nigel's troops if there is internal strife because of Warin. Nigel is loved and respected throughout the Eleven Kingdoms. There is no taint to his name.

"And as for the north," he glanced at Jared and smiled reassuringly, "I believe that Dukes Jared and Ewan can defend us adequately on that front. The Earl of Marley can be recruited also. That still leaves us the crack Haldane troops in reserve, for wherever they're needed. What think you, my prince?"

Kelson grinned and released Morgan's arm, slapped his shoulder enthusiastically. "Now, that's what I wanted to hear. Jared, Derry, Deveril, come with me, please. We must get dispatches off to Nigel and the rebel bishops within the hour. Morgan, are you coming?"

"Shortly, my prince. I wanted to wait for Duncan."

"I understand. Whenever you're ready."

As Kelson and the rest departed, Morgan turned and reentered the Church of Saint Teilo. Treading softly, so as not to disturb the few mourners still praying in the stillness, he made his way down the clerestory aisle and along the ambulatory until he reached the vesting chapel where he knew Duncan would be. Pausing, he peered through the open door.

Duncan was alone in the chamber. He had put aside his priestly garb and was lacing the front of a plain leather doublet, his back to the doorway. As he finished with the lacings, he reached for his sword and belt lying across a table beside him. His movement stirred the vestments on the rack to his right, jarring the silken stole from its peg. Duncan froze as the stole slid to the floor, bent slowly to retrieve it. He straightened and stood without moving for several seconds, the stole clasped in stiff fingers, then touched it to his lips and returned it to its place on the rack. The silver embroidery caught the light from a high window as Morgan stepped quietly into the doorway and leaned against the doorjamb.

"It hurts more than you thought it would, doesn't it?" he said in a low voice.

Duncan's back tensed for just an instant, and then he bowed his head.

"I don't know what I thought, Alaric. Perhaps I believed that the answer would come to me of its own accord, that it would make the parting easier. It docsn't."

"No, I don't suppose it does."

Duncan gave a sigh and picked up his sword belt, turned to glance at Morgan as he buckled it around his slim waist.

"Well, what now?" he asked. "When you're Deryni, excommunicated from your Church, and exiled from your king, where can you go?"

"Who said anything about exile?"

Duncan picked up his cloak and flung it around his shoulders, furrowing his brow and glancing down as he fumbled with the clasp.

"Come, now. Let's be realistic. He doesn't have to say it, does he? You and I both know he can't let us stay when we're under the ban of the Church. If the archbishops found out, they'd excommunicate him too." The components of the clasp snapped together with a sturdy click, and Morgan smiled.

"They may do that anyway. Under the circumstances, he really doesn't have much to lose."

"Not much to—" Duncan broke off in amazement as he realized what Morgan was implying. "He's already decided to take the risk?" he asked, watching his cousin's face for confirmation. Morgan nodded.

"And he doesn't care?" Duncan still seemed unable to believe what he was hearing.

Morgan smiled. "He cares. But he recognizes the priorities, too, Duncan. And he's willing to take that risk. He wants us to stay."

Duncan stared at his cousin for a long moment, then nodded slowly.

"We ride against tremendous odds—you know that," he said tentatively.

"We are Deryni. Such has always been our lot."

Duncan took a final look around the chapel, allowing his eyes to touch lingeringly on the altar, on the silk vestments hanging on their rack, then walked slowly to join Morgan in the doorway.

"I'm ready," he said, not looking back.

"Then let us join Kelson," Morgan said with a smile. "Our Deryni king has need of us."

About the Author

KATHERINE KURTZ was born in Coral Gables, Florida, during a hurricane, and has led a somewhat whirlwind existence ever since. She was awarded a B.S. in chemistry from the University of Miami, attended medical school for a year before she decided she really wanted to write about medicine rather than practice it, and earned an M.A. in medieval English history from UCLA while writing her first two novels.

Miss Kurtz is interested in just about everything except baseball and business, and has worked in such fields as marine science, anthropology, cancer research, cataloging of Chinese painting, educational and commercial television, and police science. She is also a professionally trained hypnotist, an avid horsewoman, and an avowed cat person, though she has nothing against dogs. She is currently a designer of instructional materials for the Los Angeles Police Academy.

Miss Kurtz is active in the Society for Creative Anachronism, an organization which attempts to recreate the middle ages and renaissance through tournaments, banquets, revels, and classes in medieval arts and sciences. As Bevin Fraser of Stirling in the SCA, she is an accomplished costumer, calligrapher and illuminator, herald, and expert on court protocol, as well as a student of medieval fighting forms (from the sidelines only; she bruises easily).